Beaded Hope

Beaded Hope

❖ ❖ ❖

CATHY LIGGETT

 Tyndale House Publishers, Inc. Carol Stream, Illinois

Visit Tyndale's exciting Web site at www.tyndale.com.

Visit Cathy Liggett's Web site at www.cathyliggett.com.

TYNDALE and Tyndale's quill logo are registered trademarks of Tyndale House Publishers, Inc.

Beaded Hope

Designed by Beth Sparkman

Edited by Lorie Popp

Published in association with the literary agency of Spencerhill Associates, PO Box 374, Chatham, NY 12037.

Scripture taken from the *Holy Bible*, New International Version,® NIV.® Copyright © 1973, 1978, 1984 by Biblica, Inc.™ Used by permission of Zondervan. All rights reserved worldwide.

This novel is a work of fiction. Names, characters, places, and incidents either are the product of the author's imagination or are used fictitiously. Any resemblance to actual events, locales, organizations, or persons living or dead is entirely coincidental and beyond the intent of either the author or the publisher.

Library of Congress Cataloging-in-Publication Data

Liggett, Cathy.
  Beaded hope / Cathy Liggett.
    p. cm.
  ISBN 978-1-4143-3212-3 (pbk.)
    1. Americans—South Africa—Fiction. 2. Women missionaries—Fiction. 3. Women—South Africa—Fiction. I. Title.
PS3612.I343B43 2010
813'.6—dc22   2009044910

Printed in the United States of America

16 15 14 13 12 11 10

7   6   5   4   3   2   1

For Mark
How do you do it? After all these years,
you're still making this girl's dreams come true.

Acknowledgments

My first words of thanks and praise must go to my heavenly Father, who in His ever-wondrous, masterful, and incredibly loving way has brought so many special people into my life.

To Jennifer Davis, founder of Beaded Hope, thank you for sharing your passion for South Africa in a way that led me there; and, ladies of South Africa, thank you for being everything Jennifer said you would be—gracious, inspiring, and completely irresistible. Also much appreciation to the behind-the-scenes volunteers at Beaded Hope who pour their time, talents, and love into the organization and set an example for us all.

To my agent, Karen Solem, I know we're in the word business, but I honestly don't know the right ones to adequately thank you. Without your expertise and your belief in this story, none of this would have come to pass. I'm humbly grateful to you for leading the way on this journey. Simply put, you're the best!

I'd like to express a very special thank-you to Jan Stob not only for your insights regarding this project but also for your capacity for caring that extends far beyond this book. And to Stephanie Broene, your dedication has been very much appreciated. Thank you for your guidance and kindness along the way. Also to my editor, Lorie Popp, or should I call you my miracle worker? I'm so grateful for all your hours of hard work, for taking so many pages and pages of story and turning them into "just the right ones," and for even making it pleasurable in the process. Thank you, too, to Babette Rea and all the others in marketing, copyediting, art, and sales at Tyndale who played a role in the making of this book and, in turn, have created opportunities for the people of South Africa. Everyone's efforts are so appreciated.

To Dr. Kurt Froehlich, Cathy Flaten, Nancy Bentz, Annie Erickson, Sonya Hensley, and Jerry Lane, thank you for your medical and technical advice, for your willingness to share your time, experiences, talents, photos—whatever I needed, whenever.

And then there are my writing buddies: Shelley Shepard Gray, Heather Webber, Hilda Knepp, and Julie Stone, so much is better because of you and your friendships—my manuscripts, the highs and lows of writing, and of course, bagels every other Friday morning.

Since this project has been years in the making, I'd be remiss in not thanking many people who never seemed to tire of encouraging me— my sweet girlfriends near and far, Chip and Melody Wilt, friends at Bethesda North Hospital, and my ladies' Bible study group. Your heartening words and prayers have meant a lot to me.

And nearly last but always closest at heart—to Mom and Dad, Joni, and the rest of our clan, thank you for always being so supportive. You make it easy to write about loving families.

Of course, nothing could ever be as special without my husband and best friend. To you, Mark, your love is the richness in all of my days.

And to my children, Kelly and Michael, who are no longer little but still the greatest part of my heart—you will never know all the ways you inspire me. All the ways you give me hope.

Now faith is being sure of
what we hope for
and certain of
what we do not see.
HEBREWS 11:1

1

Suburb of Columbus, Ohio

"Hey, Gabby, what are you doing?"

Even after all their years together, the sound of her husband's voice could still make Gabrielle Phillips's heart skip a beat. She pressed the cell phone closer to her ear. It had been such a long week without Tom at home. "I'm running into Hirscham's to pick up a shirt for Dad's birthday."

"Running? *You're running?*"

His overly cautious tone brought a smile to her face. "Not running, silly, although I could run, you know. I'm walking briskly. Hurrying. I have to be back at church by 1:30 for a meeting with the other directors."

"Is everything . . . ?" His hesitancy to finish the sentence told her everything he feared. How many times had he asked the same question only to hear the worst? No wonder Tom could barely ask anymore. Only fools got too close to a fire after getting burned time and again.

But at least today she had good news.

"Everything is fine. Absolutely fine. Wonderful. Really." Closing her eyes, Gabby whispered her thanks to God. Tom's audible sigh and then silence made her think he might be doing the same. "Except for . . . I miss you terribly."

"Yeah?"

"When does your flight get in? Soon, I hope. It's supposed to storm today."

Dressing for work this morning, she'd seen the weather report on the small television sitting on top of the dresser in their bedroom. The meteorologist hadn't just predicted rain; he'd more like ranted about it, threatening a downpour, pointing to patches of colors ranging from alarming yellow to raging red on his Doppler 10 radar screen.

"My plane gets in around five. But I looked online. I don't think the rain's supposed to start till later tonight."

"Oh? Well, good." That concern dismissed, she thought ahead. "Pizza for dinner?"

"Should you eat pizza?"

Smiling, she rolled her eyes though no one was nearby to notice. "How about half-veggie, half-pepperoni?"

"Perfect. Just like you. Love you, Gabby."

"I know."

Somehow through all the pain and drama and disappointments over the years of their marriage, they had survived, shakily at times, but together just the same. And now they'd been rewarded.

So rewarded! She let out a contented sigh.

As her boots scuffed against the dry parking lot pavement, Gabby had to admit she must've heard the weatherman wrong. At the moment, nearly white clouds with only hints of gray streaked a blue-brushed sky, looking far too benevolent for any monstrous storm to crackle through the heavens anytime soon.

But Gabby still felt glad she'd decided not to take any chances before she'd left home this morning. No way she wanted to risk slipping and falling on a rain-slicked floor. Not with their baby growing inside her—the baby she and Tom had waited for for so long. *So painfully long.*

Instead, she'd tossed her black ballet flats back into the closet she shared with her husband, opting for ragged but sure-footed snow boots from the garage. Not so attractive, but luckily she worked at a historic stone church and not in some glossy corporate tower. Everyone at work dressed neatly but casually. No one at Graceview cared as much about her fashion statements as they did about her dedication as head of the church's children's ministries.

When Gabby reached Hirscham's entrance, she held open the door for a young mom struggling to push a baby stroller while tugging on the hand of a squirming toddler.

Not exactly an idyllic Norman Rockwell scene, but still Gabby could feel the jealousy. Rearing. Scratching. Trying to catch hold. Wanting to seep in and creep through her like a heart-strangling vine.

But it couldn't control her anymore. These days she refused to let it. Now hope wasn't just some fuzzy mirage in the distance. It had become more of a reality. On days when the green monster reared, she could more easily shoo it away with a genuine smile, not a false one. With positive thoughts, not negative ones. And by counting blessings, not subtracting them.

Heading for the men's department, Gabby already knew exactly what to get her father. Her mother had been explicit about the size, brand, and color of shirt Gabby's dad would like from her and Tom. Even though Gabby thought a shirt sounded less than exciting, she and Tom couldn't afford much more than a shirt anyway. Tom's new job with a national nonprofit organization had been a step up, but they still didn't have a lot of disposable income, especially not with all the medical bills from the past—or the present.

Besides, next year would be different. By the time her father's birthday rolled around again, she'd already have given him a special gift. A precious one.

Something money just can't buy!

The salesperson couldn't have been more efficient, and package in hand, Gabby glanced at her watch. She could slow down a bit. She still had ten minutes to kill before she had to head back to Graceview.

Strolling through the store, she took in the new spring fashions.

It looked as if pink might be a big color again this season. But the women's clothes held little interest for her, so she meandered over to the baby department and stood at the edge, looking in. Did she really want to venture into that sea of heart-tugging adorability?

Then a sleeper caught her eye. A pale yellow sleeper, almost the color of the underside of a lemon peel, with the cutest fuzzy lamb embroidered on the chest. Even from a distance it tempted her, seeming to promise a high cuddle factor.

Could the sleeper really be as soft as it looked?

Inching her way over, Gabby tried not to notice the endless racks and shelves of pastels, the cotton candy pinks and hushed baby blues of the infant clothes, the girlie lavenders and boy-bold navies of the toddler outfits. Instead, keeping her eyes focused on the sleeper, she made a straight path. She just wanted to touch it and feel its softness. That was all.

She took the foot of the sleeper in her hand and rubbed it between her fingers. Exquisite. Addicting. As soft as a downy feather but not feathery at all, of course. Holding it up to her cheek, she could almost imagine she smelled the unmistakable scent of baby powder. Could almost swear she felt the weight of a tiny foot wrapped in the velvety fabric.

"Soft, isn't it?" A salesperson appeared out of nowhere and smiled at her knowingly.

Gabby attempted to let the fabric drop from her fingers, but she couldn't let go. "Unbelievable."

"And they're on sale."

Glancing at the price tag without really seeing it, Gabby tilted her head, pretending to do a mental calculation. But really her decision—or rather indecision—had nothing to do with money. Not this time.

As she clasped the material tighter and tighter in her fingers, she already knew there'd be an aching sadness that would spread to her limbs and then, without a doubt, find her heart if she let the fabric slip from her hand. Oh, how she didn't want to let go.

But should she? Should she really *buy* it?

But then . . .

It had been ten weeks. She'd almost made it through the entire first trimester. She had never, ever, carried a baby that long before. Not in all the eight years since she and Tom had tried to conceive.

Even though everything indicated the in vitro fertilization had worked, even though her belly had the slightest protrusion and her breasts felt more tender than usual, still, after so many years, so many tests, failures, and tears, it seemed too hard to believe, too good to be true.

But Gabby couldn't go on thinking that way. This baby—their baby—was real.

The thought made her tremble with a thrilling excitement that lifted her heart sky-high.

Until the other tremors came too, clutching at her throat, bringing fear and trepidation. Sadness of remembered losses. Feelings so easy to give in to, such a familiar place to be.

Her baby couldn't thrive in shadows and fear. A protective feeling, stronger than anything she'd ever felt before, surged through her. She needed to shove those feelings away. Her baby needed light and love. Positive thoughts and prayers. Nourishment. Gentleness. And softness.

"I-I want it," Gabby stammered. "I want it," she repeated, taking the sleeper, handing it to the salesperson. "I'm going to get it."

But as she watched the salesperson wrap her precious purchase in white tissue paper, horrible thoughts struck again. What was she doing? Something wrong? Something that might possibly jinx their baby?

No, she wouldn't let herself believe it. After all, she'd bought baby clothes ahead of time for friends before. And had anything awful ever happened to their babies?

Besides, if she'd learned anything through the trials she and Tom had endured together, it had been that there were no signs. No spells.

No talismans. No right words to chant. No fairy godmother's wand. Nothing that could create a baby.

Nothing beyond the ability of her body . . . and God's gracious will. Every minute of every day, Gabby prayed they were one and the same.

2

Heidi Martin bolted upright from her dozing on the couch. She pushed the afghan from around her waist, then the hair from her eyes, trying to get her bearings. The pinkish glow of a TV sitcom lit the dark family room, canned laughter piercing the quiet. But hadn't there been something else? something that had brought her to attention?

Oh, there it was. A phone ringing. She squinted at the orange numbers on the cable box digital clock—12:50.

Katie had missed her curfew again. This time by fifty minutes. The realization woke Heidi up like ice-cold water splashed on her face. The girl was getting later and later all the time. And more brazen.

Seventeen-year-olds. Give 'em an inch and they'll run right over you. Heidi stomped to the kitchen phone. *Well, this is it, young lady!* Jerking the cordless phone from the cradle, she pushed the Talk button, not even bothering to say hello. "What's up, Katie? What's your excuse for being late this time?"

Heidi had attempted to keep the curt, unforgiving tone from her voice so many times before. But tonight she was so tired and frustrated she didn't even try. Raising a teenager sucked the life right out of you, and raising one by yourself could be so overwhelming, exhausting, worrisome, and . . . well, she couldn't think of a single word that could adequately describe it.

Besides, her phone greeting wasn't nearly as harsh as the derisive thoughts that jumped to the forefront of her mind and wanted to leap straight from her lips. What she really wanted to say was *"What lame excuse have you and your irresponsible group of friends thought of now? And while we're at it, when are you going to stop hanging around with such a going-nowhere-fast bunch of . . ."*

Heidi hated to use the word *losers*. After all, she *was* a first-grade teacher, and that wasn't a kindly, teacherlike thing to say. But were her impressions so far off? The kids Katie had started hanging out with the past year certainly weren't recognized as the greatest students in their class. Or the athletes. Or the cheerleaders she'd always been friends with.

"Ma'am?" a man drawled in a low, somber voice. "Am I speaking with Heidi Martin? Katie Martin's mom?"

She could sense the man had been trained to keep his tone direct and calm. That was what made it even worse, causing the phone to tremble in her hand. "Y-yes."

"This is Trooper Steven Kirkpatrick, Ohio State Highway Patrol. Ma'am, there's been an accident."

The word drained every bit of life from her limbs. Heidi sank to the cold, tiled kitchen floor as the trooper said other things. *I-71 overpass. Rain. Crossed the line.* None of it made any sense. The only words that stuck, the only ones she could wrap her mind around, were *Lazarus East Hospital.*

He was still saying something when she clicked off the phone. But she couldn't listen anymore. She had to get there. To the hospital. To her Katie.

Weak with fear, Heidi managed to pull herself up off the floor, locate some slip-ons, and find the car keys. It had been raining all weekend, but she didn't even bother with her slicker hanging on a hook in the mudroom.

Somehow she backed out of the driveway without hitting the mailbox, without running over the sprinkler heads. Someway she drove down Edwards Road, even though her tears and the rain made it nearly impossible to see.

She'd grabbed her cell phone on the way out the door, but it lay silent on the empty car seat beside her. Sadly, she couldn't think of anyone to call. They didn't have any relatives close by, and so many close friends seemed to disappear when Jeff died.

Oh, please, Jeff, please. Can you hear me? I need you! I need you so much! Sobs tore at her chest while her tears flowed as furious as the heavy drops of rain. *This can't be happening! Not Katie too!*

Fear and desolation welled up inside her, battling with every breath she had, nearly stealing it all away. As she blinked through the tears, she was hardly aware of the blurry world around her. Not until a semi passed by at breakneck speed, burying her windshield under a heavy blanket of water. The force jolted her back in the seat like a slap across her face. Tears stopped instantaneously as she gripped the steering wheel to keep the swerving SUV from sliding off the road into a ditch.

That's it. No more crying! She had to be strong. She needed to get hold of herself. Had to concentrate. Had to get there. For Katie.

Please, dear Father in heaven, please get me to Katie. I need to get to her, Lord, please.

The litany echoed over and over in her head while raindrops pounded at the windshield. The blackness of the stormy night made it difficult for her to find her way, even on roads she'd traveled so many times in her life.

After what seemed to be an endless series of curves, the street finally emptied onto a straight stretch of pavement. Dim-burning lights from a gas station in the distance helped her see the way. Little by little, it seemed her plea was being answered. The rain began to ease just as red letters on the hospital Emergency sign glowed brightly ahead.

Heidi parked the SUV and raced through the emergency room door. Surely she was getting help from somewhere because on her own nothing was really working. Not her legs. Or her mind. Barely her lips.

"Katie Martin?" She braced herself against the registration desk, biting back a sob.

A twentysomething registrar in a navy smock stared at her. "You're her mother?"

"Yes. Yes, I am." Her insides tightened, thinking of all the times people had asked about Katie's "real" mother, though in her mind, she'd always been Katie's real mom. *I'm the one who's always been there. I'm the one who raised her, who always cared.* "Where is she? I need to get to her."

"Sure, sure," the girl said, reaching for a packet of papers. "First I'll need you to sign a consent form, and I'll also need your driver's license, insurance card. The copayment can be made by credit card or—"

"Look, there's only me, okay? No one else. And for me, there's only Katie. I can't do papers now. Push the button on the door. Please." She felt a string of curse words rising in her throat. "Now. I want to see my Katie now."

"It'll only take a minute to—"

Heidi hit the counter. "Let me see my baby!" Tears formed in her eyes again.

"Open the door." A male voice boomed from behind Heidi, addressing the girl. "You can do the paperwork in a minute."

The girl looked peeved but answered politely, "Yes, Doctor."

Heidi turned to see who her savior was, ready to offer her thanks.

Surprisingly it was a man she recognized. Kevin Peterson. She knew his face far better than she knew him. She'd seen him in passing when Katie and his daughter, Natalie, had been on a basketball team together back in elementary school. Prior to so many things . . .

"Thanks," Heidi murmured as the metal doors magically folded open. Swiping at her eyes, she rushed through the doors, taking giant steps toward her Katie.

3

Cassandra Albright assumed everyone had their designer tracksuits tailored, but once she found out they didn't, that didn't stop her from making sure hers fit snugly, yet tastefully, showing off her fit, slim figure. After all, she got up every morning at 3 a.m. to exercise before airtime. Not because she particularly enjoyed watching reruns of *The Andy Griffith Show* while she worked out on her elliptical machine but because she had to. Both her job as lead anchor at the number one station in Ohio's capital city and her status as a local celebrity demanded she look her best at all times.

That was also why she never bought a pink, baby blue, or lavender jogging suit. They were just too cutesy, too bourgeois. Comfort should never be at the expense of good taste, so she chose the classics—chocolate, charcoal, or black for fall and winter. Crisp white for summer. And for spring? Tans, beiges, or a rich, creamy latte color like the one she'd selected from her closet on this overcast but dry Sunday in early March.

Accenting her outfit with darling off-white canvas slip-ons trimmed in gold and a white and yellow gold braided bracelet with matching small hoop earrings, she felt really good about herself as she carried hefty Sunday editions of the *New York Times* and *Columbus Dispatch* into Max's Bagel Shop. True, the papers were cumbersome and the ink could even be quite messy. But she'd been in broadcast news for the past twenty years and always strived to look the part.

After hoisting the newspapers up on a stool at the counter, she slipped onto a nearby seat. Before she could even undo her nylon zip-up and display her toned shoulders exposed by a sleeveless spandex racerback top, a college-age kid behind the counter showed up to take her order. Or rather to give it.

"Don't have to tell me, Ms. Albright. I already know." He swiped the counter with a damp rag. "You'd like a blueberry bagel, very, *very* lightly toasted with just a smidgen of low-fat cream cheese. Also a small orange juice, pulp-free with a spoonful of crushed ice. And a mug of coffee, house blend with one-quarter-inch room for cream. Hold the sugar and especially any artificial sweeteners since they can cause cancer and mimic symptoms of MS. Plus, you'd like a spoon to stir your coffee with, not some chintzy plastic stirrer. And make it a clean spoon, not one with food particles or smudges, thank you very much."

At first, Cassandra assumed the kid was being impudent, spouting her usual order that way and with all her inflections to boot. She was just about to ask for the manager to see about having him fired when she noticed how pleased he was with himself as if he'd just recited the Gettysburg Address backward. More importantly, out of the corner of her eye she also spotted a middle-aged couple eavesdropping. That was when she switched gears.

"Ah, let me guess." She smiled at the shaggy-haired, unshaven guy. "You're majoring in broadcast journalism. Am I correct? And you're trying to get on my good side?" She winked. Honest to goodness winked, and she detested winking.

"Yeah—uh, yes, ma'am." The kid nodded, a nervous half smile twitching at his lips.

"Well, first hint, young man. A shave and a haircut go a long way. So when you're ready for an internship and after you've paid a visit to the nearest men's salon—" she smiled most graciously—"feel free to e-mail me."

Pulling her tan knapsack-style leather purse off the back of her stool, she rummaged through it for a pen and a business card. "What's your name?"

After his smooth-sailing monologue, the kid suddenly seemed to have developed a case of the jitters, his answer coming out in a stutter. "J-Jimmy W-Watkins."

"Well, here you go, James." Cassandra handed him the card. "Don't lose it. I'll be expecting to hear from you."

"Th-th-thank you. Thanks so much." He waved the card in the air like it was a winning lottery ticket before going to place her order.

Cassandra knew full well that when he did e-mail her, it was doubtful she'd even notice or reply. Not with the zillions of e-mails she got each day. *Thank goodness for the Select All and Delete buttons,* she mused. Besides, internships at WONR were coveted and few and sometimes used as favors for relatives of major advertisers.

But everyone needed a sliver of hope from time to time, didn't they? And that was the gift she'd given James Watkins today. And it was good PR for her and the cheapest kind, she thought, looking to see if the couple next to her had noticed her generous offer.

But they were slathering their bagels with extra cream cheese and gabbing to each other. Just like the rest of the patrons, she realized disappointedly, glancing around the room. Many of them appeared to be churchgoers. The same sets of people that frequented the place week after week. They all appeared involved with themselves, their own conversations. No one seemed to have noticed her friendly gesture.

Maybe I've been coming here too often. Too much a part of the scenery.

Well, she could switch bagel shops, for sure. In fact, hadn't a new place just opened down the street from her luxury condo development?

"If there's anything else, Ms. Albright, just let me know." Jimmy's voice broke through her thoughts as he set a bagel basket, juice, spoon, and a mug of coffee in front of her.

"Thanks, James." Deliberate in her routine, she picked up the spoon and, though it appeared to be clean, wiped it with a napkin before stirring two containers of cream into her coffee.

As she blew at the cup, waiting for the coffee to cool slightly, she glanced at the TV hanging from the ceiling in the corner, immediately wishing she hadn't. There she was—Lisa Delacroix, WONR's new weekend anchor. *Ms. Up-and-Coming. Ms. Junior All Right.* At first, Cassandra had heard a whisper here and there. But lately, praises for Delacroix and predictions about the young newswoman occurred on a daily basis.

Maybe Cassandra wouldn't have been so nervous if she hadn't started out the same way. Twenty years ago she'd walked into WONR as the weekend gal too. And it wasn't long before she dethroned the weekday queen. Sure, Elizabeth Gould had more experience and credentials. But Gould also had more wear and tear on her face and body. Maybe it shouldn't have mattered, but apparently it did. Thoughts like that had been keeping Cassandra up at night lately— not so good for her own forty-plus, aging face.

"Excuse me." She felt a tap on her right shoulder a second before an older, bald gentleman wearing a shiny, worn-out suit sidled up to the counter next to her. "We were just about to leave, and I said to my wife here—" he pointed to a fragile-looking woman behind him— "I wanted to stop and ask you a question."

"Of course," Cassandra answered kindly, thinking he might want an autograph.

"I just want to know why you news folks are always focusing on the bad stuff and bad people out there," he said, pushing his wire-rimmed glasses up his nose. "I know my wife and me, we'd sure like to have some good stories about good people to listen to before we go to bed at night. And we'd like to hear 'em when we get up in the morning too."

Oh, please. Not another one. Cassandra had heard this complaint so many times before. She could hardly fathom that people didn't under- stand the competition out there. Of course they had to scare people and sensationalize stories. How else could they be sure anyone would tune in?

Still, she answered in the same diplomatic way she always did.

"Why, there's nothing that would make me happier than to make you happy. So I'm going to write a note with your request." She grabbed a paper off the counter, a church bulletin someone had left behind, scribbling a note on it. "I'll give your message to our program director first thing."

As the elderly couple left, she stuffed the note in her purse and gave another surreptitious glance around to see if anyone had been watching her gracious encounter with the old man. But no one seemed to notice. No one seemed to care that a true celebrity was in their midst.

It's happening. I'm blending in. Too familiar. Losing a hold on my audience. Coming to me with job requests and complaints, like I'm the human resources girl or a suggestion box!

And with Delacroix nipping at her Etienne Aigner heels, she'd soon be relegated to the shadows . . . before disappearing altogether. She couldn't let that happen.

Something had to be done.

4

"Katie?" Heidi's hand trembled as she bent over the hospital bed and tenderly pushed straggly wisps of hair back from her daughter's brow, trying not to touch the gauze bandage there.

But the girl didn't respond to her hand or her voice. Her eyes remained closed, her head turned away on the pillow.

"Is she . . . ?" Heidi didn't know exactly what to ask the nurse who was busy evaluating the monitors behind Katie's bed. In a way, she felt too frightened to hear any answers. *Is Katie sleeping? medicated? unconscious?* Anxiety welled up in her as each word—more and more severe—pressed on her mind.

"We stitched up the cut above her eye and gave her a little something for the pain. She had some other complaints, but Dr. Peterson will be in to go over that information with you." After checking Katie's pulse, the nurse typed something into a bedside laptop, then excused herself, drawing the curtain behind her.

Dread and anxiety seemed to quickly fill the small space lit up by a sickeningly yellow fluorescent overhead light and the green and red squiggles on the monitor. Both threatened to make Heidi crumple, but she stood as firm as she could on shaky legs, staring at Katie, willing her to open her eyes. To acknowledge her. To speak—utter anything. To say a word that would make everything all right again.

At the moment, though, hope seemed distant. As elusive as the years that had turned Katie's chestnut curls into a head of hair dyed defiant shoe-polish black. As intangible as the events that had taken their relationship from nights of cuddling to days of barely tolerating one another.

How? How did that happen?

Katie had seemed as good as could be expected for a long time after Jeff's illness. And then suddenly . . .

For some time now, Heidi had been searching her memory for the turning point. So often she awoke in the middle of the night, lying there in the dark, trying to pin down the incident that had started it all, struggling to figure it out. But there never seemed to be an answer. It felt as if she and Katie had gone to bed one night and woken up the next day as two different people. *Estranged by what?*

It was a question her mind kept coming back to, time and time again. As with an unfinished crossword puzzle, she could put it aside for only so long before she had to pick it up again, compelled to fill in all the blanks.

Even now, the bewilderment of it all made her feel weary. Sighing, she slumped down, sat on the edge of Katie's bed, and stared at her daughter's soft-cheeked face.

She looks so peaceful. None of the angry, contorted features Heidi had become accustomed to lately. So much arguing. Could they ever get through a day without bickering about something? What had they argued about tonight before Katie left? . . .

"Katie, that's crazy. Do you forget how old you are?"

"Old enough. I'll be eighteen in less than a year and a senior. Then I can do anything I want."

"Well, you're not eighteen now. And you're not driving to Florida for spring break with your . . ."

"Friends, Mom; they're called friends. Why do you have such a hard time saying it?"

Glaring at each other, they had both drawn their hands to their hips simultaneously like gunslingers drawing their pistols.

Heidi gave in first, letting her hands fall to her sides, not wanting their disagreement to escalate. "Look, arrangements have been made. I've already put down the money with church. We're going on Graceview's mission trip to South Africa over spring break, and that's final."

"I can't believe you. You treat me like . . ." Disgust narrowed Katie's eyes, and she shook her head. "You've changed so much."

"*I've* changed?" Heidi eyed Katie's free-spirited outfit consisting of multicolored striped tights and a short denim skirt with a black lace slip underneath, topped off with a purple tank top and a black hoodie.

If she were honest, she'd have to say that even in such a hodgepodge of an outfit, Katie still looked cute in an odd sort of way. But then Katie's looks were so classic and pretty, how couldn't she? She had Jeff's expressive iridescent blue eyes fringed with long lashes. Her nose fit her face perfectly, and her carnation lips didn't need gloss.

"Never mind." Katie's mouth twisted, looking as if she could either cry or spit nails at any second. "I can't even talk to you anymore."

And I hate it! I hate it so much! Heidi wanted to reach out to her, but Katie had already started stomping to her bedroom and was too far for Heidi's arms to stop her. But maybe her words would?

"Carol Singer said when she and Megan went on a mission trip to Nicaragua last summer with their church it was the best thing that ever happened to them."

Katie kept walking.

"Megan loved playing with the kids. Helping the moms. That's why I signed us up for the Women Helping Women team on the Mamelodi mission. I figured you'd really like—"

"Ha!" Katie stopped in her tracks and turned. "Are you serious? You really want me to be like Megan Singer? That's it?"

"What's wrong with Megan? She's been cheering forever, and Carol told me she's one of the leads in the spring musical."

Katie rolled her eyes. "You think Megan's perfect just because of her blonde ponytail and the hair ribbon she has to wear at the games. But you don't really know her. That's not the real Megan. So maybe she was nice to a bunch of Nicaraguan kids. But she sure isn't nice to the ones who go to her own school."

"You've never once mentioned Megan being mean to you."

"She's mean period. You should see her in the cafeteria. Sometimes I can't even eat my lunch—the whole group of them make me so sick. All picking on this one overweight girl who's a freshman. Or if it isn't her, they hit the lunch trays of younger kids that pass by. You know, the dorky ones, so they spill their food all over the floor."

"Megan Singer? Megan does that? I just can't believe . . ."

The curtains flung open, and Heidi jumped from the hospital bed.

"I'm sorry to keep you waiting," Kevin Peterson said. "A lot going on as usual."

She'd been oblivious, not at all tuned in to anything or anyone but Katie. But now that he mentioned it, she could hear the scurrying of feet beyond the curtain as well as bleeps echoing from various cubicles, telling the tales of other patients' vitals.

"How does she seem to be doing?" He moved closer to Katie, to the opposite side of the bed.

Wasn't he supposed to be the one telling her? "She hasn't opened her eyes."

Nodding, Kevin took the stethoscope from around his neck, checked Katie, and put it back in place. "The squad at the scene called in the accident as critical. I believe Katie and another passenger in the backseat were the only two restrained, but as I understand it, the car was in pretty bad shape."

"How are the others?" She hated saying *others*. Even though she knew the names of Katie's new group of friends, she could hardly put faces and personalities with their names.

"The driver isn't as bad off as the front seat passenger. As far as the details, it's best to get the information from their parents."

Heidi crossed her arms over her chest, bracing herself. "How is Katie?"

"When they brought her in, she was complaining of pain in her head, neck, and shoulder area. After we stitched her up, I took the liberty of running some initial tests. Obviously it was done without your consent, and I hope you don't mind. But I took one look and recognized her. And, well, if it had been Natalie . . ." Kevin drew in a deep breath. "I treated Katie as if she were my own."

The two shared a look of understanding that surpassed any words, and a lump formed in Heidi's throat. "I'm so glad. Glad that you were here. Thank you."

"Oddly enough, I wasn't supposed to be. One of the other docs had an emergency in her family and couldn't come in. I was at home not doing much, so . . ."

Over a year ago, Heidi had heard about the Petersons' divorce through the grapevine at school. At the time, she hadn't thought much about it given the fact that divorces seemed to happen so frequently.

Now that she stood across from Kevin Peterson, she had to wonder why. Here he was, a good-looking man with just a hint of gray at his temples, promising he'd be just as pleasing to look at in years to come as he was now. And even better, he seemed so sweet and dedicated, not at all arrogant or pompous. But who knew what went on inside marriages or behind closed doors?

"I was concerned that Katie might've suffered severe trauma to her brain. At first, she was . . ." He paused, softening his voice as if trying to lessen a blow. "She was crying out for her father. For Jeff."

At the mention of her deceased husband's name, Heidi closed her eyes and grasped the bed frame, steadying herself. She could imagine the scene—Katie wailing, scared and confused. It took her a moment before she could open her eyes.

Kevin went on. "I have the results of the CT scan of her brain, which seem to be normal, so I'm thinking that was possibly due to the frightening circumstances. Obviously an extremely traumatic situation, to be sure."

A sigh of relief escaped Heidi.

The tone in Kevin's voice told her to steel herself for more. "I am, however, ordering films of her neck and shoulder."

"What are you thinking?"

"It may be nothing. But given the severity of the crash and her complaints, I want to make sure there's no internal damage."

Suddenly Heidi felt chilled, as if the air in the room had dropped ten degrees. She rubbed her forearms vigorously to warm them. "It's so hard to see her like this. And the call. It was so . . ."

Stepping around to her side of the bed, Kevin placed a comforting hand at the top of her arm. "She's going to be okay. She'll get some rest, and she'll be fine. These tests are precautionary. I'm not saying there's anything wrong. I'm just making sure."

She felt moved, grateful for his compassion as well as his thoroughness. "Thanks, Doctor."

"Kevin."

"Kevin."

Squeezing her arm in a supportive gesture, he gave her a consoling smile before he turned to go. "Oh." He held on to the pushed-back curtain. "I know you want to stay by her side for now. But when they take her to radiology, will you do a favor for me?"

Heidi looked at him expectantly.

"Will you go out and sign the consent and get the paperwork done?" he pleaded good-naturedly. "Otherwise, they'll have my head out there."

"Definitely. Then after the X-rays—I mean, if those come back normal—will she be ready to go home soon? Will that be all of the tests?"

"Actually—" Kevin drew out the word—"there's one more."

Noticing his jaw suddenly tighten, she felt hers tense too. "Another test?"

"A urinalysis." A sympathetic look darkened his eyes. "Apparently from the evidence at the scene, drugs and alcohol are suspected."

5

"There you are. Finally a moment alone with my feisty redhead."

Coming up from behind, Tom wrapped his arms around her waist, and Gabby had to admit it felt good, especially since they'd been apart most of the week.

She set down the oversize, steaming bowl of penne pasta she'd been sent into her mom's kitchen to fetch, letting herself sink into him, allowing herself to be drawn back to the past. Back to earlier, simpler times—their college days when they'd head to her parents' house for a weekend visit. Even though there was an unspoken rule they'd be in separate bedrooms at night, that didn't seem to lessen their passion for each other by day.

Especially not Tom's. Back then, he was always pulling her into an empty room for a quick cuddle. Or drawing her close for a kiss when he thought her parents weren't looking. Even now, the thought of her husband's desire in those days could make Gabby smile. And she did as she nestled her body closer to his while weakly protesting his reference to her hair color. "First off, I'm not a redhead. I'm a strawberry blonde."

They'd bantered about the same thing many times before. Tom never ceased to be amused by the fact that Gabby's mom, Rosalie DeFazzio, determined to hold fast to her Italian heritage when she married Johnny O'Malley, had named her offspring Gabrielle, Mario, and Salvadore, even though each baby came along with red hair more flaming than the last.

"Red, blonde . . . whatever." He chuckled huskily and started to pull her tighter. But then, just as quickly as his ardor sparked, it defused. Loosening his hands from around her, he placed them lightly on either side of her waist. "Are you sure you don't need to go home soon and rest?"

With a light giggle, Gabby turned around in his arms, coming face-to-face with the man it seemed she'd loved forever. "Go home and rest?" She pushed a tuft of his sandy hair back into place, trying to read his eyes. "Oh, I get it. There's a basketball game on this afternoon, right?"

"No. I just figured you're probably tired."

"Actually, I'm feeling good today. Besides—" she glanced around the kitchen at the messy counters, sauce-splotched stove top, sink full of colanders and pots, all evidence that her mom had gone to a lot of trouble to prepare a major culinary feast for the entire family— "we just got here, you know?"

"Yeah, but you can't blame a guy for watching out for his girls. I mean, girl."

His slip of the tongue caught her off guard. Considering all they'd been through over the past years, it had seemed almost taboo in these last couple of months to talk about the baby much, especially to mention something as specific as the baby's sex or to rehash favorite names they'd thought about when they first set out to become parents. But now that Tom had accidentally brought it up, a feeling of relief washed over Gabby, making her even more aware of how tight-lipped they'd both been in the past weeks.

"Or boy," Gabby countered, more eager to say the words out loud than she'd even realized.

"Or boy," Tom agreed, smiling. He just barely touched the slight protrusion of her belly beneath her off-white corduroy jeans. "It's going to be all right."

"I know. I know it is. Everything's going to be fine."

Their words felt solemn, like the vow between blood brother and sister or between a groom and bride. But then, the bond between them had always been strong. In fact, at first it had shocked her when they'd struggled with her inability to conceive. Loving and caring for each other had always seemed so second nature to them. She'd never have believed their marriage could become strained, that the two of them would ever succumb to stress in the same way other, *normal* couples did.

And yet they had. Through the years of excruciating bleeding, fertility meds, hormonal ups and downs, negative pregnancy tests, and miscarriages, they'd almost lost their way.

Oh, they'd soared at times—their faith and their hopes, all bolstering their dreams of having a family. But then the same things always followed. The heartbreak, the depression, the unbearable disappointment.

Often it felt as if they'd been led into a long, dark tunnel, and it was so, so hard to find their way out to the other side. Sometimes they walked side by side holding hands, trying to plod the path together. But too often, when the pain of it became too much, it almost seemed easier to let go of each other. To take separate paths through the darkness.

Through it all, she had wondered if they'd survive, if they would ever find their way out to the light. If they would ever come up for air. And if they did, would they still know how to breathe? to walk? to hold on to each other?

"It makes you wonder, doesn't it?"

"Wonder?" Her forehead scrunched. Had Tom read her thoughts? Not that it would be the first time. "Wonder about what?"

"About the genetic thing. The red hair. What are the chances, do you think?"

Gabby laughed. "You're asking me?"

"You're the education major."

"*Elementary* education." She tapped his chest with an index finger. "But you're the botany major. Wasn't there something about Mendel's laws and all that? You should know better than me."

"I'm sure I do if I could remember."

"What were you planning to do with a major in botany, anyway?"

"Hmm. Marry you and live happily ever after?"

"Wow—after all these years, you still always say the right thing, don't you?"

Tom pecked her on the nose, his mischievous grin sending a sparkle to his eyes. "Does that mean I win a prize? We get to head home early?"

She knew Tom loved her family just as her parents and brothers had taken a liking to him from the first moment he'd set foot in the O'Malley house many years ago. Even so, with all his business travels lately, they hadn't been able to spend much time alone together, and they didn't have to talk about it for her to know how he felt. These were special days, not just because she was finally carrying their baby but also because they'd both agreed that with the financial drain of the in vitro fertilization, not to mention the compounded emotional drain, this was their very last chance at becoming parents.

Somehow it felt so much better and safer being close to each other. So often she wished the three of them could be safely nestled, wrapped together in a cocoon for the next six-plus months only to be birthed at the exact same time.

"We'll leave right after Dad opens his birthday gifts," Gabby told him.

"That's our cue?"

"Yes, definitely."

Tom bent down to kiss her lips but didn't quite connect before Salvadore's oldest son, Mikey, came barreling into the kitchen.

"Grandpa said he's going to start eating anything that moves if you don't hurry!" The five-year-old hugged and tugged at Gabby's leg.

"He what?" Both she and Tom burst out laughing.

"And Grant can't stop moving!" His eyes were as huge with fear over the possible demise of his two-year-old brother as their smiles were wide with amusement. "Grandpa's going to eat him."

"Well, we can't let that happen, can we?" Gabby picked up the pasta bowl from the counter.

Tom instantly took it from her hands. "Let me get that," he insisted before turning to Mikey. "Come on, dude! Let's save Grant!"

Mikey squealed excitedly as Gabby watched him tag after Tom. She couldn't help but have visions of their own kids, prancing behind their father one day. What a wonderful father her husband would certainly be someday. Soon.

"Aren't you coming?" Tom looked back at her.

Gabby nodded. "I'm just going to grab some extra napkins."

But as she crossed the room to her mom's napkin holder, a twinge of pain flitted across her stomach, and she clutched at her belly.

Could it be . . . ?

No, it couldn't be. It was probably just the orange juice. It *had* to be the orange juice, didn't it? It had looked so good and fresh in a glass pitcher in her mom's refrigerator. But she should have known better. It was far too much acid on an empty stomach. She should've eaten something first.

6

The City Grille really did make the best salmon, Cassandra
thought absently as she laid her near-empty carryout container
on the ebony coffee table, then searched her cranberry sofa for
the remote.

Finally finding it behind her left hip, she pointed it in the air
at the television like a deadly weapon, unable to stand the cable
network news one more second. It was ridiculous how young most
of the female newscasters looked on those stations. So wet behind
the ears. When had the world gotten so lax? When had glam and
cleavage become more important than knowledge and experience?

Tossing the dolled-up creatures out of her family room with a push
of a button, she surfed the other channels until she found a news crew
more to her liking.

There, that's better. 60 Minutes. Now she could relax and visit with
some old familiar faces. Some mature professionals worthy of their
vocation.

Cassandra settled back on the couch and listened to the windup of
a segment on gun lobbyists before picking up the week's pile of mail
from the cushion beside her.

Dividing her attention between the news show and the packet
of envelopes, she mindlessly sifted out the bills, laying them on the
coffee table. Next she rummaged through the remaining stack, tossing

leaflets and catalogs—all except for the Coach advertisement—onto the floor to be discarded later.

That still left a few miscellaneous items to deal with. Such as an invitation to a wedding from someone at the station. Someone she hardly knew who apparently felt obliged to invite her, and now for the sake of proper etiquette, she'd be obliged to buy them a wedding gift. But to actually go to the wedding? She held the lavender-trimmed invite up to her cheek for a moment, then flipped it on top of her stack of bills. It sort of fell into the same category, didn't it?

Commercials had come and gone, and the new segment was one she could stand to miss—statistics on the religious beliefs of the American people.

Cassandra had heard it all before and was about as interested in the topic as she was in the final piece of mail sitting on her lap— another bulky letter from Trudi Miles. Tucked in a tan envelope with childlike printing, it looked about as uninviting and bland as the place it originated from—Plaines, Indiana, the town Cassandra had grown up in.

Why on earth was Trudi always sending her things? On practically a quarterly basis, those unexciting, jam-packed, and usually smudged envelopes would arrive with a two- or three-page letter about Trudi's rather dull family life. Unfortunately the letters were always accompanied by photos of Trudi and Bobby's kids—who hadn't morphed into the most attractive teenagers on the planet—directions for creating a hummingbird garden, or a recipe for a quick and easy pineapple upside-down cake. Was the woman kidding?

Cassandra and Trudi had been so-called best friends when they were little girls. Very little. So young, they didn't have anything more in common than living next door to each other. But Trudi's house and the foster home Cassandra grew up in didn't resemble one another at all. Oh, maybe on the outside with the worn, shoddy paint. Missing shingles. Storm doors coming off the hinges. And scruffs of burnt grass that scratched the backs of their legs on summer days when they had nothing more to do than sit there on the patchy lawn and dream of being somewhere else.

But on the inside . . .

Like a twister under the radar, gathering force and unstoppable, anger and humiliation built inside Cassandra. The bile that rose to the back of her throat, the pressure that filled her head till she thought it'd burst into a million pieces seemed to come from nowhere.

But that wasn't true. It had come from somewhere. From him. That awful, disgusting, prickly-cheeked excuse for a man who had the audacity to call himself a foster parent. She could still feel his calloused, filthy hands scrape along her cheeks. Could still smell the rancidness of days-old body odor that sickened her as much as his rubbing up against her thigh. He may not have taken everything away from her, but he'd taken enough. Finally at sixteen, after eleven years, she'd left before he could take it all . . . every secret, special part of her.

Stashing a wad of bills in her pockets, tips her foster mom kept in the cookie jar, she'd practically crawled out of town, sneaking through the dark streets, behind the diner where her foster mom worked double shifts, until she got to the highway.

No one came looking for her. And for once she felt lucky that no one cared.

Except for Trudi, apparently. Trudi had tracked her down a few years ago and had been writing to her ever since, signing her letters with inane phrases like "hugs from your best friend."

Well, if she were really a best friend, she'd know better. She'd know that I never want to be reminded of anything that has to do with that place or those years again.

Could it be any simpler than that? Cassandra almost chucked the envelope to a spot on the coffee table designated in her mind as "Later; possibly never."

Cassandra stared at the envelope on the table for a moment, then forced herself to look away. She pressed her right palm to her forehead and took in a couple of long, deep, cleansing breaths, letting each out slowly. Through the years she'd gotten so much better at tucking the past away. Far, far away.

As she regained her composure, she looked around once more, considering each of the stacks that surrounded her. Then, retrieving the envelope from the table, she tossed Trudi's epistle on the floor into the pile of papers meant for the trash.

7

Leafless branches of a white birch wagged delicately in the slight midday breeze. Like lithe arms of graceful ballerinas, they seemed to wave to Heidi as she sat in a high-backed, ivory-colored chair next to the bay window of her living room. But she was in no mood to be lulled into a still contentment by the sight or to enjoy the sun, pouring in the window, warming the arms of the chair and the mocha carpeting beneath her feet. Warming everything but the prickles of cold dotting her forearms . . . and the constant anxious chill in her heart.

Dry, shriveled leaves seemed a better focus instead. Drained of their autumn glory, then buried for a while under winter snow, the leaves were now set free under the sun, skipping over the lawn in messy scatterings, reminding her of all that Jeff had left behind for her to do.

Messes and work everywhere. From clearing leaves trapped around the shrubs and preparing the beds for spring to filling the void she felt when she looked at the bed they'd shared, his chair at the kitchen table, or the side of the couch where he'd always sat.

And then, of course, to taking care of Katie. His daughter. Her inherited child. More work to do. So much more. After this weekend, more than she'd ever imagined.

It's so unfair of you, Jeff. . . .

She squeezed her right hand with her left to release the aching from her knuckles and wrist. She flexed her feet. Rolled her neck from side to side. But nothing seemed to relieve the dull, allover pain. Tension and worry rammed her from all sides, leaving her feeling like she'd been in a wreck Saturday night too.

So unfair . . .

A creak of a stair step made her already-nervous insides jolt even more. Looking up at the set of stairs that cut through the foyer, she almost wished it were a toddler Katie coming down the steps in a cotton nightgown, dragging her stuffed lion behind her. But no, it was teenage Katie—all grown and dressed in too-tight blue jeans and an equally snug maroon T-shirt, a silver-studded belt wrapped twice around her hips.

Katie seemed to startle at the sight of Heidi sitting somewhat camouflaged by the silence of the living room. Pausing midway down the staircase, Katie glanced at the front door more than once as if considering her next step. But then slowly she descended the remaining stairs and dutifully trudged into the living room. "It's so sunny." She squinted, blinking out the window.

Heidi nodded. "It really is."

"It's weird. Like, the other night was so awful and stormy. And now . . ."

"Now, it's like it never happened."

"Yeah. Exactly."

Well, there's one sliver of something we can agree on.

Honestly, how *did* God stand it? The ups and downs. The storms, the sunshine. The trials, the triumphs. Over and over and over again. With millions and millions of children. How did He manage? Because Heidi was growing weary of the whole thing. The roller-coaster ride had been too wild for her in the past years, knocking her around too much, nearly throwing her out of the seat.

"How's your head?"

"Better." Katie lightly rubbed her forehead. The large gauze pad had been removed before she left the hospital. Now just a small Band-Aid covered her stitches.

Ha! A Band-Aid. If only that could really cover all that's wrong. . . .

"I guess I was really lucky, huh?"

"I guess." Heidi shrugged, her shoulders so taut it made her long for Jeff again. If she closed her eyes tightly enough, could she still feel the relaxing, comforting touch of his hands?

Silence hung between them until a school bus, coming to pick up afternoon kindergartners, screeched outside. Heidi felt like she hadn't been at her job for a million years, even though she'd only taken off the day. "You look like you're going somewhere."

"Jessica's picking me up. We're going to go see Mark at the hospital."

Mark. The driver. The boyfriend. Oh, I don't even want to think about it. Jeff, how could you? How could you leave me? Saving her breath for the verbal combat she knew would ensue, Heidi shook her head.

"What?" Katie's eyes narrowed. "Are you serious? But I feel fine."

"I'm really glad you feel fine. But the answer is still no."

Katie's mouth dropped. She turned her head from side to side as if trying to clear it so she could process Heidi's words. Her hair flew in all directions, mostly out of her face, revealing the contempt in her eyes. "So I'm okay, but my boyfriend's still in the hospital. And you're not going to let me go see him? What about that 'do unto others' thing you always say?"

Heidi bit her lip.

Katie stuck hers out in a pout. "I don't get it."

"It's simple. I don't want you to see him. Not right now."

"Now?" Contempt turned to frustration, tears welling up in Katie's eyes. "Or do you mean never again?"

Heidi's heart wrenched as she watched a tear escape down Katie's cheek, knowing there would be more. "Look, I don't want to argue about this. It's just that—"

"Just what? Everyone's tests came back clean, right? No one was doing anything that night. No drugs, no alcohol."

"*That* night?"

"I can't believe you! You act like kids are supposed to be perfect. Like you were perfect. Like you *are* perfect."

"Believe me. I realize none of us is without faults."

"So, why are you being like this? The stuff in the car—it was his brother's. They proved it."

"I know."

At that, Katie threw back her head and let out a bewildered cry. "It wasn't drugs. It was the rain. And the drug tests were negative. Jessica's mom is ready to throw a party and buy her anything she wants, and you're just being plain mean." She flung her arms in the air, reminiscent of tantrums of her younger days. "I don't get it. Why do you hate me so much?"

"Hate you? You think I sat by your bedside all night because I hate you?"

"Well, what's your problem then?"

"You really don't know?"

Katie glared at her, eyes blazing. "Uh, no." Her tone suddenly smacked of teenage derision, while her hands defiantly shot to her cocked hips. "But I'm sure you're about to tell me, right?"

"When you were in the hospital, the urinalysis . . ." Heidi took in a deep breath, letting out an equally long sigh. "Katie, you're pregnant."

8

"Did you find religion over the weekend, Albright, or what?"

Jack McFadden's voice crackled through his office with conde-
scending amusement, the kind Cassandra loathed but had endured
from him for years. With only a glance, her boss disregarded the
church bulletin she'd handed him, flipping it onto a mound of papers
on his desk.

"Not exactly religion. Just a sort of epiphany." Picking up the
bulletin, she stood staunchly in front of his desk and waited for his
comeback.

"Epiphany, huh?" He croaked again, rolling his eyes, which drew
her attention to those nauseatingly bushy eyebrows of his. Eyebrows
with so many wild white hairs sprouting every which way she imagined it'd take a weed trimmer to tame them. "That's a religious word,
I'd say."

"Yes, I suppose," she agreed, not bothering to mention that she'd
never set foot in Graceview Church before. "Do you prefer 'spiritual
awakening'? Or how about this word? *Ratings.* As in Nielsen. Like
that better?"

"You really think people care?" Jack leaned back in his desk chair.
"I mean, seriously . . . South Africa? I think our viewers are more
interested in the weather than they are in people dying of AIDS somewhere on the other side of the world. We're just a local news station."

"But we can be bigger than that. The station with heart. It's a global world out there these days, and all we talk about are overturned tractor trailers on I-270."

Jack sat up in the chair as if he'd been attacked. Then he counter-attacked. "People care about overturned trucks and traffic jams. It messes with their travel time. And when it messes with that, it messes with everything else in their harried, hassled lives."

"You don't think people care about other people?"

"Ha! Do *you* even care?"

Did he really expect her to answer that? "I'm willing to split the cost of the mission trip with the station. That says something, doesn't it?"

"Pretty cheap self-promotion if you ask me."

"And you're implying . . . ?"

"Look, Cass." He used the shortened version of her name, knowing full well how much she despised it. "I'm not stupid. Incorrigible maybe. Totally rotten. And not as good-looking as I used to be. In fact, I'm getting uglier by the day. But I'm not stupid. We're both in the same boat here. Been at the same game a long time. Too long. And it can't last much longer, baby."

"That's why by showing our soft side—"

"Soft side?" Jack held up a hand to stop her, one of his bouts of laughter polluting the air. "Please. Cut the garbage. It's all about survival—ours. Believe me, I get it. That's why I'm going to take your suggestion to the powers that be." His eyes suddenly bright-ened. "You know what? Forget the big guys. I'm going to roll the dice with you on this one. I'll personally pay for the other half of your trip to Mama, Mamo, whatever the place is called. What can it be? A little over a grand? Take the two weeks as vacation, and bring me back a great news story. Something huge. Maybe even dig up some dirt on the church."

"Dirt on the church? Really? I'm thinking more along the lines of a squeaky-clean, tear-jerking—"

"You're right; you're right. Old habit. Okay, go for the heart-wrenching stuff." He waved an approving paw at her. "Something to endear you to viewers, a story that'll make the station shine. It better be something major that will put me in good with management for another few years. Or maybe even take me all the way to retirement."

"Seriously—" she arched her brow, fanning the wrinkled church bulletin in the air—"do you really think I'd travel to some godforsaken place on the other side of the world for anything less?"

Sliding open the top drawer of his cluttered desk, Jack retrieved an unwrapped cigar from its hiding place. "A self-serving player like you? No way."

Cassandra left her boss sniffing at his expensive cigar, his customary response when conversations or events left him feeling particularly good. She felt more than happy too, as if her career—her life—had been rejuvenated, given a B_{12} shot of the biggest kind.

As she headed to her office, sunshine pouring in the windows along the corridor, she studied the blurb in the bulletin again. It seemed this venture was a pre–mission trip for the church's major mission trip in the summer with mini teams being sent to Mamelodi to "work closely with South Africans to better prepare for the project needs of the summer mission."

Well, whatever. Did the reason for the mission even matter? She needed a story. Something extraordinary. And from what she knew about South Africa—what with AIDS, poverty, crime, and all that—she'd be sure to get her money's worth.

Now she needed to get the pastor to okay her filming the trip. Why would he mind, anyway? It would help boost the church's image as much as she was hoping it would hers.

Scanning the bulletin, she found the number for the church and thought about calling the pastor, but better yet . . . She glanced at her watch. The five o'clock news was still hours away. She had plenty of time to run over to Graceview Church and pay a visit in person.

After all, she was never one to let an opportunity slip through her fingers. And this one had been handed to her on a silver platter. Or truth be known, on a bagel tray. If that old man hadn't stopped to complain to her in Max's Bagel Shop and if she hadn't pretended to care about his request, she would've never picked up the church bulletin and glimpsed the announcement about the upcoming South Africa trip. She certainly would've never thought of such an idea on her own.

Yes, it was all falling into place. She'd been so concerned about her career, her future, and then out of the blue, the answer appeared. Almost like it was meant to be.

That is, if a person believed in such things.

Cassandra struggled to remember if she ever believed like that. And if she had, what it had felt like. But it was senseless. Even years and years ago, she'd never been that naive.

9

Heidi knew going into the high school and asking for Katie wasn't the cool thing to do. But she'd waited in her SUV at the curb for Katie for as long as she could and finally decided she couldn't wait one minute longer or they'd be late for their appointment with the obstetrician. Dr. Stephanie Riggsby was clear across town in an area Katie wasn't familiar with, so they'd decided to ride together instead of meeting there. Surely Katie hadn't forgotten, had she?

The first set of metal-frame doors Heidi tried was locked, but a second set wasn't. She pulled open a cumbersome door. Entering the school, she was instantly reminded of Katie's elementary school days when Heidi had always felt a part of things and she suspected Katie had too. Despite her own teaching position, Heidi had volunteered anytime she could. Once in a great while, she and Jeff had even chaperoned field trips together, taking doses of Advil after the noisy bus rides with the kids but still loving every minute of it.

Back in those years, lots of friends had surrounded Katie. Heidi knew all of their freshly scrubbed faces by name and their parents' names as well. Their community seemed like one big family—and a happy one at that, with so much to hope for, so much to look forward to.

But the teenage years had nothing in common with those idyllic elementary days. Though Heidi knew it was wrong to wish time away, she didn't think she'd be too awfully sad when the current stage they were going through became a thing of the past.

Far too often she felt as if she were treading in foreign territory. Sometimes even enemy territory, she thought, walking into the main office of the school, where no one bothered to greet her, not the secretary nor the pair of student aides in their matching navy and gold lacrosse uniforms.

"Excuse me."

"Hmm?" The secretary tapped away at her keyboard.

"My daughter. She was supposed to meet me outside."

The typing continued. "Do you know what class she has this period?"

Heidi had an idea of the courses Katie was taking but certainly didn't know her class schedule offhand. "I'm not sure."

"Girls, can one of you look up a student for me and call her down to the office?"

Both of the helpers turned at the sound of the secretary's voice, but only one plopped down in an empty desk chair and clicked on a computer screen. The girl glanced at Heidi. "What's your daughter's name?"

"Katie Martin."

Everything seemed to freeze. Time. Action. The movement of the air. Or was Heidi just imagining that the secretary finally stopped typing and looked at her? Or that the girl's fingers appeared to hover over the keyboard and that the other office aide couldn't seem to find a place between A and Z where she could file the folder in her hand?

They know, don't they? Or did they? Was she just being paranoid, conjuring up something that wasn't so? Or did she really feel it? Something that told her the secret between her and Katie wasn't just theirs anymore. That the news had spread, scattered like puffy seeds of a dandelion blown by the wind.

Heidi's heart pounded as she waited for the girl's fumbling hands to type in Katie's name. But before the girl could do that, Katie came hurrying into the office, a bulky backpack flung over her shoulder.

Grabbing the dismissal clipboard, Katie signed her name without making eye contact with anyone, including Heidi. Then she briskly walked out of the office, her face blotchy red, a flustered, mortified look Heidi remembered well from times when Katie played basketball and would miss a basket in front of a hopeful crowd.

Katie's strides were so long that Heidi could barely keep up with her. Maybe she was embarrassed by Heidi's being here. Or was she possibly trying to avoid the two girls walking down the hall opposite them? They eyed Katie conspicuously, whispering to each other with their hands cupped to their mouths. Or maybe—hopefully—could Heidi be imagining that too?

It wasn't until Heidi had pulled out of the parking lot and had driven a half mile to the expressway that either of them spoke.

"How did your quiz go today?" Heidi asked, trying to ease into a conversation while merging onto the highway at the same time. Not that she cared about the test. Not that it mattered at this point. But if there was one thing Heidi had gotten good at over the past several years, it was pretending that things were normal even when they weren't. In all honesty, she didn't know how Katie could concentrate on her schoolwork at the moment.

Katie wasn't having any part of the idle chatter. She shot Heidi a cross look. "Why did you have to come in?"

"I thought maybe you'd forgotten."

"Oh, like I could forget being pregnant? You really think I'm that stupid?"

"No. I thought maybe you'd forgotten about the appointment."

"Like I said, you think I can forget being pregnant?"

Heidi glanced at Katie, and the torture she saw on Katie's face took the air right out of her lungs. She so badly wanted to ask Katie if anyone knew. And if they did, was Katie bearing the burden all by herself? Were they making fun of her? feeling bad for her? Were her girlfriends standing by her?

But somehow they never spoke to each other that directly about things anymore. It was always a tap dance. No, that wasn't right. It was more like a minefield. She tried to tiptoe around to get at the truth before there was an explosion.

So Heidi would keep inching along. Nudging. Scratching at the surface of things, knowing eventually she'd uncover the sore spot, the source of the pain. While hopefully not creating pain where there hadn't been any.

The questions began innocently, but Heidi knew exactly where she was going. "Are you and Jessica still planning on going to the mall tonight?"

Looking out the window, Katie flipped a shoulder at her. Then shook her head.

"Can't she go?" Heidi pried.

"Probably. But I don't think she wants to."

Heidi held her breath. True, she'd never much liked Jessica. Nothing specific really, just a feeling that she got from her. But here she was anyway, as sick as it was, wishing Jessica hadn't abandoned Katie. And maybe she hadn't. "Does she have too much schoolwork tonight?"

"Jessica?" Katie rolled her eyes. "Are you serious?"

Katie had never uttered even the slightest disparaging remark about Jessica before. Heidi was surprised and decided it best not to press the topic of Katie's best friend. Emotions were running too high. A concoction of anxiety. Impatience. Sorrow. Fear. Either of them could erupt at any moment.

"Well, if you really want to go," Heidi treaded lightly, "is there someone you can call?" *Tell me you have a friend. Just one other friend.*

"Mark. But you'll hardly let me see him."

"Guys don't like going to the mall anyway. What about one of the other girls?" She had to ask. Had to dangle it out there. She couldn't help herself. She couldn't care less about the mall, but she had to know. Were there any girls still talking to her? Or only about her?

"There are no other girls, okay?"

So there it was. Katie was telling her she had no friends. Now was she happy? Still, Heidi didn't want to believe it. On top of everything else, it was just too painful. "Come on. There's an entire high school full of girls."

Oh, she hadn't meant to say that out loud. It sounded so mean and awful. Not hopeful in the way she had intended it to be, as in, "Look around, the glass is half-full, not entirely empty."

The agony on Katie's face only seemed to intensify till Heidi thought her heart would break.

"Oh, well, it doesn't matter." Heidi tried to find words that would sweep away the damage. "You can go to the mall anytime."

"Whatever." Katie resumed her study of all things on the outside of the car rather than the inside.

As Heidi drove in excruciating silence, her stomach clenched. As much as she didn't want to keep probing, didn't want to know or hear of more sad, awful things, she knew she couldn't stop here. She needed to know for Katie's sake as much as her own. She tried another tack. "So, any new scoop? What's Megan Singer up to these days? I hope she doesn't have any new victims in the cafeteria."

"Only one."

"Oh no, you're kidding. That's awful. If Carol knew her perfect daughter was doing that, she'd have a cow. She's not picking on the overweight girl again, is she? Or you mentioned there was a boy— a freshman who's kind of underdeveloped?"

Katie had been so silent, staring out the window, that the sudden wrath in her voice rocked Heidi to her core. "How could you tell her? I can't believe you did that!"

"Tell who? What are you talking about?" Fixed on the tears brimming in Katie's eyes, Heidi barely noticed the car slowing down in front of her. She had to slam on the brakes to keep from hitting it.

"Mrs. Singer. How could you tell her?"

"Tell her what? About you? I've never said a word to her. I'd never say a word to anyone."

"She told Megan she ran into you in the bookstore and you were looking for books on pregnancy. And then you said because of me we couldn't go with them to the mother-daughter overnight at your work."

"What? I never said that! I just said that I'd forgotten about the overnight. There have been just a *few* things on my mind lately," she said, feeling defensive in more ways than one.

Yes, she'd been looking at books on pregnancy when Carol spied her in the Little Owl Bookshop. She'd never been pregnant and felt a need to be more informed. But she hadn't said anything close to that. "As for the books, I told her I was looking for a baby shower gift. Anyway, what right does Carol Singer have to be starting rumors like that?"

"If it's true, it's not exactly a rumor, is it?" Katie countered sarcastically.

"But still, she doesn't know it's true. It's just her way of controlling things, of making herself feel important. It's conjecture on her part. That's what it is—conjecture."

"Not anymore," Katie said, her entire young body looking slumped and world-weary. "Mrs. Singer asked Megan, and then Megan got to Jessica."

Heidi nearly gasped out loud. "Jessica?" *Katie's best friend. Her only friend. Jessica betrayed her?* "Jessica told Megan?"

"Jessica said Megan made it sound like she already knew the truth."

And now *everyone* knew? So her instincts, everything she'd been feeling back at the school, had been dead-on. She and Katie hadn't even had a chance to get accustomed to the idea themselves, and now they had to do it under the scrutiny of the entire town?

This can't be happening. It can't be real.

Every day for so long she'd woken up thinking she wasn't a widow. That it wasn't her reality. That Jeff was still alive and it was all a bad dream. And now this. Her precious Katie! This seemed surreal too. But even worse than the reality of it was the pain she knew Katie must be feeling. Pain no teenager should have to bear.

Why, Katie? Why were you so careless? She wanted to scream at her. Katie knew better. Why hadn't she stopped to think of the consequences? Why couldn't she be like other teenagers having fun, enjoying friends? Why did it happen to her?

"Why are you looking at me like that?" Katie spat at her.

"Like what?"

"Like you always do."

"I don't think I was—"

"Yes, you were. Like I'm so pitiful. Such a mess. That's how you always look at me. I'm sorry you wanted me to be homecoming princess and a champion basketball player. I'm sorry you wanted me to go out with someone like Chad Stewart. And I'm sorry—"

"That's not true," Heidi interrupted.

"Yes, it is. Admit it. Just admit it! But that's not who I am! Don't you get it? I'm just Katie. The kid whose father died and everyone looked the other way when I walked down the hall. And now I'm pregnant. I'm the girl . . ." Katie's voice cracked, her lips quivering as tears spurted from her eyes. "They all just stare. And I feel so . . ." She sobbed, gulping for air. "I feel so . . ."

"Katie . . ." Heidi reached across the front seat, placing a hand on Katie's knee.

"I feel so alone!" Katie's strangled scream rang out in the SUV, sounding like a wounded animal caught in a trap.

Wailing, shaking, sobbing . . . every moment of Katie's painful outburst seemed like an eternity that would forever remain in Heidi's heart.

As she pulled over to the shoulder of the highway, uncontrollable tears ran down Heidi's face too. Years ago, with Jeff's passing, their strong, brave hearts had shattered into a million little pieces. But over time, healing had started, and though not yet whole, they had begun to put the fragments back together as best they could. Until now. Now their fragile hearts had been broken all over again, crumbling into finer, more delicate particles. And somehow, someway, they had to keep those particles contained until their mending could start once more.

"You're not alone, Kay-kay," Heidi whispered the name she'd called Katie as a little girl. "I'm here, honey." She pulled Katie into her arms. "I'll always be here. Always."

Their tears flowed and blended as they held on to each other tight.

No doubt the doctor's appointment would have to wait for another day.

16

"Thanks for having me over for dinner, Mrs. Martin." Mark Lender wadded up his napkin, setting it alongside his empty plate. Then, with a jerk of his head, cleared the bangs out of his eyes. "It was really good," he added as shaggy clumps of hair slid right back down over his forehead.

"It's a quick, easy meal," Heidi told him. "A dinner Katie's always liked."

Even so, Katie had scurried to the bathroom only moments before. It seemed one of her old favorites hadn't quite agreed with her new condition. Meanwhile, Heidi was left alone at the table with the boy who had played a major role in it.

Suddenly not feeling so hungry either, she set down her fork.

"Think you could teach me to make chicken and rice like that?" Mark asked, apparently the only one who had much of an appetite.

"Well, I . . ." Heidi stared at him, not really sure who he was or what he was all about. There were only a couple hundred kids in Katie's class, and Heidi had come to know a majority of them. But she couldn't recall ever hearing Mark's name or seeing it on a team roster or on the honor roll list printed in the local paper. She couldn't remember meeting his parents at a game or a rally. Or at a car wash or any other type of fund-raiser.

She didn't know where he lived or where he'd come from. She just knew as he sat there with his longish, wild hair and the bulky restraining sling on his right side wrapped around his fractured collarbone, he looked sort of scruffy, like damaged goods. And not exactly like the type of person she hoped Katie would bring home to meet her one day.

"There's not much to it," Heidi said. "You need chicken breasts, rice, and some Campbell's mushroom soup. The recipe is right on the can. Just throw it all in a glass dish and bake it."

"Seriously?" Mark's eyes widened as if she'd bestowed the secret of the universe upon him.

"Seriously. That's it." She shrugged.

Waiting politely for Katie's return, Heidi folded her hands in her lap and watched Mark toy with a corner of his place mat. The wall-mounted verdigris rooster-shaped clock ticked off the minutes. Absurdly she wished the thing would crow just to fill the void and awkwardness.

Of course, she'd thought letting Katie have Mark over for dinner would do the same thing.

After Katie's soul-wrenching breakdown this afternoon, Heidi had driven them home, a sad, desolate silence heaping its weight on their already-heavy hearts. She couldn't wait to get back to their neighborhood, back to the safe harbor of their home on Old Sunberry Lane. But once they did, even that usually comforting place felt oppressive. The familiar tree-lined streets seemed far too quiet and tranquil. Their tidy house felt too hushed, so noiseless. All of it seemed to epitomize isolation, to cry out loneliness just as Katie had in the car. So much so that when Katie's cell phone rang an hour later, it was a welcome sound rather than the usual intrusion.

Holding her breath, Heidi had hoped it was Jessica calling to apologize. But it wasn't a girl. Heidi could tell by the inflections in Katie's voice. It was Mark, asking if Katie would pick him up so they could grab some fast food together.

Heidi's eyebrow automatically cocked in disapproval. But when Katie kept begging permission, Heidi's resolve eroded much the same way Katie's tears had melted the layer of makeup from her cheeks. Mostly it was the echoes of Katie's pitiful sobbing still resonating in her mind—and heart—that did it.

Would it be so awful if Mark came to dinner? It wasn't like it meant Heidi condoned what they'd done.

Really, what *was* she proving by not letting Katie see him? As if they could do anything more or worse? As if Katie could be impregnated twice? Besides, as much as she didn't want to, Heidi had to face him and his family sometime.

She'd finally decided to meet Katie halfway. "Why don't you pick him up and come back here? I'd planned to make a decent dinner tonight."

"He can come here? Really?"

"Yes, really."

Heidi had felt like the worst kind of mother when Katie eyed her so warily. But she'd been just as shocked as Katie that she'd blurted out the invitation.

She couldn't even remember Mark visiting the house. Katie and her friends would typically meet up somewhere. Heidi had always wanted to blame it on the newfound freedom that came with a teen's driver's license, but was it also because Katie didn't think she would totally approve?

"So, Mark, do you like to cook?" Heidi couldn't stand the solitary sound of the ticking clock any longer.

"I never really tried it. My mom works two jobs. She doesn't get a chance to cook much. So I never learned."

"That's understandable."

"Yeah. I had a job too. At Homeland Lumber after school. Well, I mean, I did before the accident."

"Oh yeah? How much longer in the sling? Can you go back to Homeland after that?"

"About three weeks. But I'm not sure how I'll get to work since the car is totaled. We didn't have any collision insurance."

"That's awful." Heidi suddenly had a vision of Mark Lender twenty years into the future sitting at a kitchen table. More than likely with much thinner hair. The pressures of life bending his shoulders into a permanent stoop.

"My mom . . ." He rubbed his injured shoulder. "The thing is, she doesn't know about the baby. After the accident, I couldn't tell her. She was too upset about the car, and there's no money to get another one."

It wasn't as if Heidi hadn't thought about contacting Mark's parents. She'd wanted to get her bearings on things first. She hoped she and Katie could adjust and make a decision about what they wanted to do about the baby before dealing with the other set of grandparents.

Of course, she'd wanted to have a minute before facing the rest of the community too. But thanks to Carol Singer and her daughter, that wasn't going to happen, was it?

That thought alone made the mushroom sauce turn over in her stomach. Enough so that she considered joining Katie in the bathroom.

But then Katie walked into the kitchen, giving both Heidi and Mark a wan smile before sinking quietly into her chair.

"You okay?" Mark asked Katie before Heidi could.

"Better." Pushing aside her cold, food-laden plate, she turned to Heidi. "You're not going to tell Mrs. Lender, are you?" Her voice was nearly a whisper. Apparently she'd heard Mark's confession and was prepared to come to his defense.

"Guys, you have to realize, this baby is a grandchild." Heidi looked back and forth between the teenagers. "Mark's mom has a right to know. She'll want to know."

Mark shook his head, his eyes downcast. "I don't think so. And I'm not just saying that. My mom threw my sister out when she got pregnant. I don't even know where she is. Haven't seen her for four years. Mom keeps trying to throw my older brother out too, but he keeps coming back. Those were his drugs in the car, you know. He's pretty much in trouble all the time. And then there's my little brother. He has really bad asthma. My mom's always rushing him to the hospital. Plus her jobs. My mom's not a bad person. It's just that . . ."

Heidi didn't need to hear any more where his mother was concerned. She sounded like a woman who had her hands full, to be sure. "What about your dad, then?"

"My dad? What about him?" Mark's jaw visibly tightened. "The last time he came around was like seven years ago. I think he just showed up that day to beat on my mom. That's all I can remember, anyway."

Without meaning to, Heidi let go of a sigh so heavy she imagined her neighbors heard her down the street.

"I told Katie I'd give her money from my check. To buy baby stuff. I mean, if I still have a job once my shoulder is well and if I can find a way to get there." Mark looked at Heidi, his eyes pleading. "I don't want to tell my mom. What if she throws me out too?"

"That's great you want to help support your baby," Heidi said, though deep down she wanted to roll her eyes. Kids had no idea how expensive a child was. A part-time job after school would make only the smallest dent. "But don't you think your mom might wonder where your money is going? And won't she think it's odd when she sees your girlfriend pregnant?"

Katie laid a hand on her arm. "You don't understand. We're hardly ever at Mark's house. If we do go over there, it's not like his mom's around anyway."

Funny how Katie felt free to be so open and honest now in her new condition. Heidi cringed, not wanting to hear more, but Katie continued. "It's not like she'd know Mark and I are together. So she wouldn't even know the baby was his." Her eyes narrowed on Heidi. "Not unless someone tells her."

Suddenly the situation seemed worse than pathetic. Not only had Katie's boyfriend gotten her pregnant, but his mother barely knew

Katie existed. True, Heidi didn't know Katie's friends that well, but at least she knew them well enough to know she wasn't all that crazy about them.

Oh, how she'd never visualized things this way. Never thought she'd be sitting here between her pregnant daughter and a stranger who had contributed to that condition.

Heidi had always imagined the fourth chair at their table being filled with some nice, upstanding guy one day. A young man with trimmed hair, highlighted blond from days spent playing soccer or baseball or golf in the sun, who wore button-downs and jeans that didn't hang halfway down his backside. Someone who adored Katie and treated her like the precious jewel she was. Someone to whom Katie wanted to promise her future without compromising her present.

But her reality was nothing like those visions. If it were, the seat at the head of the table would be filled as well. Jeff would be here with them too.

Lifting the dirty dishes and carrying them to the sink seemed like too much to think about. Still, after a few minutes of struggling, feeling like a weight lifter heaving a barbell into the air, Heidi managed to push off the heavy listlessness of self-pity and get to her feet.

To her surprise, Mark thanked her again for dinner as he and Katie brought their dishes to the sink. Then the pair moved into the family room while she finished up with the rest of the mess.

Deliberately keeping the faucet down to a quiet drizzle, Heidi strained to hear them as she rinsed the dinner plates. Did they actually have things to say to one another? What was the attraction for Katie?

Over the hum of the television, she could catch a word here and there, but nothing she could make sense of. At one point, though, she heard Katie laugh like she used to. When was the last time Heidi had heard her laugh that way? Months ago? Years?

It was laughter that didn't seem derisive or put on. Laughter that sounded real and pure. Young and free.

For a moment, Heidi stood still, soaking in Katie's joy, a spontaneous smile bursting across her face.

But then a frown came at the thought that Mark—and only Mark—had been the one to elicit the joy left in her Katie.

Staring out the kitchen window, clutching the dishrag in her hand, Heidi wondered at her topsy-turvy emotions.

She was still trying to reconcile her feelings when the phone rang. After drying her hands on a dish towel, she picked up the phone from the granite-topped island and glanced at the caller ID. Peterson? *Kevin Peterson?* Her heart lurched. He had some other news about Katie? "Hello?"

"Katie?"

"No, this is Heidi."

"Heidi, it's Kevin Peterson. Sorry about that. Your voice sounds young."

"People say Katie and I sound alike on the phone. Do you want me to get her?"

"Actually, I just spoke to Katie the other day."

She sucked in a breath. "Really?"

"Yeah, I ran into her at the gas station. She was pretty chatty. Said you both are going to South Africa soon. That sounds interesting."

His voice sounded so relaxed and calm. She wanted to relax too, but that wasn't something that came easily to her these days.

"Well, yes. I mean, we *were* going to South Africa." Heidi turned away from the family room to make sure Katie couldn't overhear her. "But I'm not so sure now."

"Yeah? Katie made it seem like a done deal. Seemed very excited to be going, too. Some sort of women helping women thing? She said she was glad not to be heading down south to the beach for a change."

"She said all that?"

"Pretty much unsolicited."

"With everything that's going on, I just don't know." Walking over to the stove, she picked up the teakettle, brought it to the faucet, and filled it halfway with water. Chamomile tea—that was what she needed right now.

"She asked my opinion on that, too."

"On what?"

"On everything. She said she'd gotten vaccinated before she knew she was pregnant," Kevin continued, his voice still low and soothing. "She asked if I thought it was okay to travel."

"Really?" Heidi paused before setting the kettle on the burner.

"I told her the flight could get a little uncomfortable, especially if she was experiencing morning sickness, and she might be somewhat fatigued. But other than that . . ."

That answered some of Heidi's questions—the clinical ones. But there were the emotional ones too. So Katie wanted to go on the mission trip after the argument they'd had the night of the accident? That was a surprise. It seemed they'd switched places. Because now Heidi wasn't so sure she wanted to go. Did she really want to risk having their church across town find out about the pregnancy? Christians or not, would they be talking behind Katie's back, reacting to Katie the same way people at her school had? Could Katie handle more of that? Could Heidi?

"Katie's going to be all right." Kevin's voice broke through her thoughts. "She's a nice kid."

"Thanks. I appreciate that."

A silence hung between them before he spoke up. "That's not the only reason I called, though."

The teakettle began to whistle faintly. Gripping the phone tightly, she ignored the sound. "It's not?"

"Not exactly. When I saw Katie, it made me think of you, and . . ." He paused. "I was wondering if you might want to meet me for coffee tomorrow night at Kerouac's Coffeehouse. Near downtown."

The question caught Heidi off guard. "Tomorrow evening?" The kettle shrilled. She jumped and moved to click off the burner.

"Yeah. Are you busy?"

"Well, no, I'm not. It's just that I . . ." She what? Felt like a jumble of emotions right now? Didn't know if she could think of anything to talk about beyond Katie? Didn't think she'd be very good company? All of the above? She wasn't sure how to answer.

But Kevin made it easy. "Hey, sorry about that. The invite probably came out of nowhere for you."

"It's not like—"

His even, sweet voice interrupted her. "Listen. I think my timing is a little off-kilter here. I shouldn't have sprung that on you. How about this? Think about it, and if you want to get together when you get back from South Africa, you know where to find me, right?"

"Yes, I do." She smiled into the phone. "Thanks," she said before he apologized again, this time for the craziness in the ER, and said he had to go.

While sorting the remaining dishes into the dishwasher, Heidi had to admit she felt pleasantly surprised that Kevin had called her. And somewhat flattered, too. Even more than that, his easygoing demeanor seemed to have quelled her anxiety momentarily. No doubt about it, the man had a great bedside manner. He'd found his true calling in life.

She turned on the dishwasher, then grabbed her mug and her tote full of papers to be graded and started to head upstairs to her office. But then, walking past the pantry, she stopped and set down her tote and cup. She pulled a couple of items from the well-stocked shelves and laid them on the counter next to Katie's car keys.

Next, Heidi grabbed a pad of Post-its from a kitchen drawer. She wrote Mark's name on the yellow square and stuck the note on a box of instant white rice sitting next to a can of Campbell's mushroom soup.

Outwardly her gesture appeared kind, she knew. But inside her thoughts and emotions were at war again where Mark and his involvement with Katie were concerned.

Why him, Katie? Why this?
Why me, Lord? Why me?

11

Even though her black crepe skirt didn't fit quite the way it used to and her lacy white blouse could've used a quick ironing, Gabby still felt somewhat elegant as she strode across the tile floor of Mancusi's to the table where her husband was already waiting for her.

Tom's late afternoon call had come as a surprise. Not that they didn't typically touch base during the day. But this time when talk turned to dinner, he suggested they meet somewhere. And not just at one of their usual sandwich shops but at one of the city's finest restaurants.

At first she'd thought he must be teasing. She laughed, asking if after dinner they could then fly to Paris for dessert. His idea might've sounded romantic and spontaneous, but it seemed preposterous too. Had he forgotten their budget? the money they still owed from the cleanup when spring rains had flooded their basement? the stack of fertility clinic invoices? the extra funds they'd need to furnish an entire nursery one day very soon?

Gabby had started to remind him of all that, but something in his voice wouldn't let her. He sounded too much like Tom of years ago, so excited to be behaving like an impetuous male. Wooing her in the same way he had when they'd first met and had fallen in love on a lush green college campus a lifetime ago. Or when, as newlyweds, he'd bring home a small bouquet of flowers in the evening or tape weekend getaway plans to the bathroom mirror for her to find in the morning.

As she approached the table, his smile looked that way too, as if he was totally pleased with himself and also very pleased simply to see her.

Getting up, he kissed her lightly on the cheek before pulling out the maize-colored, cushioned chair for her.

Gabby felt something close to bliss when he sat down and they gazed at each other across the candlelit table. Who knew meeting her husband in the middle of the week in such a special place for no apparent reason could feel so wonderful. Marveling at her emotions, she was more than glad he'd thought of it and equally happy she hadn't spoiled his plans, no matter what kind of dent the evening was bound to put in their budget.

"Hey, gorgeous." Tom reached across the table for her hand.

"Hey, mystery man." She placed her left hand into his right one, thinking how she never tired of the tenderness of his touch.

"No mystery." His hand gently squeezed hers. "Just wanted to have a special dinner with my girl."

"Well, I agree; this is certainly out of the ordinary."

Tom smiled at her, the blueness of his eyes intensified by the peacock color of his tie. It wasn't often he wore a suit and tie since his position rarely called for either. But as Gabby well knew, for the past few weeks he'd been preparing for today's regional presentation with national executives. That sort of meeting required business attire, and she was only too happy to make sure his black suit was dry-cleaned and pressed. She loved seeing him in tailored clothes. His well-conditioned physique seemed a perfect match for a suit, his square, broad shoulders filling out the jacket easily.

"Did everything go well with your meetings today?"

"Very well." He nodded. "National is actually increasing our budget, so we'll have more operating monies this fiscal year."

"*We*, meaning the organization? Or *we*, meaning you and me?"

"Both."

"You got a raise?" She couldn't restrain the glee in her voice.

"A small one. But, yes, *we* got a raise."

"Oh, that's wonderful! So *that's* what this is all about."

"You mean Mancusi's?"

"Well, yeah."

"No, not exactly. It's sort of more than that. It's about . . ." Tom stared at her as if seeing her for the first time.

His scrutiny, loving though it was, suddenly made her feel self-conscious to the point where a girlish giggle erupted from the back of her throat. "What? It's about what?"

"I guess you could say I had a sentimental moment today."

"Really? I didn't know big, brawny guys like you had sentimental moments," she teased, although it wasn't at all the truth. That was one of the very reasons she'd loved Tom Phillips in the first place. His combination of strength and sensitivity was not so often found—or at least not so readily revealed—in most other males she'd met.

"During the meeting today, we took a break to go out to lunch. I go in and out of the building all the time, but somehow the moment we walked outside, it hit me. The scent of hyacinths blooming right next to the main door."

"Hyacinths?"

"You don't remember? Our junior year?"

"Sorry. I'm not making the connection."

"Spring break at my fraternity house and your sorority house?"

"Oh, when we told our parents we wanted to stay on campus and help paint houses so we could make extra money?"

"But all we really wanted to do was spend time together."

"Why did we think we couldn't spend time together without doing all that awful painting?"

"Who knows? Mostly, I just remember sitting on the front porch of your sorority house with you."

"You do? Why don't I remember that?"

"There was that same flowery scent in the air. And I'd look at you, and even with paint splattered on your face, I kept thinking that I could never love you more than at that moment."

Gabby sat quietly, stunned by the sweetness of his words. It wasn't as if Tom never told her he loved her. His phone calls and their nights usually ended that way. But still, she felt moved and blessed that in all these years there were still precious things left to be shared.

"Today I realized that wasn't true. Somehow I love you more and more all the time, Gabby, and I know, without a doubt, I always will."

Unexpected tears instantly moistened her eyes. "It could be a long time, you know." Her voice quaked with emotion even though she was trying her best to be lighthearted. "Maybe another fifty years or so."

"Promise?"

"Promise."

Releasing her hand, Tom raised his water glass in the air, and she did the same. As if sealing their heartfelt vow, they clinked the crystal stemware together.

Before they could even take a sip, a waiter arrived at their table, fussing over them. "Would you like to see our wine list?" He held out a leather-bound binder. "Are you celebrating tonight?"

"No, to the wine list. But, yes, we're celebrating," Tom answered. "Celebrating each other," he added, making the waiter smile, though not nearly as much as her.

◈ ◈ ◈

"Gab . . . ?"

The touch of Tom's hand smoothing her hair brought Gabby out of the gauziness of sleep more than his whispered words. Looking up, seeing the silhouette of his face bent over her in the early dawn gray of their bedroom, she smiled with a pleasure that tingled to her toes.

How crazy was it she didn't wake up every morning feeling this way?

Gabby was so lucky, so blessed to be married to this man. *Shame on me for taking it for granted, Lord.*

"I have to go," the love of her life said.

"Mmm . . . why?" she moaned.

"You know why." He grinned. "I have an early morning flight to catch."

"Why?"

"Because I have to get to Philly. And before you ask why again—" he chuckled—"because the big boss man is making me."

"But I'll miss you." Playfully, Gabby flung her arms around his neck, pulling his face closer to hers. The previous night was still fresh in her mind, and she guessed by the way he laughed, it was for him too.

"I'll miss you too."

"Thank you for last night. I felt like a princess. Everything was so . . ." She couldn't think of a word delicious enough to describe it.

"Incredible. Like you." Tom kissed her forehead. "I wish I could stay snuggled in with you. But I'm already running a little late, and if I miss this flight, a lot of people are going to be upset with me."

Freeing him from her grasp, she murmured, "I know; I know. I'm sorry."

"Me too. I'm sorry I have to go. You, however, have another thirty minutes until the alarm goes off." He fluffed their goose-down comforter and tucked it around her chin. "And you should be getting as much rest as you can, mother-to-be."

"That reminds me. I had a dream. A really good dream . . ."

"Yeah? Was I the knight in shining armor this time?" Tom snickered. "Or the football player with the huge biceps?"

"No, not about us, silly. Well, about us. But *us* as a family. It was one of those dreams you could really feel, you know? Like I can still feel it—it was awesome." Gabby sprang up in bed, propping the pillows behind her. "The sun was shining and we were at a picnic, sitting on a blanket, the three of us. You, me, and our baby. I don't know if the baby was a boy or a girl. . . ."

More light was pouring in the window with each moment. Suddenly she could see the strain on his face, could tell he was trying to be patient and listen to her narration but was also duly stressed at the prospect of missing his flight. She had to let him leave. "But I'll tell you about it later, okay? Because you really need to go. So get out of here, will you?"

"Thanks." He lifted her chin and pecked her on the lips. "I'll be in meetings all day from the minute I get off the plane," he said, crossing the room to pick up his keys from the dresser. "But I'll call you the first chance I get. I'll be catching a flight home tonight, okay?"

She watched him grab his briefcase from where it sat on the floor. "Definitely okay. I love you, Tom."

"Love you too," he said over his shoulder as he hustled from the room.

Hearing the front door close, Gabby settled back under the comforter, but there was no way she could—or wanted to—go back to sleep.

The silence of their house caressing her, she lay there savoring the quiet and the sweetness of her thoughts.

When she'd lain in Tom's arms the night before, she told him how amazing it was that they'd spent nearly a dozen years together and still had things they hadn't shared. Like his story about the hyacinths and those times they'd spent on the steps of her sorority house. For a while they made a game of it, both of them taking turns, trying to think of things they had never told one another.

Most of their secrets and memories made them laugh. Except there was one thing Gabby didn't want to tell him. Even though it kept coming to the forefront of her mind . . . even though she wanted to unburden her heart, she just couldn't make herself say it. It was something she didn't want to share with anyone, not even Tom.

So she pushed the thought back into its hiding place, the same way she had for years, telling herself she didn't want to mar their perfect evening with the real reason she'd never wanted to adopt.

Why should she? Once their baby was born, her secret—her fear—wouldn't matter anyway.

Even now, Gabby shooed away the sad memory, preferring to think about happier things, like their baby.

One thought of their little angel and remnants of her dream rushed back, flooding her already-overflowing heart. She closed her eyes and tried to focus on the three of them again, the way they had appeared in her dream. Tom was smiling, stretched out on his side on the blanket, his head propped up on his hand, gazing at her and their baby adoringly.

And there she was with their baby in her lap, the infant squeezing her index finger tightly. She could still remember the essence of it, the silky feel of the baby's hand wrapped around her own flesh. The delightful sound of the baby's gurgling. The welcome weight of the child leaning against her chest.

Was the baby a girl or a boy? Gabby tried to think back, to fill in the blanks of her vision, tried to recall clothes or colors or hair, but somehow she couldn't remember. But did it really matter? Boy or girl, it was the feel of the baby that was so special. The feel of the three of them together. As a family.

Minutes later, the alarm jarred her awake. Feeling groggier than she had the first time she woke up, she dutifully made her bed with half-closed eyes, then shuffled into the bathroom.

Gabby held her breath as she did every time she went into a bathroom these days. Past attempts and failures at conceiving a child had conditioned her that way. Always there was the worry . . . and always there was the hope that she wouldn't see signs of something gone wrong.

Forcing herself to look, she felt relief spread through her like clear, cleansing waters rushing over a dam. No spotting. *Thank You, Lord!* A new day had dawned and their baby—their family—was safe again.

She turned on the shower, letting the water heat up while she brushed her teeth. Counting absently as she always had since she was a kid, she gazed around the master bathroom.

The moment she saw it, the room reeled. Spun crazily out of

control. She dropped her toothbrush and gripped the marbled sink counter with both hands. Steadying herself, she looked down again at the crimson spot of blood on the cream-colored rug.

It took a minute before she could manage to shakily reach for a tissue, and that was when she saw the off-white hand towel Tom had used. Streaks of red were smeared on it. Apparently her husband had cut himself shaving this morning.

Oh, will he ever hear about this, she thought as she wet the Kleenex with cold water, sank to the floor on her knees, and rubbed at the spot on the rug.

12

Air caught in Gabby's lungs.

It didn't seem real. One minute she was sitting in her office still feeling euphoric from the night before. The next minute she was in one of the church's colorless, metal restroom stalls staring at the reddish brown spots of blood on her underwear. So tiny, yet so . . .

It has to be something else. It has to be! Heart pounding, she frantically grasped for other explanations. Any explanation. Maybe she'd sat in something red? Or somehow the blood in the bathroom that morning had gotten on her? Or—

Reality knocked the wind out of her. *This can't be happening. I can't be losing this baby. Oh, dear God, please help me. I felt it. I really felt this baby in my dream.*

And the feeling was still so raw, so real. The warmth of the infant nestled against her chest. The sweet, warm breath on her cheek.

A wail began to form in her gut, threatening to rise up. But she couldn't—wouldn't—let it surface. If it did, if she let it, it would surely turn her insides out, taking with it every bit of fight. Leaving her empty and void.

Gabby bit her fist, refusing to let the cry escape. She would not collapse. She would not give in to hysterics. Not now.

It took everything in her to half walk, half stagger to the sink. But it took even more than that to push all the negatives from her mind. Yes, she'd been here before. Yes, it almost seemed routine.

But this time she'd lasted nearly the entire first trimester. This time would be different.

It has to be!

"I'm fighting for you, baby," she whispered to the infant inside her as tears spilled onto her cheeks. "I won't give up. I promise."

Splashing cold water on her face, she tried to stop the tears. She stepped back from the sink and took a deep breath. Her sister-in-law had spotted with Grant, and everything had been okay with him. Not every pregnancy was textbook perfect. Things happened, and in the end, most babies were just fine.

You'll be fine too, baby. She gently rubbed her belly.

Still, her eyes filled again as she stumbled to her office to get her purse and keys. The stretch of hallway was a blur.

She'd decided not to call ahead for an appointment. Didn't think her mouth could quite form the words or that she could steady her voice on the phone. She wanted to be there with Dr. Selleck, letting him soothe her worst fears. She'd go to his office and wait for him to make things right—till the next day if she had to.

◈ ◈ ◈

The traffic was light, and Gabby made it to Dr. Selleck's office in less than ten minutes. The nurses greeted her with hopeful smiles, knowing her history well, promising an exam room any minute.

Obviously she felt too distraught, too anxious, to pick up a magazine and casually flip through the pages like the other women in the waiting room. Instead her eyes were fixed on her hands, pressed together nervously in her lap, squeezing hard till her knuckles turned white.

It crossed Gabby's mind more than once that she may have looked like she was praying. But she most definitely was not. She'd already said the same prayer—or some version of it—so many times before. Was God not listening?

The only thing she had to be thankful for at the moment was that Tom was out of town. She would save the baby on her own. No one else would have to worry. No one else would have to know.

The nurse called her name, and Gabby looked up to see Sally's familiar face. No matter the turnover in the office, she visited so often she knew many of the nurses by their first names.

She attempted a cordial smile but couldn't muster one up as she got to her feet. In four shaky strides she stood next to Sally, who greeted her warmly, not realizing—or more likely, not wanting to acknowledge—that Gabby's life might be about to change . . . forever.

"They keeping you busy?" Sally asked, and Gabby knew she was referring to church.

"Always. How about you?" she quickly replied, attempting to deflect any more questions about herself.

"Same," Sally answered as Gabby followed the woman through the doorway and down the maze of mauve hallways. "Rarely a dull moment around here; that's for sure. And if there ever is, we savor it." She laughed in a light, easy way that Gabby had to appreciate, even if it was in contrast to the heaviness in her heart.

The two of them spent the next twenty minutes together while Sally performed the ultrasound. Gabby knew better than to ask questions, since Sally would defer to Dr. Selleck for the answers.

Another twenty minutes later, and the doctor—hopefully turned miracle worker, Gabby wished with all her might—came into the exam room and took her hand. "I'm sorry to have to tell you this," he said, bowing his head. "It appears the fetus hasn't grown for several weeks."

The room spun and Gabby nearly fainted, wobbling on the exam table. Dr. Selleck caught her by her shoulders.

"Hasn't grown?"

"It terminated several weeks ago in utero," he explained. "Possibly right after your last ultrasound."

"So these past few weeks . . . ?" She grasped the sanitary paper covering the exam table, balling it up in her fists. That was why the morning sickness had suddenly seemed to disappear? why her breasts hadn't been as tender? It had all been pretend the last three, nearly four weeks? All for nothing? Acrid bile rose to the back of her throat.

"I don't understand. I thought maybe the bleeding was because of last night. We made love, and you'd said to wait for the first three months. But we were so close, and—"

"Believe me, Gabby. It was nothing you did. And nothing you didn't do. It just is."

"But that can't be. It can't be." Gabby choked back a sob. "Dr. Selleck, please. You have to do something."

Dr. Selleck took hold of her cold, bloodless hands, clasping them in the warmth of his. "I wish I had different news for you." His eyes brimmed with compassion, worry lines crisscrossing at the edges. "I really do. I know how long you and Tom have tried." He squeezed her hands. His voice sounded as leaden as her heart when he said, "I'm sure you could use a few minutes alone."

Stunned beyond words, she only managed to murmur a half-hearted "Thank you."

The tears came the moment Dr. Selleck walked out of the room, and she knew they'd keep coming for quite a long time. Elbows on her knees, she buried her mouth in her forearm, muffling the sobs that racked her chest. All this time she'd thought she'd felt life growing inside her, making her a mother-to-be, giving her a place in the world where life made sense and she had a reason for being. And now . . .

Gabby hated herself. Her body. Her life. She hated it all.

Oh, Tom, I'm sorry. So sorry. Why did you ever marry me?

She cradled her head in her hands, crying for Tom. Crying for herself. Crying for the baby they would never know.

Only . . . she did know the baby, didn't she? Suddenly the images of her dream last night came to her more vividly than ever. Tiny rosebud pink lips shaped like a bow. Wisps of strawberry blonde hair, shining in the sunlight. Chubby little hands waving excitedly. It was a girl. Definitely a baby girl. Their Madison. How many times had she lain awake at night and dreamed of a little girl named Madison?

Awed by the image, Gabby tried to memorize everything about her, pressing the infant's features to her mind and heart. Never did she want to open her eyes and lose Madison again, but a soft knock on the door startled her.

Sadly, the vision dissipated in an instant when Sally entered the room. "Dr. Selleck wanted to make sure you had someone to drive you home."

"Yes, I do," Gabby fibbed. She didn't want to talk to anyone. Besides, she had herself—her desolate, mournful self—and she wanted it to stay that way.

◈ ◈ ◈

The cramping had started the moment Dr. Selleck told Gabby the news. The pain only intensified throughout the drive home. Hunched over the steering wheel, she hoped in a sick way that she would never make it home to 488 Cantebury Court. Hoped she would die along with the baby.

I'm not pregnant. Really not pregnant. Rubbing at the spot where her baby used to be, Gabby felt the sadness overwhelm her. Although it shouldn't have been such a shock. Her body . . . her God . . . had failed her. Again. Was there anything new about that?

By the time Gabby pulled into her driveway, anger, as all-consuming as a raging fire, burned in her. She slammed the car door shut, then stalked through the house she and Tom had saved so earnestly to buy. The home where they'd planned to raise their family. Heartsick, her grieving came out in groans, primeval growls from the deepest part of her being.

Like a woman gone mad, she flung open the oak kitchen cabinets, swiping the shelves clean of fertility pills, painkillers, and prenatal vitamins. She hurled the containers against the wall, cursing and scream-ing, and threw her arms up to the heavens, not in supplication but in bitter resentment and disbelief that God could disappoint her so.

After all the children she'd served and all the ways she'd served Him, He couldn't give her and Tom this one thing. The thing nearly every person in the universe already had. A child of their own.

The cordless phone rang, and Gabby yanked it off its cradle and threw that against the wall too. She didn't want to speak to anyone. Not Tom. Or her mother. Or her brothers or sisters-in-law. Or any of her friends. She was too exhausted. Too weary of delivering bad news and disappointing everyone. Sick of hearing everyone's platitudes and pitiful sighs. Tired of being on the receiving end of pats on the hand, assuring her that everything would be all right.

It wasn't all right. Nothing was all right.

About to collapse, she tore back the comforter from her bed and fell into it headfirst, weeping into her pillow. The love and joy she and Tom had shared here last night now seemed like a distant memory. They'd never be happy again. Never.

His arms slid around her waist, spooning her against him in the bed. Even in the blackened room, even in her groggy state, Gabby knew it was her husband. She started to turn, to kiss him hello, but then . . .

It felt like a punch in the stomach, the memory of what had happened today. Needing to escape the pain, she recoiled defensively, her body tightening into itself.

"Gabby?" The worry in Tom's voice was unmistakable. Did he know? Somehow it seemed he did. She tensed even more. "What's going on? I've been going crazy. I tried calling you everywhere."

How? What did he know?

"You left your wallet at the doctor's. I had a voice mail from his office manager. Apparently she couldn't reach you. I tried to call you too. You weren't scheduled for an appointment today, were you?" Tom placed his hand on her belly.

The pain that shot through her heart felt more intense than any discomfort she'd felt that day. "The baby's gone."

"Gone?" Tom gasped, then groaned in her ear.

Gabby held her breath, waiting. For what, she didn't know. An assault? A pardon?

But instead, his arms loosened from around her, he rolled away, lying flat on his back. "You—we lost the baby? How?"

Tears clogged the back of her throat as she tried to form some words. "I don't know how."

A curse word flew from his mouth and ricocheted off the ceiling. "Gabby, honey, please! Talk to me." His voice rose. "Tell me something. I need to know why."

He was right. It was only fair for him to know everything. Only fair for him to hurt like she did.

Shooting up in bed, she suddenly found her voice and ranted hysterically. "The baby died. Right inside me. Inside my body. I thought I was pregnant. I thought it every second of every day, and I knew this time would be right. But no. It was a big, fat farce. Once again. I haven't been pregnant for weeks. Why? I don't know. Because God hates us? Because my body sucks? Because the entire universe is against us? Pick whatever reason you want. Because I don't know the answer." Her wailing came on as fiercely, as loudly, as her screaming had.

Moving toward her, Tom pulled her into his arms, trying to soothe her the same way she had always imagined she'd comfort her child when she couldn't sleep, had bumped her head, or had been hurt by the words of a friend.

"I'm sorry. I'm sorry for yelling. I'm sorry for everything. But it's okay." He kissed her forehead. "We're here. We're together. It's all right. We've been through this before. We'll figure it out."

She pushed at his shoulders, trying to break free from his caress. "Figure it out? Are you serious? There is no more 'we'll figure this out.' Remember? It was our last chance. It's over."

Even as she said the words, even though she pushed at him, he held on, not letting her go.

Fine. Tom could hug her all he wanted, could try to embrace her and comfort her. But his arms wouldn't reach far enough; his love wouldn't penetrate deeply enough. Nothing he could ever do could exorcise the pain from her heart.

13

Gabby wasn't quite sure what Tom felt. She hadn't spent much time with him over the past week. Many evenings she pretended to be asleep when he got home at night and when he left for work in the morning. Even the one day he'd taken off work, she avoided him as much as she could all day, going from one room to the next in their small house. She wasn't even sure why she'd done that. She was just so angry. At herself. At God. At her husband.

Kicking off her gym shoes at the front door, she tried to make a silent path toward the kitchen in sock-covered feet.

But Tom looked up from where he hovered over the computer, greeting her with a hesitant smile. "How was the afternoon?"

"Fine." Gabby shrugged.

"You girls get a lot of walking and talking in?"

"Walking, yeah," she told him, not bothering to add she'd never called her sister-in-law to meet her at the park. Also not mentioning she'd circled the two-mile periphery of the park only once on foot. By that time, she'd seen so many moms and dads interacting with their children, it had been too much for her. Bolting from the area, she'd gone and sat in her car in the parking lot with her eyes closed and stayed that way for hours until the sun began fading from the sky.

"What are you doing?" Curious, Gabby took a few steps closer.

Usually with anything work related, he used his laptop. For anything else, he'd get on the house computer.

"It's nothing." Tom clicked off the monitor.

But she'd already caught a glimpse. "Adoption information?"

"I just had a few free minutes. . . ."

"Everyone thinks they have the answer. Even you." It was awful to think adoption could be such an easy cure-all for other people. Gabby wished it was for her. She loved children; she always had. But adopting a child wasn't that simple for her. It was frightening for reasons she was too embarrassed to even share with anyone, including her husband.

Seeing a shadow cross his face, she knew her accusation stung. Still, Tom got up from the chair to hug her.

But her arms hung at her side. She was too numb. She couldn't bring herself to hug him back. Instead she pulled away, running a hand through her ponytail. She hadn't done her hair or put on any makeup all week. In fact, she could hardly stand to shower, hating to see her naked body, knowing it was emptied of the baby it once held.

"Don't you get it? I had the baby in *me*. It's *me* who will never deliver a baby. Never breast-feed a child. Shouldn't every woman have the chance to do those things? Why would God do this to me?"

And why didn't Tom seem more distraught that they'd just lost their last chance to have a child of their own? Why wasn't he angry at God like she was?

"I won't go there. You can't praise God when things are good and then not love Him when life turns bad."

"*Bad*? This isn't bad. It's devastating. It's wrong. It's hateful of God."

"He has a plan. You're the director of children's ministries. You spend every day at a church. Don't you believe that?"

Didn't he realize how torturous it was being in a job around children, knowing you couldn't have one of your own? And she'd tried to believe. For eight years she tried to think that way. To know it and feel it in every part of her heart that God had a plan for them if she'd only be patient. Just hang on and *believe*. Yes, it did turn out He had a plan. He planned for them not to have any children. Planned for them to be miserable without a family to call their own.

But Tom didn't see it that way. As always, he tried to comfort her. "Your mom brought over some chicken noodle soup. Can I heat some up for dinner?"

"I'm not hungry."

"Are you sure? How about a grilled cheese sandwich?"

"No thanks."

"Want to sit on the couch? watch some TV with me? I can get an afghan for you."

Gabby shook her head. "I'm kind of tired. I think I'll just go back to the bedroom."

"It's only six thirty. Sure you want to do that?"

"I need my strength for . . . you know, work."

"Okay." Tom nodded as if trying to be understanding. But at the same time, his jaw clenched, and she noticed the disappointed look in his eyes.

She felt him watching her as she crossed the room and headed down the hallway to their bedroom. Without even taking off her sweats, she slipped under the silky comforter and closed her eyes tight. The murmur of the TV echoed in her head along with her own voice asking *why, why, why* over and over again.

The next thing Gabby heard was the bedroom door scraping over the carpet as it opened.

"You know, it was my baby too," Tom said solemnly. Then he closed the door, leaving her alone in the dark.

For the first time in what seemed like an eternity, she was unable to shed a tear.

14

Cassandra tapped her brakes before guiding the Jag into a slow right turn and onto the freeway. But even the rush of traffic couldn't take her mind off where she was headed—a get-to-know-each-other meeting at Graceview Church. This was so not worth her time.

Did she really need to meet with the other people going to South Africa? commune with the other women? get to know them better?

Not to her way of thinking she didn't.

She hadn't signed up for the Women Helping Women team to make new friends or fill some void in her life. If she didn't think the group had the best potential for a news story—the woman-child-community stuff WONR's target demographic had a heart for—she would've definitely opted for something more male-oriented. She found that men were so much easier to deal with, as long as you didn't get too involved with one. Not all emotions and hormones like the majority of her gender.

But like it or not, she had to attend tonight's meeting. The mission trip itinerary had stated it was mandatory. She'd go and try to be chatty and heartfelt with the bunch of females she was assigned to, though it was the last thing on earth she wanted to do.

No, Cassandra corrected herself. *Not exactly the last thing.*

Definitely at the bottom of the list was praying. And it seemed like there might be a whole host of "prayer opportunities." At least that's what the pastor had mentioned when she'd visited Graceview the first time and talked to him about filming the trip. In fact, the man—a total stranger—said he'd be praying for her.

Praying for her? Cassandra Albright? Sure, praying might be a large part of his gig. But honestly! That had peeved her. Did she look like a person who needed prayers? Dressed in her creamy designer suit that day, with her expensive shoes and a diamond-encrusted Tiffany watch?

"You'll pray for me?" she'd questioned, her eyes narrowing on the pastor's round face.

"Yes, and the entire mission group. There will also be prayer meetings you can attend before you leave, so you can pray for the mission as a whole. Prayers for safety. Prayers that God will help you accomplish your goals—and His—for your trip."

Well, as far as the safety thing, she couldn't imagine that would be an issue. It wasn't like they were traveling to Darfur, for goodness' sake. As for her goals for the trip, she pretty much had to make those happen herself, didn't she? Not like God was going to come down from the heavens and help set up her video camera.

Cassandra slid onto the exit ramp, then made a right turn on red onto Bridgestone Boulevard. The queasiness in her stomach started up again. What had brought that on? The two Advil on an empty stomach? Or was it because she was only miles from the church?

Probably both.

The trip was going to be slightly more uncomfortable than she'd first imagined when she and McFadden had been busy plotting their career boosts in his office. How would she ever stomach it? Listening to God-talk. All that praying. Pretending to be "one of them."

Church had never been part of her life, which was probably lucky for the people of Plaines, Indiana. Most likely if her foster father had ever set foot in a church, it would've been struck by lightning and burned to the ground. God didn't exist in the house her foster parents rented. No one ever really talked about God or even mentioned His name unless it was in a string of curse words.

Still, uneasy or not, the mission trip had to be done. Cassandra had to protect herself, her interests, her place in the world. If she didn't, who else would?

With a shake of her head, she dismissed the heavy thoughts, checking the digital clock on her wood-grain dash—7:20.

When she pulled into the church lot, she realized she wasn't the only one who liked being ahead of schedule, even for events as dreadful as this promised to be. At least a dozen or so cars were already parked there.

Just as she locked the car and slipped on her Brooks Brothers blazer, she spied a woman cutting across the lot on her way to the church entrance.

Whoa! Talk about someone who looks like she needs a few prayers said for her . . .

Dropping her keys into her Bulga handbag, Cassandra stole furtive glances at the woman from behind her gold-trimmed sunglasses.

Even though the lady was at least ten years younger, she looked horribly fatigued. Totally wrung out. She might be a natural redhead, but evidently she still got highlights too, because the streaks had grown out quite a bit, which was easy to see even with her hair pulled back in a ponytail. Her gray, waist-length jacket looked a bit dowdy and her jeans as if they'd seen better days, like around the beginning of the millennium. The girl looked like she needed more than some religious mumbo jumbo spoken on her behalf. She needed a makeover. Yes, and a vacation might not hurt either.

15

Gabby leaned against the painted concrete wall and glanced around Graceview's community meeting room at the tables of soon-to-be missiongoers. Some of them seemed to be getting antsy, shifting in their metal chairs. She didn't blame them. The director of missions could yammer on and on once he had the floor.

"Again, folks," he said for at least the third time, "our summer mission trips to Mamelodi might be larger. Typically we've had three hundred volunteers each summer in the last couple of years since we've been in partnership with Pastor Shadrach. But the spring trip has a unique quality about it that you will find absolutely amazing. The thirty or so of you will be broken into half a dozen teams, each with a particular initiative in mind. Your teams will not be interacting with one another, but you will be working closely with the people in South Africa, laying the groundwork for the summer projects and volunteers. . . ."

Gabby half listened, not really caring to hear his spiel. None of it mattered anyway. She didn't need substance in her life right now. She needed distance. If there was a trip headed for the moon, it wouldn't be far enough away for her.

She'd never much entertained the thought of going on a mission before this, either too busy with the children's ministries or too caught up in trying to have a child. But when one of the team leaders had a family emergency, Gabby jumped at the chance to go in her place.

Being gone was the only thing that could get her through Easter Sunday.

Another Easter Sunday without a child of her own.

How her heart had ached each year when she saw the little girls at church in their frilly, pastel dresses, clacking white patent leather shoes, hair held back in fancy headbands and satiny bows or bonnets on their adorable heads. And the young boys, looking like miniature gentlemen in their vests and ties or sport coats, fidgeting in all that restraining clothing.

How hard it always was watching her nieces and nephews, giggling and racing around her mom's backyard in search of Easter eggs filled with candy and coins while her brothers and sisters-in-law looked after them, a proud glint in their eyes.

Knowing she'd be far, far away for the holiday . . . knowing she'd be leaving soon—if even for two weeks—had given her an inkling of hope.

The only problem was Tom.

She still hadn't told him. Not that she was trying to hide it, but they hadn't truly talked in quite a while. He'd tried to at first, but she couldn't stand the small talk, the pretense of acting normal. As the evenings went by, they barely spoke to one another. Ultimately it seemed they had forgotten how. They were just two people living under the same roof but leading separate lives. Even so, she couldn't go off to Africa without mentioning it. She needed to tell him tonight.

"We'll take a short break." The director of missions seemed to finally be wrapping up his introduction. "When you come back, please look for your team leader. That person will be sitting at one of the six tables spread throughout the room. It'll be a chance for you to get to know the members of your group." He paused. "But before we get started, let's take a moment to pray."

As he bowed his head, the others followed suit. Gabby hesitated, then lowered her head, halfheartedly focused on the words he strung together in prayer.

"Gabby?"

Gabby felt Cassandra Albright's eyes zero in on the name tag stuck to her T-shirt. Already aware that the woman would be joining her Women Helping Women team, she'd mentally prepared herself for meeting one of the city's best-known news personalities.

"Ms. Albright, it's nice to meet you." Rising from her chair, Gabby shook the news anchor's creamy, smooth hand, the unique-looking charms on the woman's gold bracelet jingling in response.

"Please call me Cassandra." She let go of Gabby's hand and settled gracefully into a chair. "We will be traveling across the world together, after all."

Everything about the woman—from the silken white blouse she wore under her navy jacket to the cream-colored shoes that matched her expensive leather bag—looked perfect. Gabby thought Cassandra's life must surely be as together as she appeared.

"How many others are in our group?" she asked.

"Only two." Shuffling through the papers in front of her, Gabby searched for the team list. "I remember there's a Katie Martin, and her mother's name is . . ." She scanned the page.

"Hi, I'm Heidi Martin."

Gabby looked up from her papers to see a pretty woman with a heart-shaped face and chin-length blonde hair standing in front of her. She guessed her to be in her late thirties but only because of the teen-ager by her side. In reality, dressed in jeans and a cropped khaki jacket, Heidi Martin looked as if she could be at least five years younger, closer to Gabby's age.

"And this is Katie." Heidi introduced her daughter, gently touching the girl's arm.

With dyed black hair, Katie looked the opposite of her mom. Except she was pretty too. Even her boxy band T-shirt and frayed jeans couldn't hide the fact. Plus, there was something sweet about her tentative smile.

"Nice to meet both of you. My name is Gabby Phillips, and this is . . ." She waved to Cassandra, who was smiling as if there were a camera or two in the vicinity.

"Oh! Cassandra Albright. It's so nice to meet you," Heidi said excitedly. "I watch you on the news all the time."

Cassandra held out her hand, all polished precision, her bracelet jangling again as she and Heidi shook hands. "Thanks. We need as many viewers as we can get." Her teeth flashed white.

"Cassandra will be coming along with our team to film a report on women in Mamelodi," Gabby informed Heidi and Katie. Then she turned to Cassandra. "I'm guessing this is for a special report for WONR?"

"The first international segment of its kind, actually." Cassandra seemed eager to let them know.

"Do you know what it'll be about?" Katie spoke up, and Gabby was surprised but glad the teenager felt comfortable enough to do so.

"Mostly I plan to illustrate the plight of South African females. And of course depict how the women from this community are attempting to make a difference in their lives."

"That sounds like quite an undertaking. I hope we meet your expectations." Heidi grinned at Cassandra before facing Gabby. "Do we know who we'll be working with there yet?"

"Somewhat," Gabby told them, thinking back to the several e-mails she'd received in the past week. "I've been in contact with Mama Penny in Mamelodi. She e-mailed me from the hospice. From what she said, she already has a group of women our team will be working with. It seems one woman in particular has an idea of how we can help the South African ladies earn money for their families."

"That sounds interesting," Heidi said.

"I know someone who stayed in an awful old hotel while they were there on a mission trip," Katie said, changing the subject. "Is that where we'll be staying?"

"As far as I know, that's where many of the other groups will be, but we'll stay at the pastor's compound."

"Do we have any details regarding those accommodations?" Cassandra chimed in.

"I wish I could say I did." Gabby glanced from Cassandra to the mother and daughter pair. "Anything else?"

"Do you work here at the church full-time?" Heidi asked.

Gabby nodded. "More than full-time many weeks. I'm the director of children's ministries."

"I thought you looked familiar. How wonderful!" Heidi said. "I love working with little kids. I'm a first-grade teacher."

"Oh, my! Are they canonizing you anytime soon?" Cassandra chuckled. "I remember doing a news story on elementary school-children. It was shot in the cafeteria. Talk about messy. One child put his hand on the leg of my white silk pants. I never got that mustard stain out."

"Yeah, well, working with children has its share of occupational hazards," Heidi chirped. "Mustard. Germs. Sticky hands. Pet gerbils running loose in the classroom."

They all looked Gabby's way, and she felt they were expecting her to relay some sort of child-oriented anecdotes too. But children were the last thing she wanted to talk about.

Instead, Gabby gathered the papers from the table and handed them out. "I've been asked to give you a list of what not to bring on the trip. You can look it over. But mainly, you don't have to bring your best clothes, and you might not want to risk taking anything too valu-able. Costume jewelry is okay, and if you want to wear a plain wedding band, that's all right too."

She glanced at the other women's hands, but she didn't see any wedding rings there. Likewise, she felt their eyes scrutinize her left hand, making her feel suddenly self-conscious. "Oh, and a couple of other things. We'll be going on a safari toward the end of the trip. It's included in your cost, and it's sort of a tradition. The South African people are extremely proud of the beauty of their country and feel God has blessed them considerably. They urge visitors to experience their land and its creatures. In keeping with their wishes, we've made arrangements to do so."

"That'll be so cool!" Katie exclaimed, her exuberance almost making Gabby smile.

"And remember," she went on, "it's the end of their summer, so at night it will cool off, but during the day it will be hot, so you'll want to pack accordingly." She paused. "Any other questions?"

"What about the Internet?" Katie asked.

"You can't be Facebooking kids back at home." Heidi looked at her daughter as if she were fourteen-carat crazy.

"Do you really think I don't know that?"

Gabby interrupted them. "You won't want to bring a laptop. Again, too valuable. We will have minimal Internet access at the hospice. The e-mail address for the hospice is printed on the sheets I handed out. You can pass it along to concerned friends and family so they can contact you if they need to."

"What do you mean *minimal*?" Cassandra said.

"From what I understand, it's a small miracle the village has access to a computer at all. Right now, there's network connectivity to the hospice but few other places. It's certainly a luxury there, not a given as it is for us," Gabby explained. "Aside from cost, apparently servicepeople won't come out to the village, and no one in the village is trained to fix the computers when they go down. And from what I hear, that's quite often—sometimes for days at a time. If we do need to use the hospice computer, they would appreciate it if we use their account." She paused before asking, "Anything else?"

The three women shook their heads, and Gabby felt thankful. She still had work to do in her office. So many things to take care of before leaving the country for two weeks. Tom was on that list too.

"So." She clasped her hands together. "Guess that's it until we meet as scheduled at the airport."

As they all started to get up, Gabby spied another team nearby, bowing their heads in prayer. *That's right!* "Before we go, we should pray." She stretched her hands out on the tabletop.

Heidi set down her keys and clasped Gabby's left hand. Did she hear Cassandra sigh before laying her purse in her lap and taking hold of her right hand? In between, Katie completed the circle.

"If there's anything you want to add when I finish, please feel free to chime in." Gabby took a deep breath. "Father God, we praise You and thank You for bringing us together. Thank You for entrusting us to do Your works and for . . ."

The words she uttered sounded good. She'd always been able to pray publicly with the best of them. But she hadn't felt like praying for weeks now. Hadn't been feeling like doing much of anything actually. Why pray when she barely believed the words she'd lived by for so long? Why pray when she could no longer feel the meaning of those words?

More than anything, Gabby felt Cassandra's loose touch, the way the woman's weight shifted away from the table and not forward. And though Heidi had seemed so lighthearted and pleasant, there was something that felt serious and needy in the way she clutched Gabby's hand as if holding on for dear life.

Gabby thought she recognized the feeling and squeezed back.

Then, finishing her recitation, she paused, waiting for one of the others to add a prayer to hers. When no one did, she led the team in an "Amen."

After the meeting, Gabby stayed at church, doing some paperwork till nearly eleven. On the way home, she hoped Tom would already be asleep when she got there. Though Gabby knew she couldn't put off telling him much longer, tonight no longer seemed like the right time. She was so, so tired. Sunday would be better. After church. Maybe they could go have a late breakfast—something they hadn't done for quite a while.

Relief washed over her when she opened the front door. It

appeared she'd gotten her wish. With the television droning in the background, Tom had fallen asleep on the family room couch. He seemed to be doing that more and more lately. Oftentimes, he slept there all night instead of coming to bed.

Slipping off her shoes, Gabby tiptoed around the house quietly, so as not to wake him. She turned off lights and double-checked the front door, then started to head down the dim hallway to their bedroom when Tom sat up on the couch and startled her. Obviously he hadn't been sleeping as soundly as she'd imagined.

"I ran into Matt Wilson downtown today."

As she faced him in the semidarkness, her heart quickened in her chest. "Really?"

Matt and Kelly Wilson had been in a small group with them years prior. She hadn't seen much of either of them lately until tonight when she'd run into Kelly at the mission meeting.

"I guess we're both going to be bachelors for a couple of weeks while you girls are in South Africa?"

Gabby could tell he was trying to keep his words light, his tone nonchalant. But he couldn't pull it off. Hurt and resentment seeped through every word.

"Tom, really . . . I was going to tell you."

"Oh, I'm sure you were. Eventually, huh?"

A stranger's voice coming from the TV hung between them for a moment.

"I'm a team leader. So the church is paying my way."

"Did I mention money?"

"No, but—"

"I don't understand what's going on anymore."

"I-I know."

"Used to be if we went a day without speaking to one another, it didn't feel right. But now . . ."

A vague memory of what that felt like clutched at her heart. Tom had always been there for her. Always. Emotion grabbed at the back of her throat for a moment; then it loosened and was gone. And there was nothing. No crying out, no tears. Just a feeling of emptiness. So dead. So numb.

"You keep pushing. You're pushing me away."

Gabby tried to think of an explanation. To deny it. But everything he said was true. "I know."

Appearing disgusted, he hung his head. A man so broken, she couldn't stand to see him like that. But still, every part of her being felt like stone. Somehow she couldn't make her legs move even though she tried. Couldn't will her mind to go to him.

For once, he didn't make a move to come to her either.

"We can't go on like this." Tom shook his head slowly. "Maybe a separation. Maybe that's the right thing."

Was he asking her? Or telling her? "Do you think . . . Will you be here when I get back?"

His face, lit up by the television, looked contorted with confusion. "I don't know. I really *don't* know."

But she had a feeling she did.

16

Coming through the airport terminal door, leaving the last whoosh of air-conditioning behind, Gabby paused on the sidewalk and squinted into the sun.

A glorious sun, like a giant tangerine hovering over the city of Johannesburg.

She'd slept during most of the eighteen-hour flight, rousing just a few times. One time to eat. A second time when a baby's cry broke out in the darkened cabin and shattered the silence. After that, she willed herself to sleep, only waking up now and then to make a wish. The same wish every time: that the plane would never stop and she would keep circling and circling the earth forever, through all eternity.

But at some point the landing gear had popped out of its holding place. The plane bounced along for a few moments, righted itself, and then inched to the designated terminal.

As she forced herself to open her eyes, a fluttering sensation took hold in her stomach. No more hiding, no more hibernating for her.

Maybe this isn't such an awful place to be, Gabby thought. Against her pale skin, the rays of sun felt intense and powerful, reminding her of how far away she was from home in such different surroundings, halfway around the world from heartache.

Maybe here she'd feel her soul warm up again. Maybe the laserlike heat could burn off the chilled layers around her heart. But it was hard to imagine that could happen here or anywhere else.

Staring at the Master's closest star in the sky, she dared Him to try.

"Doesn't this feel amazing?" Heidi pulled her luggage next to Gabby's.

"Better than Ohio." Maybe she could even make a career of this, flying to strange countries, being estranged from those she loved.

"Especially after the surprise ice storm we got hit with this week." Heidi shaded her eyes with her hand.

"Not really a *surprise* ice storm." Cassandra sidled up between them, trailing her matching luggage. "If you follow the news, it happens to us almost every year at this time."

"Mom, look! Don't they look beautiful?" Katie nodded toward a pair of women in African dress walking toward them. Their colorful, floor-length wrap skirts and matching tunic tops were breathtaking in the light of day. Bright orange and red circles on an olive green background surrounded one lady, her flared three-quarter-length sleeves adding a feminine touch to the bold, eye-catching colors. Her companion, dressed in sweeping swirls of blues on white, wore a matching head wrap that looked mystic and attractive at the same time.

Gabby was sure the women couldn't help but notice the four of them staring. Casting smiles their way, the ladies bowed their heads in a demure pose. Gabby felt like bowing her head too. The atmosphere was so different.

Cassandra went right to work. She seemed to have no inhibitions about grabbing her formidable-looking camera with its nearly foot-long black lens and snapping a few pictures of the ladies.

While she was at it, she got a few photos of the rhythmic trio playing xylophones a few feet away. Or at least the musical devices resembled xylophones, with bars made from different widths of wooden rectangles tied with strings to an A-shaped frame. The musicians appeared as primal as the instruments they played, wearing animal hide vests and furry pelts strapped to their legs like chaps, all sporting some kind of tribal headband.

Katie studied the musicians and then turned to her mom, laughing. "What do you think? A new look for me?"

"Ha! Let's not even go there, okay?" Heidi waved a hand at her daughter and smiled.

"Who are we looking for again?" Cassandra asked as soon as she had her camera back in its case and the case deposited in a shoulder bag.

"A woman is supposed to meet us," Gabby answered. "Mama Penny."

"Mama Penny?" Cassandra lifted a waxed brow.

"The lady you mentioned at our meeting," Heidi clarified.

"Right." Gabby nodded. "From what I understand, she seems to be in charge of a lot of things."

"Like those Women of the Year who get their pictures in the paper? Always on at least twenty committees? With a husband and children to take care of?" Heidi adjusted the purse sliding off her shoulder. "Can one person really handle all that?"

No one seemed to have an answer, but Gabby figured Heidi wasn't really expecting one. "Mama Penny is sort of *over* everyone, like a mayor or a matriarch or . . . I'm not sure. She's more educated than many of the people in Mamelodi."

"Really?" Heidi said. "Like a nurse or a teacher?"

"Again, I guess we'll find out." Gabby shrugged. "I was given a brief overview. It sounds like Mama Penny counsels at the hospice. Tracks down money and donations from businesses for various things. And is a sort of liaison for the community, a woman-of-all-trades. I get the impression a lot of people depend on her for help."

"How do we find her? Do you know what she looks like?" Cassandra pulled at her linen blouse, flapping it against her chest. "It's downright hot out here. And I'm ready to unload this stuff." She pointed over her shoulder at her luggage.

Oh, two weeks with Cassandra Albright. No, make that twelve and a half days since we've already spent one and a half traveling. It was going to be a challenge, for sure. Gabby had experienced evidence of that in the Columbus airport with Cassandra preening for everyone who walked by as if she were campaigning for the presidency or the Miss Congeniality award. It had made Gabby want to groan out loud. "No, I don't know," she admitted.

The curbside bustled with activity, which made sense, since the airport, as a person in baggage claim had mentioned, happened to be the largest on the entire continent.

Gabby glanced up and down the sidewalk. A stout lady, standing next to a young girl and a white van parked about ten yards away, caught her eye. The woman's coral blouse looked stretched to its limits as did the flared, brightly colored patterned skirt she wore, both a beautiful contrast with her dark skin.

But more than the clothes Gabby noticed the way the woman stood so solidly, unfettered, stoic, while all around her was chaos. Her shoulders, square and broad, looked ample enough to carry the weight of the world on them.

It seemed worth a shot.

Gabby turned to the others. "Follow me."

She led her crew, suitcases rolling behind them, toward the woman. But the mystery was solved before they even reached the van when the driver, a young male with black-brown skin, hopped out holding a cardboard sign. The words *Gabrielle—Graceview Church* were written in bright blue marker.

What an unlikely-looking welcoming committee. A woman in her fifties or sixties. A driver who looked to be in his early twenties. And a girl about nine years old.

Maybe we look just as odd to them, Gabby considered. Four women coming from the other side of the world—to do what? Save them? Save South Africa?

If they only knew. Gabby frowned. She couldn't speak for the rest of her group. But didn't she need someone just as badly to save her from herself?

Trying to shake those awful thoughts away, she tugged her suitcase up to the woman and to a halt. "Penny?"

"Mama Penny."

"Mama Penny, I'm Gabrielle Phillips."

She held out her hand, and the woman took it, shaking for only a moment. Then, before Gabby knew what was happening, Mama Penny pulled her toward her bosom, enclosing her in the warmth of a full embrace.

"Welcome, welcome, Gabrielle." Mama Penny patted her on her back. Loosening her hold on Gabby, she spoke to the others. "We are so happy you have come with Gabrielle. All of you." She turned to Gabby. "What are the names?"

Gabby couldn't help but smile, both from Mama Penny's overt friendliness and relief that she could actually understand the woman. She'd been worried about them communicating, but the gregarious Mama Penny spoke English just fine. At times her emphasis on syllables was a bit off and her accent was rather thick. Still, Gabby managed to comprehend most of what she said.

"This is Cassandra." Gabby pointed to the newswoman.

Cassandra nodded to Mama Penny while the matriarch gave her the once-over. "Striking," Mama Penny commented as the two shook hands. "Welcome, Cassandra. Thank you for traveling far."

"And this is Heidi and her daughter, Katie."

"It's nice to meet you." Heidi held out her hand.

"You too, Mama Heidi." The older woman winked. She clasped Heidi's hand before turning to Katie and giving her a warm hug. "Tell me, what does Katie mean?"

"What does it *mean*?" Katie glanced at her mom for help, but all Heidi could do was shrug, so Katie did too.

"In Africa," Mama Penny explained, "often the names we give our children stand for something. For example, my grandson's name is Rapala. It means 'pray.'"

Katie still looked stumped. "Well, the only thing I know is my real name is Katherine. Katie for short."

"Katherine, you say?" Mama Penny's brows furrowed. "Let me

tell you another name. This is Sipho." She reached a hand up to the driver's shoulder. He was at least four inches taller than Mama Penny. Gabby judged him to be close to six feet.

"*See* what?" Gabby asked him.

He smiled, white teeth contrasting against his smooth, dark face. But even with that bright grin, he seemed shy, Gabby thought, his eyes downcast. *"See-poe,"* he answered.

After another round of hand-shaking and hugs, Mama Penny explained, "Sipho has been driving for Pastor Shadrach for many years, since he was a teen boy. Because you will be staying at Pastor's compound, he will be driving you where you will need to go. He is a good driver. But sometimes you must say, 'Slow down, Sipho. Slow down.' Even I say to him at times, 'You drive like we will be meeting Jesus very soon!'"

Everyone laughed.

"This is sometimes true." Sipho chuckled. "But I will be careful with you, I promise."

"Thank you." Gabby smiled, adding teasingly, "We appreciate that."

"And who is this?" Heidi crouched in front of the thin girl standing next to Mama Penny.

Gabby had noticed how patiently the child waited for the adults to finish their introductions.

"This darling girl is Nomvula." Mama Penny put her arm around the girl's shoulders.

Nomvula's dark eyes were large and round, and she had the most beautiful pecan-colored skin Gabby had ever seen. Someone had taken a lot of time to cornrow her hair, an elegant look that seemed somewhat out of context with her faded blue skirt and pink T-shirt that read *Dugan Dodgers*. No doubt the shirt had been in the heaps of clothes donated from Graceview Church, a part of some other child's baseball uniform. Had Nomvula worn it in honor of them?

Or because it was all she had?

But whatever the child didn't have, Mama Penny seemed to make up for. The plump woman gazed at the child, and Gabby could easily see the way Mama Penny caressed Nomvula with her eyes.

Gabby shifted on her feet, a sense of inadequacy sweeping over her. It had been a while since she'd looked at a child at Graceview that way, hadn't it?

Mama Penny's show of love wasn't lost on Nomvula. It seemed to spark a confidence in the little girl that lit a smile, which she beamed on the rest of them.

"If it is all right with you," Mama Penny announced, "we plan to drop off your things at Pastor's; then we will take you to see Nomvula's mother, Jaleela. She is one of the women you will be working with. She is feeling better today. She would like you to come to her home so she can share some pap with you."

"Pap?" Katie asked. "What is *pap*?"

"Ah, you will see, Katie Blue Eyes." Mama Penny put a hand to her chest, her eyes widening as if she'd experienced a revelation. "That's what your name means, I think. That's what I will call you—Blue Eyes!" She laughed with ease, not seeming to care that she might be amusing only herself.

But that wasn't true. They all joined in with Mama Penny, and Gabby thought Katie looked particularly happy.

"All right," Mama Penny asked, "shall we go, then?"

Nomvula tugged at Mama Penny's long skirt.

"What, child?"

The girl held up a plastic bag.

"Oh, that is right. Nomvula and her mother made welcome gifts for you." Mama Penny touched Nomvula's back. "Go ahead. You may give them now."

Nomvula opened the bag and pulled out four dolls, each less than three inches long. Gabby couldn't believe how intricately made they were. All starting with just a cork wrapped in colorful cotton material for the body, Mama Penny explained, and heads made with a ball of foil covered in black cloth. The neck area where the two cloths met was embellished with rows of miniature seed beads strung together, resembling a necklace. Beads also were used to make the eyes, and black yarn, the braided hair.

"Welcome . . ." Nomvula started off ceremoniously but had to stop almost immediately, looking back at Mama Penny.

"Cassandra," Mama Penny told her.

"Cassandra." The girl held out a doll.

Cassandra accepted it graciously. "Thank you, Nom—" She glanced at Mama Penny too.

"Nomvula," Mama Penny answered.

Cassandra nodded, repeating after her.

Nomvula stepped down the line. "Welcome, Mama Heidi. Welcome, Katie Blue Eyes." She handed an orange doll to Heidi and a teal one to Katie, both of whom bowed and hugged her.

Nomvula hesitated before stepping over to Gabby, though Gabby wasn't sure why. "Gabrielle?" she whispered almost reverently, holding out a lime green doll.

"Thank you so much." Gabby bent down to hug Nomvula.

"Your name is really Gabrielle?"

"Yes, it is."

"You are like the angel? the one who came to bless Mary?"

"Well, yes, it's a form of—"

But before Gabby could finish her answer, Nomvula grabbed her hand and wouldn't let go. "Thank you for coming to my mother." She glowed. "Yes, you will meet my mother today."

17

Sipho sounded almost apologetic as he started up the lengthy passenger van and told them it was a forty-five-minute ride from the airport to Mamelodi. But Gabby didn't mind at all. The warm breeze blowing in the window of the van caressed her face, almost like a lover's touch. Only better, without any complications or conversations attached and no involvement required.

Closing her eyes for a moment, soaking up the soothing feeling, Gabby wished she could fold her whole being into the soft flutters of wind. Wished she could drift off into a never-never land of sleep again like she had on the plane. But it wasn't an option, was it? She was the leader of this crew, the price she had to pay for an escape to the other side of the world. And being the lady in charge meant taking charge. Although, half tuning into the chatter going on around her, it seemed her team was doing just fine without her guidance at the moment.

She settled deeper into the seat. She had so little interest in being a part of anything right now. Not a part of these women. Or a part of today. Or tomorrow. Just the thought of it made her feel weary. And so much more emotionally drained than she already was.

Trying to come to terms with her loss had been one thing, but she'd been too numb to deal with Tom too. He hadn't even offered to drive her to the airport. Not that he should've, she knew. In fact, he left for work that morning as if it were any other day, except he left earlier and without even mumbling good-bye.

It had felt so strange when the taxi arrived and she'd stood at the front door of their house, key in hand, ready to slip it into the dead bolt. She lingered there, paralyzed for a moment, feeling like she might never recognize her life again if she left that way.

But what could she do? Leave a long note to Tom? To explain what? Call his cell phone? To say what?

Weeks earlier, her heart would've immediately turned to her Father in prayer, imploring His help and intercession. But that was weeks ago. Instead, after pausing with the key in her grip, she had finally turned it clockwise, locking the door behind her.

Gabby let go of a long, pitying sigh but didn't even realize it until she felt something tugging on her, drawing her attention, making her turn to the right. It was Nomvula's eyes. Gabby had felt the girl staring from across the van, her fixed look pulling on her like a magnet.

Ever since Nomvula had been introduced to Gabby, she kept glancing at her, almost as if Gabby were her captive or an illusion that might slip away if she didn't stand guard. But at the moment the look in Nomvula's eyes was something altogether different.

How could young eyes look so old? How could this child make Gabby feel like one herself? Gabby squirmed and tried to make conversation with Nomvula. "It's a long ride from the airport."

"It is all right. I do not mind."

The smile Nomvula gave her was so unconditionally forgiving and kind that Gabby felt compelled to sit up a little straighter.

There should be something more she could say to the young girl. Couldn't she think of something? But what do you say to a nine-year-old who looks as wise and self-possessed as your white-haired grandmother?

Unable to think of anything, Gabby tuned in to the talk going on around her.

"This place reminds me of Dallas," Katie said, her face pressed against the window in the seat in front of Gabby. "You know. Outside of Dallas. Like after you leave the city part."

Katie's observation made Gabby look out the window too, and she took in the passing scenery for the first time. To her, the soft, rolling ground topped with golden, sunburnt grass seemed as if it could be anywhere. As if they could be journeying down some state route anywhere in rural America.

They'd left behind Joburg—she'd quickly caught on to Johannesburg's friendly nickname—with its shiny modern skyscrapers, plethora of shopping opportunities, and sobering Apartheid Museum. The country's largest city, it was a place she could relate to.

Who knew what sights awaited them in Mamelodi, though? Would anything seem familiar there? She'd heard enough to know that the stretch of road they were traveling on wasn't the only thing that divided the village and the city, the two cultures, the two worlds.

"Yes, it kind of does," Heidi answered Katie from the other side of the van, breaking into Gabby's thoughts.

"Remember when we went on vacation there with Dad?" Katie asked, her tone wistful, her face turned away from her mom.

"I do. You went to Six Flags with your cousins. Seems like a long time ago, doesn't it?"

Heidi's voice seemed to echo Katie's same reflective sentiment, making Gabby wonder once again about Katie's father. From their tone and the fact Heidi didn't wear a wedding ring, she got the impression he was missing from their lives. But in what way, she couldn't be sure.

"Dallas?" Mama Penny's head turned from the passenger seat in the front of the van.

"Dallas, Texas," Katie explained.

"I have heard of that place. From missionaries." Mama Penny smiled. "That is where they have those people. The cowboys. But we have no cowboys."

"What they have in Texas are oilmen. Very wealthy oilmen. I had the pleasure of meeting a few when I went to a broadcast symposium there several years ago." Cassandra touched her fingertips as she spoke as if to see if each acrylic nail had made the trip safely. "They also have some of the most fabulous shopping I've ever encountered. Between Dallas and Houston, it's remarkable. The malls in Ohio pale in comparison. Did you go to the Galleria when you were there?" she asked Heidi over her shoulder.

"No. We were mostly visiting family."

"Oh, well, too bad." Cassandra flung a hand in the air. "You missed some of the greatest shopping of your life."

Gabby couldn't believe Cassandra was talking about ultimate shopping experiences. Did the woman have no censor in her brain? Didn't she realize where she was, who she was with? Luckily Mama Penny appeared unfazed by Cassandra's reality, which was, no doubt, nothing close to her own. Still, Gabby had enough problems of her own. She didn't have the energy or inclination to teach Cassandra social skills, for goodness' sake.

"What about you?" Mama Penny asked Gabby. "Have you ever been to Dallas?"

Though she'd been listening to the conversation, she really had no desire of being sucked into it. "No. The only state we've seen out west is Colorado. We went hiking in the Rocky Mountains one summer."

"We? You have a family?"

"Um, well, my husband and myself."

Mama Penny's eyes took on a knowing look. "Ah. Do you two do a lot of traveling?"

"Not so much." Although they'd wanted to. In the early years of their marriage they'd bought a calendar each January with full-color photos of some of God's greatest landscapes in the U.S., plotting out which they'd like to travel to most. But as time went on, they traded in those dreams for dreams of a family. That was where all their money, time, and focus went. And in the end, where had that gotten them? Not very far. "At least not recently."

"What is your husband's name?"

"My husband?"

"He let you come around the world without him, didn't he?" Mama Penny gave her a curious smile. "I want to thank God for him."

Gabby could feel Nomvula's eyes on her again. The other women had turned around in their seats and were looking at her too. "His name is Tom." She felt almost guilty mentioning him. Did she even have a claim on him anymore?

"He is happy for your trip?"

It was great that Mama Penny was being so kind, but she was getting a bit personal. Besides, these weren't easy questions with easy answers. At least not lately. "It was very last-minute, so . . ."

"Did you have time to pack a picture of your Tom?"

Yes, the lady was indeed being far too personal. "I-I didn't bring the wallet I usually carry." Gabby scooted her backpack closer to her side, feeling suddenly exposed. As if everyone could see the contents of her bag. Her heart.

For a moment when she got off the plane, she thought maybe she'd found a place on earth where she could hide away from everything past. Where the emptiness might be filled with something new. But now, after just a few questions, just a few reminders, that hope seemed gone. The hollowness was there in the pit her stomach again. It felt even worse than before.

"I'll bet he looks like David Beckham." Katie had hoisted herself up, looking over the back of her seat, smiling at Gabby.

"David Beckham?" Heidi mused. "Where did you come up with that?"

Gabby could tell Katie wanted to relate to her. Even though she was twice her age, Gabby was still closest to Katie's seventeen. The one who might remember what it felt like to be that young. For a moment, she wished she really could go back to where Katie was. At least that way she and Tom could have another chance. They could start all over again.

"Does he?" Katie prodded. "What does he look like?"

Everyone stared at Gabby. They all stretched around in their seats with curious smiles and a look in their eyes that appeared half-hopeful, half-envious. Like she had it all. Like she was the lucky one. Oh yeah, if they only knew . . . "I don't know. He just looks like Tom, I guess."

Her anticlimactic response seemed to have caused everyone to turn back around in their seats and look out the windows. Cassandra pulled a small camera out of the black bag next to her. Maybe a video camera?

Now that they were off the main road, getting closer to the village, Cassandra recorded whatever there was to be seen when the van came to a stop at a traffic signal. And, no, Gabby was fairly certain the surroundings didn't resemble the Dallas landscape anymore. It seemed the forty-five-minute ride that separated Johannesburg, or Egoli, "City of Gold"—the capital's other nickname—from the village of Mamelodi was a monumental distance indeed.

In fact, Mamelodi looked quite the opposite of the city, she thought as they passed an area of huddled-together shacks known as Squatter Camp, according to Mama Penny. Long gone were the gold and silver skyscrapers gleaming in the sun. Here, scraps of tin formed roofs, held on by a few broken bricks or a discarded car tire. Heaps of dirt and waste sullied the roadside. Signs hanging on dilapidated structures about the size of most master bedroom closets back home advertised a hair salon or a first aid station.

Gabby couldn't believe it. Her brothers' kids had playhouses in their backyards more solidly built and inviting. Where did the children play? she wondered. Or maybe they didn't, she realized, watching young boys who didn't look old enough to be out of their mothers' sights roaming the streets, appearing aimless. And little girls holding hands with children even younger than themselves, tugging them behind. Once in a while a woman in African dress and a scarf wrapped around her head walked down the street looking purposeful about her mission. Maybe going to a job? or to find food for her children?

Gabby looked away, not wanting to see anymore.

After another ten minutes and another stretch of road, Mama

Penny turned around in her seat. "We're here. This is Pastor Shadrach's compound."

Sipho turned the van left into an enveloping lush greenness where there was at first no sight of any houses or buildings, just tall, palmlike trees and a variety of other leafy shrubs and trees spread out on flat, green grass as opposed to the tall, burnt grasses by the roadside. It might have seemed like a miniature Eden, except for the fence surrounding the area. At least ten feet high, the impenetrable-looking metal enclosure would have been considered a nice decorative addition to the property if it hadn't been laced with large, menacing, curlicue loops of barbed wire and further enhanced with strands of a thin, straight wire that warned of an electric fence.

Gabby gasped, then heard echoes of shock reverberate throughout the van as everyone else noticed the tangles of wires.

"Is that an electric fence?" Katie couldn't disguise her disbelief.

Mama Penny faced the teen, her eyes firm. "It is."

"But why?" Katie asked the question Gabby was sure everyone was thinking.

"Crime is very high in South Africa, child. There are gangs. Many lost souls. You would not like the curfew here, I am sure. My grand-daughter Mpumi, she is nineteen. She must be home by dinnertime. That is six o'clock, when it starts to become dark."

Katie's eyes were wide. "You're kidding."

"It is not a joke," Mama Penny said matter-of-factly. "We must keep from being harmed by others. That is why you will see gates and fences on all the houses here. That is our way of shutting people out." She paused before adding, "But we all have ways of shutting out people, don't we?"

Even though Mama Penny addressed Katie, Gabby felt as if the matriarch was looking over the teenager's head right at her.

18

The luggage stacked at least four feet high in the trunk of the passenger van. Heidi bumped elbows with Sipho as they stood at the rear of the vehicle, reaching inside at the same time to retrieve suitcases.

"Ma'am." His teeth showed through his smile. "Your suitcase, it is almost the size of you. I will be happy to get it down."

"Yes, let Sipho do his work," Mama Penny chirped from the side of the van. "He needs his muscles. He gets mushy driving Pastor's van all day." She waddled a little closer to them. "Your girlfriend, she likes big muscles, eh, Sipho?"

At the mention of his girlfriend, Sipho's eyes lit up. Still, seeming respectful of Mama Penny, Heidi noticed, he didn't offer a comeback. Instead, saying nothing, he chuckled and continued his work, unloading the cargo.

Each woman thanked Sipho as he kindly set their suitcases at their feet, releasing the handles toward them. Watching the young man perform his tasks with such ease and grace made Heidi think of how she'd struggled with her suitcases and Katie's the day before.

Only it hadn't been just the weight of the suitcases that she'd struggled with. It was the memories. Memories of Jeff. They were always there, lurking beneath the surface, but yesterday they'd flooded her. Thoughts of him had caught her by surprise, causing her breath to catch. For a moment, she'd grabbed on to the trunk of

the car for support, though it wasn't physical support she'd craved.
No, at that moment, she would have given the world for someone
to lean on emotionally. Someone to confirm that she was doing the
right thing, taking her daughter—her pregnant daughter—clear
across the globe.

"Katie's going to be all right." Suddenly Kevin's comforting words
came back to her. The memory of his soothing voice, his concern—
even his invitation—made her flush. She hoped anyone who noticed
would think it was merely the heat that was affecting her.

But no one seemed to be watching her anyway. Everyone was
focused on Mama Penny, who was pointing to the only house on the
property. It was a modest brick home nestled in a cradle of palm trees.

"That is Pastor Shadrach's house," she told them as their trailing
suitcases came to a halt on the dirt and pebble drive.

Even though the pastor's house appeared to be partly under
construction with a wheelbarrow in the front yard and ladders and
tools scattered all around, someone had attempted a flower bed along
the walk and had placed a cement water dish on the porch where birds
were gathered. Both of the additions exuded a warm feeling, portray-
ing a welcome haven for weary souls and tired travelers, including
those of a feathered variety.

"Pastor and his family come and go much, but that is not true of this
week. He has asked me to share his sorrow that they could not be here.
A pastor dear to him lost his church last week in Nigeria. It was burned
to the ground," Mama Penny reported solemnly. "Pastor Shadrach's
family has gone to help and to pray with the pastor and his wife."

"You mean someone started a fire?" Katie blurted.

Mama Penny nodded. "That is what is thought."

"But who would—?"

Before Heidi could finish, Mama Penny answered. "There has
been unrest with some youths of another faith." She pointed straight
ahead to a row of identical two-story brick buildings. Like miniature
dormitories, they were fairly plain, except for the thatched grass roofs

that gave them the slightest bit of tropical flair. "That is where you will be staying. Come."

Dust swirled around the wheels of their suitcases as their procession ambled wordlessly up the drive toward the buildings. The only sound breaking the silence was the loud, piercing cry of a bird repeating its noisy message over and over again. Heidi startled at the alarming noise, feeling as if a pterodactyl might swoop down on them at any minute.

Mama Penny noticed and half smiled. "It is the go-away-bird."

"Go-away-bird?"

"The gray lourie. It calls out loudly, *gaa-wayrr, gaa-wayrr*, alerting animals when a predator enters the territory."

"Oh." Heidi's shoulders relaxed some as she looked into the trees surrounding them, trying to spot the vocal warbler. She almost ran into the back of Katie when she halted dead in her tracks.

"Awww . . . ," Katie cooed. Letting go of her suitcase, she drifted like a sleepwalker over to a dog, lazing under a nearby shrub. "Isn't he precious?"

The gray, short-haired creature looked anything but precious to Heidi. But then, unlike Katie, she was a discriminating dog lover, since her allergies typically got the best of her. The only time she was willing to bring on an attack of sneezes was when an exceptionally irresistible fluffy puppy crossed her path.

Katie, however, had always been moved by anything on four legs, even a mangy creature like this that Heidi hoped not to come within ten feet of during their stay.

As soon as Katie got closer, the dog showed its less-precious side. Leaping up on all fours, the mutt bared fanglike teeth. Seconds later its low, grumbling growl accelerated into a fierce, high-pitched bark.

Even though Heidi spotted the rope around its neck and knew it couldn't attack Katie, her heart jumped in her chest, and she took a few steps back from the wildly barking animal.

Gabby and Cassandra stepped away too, Cassandra even letting out an unladylike curse.

But Katie remained where she was. Facing the animal head-on, she whispered to it. When the animal growled again, it looked as if Katie was about to hold out her hand.

What if it bit her? What if it hurt her, hurt the baby? "Katie!" Heidi called out.

"I'm fine, Mom."

"You might not be," Sipho said from behind them. "I wouldn't get too close."

Katie still hadn't lowered her hand. "Oh, he'll settle down."

"I would stay a distance," Sipho warned again, his voice raised a bit as the dog's growls intensified. "That dog is not so smart."

Katie turned to look at Sipho. "He isn't?"

"No, he is not. He still barks at whites. I do not think he knows Apartheid is over," Sipho said.

Surely he's kidding, Heidi thought. Although when Nomvula approached the animal, the dog didn't seem bothered. Certainly that was because the creature was familiar with Nomvula. No way the dog could actually distinguish, right?

"What's his name?" Katie asked.

"Hazard." Nomvula rubbed the dog under his neck, placating him.

"Well, we'll be friends by the time I leave, won't we, Hazard?"

That promise made, the women fell back in line with Sipho bringing up the rear. Heidi watched as Nomvula and Katie walked alongside Gabby. They both had taken a liking to the church director, but at the moment Gabby didn't seem as interested in them. She acted more standoffish than when they'd first met at the church. Less talkative. But maybe Gabby was just fatigued from the trip.

Heidi felt relieved that Katie liked Gabby. She was the type of woman anyone would admire, and it might turn out to be a positive thing for Katie, who could use another friend at the moment.

Surely she had to be sick of hanging out as a mother-daughter duo the past couple of weeks. Though Heidi enjoyed their time together, or at least having Katie around the house more, she knew it'd been upsetting to Katie to be stuck at home. The girl was so used to running with friends nonstop that the lack of activity had to have been a hard adjustment.

But that was how it had been since the news got out about the pregnancy. Her cell hadn't been ringing as much lately. Mark was about the only one Katie spoke to anymore, and whatever they'd been texting back and forth about at the Columbus airport hadn't seemed to make Katie very happy.

At least she'll get a break from the drama back home for a little while. Maybe we both will.

They were certainly overdue, Heidi thought, watching Katie pluck a hot pink flower from a vine circling a tree. Hopefully memories of this trip would be comforting for them long after they returned home.

"Well, this looks better than I thought it would," Cassandra remarked quietly to Heidi as they reached the threshold of their building. "You wouldn't believe the stuff I was imagining. Practically barbaric conditions, dirt." She laughed. "Mice."

Once they stepped inside, however, the stale smell of days-old rot and mildew greeted them.

"Wow." Cassandra coughed. "Let me take that back. This is exactly what I thought this place would be. I hope my can of Lysol survived the trip."

Heidi tried to think of something complimentary to say to Mama Penny and Sipho to compensate for Cassandra's outspokenness, and by the look on Gabby's face, she was trying to do the same. But nothing came to mind.

But then how could it? Her brain was on overload, processing everything before her eyes. Taking in the broken-down, stained couch; the unfinished walls; and the wires hanging from the ceiling. It appeared that money and manpower had run out, like at the pastor's house.

What had she expected? She knew they weren't staying in a hotel like most of the other groups from Graceview. And that was all right. They'd figure things out and make the place more comfortable.

Luckily Heidi had dedicated the better portion of her second suitcase to some comforts from home and goodies. She'd stuck in a couple of dish towels, plastic containers filled with snacks to share with everyone, plus some playthings for kids and a couple of aromatherapy candles, which would work out quite well at the moment. Seriously, what *was* that awful smell?

"What on earth?" Cassandra uttered Heidi's thoughts out loud. "It smells like a rat died or something." She put a hand to her mouth as if she'd be sick any moment. "Okay, I'm not kidding. That smell has to go or I do."

It took only a minute of investigation to discover an overflowing bag of trash in a corner of the kitchen, where insects of every kind had discovered it too.

Mama Penny groaned. "I apologize for Dominic. He has been gone for a few days to help his mother. It is usually his job to clean when guests depart, but he maybe was in a hurry." She turned to Sipho. "Did his father pass?"

"I believe so."

"Oh, Lord God of all comfort—" Mama Penny closed her eyes and lifted her arms to the heavens—"please give Dominic and his family the strength they need. The kind of strength that is only Yours to give."

Sipho whispered, "Amen" before opening a few windows and then retrieving the trash.

Mama Penny frowned. "Katie Blue Eyes, suddenly you do not look so good. I hope the awful smell has not made you ill."

Heidi's gaze shot to her daughter, and her pulse quickened. It was true. Katie may have jauntily approached Hazard just minutes ago and practically skipped up the drive picking a flower or two along the way, but now she looked peaked. Beaten. Her lips crumpled, her face contorted.

It was a look Heidi knew all too well—from the morning sickness. The nausea seemed to have disappeared a couple of weeks ago, and they'd both been so thankful. Now it was back? Would they have to work to keep their secret here too?

"Oh, I'll be all right," Katie said weakly.

"How about a cracker?" Heidi unzipped her smaller suitcase. "Or maybe a granola bar?"

Katie looked like she barely had the energy to shake her head. "No thanks."

"I think it is best to give you ladies a moment. Some time to put your things away," Mama Penny said, holding out her hand to Nomvula, who was standing by Gabby's side. "Come, sweet girl."

Nomvula stood still.

"Vula," Mama Penny repeated.

The girl gave Gabby one last look before taking Mama Penny's outstretched hand.

"We will return soon, child. Do not have a sad face. This is a good day for you. For all of us. We have angels around us we cannot see. And angels who have come from America too."

"This place would never pass building code inspection." Cassandra paused from yanking her massive black suitcases up the uneven concrete steps leading to their bedrooms.

Since Cassandra had been first to forge up the steps, that meant everyone else had to pause on the stairs too, trying to steady their suitcases behind them. Heidi wished Cassandra would just keep moving. Her legs felt too shaky yet from the flight to be balancing on the precarious stairs, let alone keep her grip on the two weighty suitcases behind her. She was beginning to lose the battle with gravity. And then there was the matter of Katie.

"You feeling any better yet?" she whispered to Katie behind her.

The way Katie clenched her teeth gave Heidi the answer. As did Katie's ashen face.

Things were going to get even messier around this place if the bigmouthed anchor didn't get a move on and if Katie didn't make it upstairs to the bathroom before the turn of the century.

"Maybe they don't have building codes here like we do," Heidi suggested, trying not to look down but having a hard time looking up at Cassandra.

"No kidding. That's quite apparent. It reminds me of an investigative piece we did on a builder who was saving money by—"

A rush of air passed over Heidi's sweat-outlined face as Katie bolted past her up the steps. She nearly knocked her over and bumped into Cassandra's suitcases, leaving the woman wobbling in her wake.

They heard a door close overhead.

"What's her problem?" Cassandra's pinched expression conveyed her annoyance. So did her tone. She gave Heidi a disapproving look, as if she was a mom who couldn't control her child.

"She's not feeling well," Heidi ground out, not sure how much longer she could control herself.

"Her stomach?" Gabby chimed in from below.

Heidi nodded.

"Well, who does feel well?" Cassandra cut in. "The flight was ridiculous. Eighteen hours. And what was the reason we couldn't get off when we stopped and refueled? My J Brand jeans will never be the same again. I really should have worn—"

"Honestly," Heidi interrupted. "I really can't handle hearing it right now, okay?"

Abandoning her suitcases on the steps, like Katie, she practically took her life in her hands too, leaping up the narrow, treacherous stairs with no railing to catch her. When she reached the top, a wave of dizziness swept over her. A common landing area, only about six feet square and again with no railing, branched out to three bedrooms and the closed bathroom door.

With a thatched roof coming to a point about twelve to fifteen feet overhead, there were no ceilings to any of the rooms. No privacy. Sounds of Katie's retching could easily be heard from outside the door.

Heidi thought about knocking, but why bother? She figured she was barging into the bathroom whether Katie said she needed her or not.

Looking around the tiny, cramped space, Heidi almost wanted to be sick too. Katie sat on the gritty, grimy floor, gripping the toilet streaked with permanent stains of who knew what?

Oh, why on earth had Katie ever pushed for them to come here? Heidi had been ready to abandon the trip in a heartbeat. Why, in her condition, had Katie changed her mind, wanting to come so much?

Katie certainly didn't look so happy to be here now. Wiping her mouth with the back of her hand, she sat slumped on the floor, staring at Heidi, her hollow eyes filled with nothing but disappointment.

Heidi's own eyes began to mist. It was pathetic seeing Katie this way. Heart aching, unable to look at her daughter any longer, she glanced around the bathroom, searching for a washcloth, anything she could wet to cool Katie's forehead.

Gabby had said there would be linens supplied for them. Heidi supposed the stack of four towels on a mud-covered plastic chair that looked as if it belonged outdoors on a patio must be them. She grabbed one from the top, the pale green thing like a rag in her hands, and for a moment Heidi thought of her linen closets at home. She could also picture the two white fluffy washcloths she'd packed for the trip. But now wasn't the time to riffle through her suitcase for them.

Heidi turned on the antiquated faucet. It sputtered and spat till a trickle of water emerged, allowing her to wet the corner of the towel with cold water. She knelt and held the cloth against Katie's brow.

"Everything all right in there?" Cassandra tapped on the door.

Katie's forlorn expression clutched at Heidi's heart. "We're fine," Heidi answered, knowing from Katie's look that they were feeling, thinking the same thing.

Would they ever be free of this? All these miles away from their hometown, from the scrutiny there, couldn't they just relax and not be worried about others finding out? and what they might think? how they might judge them?

"We put your suitcases in the bedroom for you," Gabby told them through the door.

"Oh, you two didn't have to do that."

"No problem."

"She's vomiting," Cassandra said in a low voice to Gabby. "And here I was worried about germs from the passengers on the plane. Thankfully I packed my echinacea" was the last thing Heidi heard Cassandra say before she walked away.

Heidi moved the damp cloth, pressing it to the side of Katie's face.

"I'm so sorry," Katie whispered, her voice trembling.

"Oh, Katie . . ." She wrapped the broken-looking girl in her arms. What could she say? She was sorry too.

19

Cassandra swatted at a mosquito that appeared to be delighting itself in the flesh of her forearm.

How dare the thing! Already being pesky and she hadn't even settled in yet.

Although settle in to what? Her matching ebony Louis Vuitton suitcases stood upright in the center of the closet-size room alongside her camera bag and silver purse. Surrounded by speckles of ants traipsing back and forth on the dust-covered wooden floor, the luggage looked like a pair of sentries over the only other object in the room, a twin bed minus a headboard, slammed up against the wall.

Talk about sparse! Cassandra had stayed in Super 8 Motels that were more furnished than this place and far cleaner, too. Not that she'd ever admit that to anyone—about the Super 8s. But she hadn't exactly started out at the top of her profession. There had been a few Podunk stations before WONR, places that didn't have much of a budget when sending eager new reporters out on assignment. A young, aspiring newsperson, she'd worked harder than the rest—and stayed wherever necessary to hold on to a job. Even if it sometimes meant an uncomfortable night of sleep with one eye peeled on the metal motel door or covering the bed with towels so her skin didn't have to touch the sheets.

But it didn't matter. She'd have done nearly anything in those days to launch her career. And now she'd come full circle, hadn't she?

Now she was doing just about anything to save it.

Although it was harder the second time around, Cassandra thought, picking up the smaller suitcase of her high-priced set and heaving it onto the bed. She'd become spoiled by the fruits of her labor and by the successful lifestyle she—and only she—had created for herself. Once people thought of you as rich and successful it was difficult to be viewed as anything less.

It was also difficult to view yourself as anything less. Who wanted to?

The zipper sounded unusually crisp and bold in the quiet of the nearly barren room as she opened a front pocket of the suitcase to remove a battery-operated clock and another necessity, a light-up travel mirror, also battery operated.

Holding both items in her hands, she peered around the space wondering what to set them on. She felt like a kid on Christmas morning when she spied a cardboard box in the corner. After laying down the mirror on the stained bedspread, she reached for the box, turned it over, and placed it next to the bed. *Voilà!* Her room now had a nightstand. A little low to the floor, but it would have to do.

If only there were something to make the bed more inviting or even a little less scary to sleep in. She hated to imagine what the sheets might be like, because the bedspread certainly didn't look appealing or clean. The lace-fringed, tattered thing was covered with brown, streaky stains. Worse than Jack McFadden's teeth, and that was saying something.

Jack. He couldn't wait for her to leave so she'd get back soon with the story that would breathe new life into his stagnating career. Yeah, good old look-out-for-himself Jack, just like every other man. He was probably at Rolling Meadows Golf Club right now finishing a round of golf or enjoying an icy vodka tonic and a portobello mushroom appetizer.

While she was here in this godforsaken place.

Feeling another mosquito guzzling with fervor, Cassandra smacked the left side of her neck. The jarring let loose a trickle of sweat, dripping down her chest all the way to her belly button.

It had to be at least ninety degrees in the upstairs area. What she wouldn't give for a ceiling fan. But there'd have to be a ceiling first, she reminded herself, craning to look at the pitch of the thatched roof.

How many varieties of insects was that thing home to? She shivered at the thought.

Yes, she could definitely use a vodka tonic herself about now. Would sell her soul for one even. Cold, smooth, and numbing. It sounded like the perfect end to her long day of traveling. But that wasn't going to happen, she knew, since there was no alcohol on the trip. Drinking was rude to the natives or something like that.

Cassandra sighed. Churches and God sure knew how to make rules. Usually she knew how to get around them, but locating a cocktail at the pastor's compound in a small village in South Africa seemed beyond even her typically resourceful skills.

"Is Katie feeling better?" she heard Gabby ask Heidi.

Inclining her ear toward the hollow wooden door, she strained but couldn't make out Heidi's answer.

Oh yes. It was all going to shake out the way it normally did, wasn't it? By the end of the trip, Gabby and Heidi would be the best of friends. And she'd be on the outside . . . as always.

Most of her growing-up years and even her on-her-own twenties had found her on the outside looking in. She'd learned in those days that not many people wanted to include outsiders. Once you were one of the outs, people just knew that about you somehow. They don't choose you. They don't want you for a friend.

But who had time for frivolous things like friends? Cassandra certainly hadn't. She scraped by and worked at all sorts of jobs throughout college while the only job most of the other girls seemed to have was attending frat parties.

And once she got hired on at the first TV station, she'd worked many long hours trying to prove herself, to get ahead. She got used to being on her own. In her line of work it was better anyway. After all, too much accessibility caused the downfall of many a celebrity. You needed just the right amount. Like a tease. Bop into the bagel shop on Sunday morning and people will feel like they've experienced a star sighting. Do it every day and there's no mystique left.

Picking up the portable mirror, she inspected her teeth. All good there. She fluffed out the sides of her hair with her hands.

Cassandra didn't want to be included with that pair anyway. The Heidi woman was such a mom, so hands-on. She could really get on one's nerves after a while. No wonder her daughter did that rolling-eye thing all the time. Cassandra could empathize. And then Gabby, Miss Holy of Holies, Director of Children's Ministries. What was up with her? Good job, supposedly a nice husband, a great relationship with her Savior, right? For all that, the woman sure looked down and out most of the time.

Oh, well. Not my problem. She wiped at a smudge of mascara from beneath her left eye.

"Can I come in?"

Cassandra straightened at the sound of Heidi's voice and the light rapping on the thin wood door.

"Sure." She set the mirror aside. "Good luck on the door not caving in. It's off the top hinges." Too bad she hadn't packed a small tool kit.

Slowly Heidi opened the door, peeking inside. "It looks pretty much like our room. Only we have two beds."

"Really? And here I thought this was the luxury suite. Bet you don't have a nightstand like that one." She pointed to the upside-down box.

Heidi cracked a smile, surprising Cassandra that she didn't try to reprimand her for the smart-aleck remark. "There were four towels in the bathroom. So I brought you one. Your *linens*, ma'am." She offered the towel.

So even she lets loose of the reins once in a while, huh? Cassandra took the threadbare piece of cloth out of her hands, noting that, like the bedspread, it was stained and the hem was missing from the edges. "And room service too. Um, thanks."

Heidi rocked back in her sneakers. "I know what you're thinking."

"I'm not thinking anything." Okay, so she was. She was wondering why Heidi was being so nice to her.

"Sure you are. And that's okay. But truly all the towels are in that bad of shape. I didn't shortchange you. Actually, sort of the opposite."

Cassandra cocked her head.

"I picked out the best ones for you and Katie."

"For Katie and me?"

"I'm used to messy. Gabby probably is too. We're around little kids all the time."

"Well, I—thanks. Again."

"You're welcome." Heidi slid her hands into the pockets of her khaki capris and turned to walk away.

No, it didn't make sense that Heidi was being nice to her. But she'd take anything she could get her hands on to make the trip easier on herself. After all, there were givers and takers in this world, and there was no mistaking which camp she belonged to.

And which one Heidi seemed to fit in, too. Maybe she was one of those moms Cassandra only knew from watching television who always felt compelled to smooth things over, make things comfortable for everyone. It could get nauseating, she supposed; but then again . . .

"I have some echinacea," she found herself blurting out. "An entire bottle." She bent over, pulling a container out of her smaller suitcase. "If your daughter is feeling like she's getting sick."

Heidi stopped to face her. "She'll be okay. She just had an upset stomach. But thanks. Maybe I'll try some later."

"Try what?" Gabby poked her head into the room.

"We were just talking herbs," Heidi told her.

Gabby nodded. "Hey, Sipho just stopped by, and plans have changed. We won't be going to see Jaleela until tomorrow morning. Evidently she isn't feeling well."

"I thought Mama Penny said she was having a good day." Heidi looked confused.

"Is it from AIDS?" Cassandra asked. Admittedly, the thought made her squirm inside.

Gabby shrugged. "I suppose."

"Well, it's probably for the best. It's going to be getting dark soon anyway," Heidi answered, sounding like the reasonable mom she was. "She can rest and we can get settled in."

But as Heidi and Gabby both retreated from her room, Cassandra looked around, feeling her shoulders sag, her mouth curl up in distaste. It didn't look at all like a place where she could get her beauty sleep.

20

Gabby's eyes shot wide open, instantly flooded by daylight. She lay stiff in bed, listening.

Screaming. She'd heard screaming.

Why wasn't Tom doing something about it? Why wasn't he—?

Head still flat on the nearly featherless pillow, she blinked at the bare, unpainted Sheetrock wall next to the bed.

What on earth? *Where* on earth?

Oh! South Africa—

She bolted out of the twin bed.

But she didn't have far to go. Three steps across the landing, and she was at the bathroom. That was where the screaming had come from.

Heidi and Katie came running from their room too. Katie in a tank top and boxers, her hair in a flop-top ponytail, and Heidi in a loose, cotton sleeveless nightshirt. Gabby could've sworn they looked as stiff as she felt. Too scared to move, not sure what they'd open the door to. A burglar maybe? A ten-foot python?

Heidi was closest to the door, and she glanced Gabby's way. Sucking in a breath, Gabby nodded. Heidi turned the knob, then flung the door wide open.

"*Excuse me?*" Cassandra shrilled at their quickly formed rescue team. "Excuse me?"

The anchor stood stark naked in an old-fashioned claw-foot tub, void of the luxury—and privacy—of a shower curtain. Though the water had been shut off from the handheld showerhead, her entire body and the tips of her short, styled hair dripped with water. Hands shooting up from her sides, she worked to cover herself with one hand flying over her chest and one below her waist.

"Are you okay?" Gabby tried to avert her eyes, look anywhere but at Cassandra.

"Of course I'm okay." Cassandra sounded duly disgusted.

Heidi shifted on her bare feet. "Well, you—we came running because you screamed."

"Well, of course I screamed!" Cassandra flared. "You would too if you had arctic cold water spraying out on you." She clutched herself tighter, nodding at a towel sitting on the closed commode. "Would someone kindly hand me that thing?"

"Your linen?" Heidi grinned, handing Cassandra the towel.

"Oh yes, my linen. And you all are my maidservants, right?" Cassandra squinted down her nose at the three of them. Even given the uncomfortable situation, she still managed to easily look imperious.

They politely turned to leave, and the three of them were almost outside the door when she called out. "Oh, and don't get after me, you all, acting like I used up all the hot water. FYI, I couldn't use up all the hot water because there is none. Nada. Or however you say that in Zulu."

Simultaneously their trio swung back around at the sound of Cassandra's voice.

She was already dried off and wrapped in her honey-colored silk robe. "I'm serious." She tightened the sash at her waist. "The water was tepid at first. Well, for about a millisecond or . . . Whatever's possibly smaller than that?"

"A microsecond?" Katie came to life. "A nanosecond?"

Everyone turned to look at her.

"Well, she asked."

Heidi gave her daughter's ponytail a tug. "I think she meant it as rhetorical."

Katie's face scrunched. "Everything with you older people is rhetorical."

"So while we're debating that issue . . ." Cassandra removed her stretchy deep purple headband, and Gabby couldn't believe how beautiful she looked without her usual amount of well-applied makeup. Sure, age etched the slightest lines around her eyes and lips, and her uncovered forehead exposed a slightly noticeable crinkle. But still, how many females at any age could look so attractive without the benefits of a little foundation, concealer, and lipstick?

"Has anyone thought about breakfast?" Cassandra asked, fluffing her semidamp hair with her polished fingertips.

Gabby shook her head and Heidi tilted hers. "Oh, wouldn't a big breakfast be wonderful?" Her expression turned dreamy. "Eggs over easy. Canadian bacon. Waffles."

"With whipped cream and strawberries," Katie added.

"Don't I wish." Cassandra chuckled, streaking her toothbrush with paste.

"Don't we all wish!" Gabby nodded.

"Ugh. No coffee. And the thought of no hot showers . . . ," Cassandra murmured as she turned on the faucet, which hissed at her. "I can't believe it. Just dreadful. How many more days of this till we're home again?"

"Twelve," Katie spouted, and everyone looked her way. "Oh, I get it. Rhetorical again, right?" She smacked her forehead with the palm of her hand and burst out laughing.

The total spontaneity of Katie's laughter was contagious. All the ladies joined in, Gabby included, feeling some of the strain between them break away.

As the three of them moved all the way onto the landing, closing the bathroom door behind them, giving Cassandra her due privacy, Gabby felt some of the hurt within her break loose too.

After losing their baby—losing their last chance for a family—she never thought she'd laugh again and had never really wanted to. But there it was, whether she wanted it or not, whether she wanted to cling to her desolation or not. Out of nowhere. Unsolicited. Unprovoked. The first hint of laughter after her loss. Hardly anything, but it was the start of a line crossed.

Without a moment's thought, she hugged Katie, thankful the teenager had come with them. And suddenly awed by the girl too. She couldn't have imagined being Katie's age and traveling with a couple of women and her mother with no other teenagers around. Even after being sick the day before, Katie seemed to be making the best of things.

"You mentioned you liked my hair yesterday," Gabby told her. "Do you want me to braid yours like that today?"

"Seriously?" Katie pulled the ponytail holder from her head, shaking out her dark hair. "Awesome."

Heidi nodded to her daughter. "That would look so cute on you, Kay-kay. Your hair's just the right length."

Cassandra emerged from the bathroom, cosmetic bag in hand. "The bath is all clear and ready for the next victims," she informed them.

And they all laughed again.

◈ ◈ ◈

During their Colorado vacation, Gabby and Tom had done everything they could afford to do, which included a two-hour Jeep tour so they could explore some of the rarer sights that glimpses from the roadside couldn't provide. Gabby remembered laughing as the Jeep bumped over the uneven mounds of earth. Even holding on to the grab handle, she'd flown up in the backseat, her body flailing, pitching from side to side. And Tom had always been there to catch her. To hold her hand, pull her close. Smile into her laughing eyes.

For a minute, Gabby had a sense—or more like a wish—she and her group were on an adventurous, carefree Jeep tour too.

But no. Sipho was at the wheel of the dust-covered, indistinguishable white passenger van again, same as the day before. Their group had filed into the van, taking the same seats they'd laid claim to the day before. Only this time, instead of easing down the wide-open road from the airport, flanked with rural, rolling mounds of earth and tall golden grasses that had flourished in the sun, the van went off road to enter Squatter Camp.

The sun beat down on the red dirt, the foundation of Squatter Camp, offering a fleeting memory of something Gabby had seen before on another trip, another time. The van jostled and lurched, lumbering over the unforgiving mounds of brick-colored clay, as Sipho worked hard to control the wheel, nearly bottoming out in the deep grooves in some places. The van had nothing in common with the agility of a Jeep. But then, the direness of the scene outside the window bore no resemblance to the breathtaking, vibrant sights of Colorado.

Only a smattering of green could be seen every now and then. And that was from clumps of weeds, looking unhealthy and sadly worn as if it had taken every bit of energy conceivable to sprout through the nearly rock-hard soil. A lone tree could be seen every so often too, but those plants also seemed to be striving, not thriving, low to the ground and stunted, as if too depressed to raise leafy arms over the surrounding shacks.

The shacks were constructed from scraps of found material—wood, siding, and tin—in dull, lifeless grays, dirty yellows, too-bright blues, and sick pinks the shade of indigestion medicine. A patchwork of scraps to harbor their patchwork lives and families. Families that had been fragmented by HIV, AIDS, lack of food, lack of jobs . . .

And lack of hope?

As the van's tires clawed over the bumpy, uneven landscape, Mama Penny told them stories about a woman whose husband was into witchcraft and voodoo, who would drag her into the woods at night, doing strange things to her to try to rid the virus from her body—the virus that he'd given her, that plagued his body too. About a girl named Mighty, around Katie's age, who had spent most of her childhood caring for younger siblings after their parents died, and now she was all alone because her sisters and brothers had died of AIDS too.

And just as she began to tell them more, she poked her head out the window and waved to a woman who looked to be in her late forties. The lean woman sat on a stool in front of a hut made of pieces of wood, crisscrossed and nailed every which way. "Hello, Rebecca. You are good?"

A broad smile instantly lit up the woman's face at the sound of Mama Penny's voice. "The sun shines," she uttered in simple explanation.

Mama Penny chuckled and waved again as the van continued on; then she turned to them. "I do not know why I wave to her. Rebecca is blind. A blind grandmother. I tried to save her daughter, Grace, from AIDS, but she waited too long to admit her sickness. It is a shame too. Her son, Blessing, is so precious, just three, and now Rebecca must raise him. It is so often that way for grandparents now—the ones who are lucky enough to live to their forties and fifties. There are the grandbabies and the grandparents. The middle generation is becoming less and less."

"How can she raise him if she's blind?" Heidi spoke up.

"How can she not?" Mama Penny said, but then she softened. "I do not know how she manages. I can only tell you if you would see inside her home, it is immaculate. I have two seeing eyes and cannot say that for myself."

More stories flowed from Mama Penny. About young nieces caring for sick aunts and the estranged caring for strangers. She talked, too, of the still-prevailing embarrassment associated with the disease that isolated people from each other.

It seemed like too much for Gabby to take in. All that striving going on inside the dreary, ten-foot rectangles of tin. While outside, the garbage—discarded pieces of tin, cardboard, rusted-out cars, and trash—thrived. She imagined the white clumps of litter might look like polka dots from an aerial view.

She looked away for a moment and focused on the ladies in her group. They'd had such a fun morning. Cassandra's drama and screaming had been a catalyst for laughter and sharing for all four of them. Gabby hadn't felt a kinship, hadn't felt anything like that for a long time. But that feeling had dissipated. Now only a definitive somberness hung over their group. She could feel it. She could see it too. Katie staring out the window, biting her thumbnail. Heidi's forehead pinched, her eyes downcast. Cassandra, too, sat still, her camera at her side, looking outward, keeping her thoughts inward for a change.

Only Mama Penny, riding shotgun, seemed able to muster any kind of positive body language in spite of the surroundings. Her sight didn't waver from the view outside the window. Her lips remained straight, firm, not turned down. Her eyes reflective but determined.

But mostly Gabby noticed the way she held her head—high, so high—as if this too would be overcome. This too would pass. Someday.

No wonder the woman had beaten the odds. Gotten an education. Lived to educate others. No wonder she'd been named Woman of the Year.

Gabby lifted her chin, attempting to mimic the older woman. Then, through the window, she noticed a string of ragged garments hanging on a limp clothesline in the heat of the sun. In another place, it might look like a mother's attempt to do her chores, to do right by her family. But here that attempt looked so futile, it made Gabby's head hang. After all, how clean could the clothes be in this place? Wouldn't they get stained from the red clay? Wouldn't the children sweat in their shirts the moment they put them on? Especially if they were inside the tin huts?

Gabby wished she knew more about the way things worked. As in, did the tin roof reflect the sun? How hot could it get inside? And in the winter, how cold? Were the families virtually homeless when chilly winds blew? with no shelters to give them aid? Tom would know how tin conducted heat or let in air. He always knew things like that.

Tom . . . If he were here . . . "How cold does it get here, Mama Penny?" The words were out of her mouth before Gabby knew it. And by the way the others turned and looked at her, she imagined her voice might've been a welcome reprieve from the sights outside the window.

Mama Penny swung around in the seat, speaking over the top of her broad shoulder. "June is our coldest month. Sometimes it is one degree."

"But that's Celsius, right?" Heidi asked.

"Celsius?" Gabby repeated. "I forget how to calculate that."

"I know." Heidi nodded. "I forget too."

"One degree would be a little over our freezing point." Katie shifted in the seat, sitting with a leg bent underneath her. "About thirty-four degrees."

Heidi gave her daughter a puzzled look.

"What?" Katie frowned at her. "That wasn't rhetorical too, was it?"

"No. I'm just wondering how you know that. And about that nanosecond stuff."

"I just do." Katie's hand fell over a braid, feeling the tip of it.

"Thank goodness we have someone with us who can still think," Cassandra murmured. Picking up her video camera, she aimed it through the open window of the van again.

Gabby watched her, wondering if the camera buffered the stark scenery in any way. Lost in thought, she didn't notice the van's slowing down until it stopped.

"I must check on some children." Mama Penny opened the passenger door. "I very much appreciate your patience." She struggled down from the high seat of the van with much effort.

Gazing out the window, Gabby saw the three children Mama Penny was referring to. A young boy in between two girls stood in a row, like stair steps, in front of the hovel that was their home. Gabby guessed their ages to range from seven to eleven years old. The oldest had a protective hand on her brother's shoulder while the brother held hands with their baby sister.

Their eyes seemed to brighten some at the sight of Mama Penny, but other than that, their faces remained expressionless. Just a slight smile tugged at the older girl's lips when Mama Penny reached into her canvas satchel and presented some fruit and bread. The girl's face hardly changed as Mama Penny pulled some money from the pocket of her skirt and pressed it into the palm of the girl's hand.

What did change their expressions was when Mama Penny hugged them. It seemed to be the best of all the gifts she had to offer, the thing the children were starved for more than food. None of them shirked the moment of love Mama Penny shared with them. Each seemed to want to linger in the fold of her embrace. And when they finally stepped back from her, they looked almost awakened. Alive again. Like they could go on another day.

As she witnessed the change, Gabby's cheeks tingled. But she didn't realize what she'd seen until Mama Penny hoisted herself back into the van.

"They are a child-headed family," she explained as if they all knew what she was talking about.

Cassandra pointed the camera to Mama Penny at that bit of cryptic information.

"What does that mean exactly?" Katie wasn't shy about asking.

"I am sorry. I forget all do not know of such things," Mama Penny said as the van lurched forward. "The children's parents have died of AIDS. They have no mother. No father. They must raise themselves. It is a child-headed family."

"Oh." Katie's brows furrowed. "Are there many kids like that?"

"Yes, unfortunately. There are over a million orphans in South

Africa alone. It is often the way here. Too often. That is why they speak of the children these days as the 'lost' generation."

"But how do they survive?" Heidi wanted to know. "What do they eat?"

"Whatever they can." Mama Penny shrugged, adding with a sigh, "They must depend on each other and the kindness of those around them. Their lives are difficult, and sadly, they live in fear. Of survival. Of the virus that took the lives of their mother and father. It is not just food that is missing for them."

Gabby had seen as much during Mama Penny's exchange with the children. "Did I hear somewhere that one in three pregnant women with HIV passes it along to her child? Do many of these children have HIV too?"

Cassandra had shifted the camera to Gabby, who was only too happy when the anchor turned it back on Mama Penny.

"Yes. I do not have an exact number for you. It is always changing. I can only say I dream of the day when we have the resources to test all babies for the sickness. But families are fragmented and scattered. There are too many pregnant women. Too many still embarrassed to admit their illness. Of course, it is the children who then suffer in so many ways."

"Sometimes in my classroom, I can look at a child and just know there are problems at home. And it breaks my heart," Heidi said. "Sometimes when you look at a child, do you know, Mama Penny?"

As the tires churned through the red clay, Mama Penny nodded. "Recently a four-month-old baby was brought to us. The mother had just died of AIDS, and the baby weighed only eleven pounds. Eleven pounds at four months. It was very obvious. I wished I was not right, but I was. Often in younger children, you will see an orange tint to their hair. The hair may become fluffier, thin. I have observed many times that may be an indication too."

Self-consciously, Gabby pushed her red hair back from her face while she listened.

"I only have twenty-two kids in my class to deal with." Heidi shook her head. "And they all have guardians. I can't imagine how overwhelmed you must feel at times."

"The good news is, there is a Father in heaven." Mama Penny looked directly into Cassandra's camera. "I am not alone. Though I tire at times, He is there. And I will not give up."

Listening to Mama Penny's voice resonate with resolve, seeing her chin raised in defiance, Gabby believed the woman could save all the orphans on the continent. Or at least she had the heart and soul to.

Minutes later Sipho pulled out of another gully of red clay onto a patch of fairly level ground in front of a drab, colorless tin hut. Putting the van into park, he turned off the engine.

Quiet engulfed the van, inside and out, while everyone absorbed the condition of the shack. So this was Jaleela's home?

Yes, Gabby had seen pictures of places like this before in magazines and in world hunger brochures that came in the mail. But even in person, it was difficult to grasp.

And to think within seconds she would be walking inside . . .

Could it really be possible the woman lived here with her children? in this space the size of Gabby's dining room at home, only not in the least as inviting?

Finally Mama Penny broke the silence. "The people here—they have seen few whites before. But no white has ever been in their home. You are the first. You care to come. Jaleela cares to trust in your coming. Let us have you meet Jaleela now?" she said, her sentence both a declaration and a question.

Gabby didn't know about the others, but when she stood to exit the van, her legs felt strange. Even worse than after their long, transatlantic flight. Could her legs really feel leaden and hollow at the same time?

She was glad to be in the backseat, glad to be the last one out, hoping to hide her wariness and herself behind everyone else. Right at the moment, she didn't want to be here. No way could she handle all of this. Not when she was still feeling this fragile . . . so broken already.

But as she regarded the shack, her spirits sinking even lower, Nomvula burst out the doorway of her home.

Wearing the same pink T-shirt from Ohio as the day before, she waved. She smiled. She laughed. She jumped so excitedly around them, Gabby could feel their graveness dissipate as quickly as a firework in a Fourth of July sky.

"*. . . and He separated the light from the darkness.*" The line of Scripture flitted across Gabby's mind. *From where?* It felt like forever since she'd read her Bible or given thought to such things.

But Nomvula looked like sunshine and light and everything bright emerging from the dark, dingy tin can of a place where she lived.

A younger boy, about six years old, stood behind her, smiling, watching as she hugged Mama Penny's and Sipho's waists, then as she gave her new American friends the same warm greeting.

The boy probably didn't even know what he was grinning about, his sister's exuberance a good enough excuse to be smiling too.

"This is my brother, Tumi." Nomvula pulled him to her side, hugging his narrow shoulders. "Tumi, this is Cassandra." She pointed with her free hand. "And Katie Blue Eyes. Mama Heidi and—" she paused to smile at Gabby—"Gabrielle."

Tumi gave the women a somewhat-guarded smile. He may not have been as demonstrative as his sister. Still, he was undeniably adorable, even with thin arms and few muscles in his legs. Gabby thought he and Nomvula had the most beautiful golden-brown skin she'd ever seen. They also shared the same eyes, rich and round as chestnuts.

As Tumi cocked his head in an endearingly shy way, she was surprised to notice a small patch of orange in his hair. But apparently it wasn't the same kind of orange Mama Penny had been talking about, because she hadn't said anything to them about Tumi's ill health. And the child looked more than fine, and in a way, fun-loving too. Whereas the sure look in Nomvula's eyes made her look older than her years, Tumi still had evidence of a boyish glint. Something in his eyes reminded Gabby of Mama Penny. Something shiny and sparkling, resistant to hardships, defying anything that would make him grow up too quickly, steal his childhood before the ripe age of seven.

"They are here!" Nomvula called out to her mother, still unseen in their dark home. "Mama!" Her voice spilled over with exhilaration, making Gabby feel humbled. "They are here!"

Nomvula's mother, Jaleela, came to the entry of their home, smoothing out the faded folds of her pale yellow cotton skirt. She too looked to be rather thin and about five feet six, taller than Gabby imagined.

Jaleela started to say something, but then her breath seemed to catch. Instead, she held up her arms to the heavens. And tears rained down her cheeks.

21

"You have come. Truly, truly, you have come."

Jaleela's tears muffled her greeting, but Gabby could still make out everything she said. More than that, Gabby felt moved by her words.

Maybe because of the woman herself?

Even though the air all about them was warm, Jaleela's smile seemed even warmer. And though Jaleela's dark hand was smooth to the touch, the open trust in her embrace was actually touching. Going deep to a place inside Gabby—a place that needed rekindling. All of that in a moment. From a stranger. Could that really be?

Stunned, Gabby studied the woman, wondering how.

With an afro like a halo crowning her head, Jaleela had a tranquil, elegant quality about her, and immediately Gabby knew where Nomvula got her aura of serenity. Gabby found herself enamored of the woman's gracious demeanor, the way she shone amid such awful, stark conditions.

"Welcome, welcome," Jaleela said over and over again as she hugged each of them to her heart. "I have prayed for this very long. So long have I prayed for you. For this day."

Gabby didn't doubt that to be true. The first thing she spotted upon entering Jaleela's home was a wooden, not-so-symmetrical cross with some beads wrapped around it. A rosary maybe? Though it didn't look long enough to be. The cross dangled from a two-by-four piece of wood, one of several two-by-fours giving structure to the shack made of tin.

There were no walls really—no plywood, no drywall, no insulation—just the exposed underside of the tin exterior showed. A few electrical cords draped across the walls and hung from the tin ceiling, providing a current to an overhead lightbulb and a small, toylike stove. Earlier Mama Penny had mentioned that none of the shacks had heat and many of them had no electricity whatsoever. The people who lived in those huts cooked over an open fire. And only the stars provided light for them at night.

Apparently Jaleela was one of the lucky ones. Gabby couldn't imagine.

"Sit. Sit." Jaleela directed them to a primitive block of wood on pedestals with benches on either side, sitting right inside the doorway.

The table fit the four of them perfectly while Nomvula and Tumi stood at their sides, and Mama Penny and Sipho lingered at the door. Obviously the two of them had realized the cramped quarters couldn't take more bodies.

The house was so tiny, Gabby could've reached out from her place at the table and touched the lone bed if she'd been so inclined. A worn white chenille bedspread covered the neatly made bed, a pillow precisely in the middle. It was a sweet, touching sight. But that image turned sad when Gabby started wondering if they all slept in the same bed. And on days when Jaleela didn't feel well, where did the children go? Did they have to sit at the table and watch her suffering?

"I have made pap for you," Jaleela offered. "And a bit of stew."

"Oh, Jaleela, you needn't go to any trouble," Heidi spoke for the group.

"Trouble? You have come all the way from America. You have come all the way to my home. There is no trouble," Jaleela answered with a serene smile as she turned to the black pot on the old-fashioned, fifties-style stove.

And yet, it appeared Jaleela had gone to a lot of extra work. Besides being filled with the aroma of her savory cooking, the shack was absolutely spotless. Even the two buckets sitting by the walls presumably to catch raindrops coming down the seeping interior looked neatly placed. Yes, it was pristine. Truly a miracle, Gabby thought. How could that be in these conditions, with all that red dirt outside? Although she sensed Nomvula and Tumi had been trained well. She'd seen them automatically wipe their bare feet on the pink rug by the doorway. None of their dusty footprints tracked across the painted concrete floor.

"Nomvula," Jaleela called.

Nomvula took her eyes off the four of them just long enough to turn to her mother, who held out a folded piece of fabric that Nomvula took into her arms. She stepped over to them again and said, "Excuse please," before placing an off-white piece of material bordered with flower-shaped eyelets over the picnic-style table. "This belonged to my grandmama," she told them proudly.

"It's pretty." Gabby smoothed the cotton cloth.

"Nomvula's grandmama liked to work with her hands," Mama Penny said from the doorway. "She did beadwork and stitching. That is where Jaleela comes to her talent."

"She lived to be almost fifty-five years old," Nomvula informed them, her eyes wide as she sat down on the edge of the bench next to Gabby.

As the comment settled over them, everyone seemed to pause. Gabby was certain they, like her, were recalling how Mama Penny had mentioned the low life expectancy in South Africa—forty-nine years old for men and fifty for women. No wonder fifty-five years old here sounded as incredulous as ninety years back home. Each day, each moment, really was precious, wasn't it?

Meanwhile Tumi helped Jaleela bring plates of pap and gravy stew to the table and set it down on the family heirloom.

"I have only three plates," Jaleela apologized, and for the first time Gabby thought she saw the slightest look of shame cross the woman's face.

"That's perfect. We'll share." Heidi nodded across the table at Katie. "We're family."

Gratefulness appeared to erase the momentary stress from Jaleela's face. She smiled. "The pap is made of mielie-meal—maize," she explained. "You may tear some off and roll it into a ball. Then dip it in the sauce."

"Oh, like chips and dip." Even Cassandra appeared to be touched by the woman's efforts. "Sounds great."

"You would like to say grace first?" Jaleela glanced around the table at the four of them.

"Gabby works at the church. She is a director there," Mama Penny told Jaleela. "Maybe Gabby would pray for us."

Jaleela put her hand to her chest. Her eyes lit up, brighter than ever. "You work at the church?" She beamed at Gabby. "Graceview Church?"

"Yes," Gabby said tentatively. "Yes, I do."

"That is where the bracelet came from." Jaleela pointed to the beads wrapped around the crude cross on her semblance of a wall. "From your church. In a Christmas box. Nomvula brought it to me."

"It has pretty colors," Katie noted. "All those blues."

Jaleela nodded. "It came a few days before Jesus Christ was born. The day I lay dying in my bed. It came to me like Jesus. Like hope."

They stared at the cross and bracelet in silence, Gabby suddenly feeling disturbed she couldn't see—or feel—the same thing Jaleela did at the sight of the coarse cross and string of beads affixed to the piece of wood.

"Would you pray for us, Gabby?" Jaleela broke the silence and Gabby's sullenness with her request.

Gabby's pulse quickened. She used to be completely accustomed to this. Used to revel in leading a group prayer. It was one of her gifts. Bringing hearts together to God in prayer. But now, she was so far away. So distant from Him. What words were there? She couldn't think of anything to say.

But everyone was staring at her. Waiting on her. Nomvula especially looked at her expectantly, and Gabby felt an immediate sense of dread. An overwhelming sense of responsibility. She didn't want to have the young girl disappointed about something—or someone—again.

Finally her mind lit on a grace she'd been saying since childhood. "Bless us, O Lord . . . ," she recited mechanically, the prayer rolling off her tongue with phrases that held little meaning after so many years of repetition.

But Jaleela appeared satisfied and touched. "Now we are *all* family," she said when Gabby finished, then winked at Heidi and Mama Penny before her smile spread like a ray of warmth around the table to the rest of them.

"Oh, these are beautiful!"

Gabby couldn't believe Jaleela's intricate, flawless beadwork. She'd never have the patience or the talent to create such unique pieces of jewelry as the angels, bracelets, earrings, and necklaces that Jaleela spread out on the table once the plates of pap had been cleared away and the cook had been complimented.

The beaded samples had been bundled up in wrapping paper dotted with colorful angels and tucked beneath Jaleela's bed. They'd been stored like secret treasures, she explained, just waiting for the women from Ohio to get here.

"You like them? It is good, then?" Jaleela stood with one hand on her hip and one over her mouth, her eyes uncertain.

Meanwhile Nomvula's eyes searched Gabby's hopefully and Tumi clung to the side of the table, both seeming to hang on every word of the women's exchange.

"Better than good," Cassandra said, surprising Gabby. She held up a three-strand bracelet for inspection. "The colors are tasteful. And I love the metallic sheen to some of the beads. Very pretty. Masterful job."

Jaleela let out a sigh, sounding much like relief.

"I told you she inherited her mother's artistic abilities." Mama Penny smiled knowingly, inching her way closer to the table.

Katie picked up a pair of earrings done in bold traditional colors. "I wish they sold stuff like this where we come from."

Jaleela clapped. "Yes? You truly do?"

"Yes." Katie held up one of the earrings to her lobe. "What do you think, Mom?"

"It's lovely. Ladies in my neighborhood would love authentic pieces like these," Heidi added.

"Yes?" Jaleela asked again.

"Definitely," Heidi answered.

As they all nodded in unison, Jaleela shuffled her feet, doing a little dance. Katie and the younger kids laughed. "It is like my dream, then. My dream from God."

"Your dream from God?" Cassandra blurted.

Gabby had noticed that all morning Cassandra had been tempering her words, her tone. But Jaleela's mention that God had supplied her with a dream seemed to cause Cassandra visible discomfort. Gabby could see it in the other woman's narrowed eyes, the way she rolled her shoulders as if shirking off the idea.

Apparently Cassandra could deal with something real like jewelry and even things as intangible and innate as good taste and talent. But what Gabby had suspected about the woman before they'd even left Columbus was that she didn't have a very developed spiritual life or relationship with God. It was far too evident in what she said and how she said it. How she wiggled every time they joined in prayer together. Not that it mattered, really. Not that Gabby was judging. Gabby was right there with her—with a mind full of questions and doubts at this point in her life.

And feelings of jealousy, too. After all, she'd had a dream, hadn't she? A dream she thought God had planted inside her. But why hadn't He heard *her* cries? listened to *her* heart? let *her* dream come true?

"I tell you, I lay in that bed." Jaleela pointed to the only refuge for sleep in her home. "My breath, it came in gasps." She mimicked the sound. "It was the virus, of course. I had been living with it for a long time. And, yes, it can kill. But really what kills most often is the embarrassment. Too afraid of what others think to get help and medicines. Mama Penny can tell you."

Everyone looked Mama Penny's way, except for Heidi, who seemed to fidget on the bench.

"I thought I would be different from others I'd seen. But I, too, lay in bed dying like a fool." Jaleela shook her head. "An embarrassed fool."

"Then I brought Mama the bracelet," Nomvula said in her shy, pleasing voice as her mama's loving gaze lit on her face.

Gabby glanced at Nomvula, sitting by her side, and in that moment saw the reasons the child's eyes looked so much older than her years. The girl had seen more than young eyes should ever see. Like the orphaned children left all alone in charge of their tin-roof shanty and each other. Orphaned children living on the streets like stray animals. How the worry of that must have consumed Nomvula!

Plus the tiredness. No doubt Nomvula's hands had performed tasks no child should have to perform, nursing her sick mother. While keeping watch over her younger brother.

And along with those worries, there was the fear that could overtake your mind and weigh down your heart. Every day, every hour, feeling afraid that the thing most precious to you in the world might cease to exist. Might be taken away from you.

Oh, Gabby knew that feeling. She knew it all too well. Surely Nomvula did too.

"I did not know Mama Penny then as I do now. She gave out the Christmas boxes to the children, and she said to me, 'I have picked a pretty box for you.'" Nomvula spoke softly, her eyes smiling gratefully at the matriarch at the door. "It was true. On the outside, angels smiled at me." She nodded at the wrapping paper, now folded in neat squares on the table. "And on the inside, the bracelet sparkled. My heart told me the bracelet could make my mama better. My heart said it would make her stronger. And so . . . I followed my heart. I wanted Mama to laugh again. I wanted her to hold me close as she used to."

Everyone seemed mesmerized by Nomvula's sweetness, waiting for her to go on. When she remained silent, Jaleela continued their story. "It is as Nomvula says. I woke up and saw her standing there. It came to my mind I was waking up for the last time. That I should say good-bye to my babies. But then Nomvula gave the bracelet to me. It had come from across the world, she said. Someone's love came from across the world."

She glanced at the beads on the wall. "I had always taught my daughter and son that God's love is like that. His love fills a heart, and then that heart touches another and another. It happens over and over until His love and hope are everywhere. It was that thought that made me smile, even in my dying. God felt close as I held the bracelet in my hand and the sickness closed my eyes again. And when I woke up, I felt surprised to be alive. I touched my precious girl's face. I looked into my son's loving eyes." Her face radiated with a childlike wonder. "I held the bold, blue bracelet. It was . . ."

"Inspiring?" Heidi spoke up.

"Yes. Everything felt different to my touch. I realized what it was. When I was sleeping, God Almighty planted a dream inside me. A dream that I would live, and I could help others live too. A dream where I and others like me, we could make bracelets and sell them across the world." She scooped up Tumi in her arms and held him close to her bosom. "Then our children will not go hungry. Then we can give to the hospice and help others. We can create a circle like the bracelet. We can do that."

"And you're sure that was God?" Cassandra asked, a teasing lilt to her voice. "Or maybe you're simply a craftier businesswoman than you give yourself credit for."

Gabby thought Jaleela might be offended by Cassandra's comment or even back down a bit. Clearly Cassandra could seem formidable and intimidating with her put-together appearance alone, not to mention her strong voice, poise, and confidence.

By comparison, Jaleela's faded clothes hung on her frail body. A cough punctuated her soft voice every now and then. And it was unlikely she'd ever had her nails done or been to a hairstylist. Yet the woman stood solid in the meagerness of her shack and laughed heartily, the merry sound drawing smiles on everyone's faces.

"Ah!" She shook her finger at Cassandra and chuckled. "You are dear. You are. But I must say, I believe it is God who puts dreams in our hearts. All comes from Him. I do not doubt that. And it is God who brings people to your life to help with your dreams."

"You think so?" Cassandra countered.

"I know so." Jaleela's eyes shone. "Don't you see? If not for God, why else would the four of you be here?"

The room was startlingly still as if a great preacher had just finished sermonizing. Gabby had no clue as to what the others were thinking. But as for herself, she knew why she'd come here, reasons that had nothing to do with Jaleela. Stabs of guilt pricking at her conscience, she scooted as far as she could to the right, attempting to make more room for Nomvula on the benchlike seat.

"How are you feeling now?" Gabby hoped to change the subject.

"On the day that I nearly died, I said to Nomvula, go find Mama Penny. Mama Penny will know what to do. Then I got medicine for the virus. Of course the virus, it will never go away, and yes, I am weak some days. Yet I am alive. I have a dream."

"Tomorrow morning it is planned that many women will come to show you their beadwork," Mama Penny addressed their group. "You will meet them at the hospice. You saw it on your schedule?" She directed the question to Gabby.

"Oh yes." Gabby had heard something about beadwork and women, but she hadn't really been in the mood to pay attention to the itinerary, figuring she'd look it over once she got to South Africa. Finally she'd glanced at the paper this morning in the van.

"Wait a minute." Cassandra put down the necklace in her hands. "Jaleela, your work alone is good enough for us to sell in the States. We don't need any other beadworkers. And it was your idea. Are you sure you want to compete with the other ladies?"

Jaleela released Tumi from her arms, holding a hand to her mouth, covering a grin. "Beadworking is a tradition. It is as old as our people, I think. I do not compete with others. They are my sisters. My friends. We must help each other."

As Cassandra looked around Jaleela's home, Gabby figured she knew what the newswoman was thinking. Who was helping Jaleela?

"So, tomorrow we get to meet more women and see more jewelry?" Heidi asked.

Katie's eyes danced. "Do we get to pick out what we like the best?"

Mama Penny said from the doorway, "Yes, what you think will sell best in your home in America."

"And then what?" Cassandra wanted to know.

"I am thinking when you see what you like from the ladies, you will make an order from them. Many have known about your coming and have been making many fine pieces. Others can make more pieces during the time you are here."

"You may choose what you like tomorrow," Mama Penny clarified. "Then the ladies will come back the day before you go home, bringing the jewelry you have ordered from them."

"But won't the ladies want to be paid that day?" Gabby searched her memory. She didn't remember anything about money. No one had given her a check, a way to pay the ladies for their work before bringing the jewelry back to Ohio to sell.

They all looked to Mama Penny for an answer. She in turn looked to Jaleela.

"It all will work," Jaleela told them. "The money will come."

Cassandra's eyes widened, though she managed to keep her tone moderate. "It will just come?"

"I have said yes to God." She smiled at all of them. "You have all said yes as well. I trust He will see us through."

Astounded silence fell over them until Cassandra let out a laugh. Gabby was almost terrified to hear what she might say next.

"I like you." Cassandra pointed at Jaleela. "You have nerves of steel. You really are quite the businesswoman. An entrepreneur."

"An . . . excuse me?" Jaleela looked puzzled.

"The person who organizes and creates a business plan," Gabby spoke up.

Jaleela smiled. "I am thankful to God for that."

"So we'll meet up tomorrow, then? At the hospice? To meet the ladies?" Gabby asked.

Jaleela nodded, a sweet smile on her lips.

But even then, with their plans confirmed, no one got up from the hard, wooden bench. As much as they'd been filled with dread when they first entered Squatter Camp, Gabby could tell that now no one seemed to be in a hurry to leave. How had Jaleela done that? How had this poor African woman in such a dire setting sold them on her dream?

22

"Katie, you don't have to do this now." Gabby sat at the kitchen table, an old-style folding table with a nicked top and four mismatched chairs, leaning back so Katie could fiddle with her hair. The morning sun penetrated the dirt-smudged window, its warmth soothing on her face.

"But you said you liked the way Kate Hudson had hers in that magazine." Katie's fingers sifted through strands of Gabby's hair, lifting up a section on each side of her head. "And you did my hair yesterday. I can at least try it."

"But are you feeling all right? Is your stomach still giving you fits?"

"I'm, you know . . ." Katie's fingers paused. "I'm doing okay."

Katie might be doing fine at the moment, but just an hour ago Gabby had heard her heaving in the bathroom again. "Maybe last night's dinner didn't agree with you," she suggested. What had Mama Penny called it? *Boerewors?*

"Mmm. Maybe." Katie's voice drifted while she gently spooled a clump of hair around her finger. "Boy, your kids are going to be so lucky."

Gabby didn't know how Katie had arrived at that thought. Just a whimsical, teenage mind at work, she was sure. But though Katie's words had a daydream quality about them, the reality of what she said hit Gabby like a prizefighter's blow, splattering her emotions every

151

which way. Yet she worked hard, so hard, to hide the fact. "Why do you say that?"

"Because, you know, they'll probably have your hair. I always wished I had red hair."

Difficult as it was, Gabby tried to steady her feelings. She didn't need to be dumping on a seventeen-year-old. "You like red hair, really?"

"Yeah."

Gabby gave a sardonic snort.

"What?"

"Oh, nothing."

"Nothing, what?" Katie prodded.

"Tom, my husband, he always likes to say my hair is red. And I always correct him and say my hair is strawberry blonde."

"For real?" Katie scooped up strands of Gabby's hair, holding them in her palm. "But it isn't at all. Your husband's right. You should see how all the reds shimmer with the sunlight coming in the window."

"I know. My brothers have red hair too. It's just something, you know, Tom and I tease about."

Or used to tease about? Gabby glanced at her watch.

Funny how she'd wanted to leave Ohio so badly, to get far away from Tom and everyone. To get away from every last reminder of the pain they'd been going through. But somehow, strange as it was, she couldn't make herself change the time on her watch. Couldn't seem to move the hour hand six hours ahead to South Africa time. And somehow she couldn't stop staring at the number on the watch face, wondering what Tom might be doing. Since it was 4 a.m. in the Midwest, he was obviously sleeping. But where? At their house? In a hotel?

"Do I need to hurry?" Katie asked over Gabby's shoulder, obviously noticing that she'd checked the time again. "Is it almost time for Sipho to pick us up?"

"Oh no, we're fine. Sipho said he'd be here at ten thirty to take us to the hospice. We still have a half hour." From Heidi's and Cassandra's movements upstairs, it sounded like they'd also be ready to leave on time. "I don't think Jaleela's beadworkers are supposed to get to the hospice until eleven or so."

Katie tucked a bobby pin into Gabby's hair. "I think you're going to like this hairstyle. It's turning out really hot."

Hot? That almost made Gabby smile. "Do you like doing hair?"

"Sometimes, sometimes not. I mean, I'm kind of this weird combination. Good at science stuff, but I really like creative stuff too."

"Do you color your own hair or go to a salon?"

"I do it myself."

"It looks like you do a decent job." Even though Katie's hair had been dyed to nearly black, the solid color was broken up with tasteful tints of auburn that seemed to be placed in all the right spots.

"Yeah? Well, Mom doesn't think so."

Gabby grinned. "I'm sure it's hard for moms to see their daughters as anything other than their little girls. It probably takes a while to transition. I can remember my mom begging me not to put anything on my hair." She paused, thinking back. "So of course I did."

Katie lowered her head and looked at Gabby. "You did?"

Gabby nodded. "I hated my red hair. But I learned it's better than orange."

Katie laughed, picking up the brush, smoothing the lengths of hair that fell to Gabby's shoulders. "My real hair color isn't really too different than this. It's a little lighter than black, obviously. More like a dark, boring brown."

"Really? That's surprising, since your mom's hair is so blonde."

"She's not my birth mom," Katie said bluntly as if she'd explained the situation a zillion times before. "She's my stepmom. My real mom left my dad and me. My dad wanted to be corporate. And she wanted to be an artist or something like that."

"Oh," Gabby stammered, totally thrown off guard by the new information. "I would've never guessed. You and your stepmom seem so close."

"Yeah?" Gabby thought Katie sounded pleased to hear that. "I guess. I mean, we argue and stuff, but . . ."

"All moms and daughters argue. I think that's as normal as the sun coming up in the morning. My brothers and dad would run out to the garage sometimes just to get away when my mom and I would get going at each other. Even with just the two of us—" Gabby shook her head slightly—"it could be a noisy, hormonal house at times, let me tell you."

Katie giggled. "Wonder why it's so normal to argue? What is it about moms and daughters, the way we sometimes can't get along?"

"Don't know. It's not like I don't love my mom, but sometimes . . ."

"Yeah, no kidding." Katie chuckled again. "Sometimes . . ."

Quiet for a moment, Gabby heard the footsteps overhead, making her feel almost guilty, as if she'd been speaking behind Heidi's back. Which she hadn't meant to do at all. "Does your dad have dark hair?" she asked Katie.

"My dad? He had brown hair. Just sort of normal, dark brown hair. Like mine, I guess."

Had? Gabby's heart sank, and she wished she'd never asked. "Oh, Katie, did he—?"

"He passed away."

"I'm so sorry." Turning in the chair, she placed what she hoped to be a soothing hand over Katie's.

"It's okay. It's been a few years since he died."

Gabby didn't feel comfortable prodding or asking more questions, so she resumed her position in the chair, letting Katie finger the long lengths of hair she seemed so intent on brushing.

It was a few moments before Katie stuck the handle of the brush in the pocket of her jean shorts and spoke again. "It's just that . . ." She smoothed the same hair she'd just brushed as if she'd lost her place. As if the mindless repetition could help form her thoughts. "I don't know. For a minute, like now, when you asked me that about my dad's hair, I couldn't remember what he looked like. I mean, not like I could ever forget my dad. At least I don't think I could. But sometimes it's like my brain won't let me see his face. It freaks me out. I don't want to ever forget him."

"I'm sure that's normal, honey. I'm sure you'll never forget what your dad looks like." Gabby grasped for some sort of explanation. "Our brains—they do funny things when we're hurt or scared."

"My mom says that too." Her voice was low and quiet as she twisted and pinned a length of hair. "She let me sleep with her a lot when it first happened. She's been a great mom, and she's not even really my mom! But I haven't always been a perfect daughter. Far from it."

"Perfect?" Gabby turned in the chair again. "No one's perfect. We all have struggles when we're growing up. Honestly, even when we think we're all grown-up." She gave a wan smile. "You've gone through some difficult things. But look at you. You're still friendly and outgoing. Bright and inquisitive. You're not bratty and self-absorbed. You're caring . . . and so pretty. And funny." Gabby felt her grin widen, recalling yesterday morning when Katie had made them laugh so much.

"I'm not always like that when I'm at home with my mom." Katie's head started to dangle. "Believe me."

Gabby lifted her brows, giving Katie an appraising look. "I believe you. Because I never was either. But I can assure you no matter what, your mom still loves you. Still loves that you're her daughter."

Katie's spirit seemed to lift at Gabby's words. Determinedly, she put a few more bobby pins into place. When finally finished, she came around in front of Gabby to judge her masterpiece.

"How does it look?"

"Well . . . not exactly like Kate Hudson's." Katie smiled. "But pretty good."

She walked over to the end of the table, retrieving the mirror Cassandra had let them borrow. Handing it to Gabby, she moved around to the back of the chair, in perfect position to witness Gabby's expression in the mirror.

The hairstyle was cute. But that wasn't what caught Gabby's eye.

No, it was Katie. The girl was a true individual. She had a maturity about her that was inspiring. Instead of camouflaging her other attributes, the funky dyed hair and smudged black eyeliner only highlighted the many other parts of her that were special.

Really special.

Heidi was lucky to have such a girl in her life. No, not a girl—a daughter. A daughter whom God had given her to love as her own.

Who wouldn't want a daughter like Katie to travel through life with? to say sweet things to? to pull your hair out over?

Even me. Even if she wasn't from my womb.

The thought struck, stunning her completely. The mirror jiggled in her hand.

Gabby couldn't be thinking that. She couldn't. Instantly her aunt's face blazed across her mind, and the familiar fear flooded every part of her. Replacing the air in her lungs. Causing her palms to sweat. Making her heart beat wildly. How could she ever forget the woman sitting at the kitchen table with her mom, weeping over the baby she'd adopted and loved so much?

"You don't like it?" Katie frowned into the mirror, nibbling her lip.

"What?"

"You look like you don't like your hair." Katie continued the lip biting.

"No, I do. It looks great."

Katie's mouth smoothed out to a smile. "Really?"

"Yes, I do. Thank you."

"I'm going to get my mom's hairspray. Hairspray's okay, right?"

Gabby nodded, trying to assimilate Katie's words, trying to still her heart, her mind. Her hand trembled as she laid the mirror on the table almost reverently.

"Okay. Be right back!" Katie darted off toward the steps, but a knock at the front door stopped her. She looked at Gabby. "Is that Sipho—do you think?"

Still somewhat dazed, Gabby held up her wrist, glancing at her watch. "If it is, he's early."

Taking several steps to the door, Katie flung it open seemingly without a thought. But instead of Sipho, another male stood there. Not as tall and not as old as their chauffeur friend. He looked to be just a couple of inches taller than Katie and around the same age. But otherwise, opposite from her in almost every way. Dark skin compared to her pale complexion, brown eyes overriding her blue ones. The only other thing nearly similar between the two was their hair. Only Katie's was even darker.

"Hello. Good morning. My name is Dominic. I came to bring tea."

Gabby got up from the chair the moment she realized the voice at the door didn't belong to Sipho. Standing behind Katie, she marveled at the young man holding a woven straw tray filled with a beautiful, complete tea service. The elegance of the china was in such stark contrast to the rest of their run-down surroundings it was hard to imagine where it might have come from. Possibly a gift to the pastor's family in return for their hospitality?

Friendly as always, Katie gave a little wave. "Hi, Dominic. I'm Katie."

"And I'm Gabby." Gabby held out her hands. "Need any help with that?"

"I am fine. May I bring in and serve to you?" He bowed his head.

"Yes, please come in," Gabby said, her voice softening, keenly aware this was the young man Mama Penny had prayed for in their presence the day they arrived. Dominic, the teenager who had lost his father.

But shouldn't he be taking time to grieve with his family?

As she and Katie stepped aside, Dominic carried the tray with sturdy hands over the threshold.

"You can set the tray on the table." Gabby directed him toward the kitchen area. "But you don't have to serve us."

"Yeah, my mom always says, 'Doesn't look like your arms and legs are broken,'" Katie chattered gregariously, to which the boy gave her a strange look. "Meaning we're fine and able and can take care of ourselves," she explained with a bright smile.

Dominic still looked somewhat confused as he set the tray on the kitchen table.

The three of them turned together at the sound of Cassandra and Heidi coming down the steps to join them.

"Ah, something hot. With caffeine?" Cassandra made brisk strides to the table and set her camera bag down beside the kitchen chair. "This could be my lucky day."

"Oh, I love tea!" Heidi looked at Dominic gratefully. "And South African tea is supposed to be great, I've read. Don't they have some kind of special red tea here?"

"Rooibos," Dominic said.

Heidi's eyes sparkled. "Roy-boss. That's right. Is that what this is?"

"It is. May I pour some?"

"You don't have to do that," Heidi started.

"But if you'd like to, by all means." Cassandra gave an authoritative nod, murmuring, "Job security" to the rest of them.

"This is Cassandra and Heidi," Gabby said. "Ladies, this is Dominic."

The boy bowed his head slightly at the introduction. "I am pleased to meet you. I apologize the garbage was not gone when you arrived. I hope it was not difficult for you."

"The garbage?" Gabby squinted. "Oh no. Not a big deal. It got taken care of."

"You had a family emergency," Heidi spoke up. "Mama Penny told us."

Dominic's shoulders slumped and his face clouded over. "Yes," he said tersely.

The stillness in the room felt awkward, but it seemed the women felt even more so, Gabby noticed. Not one of the three made a move or seemed to know quite what to say.

But Katie did. She stepped closer to him. The sorrow and empathy she apparently felt shone through the glimmer of tears in her eyes. "It's hard." She fidgeted with her hands, looking unsure about what to do with them. "It's hard. And it . . . it really, really hurts."

"Yes," Dominic answered simply again. But his eyes said so much more as he lifted them to look at Katie.

Gabby glanced at Heidi and saw her quivering mouth and the pride for her stepdaughter gleaming in her eyes. Heidi wouldn't trade her Katie for anything in the world, Gabby knew. That look said so, without a doubt.

Certainly it wasn't only genes and chromosomes, bloodlines and lineage that tied heartstrings together, was it?

But they were among the lucky ones. It didn't always turn out that way. Gabby had seen it with her own eyes. Adoption was a gamble. Love could be at times too.

She felt for the wedding band on her finger, twisting it slowly.

How much was she willing to risk?

23

Sipho arrived in the familiar white van right on time. Katie got in first, an iPod attached to her ears. Heidi deliberately lingered behind, letting Gabby and Cassandra board next, leaving her to ride shotgun to keep Sipho company. And to dodge any questions about Katie's getting sick again this morning.

Never having been pregnant before, she could only trust the pregnancy book she'd read and what Dr. Riggsby had said. That the morning sickness—which sometimes stretched to all-day nausea— typically lasted throughout the first trimester. Although Dr. Riggsby had also added the discouraging fact that some females suffered from nausea the entire pregnancy.

As the van eased over the narrow road, Heidi tensed, doing the mental calculations for the hundredth time, as if they could possibly change. Yes, one more week and Katie would be through her first three months. But until then—even after then—who knew what to expect?

In the meantime, how could she keep a not-so-discreet news reporter and a church employee from finding out? She hated the thought that they might judge Katie. That Katie might have to go through the same thing she had at school. Although she would hope that wouldn't happen since Cassandra and Gabby *were* adults and not a bunch of gossipy kids. But still . . . it would just be better if she and Katie could keep their private matters private.

"Is the hospice very far?" Heidi tried to make small talk with Sipho to calm her anxious, pounding heart, to free her mind from the problem she had no control over.

"It is several miles down the road." Sipho adjusted the side mirror. "No. Not far."

"Mama Penny said they do testing at the hospice? For HIV and AIDS?"

"Yes," he confirmed. "Testing and counseling. Mama Penny does them both."

Heidi stared out the window, wishing she could organize a committee to pick up the trash in the streets. But truly that was the least of the problems here, wasn't it?

"Does she have help?" Heidi asked, marveling at how Mama Penny did it all. The woman seemed to be everywhere doing a bit of everything.

"A few other women, yes. It seems it is the women who are educated like Mama Penny, these are the ones who have the heart to run the hospice and help others."

"I hope she gets paid for all her time and work."

"The money, it is a problem," Sipho said frankly. "The women could earn more money elsewhere in the city to be sure. And there is much work for them to do here. Too much. More outside of the building than inside."

"I'm not sure I know what you mean. To educate people?"

Sipho nodded. "And to bring them in. The ladies who work here—Mama Penny and two others—they go out to hundreds of homes, to the shacks . . . out to where people live every week. They bring medicine. They teach about the virus. They help the people live with the grieving. There is always dying, so there is always the grieving."

It didn't seem possible that so few could do so much. "What about nurses? Can't nurses help?"

"Money is so little. Right now, one nurse works only. Sometimes, if there is more money, there are two nurses."

"One nurse?" For the entire hospice? It seemed incredible—and exhausting. And she thought *she* had reason to feel tired and frazzled! Always waking up in the middle of the night wondering what to do. Should she and Katie keep the baby? Or find a wonderful home for the child, a normal home with a father and a mother? What would Jeff have said about it? The sleepless nights were so long at times. She imagined they were for Mama Penny also.

Heidi sighed for herself and for Mama Penny too. "Those ladies sound like saints."

"Oh yes." Sipho glanced at her. "Often they must use their own money for petrol to visit the sick or those who have lost others to the virus and are hurting in another way."

When they pulled off the main road onto a side street, Heidi noticed a group of white men and a woman she recognized from church. They were standing alongside a group of South Africans in front of a long rectangular structure that had been framed but not bricked in yet.

Before she could even ask, Sipho said, "That is the orphanage your Graceview is helping to build."

It crossed her mind that from what she'd already learned, no orphanage could ever be big enough to house the multitude of orphans in the country. But Sipho's mind apparently worked differently than hers. "We are thankful for the people of Graceview. Even to save one child . . . it is a good thing. It is hope."

About a quarter of a mile from the orphanage area, Sipho released a hand from the wheel long enough to point to a building—the only finished building in sight. "The hospice is there."

More red dirt took the place of a concrete parking lot, causing Heidi to glance down at her slip-on Skechers. The rust-tinted stain that rimmed the soles would never scrub clean. But it was better than wearing sandals and her toes being dyed by the dirt, she supposed.

A sandy neutral brick, the building wasn't as colorful and vibrant as the earth that surrounded it. It was interesting for Heidi to see the facility that volunteers from her church had built. She'd overheard Gabby and Mama Penny talking the day before about Mamelodi's one and only hospice that now had beds available for patients on the first floor and part of the second floor. But a portion of the building still remained a shell. Like the pastor's house, like the orphanage, more work still needed to be done, which required more donations. "It is for another day," Mama Penny had said in that hopeful way of hers. "Another day and it will be completed."

As Sipho turned in to the lot, Cassandra spoke up from the middle of the van. "Doesn't look like a very busy place. Where are all the cars?"

Heidi wondered the same thing.

"Cars?" Sipho chuckled, glancing at Cassandra in the rearview mirror. "The people have no cars."

Of course they didn't. Heidi blushed. They barely had roofs over their heads! What had the two of them been thinking?

Bringing the van to a stop at the door of the hospice, Sipho put the vehicle in park. "Some days the hospice is far busier than others. But you must understand that many with the virus are still embarrassed to come here."

Heidi shifted in the seat beside him, not totally understanding. "But don't a lot of people have the virus? I don't get it. It's not like they're the only ones, right? Why would they be so embarrassed?"

And yet even when she said the words, she realized the contradiction. The two-faced stance warring within her. So it was justifiable that she cared about what others thought regarding her and Katie's situation? that she would be so worried how the other mothers and the school officials and even people at church were judging Katie for a mistake she'd made? But it wasn't okay for someone to feel humiliated about contracting a disease like AIDS? Like they couldn't feel embarrassed—feel less than—because why? Because they didn't live in a fancy house or a prestigious community?

"Maybe they feel alone. . . ." Sipho held up a hand as if he, too, was trying to make sense of it. "As if they are the only ones? But they are coming to know the hospice more now. Coming to know that it is not just for the dying. It is for those who want to live, too."

"How many people are affected with AIDS, Sipho?" Heidi turned at the sound of Cassandra's voice. The anchorwoman pointed her camera out the window again.

Their driver's jaw tensed. "Too many."

Luckily there were women like Jaleela willing to step outside of themselves and take a stance for others.

Heidi shifted uncomfortably in her seat, grateful there wasn't time at the moment for self-reflection.

"I must run errands for the pastor's family," Sipho told them as they gathered their belongings from the van. "I will be back to pick you up later in the afternoon."

Heidi murmured her thanks, but in her heart of hearts, she hated to see Sipho go, even if only for a few hours. With his exuberant smile and easygoing way, he had quickly become dear to the women, a part of their group. Plus, they felt protected around their six-foot chauffeur; he was safe and familiar in the strange, faraway land.

The front door of the van squeaked as Heidi closed it behind her. The sound seemed noticeably loud in the quiet, and its echo made the solitude all around them appear even more desolate.

Katie piled out of the back, looking light and ready to go, her earphones tucked in her pocket, while Cassandra muscled a heavy backpack full of camera equipment. The last one out, Gabby slid the side door of the van shut. Sipho started the engine and waved before backing out of the lot, leaving the four of them standing in the heat, assessing the situation.

"It does seem strange, doesn't it?" Even to herself, Heidi's voice sounded too loud in the silence around them.

"What, Mom?"

"I don't know. I'm wondering, is the hospice like a town hall too? I mean, think about it. If we were at home meeting with a group of women, we'd be at Starbucks or a restaurant."

"Or at church or our homes," Gabby added.

"But here . . ." Heidi shook her head.

Cassandra settled the strap of her camera bag over her shoulder before fluffing the hair at the sides of her head. "I suppose we have to consider where we are in the world."

It was true. A place without e-invites and cell phones attached to everyone's ears. But hopefully somehow Jaleela and Mama Penny had gotten the word out to the beadworkers.

Hopefully?

"I'm sure wishing some beadworkers have shown up for this." Heidi found herself sighing again.

Katie bit down on a thumbnail, lines of worry wrinkling her young forehead. "Me too. Jaleela will be, like, so disappointed."

Cassandra glanced around and nodded. "The place really does look deserted, doesn't it?"

"She wants her dream to happen so badly." Katie's words were a near whisper.

Heidi drew in a deep breath, trying to think positively. "Well, at least we're here for her."

"Yes, and maybe there was a mix-up in the time," Gabby suggested. "Maybe we're here early."

But from the look on Gabby's face and everyone else's, Heidi could tell no one thought that to be true. Wordlessly, they formed a line four across and approached the entrance slowly but determinedly, reminding Heidi of the ruby-slippered Dorothy and her brave traveling companions entering the unknown.

Cassandra, on the far right, reached for the door and swung it open.

Katie, who could easily see inside the entry, let out a gasp. "It's like a surprise party! Everyone's here!"

As they stepped inside, a wave of relief swept over Heidi, and she could see the tension ease from the others' faces as well. Katie was right. It *was* like a surprise party. None of them had expected to open the door to a lobby full of nearly twenty women. Or, even more, to receive the kind of joyful greeting those women poured on them with their warm smiles, their waves, their shouts of hello.

Oh, and the colors! Heidi had to keep blinking to take it all in. Bright, bold primary blues and reds and yellows; glowing limes, oranges, and purples as rich as God's fruits. A few women were dressed head to toe in traditional African dress, displaying exquisite beadwork on their hats, their skirts, their shoes. But the majority wore colorful skirts and knit tops or silk blouses. Overall it was obvious that the South African women had donned their Sunday best for the important meeting with the Americans.

In contrast Heidi felt as drab as a piece of wood in her khaki capris and black T-shirt. And she felt awful that she hadn't returned the same courtesy of dressing up. But she'd been told to bring mainly older outfits she could afford to get ruined. At this point, she could only hope her smile would represent her excitement to meet the bead-workers since her clothes certainly didn't.

Though the lobby buzzed with commotion, there didn't seem to be a peep heard from the babies wrapped in papooselike shawls on some of the ladies' backs or even from the children, who stood quietly and politely at their mothers' sides.

Recognizing Mama Penny and a beaming Jaleela with Nomvula and Tumi, Heidi and the others made their way through the throng to their recently made friends.

"Jaleela!" Heidi was the first to hug the woman. "There are so many women here!"

"Is it not wonderful?" Jaleela laughed, holding a hand to her chest. "The ladies walked. They walk from many places, many miles to meet you."

Jaleela stood by grinning like a proud parent as Mama Penny's authoritative voice introduced Heidi and their group. Then the South

African ladies formed a single line and patiently waited to greet each one of them individually.

Had she ever been the recipient of more genuine, beautiful smiles or felt hugs that seemed more real? If she had, Heidi couldn't think of when. Every woman here in Mamelodi seemed to open her heart and arms to all of them.

She'd worked with people at her elementary school for how many years? Since before she'd been married to Jeff. How rarely did the women she worked with ever greet her or each other that way?

At the thought of people from back home, Heidi could feel her heart sinking. But she glanced at Katie, and all seemed well with her daughter. Evidently the morning sickness had passed for the time being. Katie's color looked good, her cheeks rosy and her eyes bright. And surprisingly, she looked totally comfortable with the outpouring of affection from the South African women.

In fact, even in spite of her queasy stomach, Katie had seemed almost like a different person ever since they arrived in South Africa. So much happier, more outgoing. More like . . . *her* Katie. Was it because of what she'd left behind? what she was finding here? Either way, the noticeable change in Katie made every penny of the trip seem well spent. Any concern Heidi had had about Katie missing an extra week of school beyond spring break seemed to diminish too.

"You give us dignity," a young woman said to Katie as the woman held Katie's hands in her own. "Your coming to us restores our dignity."

"But we wanted to come. We're happy to be here with you," Katie said, sounding older than her years. And looking that way, too, Heidi noted, a sudden aura of peace and confidence glowing from her.

If only they didn't have to ever go back to where they'd come from. Oh, if only they didn't!

But just as that thought came, so did another. *Oh, thank You, Lord. Thank You!* Tears crested in her eyes. *Thank You for this time, for this day, and mostly for my Katie. For her growing and glowing . . . for these wonderful women . . . for the pleasure, the peace of these moments.*

It seemed the spontaneous praise welled up from nowhere, feeling right but surprising and new. For so long after Jeff's death, she'd always prayed *for* something. Mostly for strength to get through each day. But this time, in this moment, gratitude and thankfulness overwhelmed her. It felt different but decidedly good, Heidi thought, as she opened her arms to the next smiling woman in line.

"I really like this bracelet, Chloe," Heidi told the young black mother sitting in front of her, wearing a beautiful red orange head wrap. A toddler fidgeted in the woman's lap, but who could blame him? Khomotso had had a long wait, to be sure.

For the past two hours, after all the introductions, Heidi and Katie had sat side by side reviewing the beaded jewelry samples the African women had brought. Cassandra, Jaleela, Gabby, and Mama Penny were situated in various chairs around the lobby doing the same thing. They were deciding which items might pique the interest of women in the States and which needed to be modified or improved in some way. Obviously it was their intention and their hope to be able to request something from each woman, to give each of them a chance to earn some income and ultimately a living, as Jaleela had dreamed.

How the women stretched their imaginations to create such vibrant color schemes and designs, such beauty, when there was so little of it in their lives astounded Heidi.

"Where do you get your ideas, Chloe?"

The woman shrugged. "It is a blessing. I close my eyes and they are there."

Holding Chloe's coiled, serpentlike bracelet in her palm, Heidi turned to Katie. "What do you think?"

"It's cool. Really cool. I think moms and teenagers would like it."

"How about two dozen? Would you be able to make two dozen of them for us to sell?" Heidi handed the bracelet back to its creator and wrote down a description of it on a sheet of paper meant to be an inventory. "Chloe?" she asked when the woman didn't answer.

"Two dozen?" Chloe's eyes were wide, her mouth gaping. Khomotso tugged at her lower lip though she didn't seem to notice.

"You were hoping for more?"

"Oh no. I-I have not any more wire. Just enough for the sample."

"I have wire," a younger woman said from behind Chloe. "You may have it." She rummaged through her sack and drew out a coil of wire.

"Do you two know each other?" Heidi looked back and forth from the younger woman to the young mother. "Are you friends?"

"We are now." The younger girl with dark brown skin smiled at Chloe, who graciously took the offered wire.

Thanking her new friend profusely, Chloe then agreed on a price with Heidi, promising to have more bracelets made by the end of the week.

"That was really nice of you," Heidi told the young woman after Chloe and Khomotso had said good-bye.

The girl who looked to be close to Katie's age shrugged. "She must feed her child. Besides, it is a part of our heritage. The caring, it is in our women's blood. Our ancestors lived in tribes, you know. The head of the tribe had possibly five wives, perhaps as many as twenty-five children. There was no separation. No living apart. All the women helped each other. Every woman helped every child to survive too. So we try to do the same today."

"You don't have children?" Heidi was curious about this person who had sacrificed so easily. She could tell by the expression on Katie's face that she was entranced by her too.

"No, I do not." The girl turned instantly solemn.

Heidi changed the subject just as quickly. "What will you use to make your pieces of jewelry with no wire?"

"I will figure it out. I work here at the hospice. I see many people come through these doors. Someone will have what I need."

"Are you a nurse?" Katie asked.

"No." The girl's tight lips broke into a shy grin. "But it is what I hope to be someday. I hope to come to America and learn there. It is the grandest of hopes, I know. Still it is my plan for my life. I am thinking it is God's plan too. For now, I do record keeping at the hospice. In return, they give me food to eat and a bed to sleep in."

"What is your name again?" Heidi asked.

"I am Mighty."

Mighty. Mama Penny had told them about the girl whose name seemed to personify her young life. How as a teenager she'd cared for her two brothers and little sister after their parents died. But then the virus had taken her siblings too. Oddly, she remained healthy and never had contracted the disease. But she was all alone at eighteen.

Heidi couldn't imagine being in the world by herself at that age. Having no one. Certainly it wasn't anything she'd ever want for Katie. The thought saddened her, but of course, she didn't want to act as if she knew Mighty's entire history.

Heidi felt awed and humbled by this girl who had cared for so many in her short lifetime. "It's good to meet you, Mighty. You're a very kind person." She shook Mighty's hand. "What kind of things do you make?"

"I make bracelets and necklaces. But my specialty is angels. I make beaded angels." Mighty drew several samples from her sack.

"They're awesome!" Katie held one in the air.

Heidi studied the delicate, winged forms. "You must use a million beads to make these."

"Not a million. But many." Mighty smiled demurely, appearing flattered but bashful. "I am quick to make them, though."

"That's good," Heidi told her. "Because I think a lot of people would love these."

"You can hang them anywhere," Katie added.

"Oh, I just have remembered." Mighty covered her mouth with her hand. "You are Katie, right?"

Katie nodded.

"Please forgive me. There is an e-mail. I almost forgot."

"An e-mail?" Katie tilted her head. "Here? For me?"

"Yes, you have an e-mail from the United States." Mighty smiled. "I was made happy just to see it come all that way. Would you like me to take you to the computer in the office there?" She pointed across the lobby. "You can read it and respond if you would like."

Heidi could feel her stomach drop. Everything had been going so well. And now . . . why? Why had Katie given one of her friends back home the e-mail information in South Africa? Or wait a minute— what friends? They'd all turned their backs on her weeks before they left for the trip. Just another thing to crush Katie. So it had to be Mark. Mark! Couldn't it have waited? Couldn't she and Katie have this time to themselves?

Katie hopped up, looking just as excited as Mighty about an e-mail from America, and followed the taller girl before Heidi could say anything.

So, the emotional world they'd left behind had caught up with them in only a matter of days.

Give me strength, Lord, she prayed. *Please give me strength.*

24

Gabby stood outside Heidi and Katie's bedroom door ready to knock at least half a dozen times. But each time she lifted her hand in the air, she couldn't make herself do it. Should she interrupt the two of them or not?

"What did Mark want this time?" Gabby could hear Heidi's demanding tone. "To get you near tears again? Like he did texting you at the airport?"

"What are you talking about?" Katie snapped.

"It was him, wasn't it?"

"Seriously. You're getting so mad about nothing."

"Nothing? Why did you give him the e-mail address for this place, anyway?"

"Mom, I'm telling you, you're overreacting. You don't even know what you're saying. It's not a big deal, okay?"

"It is to me. Can't we just have this time together where we don't have to be upset?"

"Do I look upset?"

The mother and daughter had barricaded themselves in their room pretty much ever since they'd gotten back from the hospice. At first Gabby thought they might be in there resting; it had been quite a busy day meeting so many South African women, examining their beadwork. But no. The pair had been going at it, their voices low but direct for the entire time Gabby had been standing on the other side of the paper-thin door.

In the meantime, she was beginning to feel like the biggest eavesdropper of all time. She needed to knock, get it over with. Pretend she'd just come up the stairs and hadn't heard the cross words between them.

"Hey, ladies!" She rapped lightly. "Just wanted to give you a heads-up. We're going to be driving out to Jaleela's friend's house in about a half hour."

The door swung open, Heidi standing behind it. Gabby noticed neither she nor Katie was making much of an effort to mask the disgruntled expressions on their faces.

"Jaleela's friend?" Heidi's forehead contorted even more.

"You didn't hear Jaleela mention her friend Lydia?"

"No, I don't think so. Katie, did you?"

Katie shook her head, looking glum. Even her spiked bangs appeared to have fallen, taking a downward turn in the past hour or so.

"Evidently her friend Lydia promised she'd be at the hospice today to show us her beadwork." Gabby kept her voice even, determined not to dampen the mood anymore. "But she didn't show up and Jaleela's concerned. She's hoping her condition hasn't gotten worse since the last time someone checked on her."

Heidi's frown deepened. "When was that?"

"Weeks ago maybe?" Gabby shrugged. "Or at least that's what Jaleela is guessing. From what she said, her friend lives a distance outside the village. So the ladies from the hospice don't get there as often."

"Do I have to go?" Katie asked her mother, hand on her hip, striking a typical stubborn teenage pose. "I have plans."

"Plans?" Heidi cocked an eyebrow, and Gabby couldn't help raising her brow too.

"Well, yeah. Dominic said he'd stop by after he finishes with his work. He's going to introduce me to Hazard. I promised him I'd be here."

"Oh, please! The dog again? I'm telling you, it's not a good idea.

The animal doesn't want to make friends, believe me. If he did, he wouldn't keep baring those fangs of his every time we walk by."

"You don't think *anything's* a good idea," Katie huffed, crossing her arms over her chest. "Really, you need to stop worrying so much. You're going to give yourself a heart attack."

"No, Katherine." Heidi likewise crossed her arms over her chest as if in retaliation. "*You're* going to give me the heart attack."

"Whatever." Katie rolled her eyes.

This felt far too awkward! Not that Gabby couldn't remember going round and round the same way with her mother when she was a teenager just as she'd told Katie earlier. But still . . .

Gabby never should've knocked on the bedroom door in the first place, even if she had only been trying to be nice, giving Heidi and Katie some advance notice. If only she could extricate herself from the scene before they caught on. She tried to slink away, but that wasn't about to happen. Nomvula came skipping up the steps at that exact same instant and stopped her, wrapping her arms around Gabby's waist.

"I caught you. You are 'it.'" The young girl's words, so innocent in light of the tension in the air, made Gabby smile. "Please will you play the tag game with me and Tumi some more?"

Gabby had started a game of tag with Nomvula and Tumi, hoping to give Jaleela a chance to rest before they took her to visit Lydia. Even though Jaleela had protested, trying to brush aside her fatigue, Gabby insisted they all take a break.

Surprisingly, her playing with Jaleela's children hadn't turned out to be merely a favor. The kids were delightful, and romping around outdoors with them brought back pleasant memories, reminding her of when she used to teach school and of the days she stood outside at recess, watching or joining in on the kids' games.

Laying her hand on top of Nomvula's head, Gabby felt the warmth of the sun and the heat being expended from Nomvula's running about. "We're going to be leaving in a bit, honey." She hugged Nomvula back. "But maybe Katie will want to."

Heidi and Katie seemed to have terminated their bickering with Nomvula's arrival. It felt safe to ask if Katie might be able to watch Nomvula and Tumi while the rest of the group rode out to Lydia's.

Heidi gave her permission easily.

Katie seemed only too happy to take Nomvula's hand and make a break for it. "Great! Let's go see what Tumi's up to." The sparkle came back into the teenager's eyes. "Dominic can join us when he gets here."

"Just don't get around the dog, please," Heidi called after them.

But Katie didn't answer as she led Nomvula down the stairs.

Heidi closed her eyes, letting out the longest sigh Gabby could ever remember hearing.

"She's a wonderful girl," Gabby offered.

"Oh, I know. With everyone else, she's great. It's mostly with me that she can be difficult at times." Shaking her head, she gave a tired smile.

"A boyfriend thing?" Gabby asked lightly, not wanting to admit she'd heard the reason for their quarreling through the door.

"It's always something. Either a boyfriend thing or yet another girl-friend thing. Teenage girls are full of constant drama. I just wish he hadn't e-mailed her. Actually, I wish she hadn't given him the e-mail address here. Couldn't they wait till we get home?" Appearing disgusted, Heidi slumped down on the bed. From where Gabby stood, leaning against the wall, she could see the mattress drooping through the slats.

"A boy you're not too fond of, I'm guessing?"

"Oh, it's . . . it's a lot of things." At that, Heidi jumped up as if she'd forgotten something. Grabbing a package of peanut butter crackers from her carry-on bag, she plopped back on the bed again. "Want some?" she asked, opening the wrapper.

"No thanks; I'm fine."

"I'm not." She bit into a cracker. "Kids! I feel like I could eat ten packs of these and all the M&M'S I brought too." But even as she said it, she half grinned, letting Gabby know she wasn't entirely serious. From the looks of her enviable petite figure, Gabby guessed Heidi rarely allowed herself to binge her frustration away.

"It's hard to understand what she sees in this boy." Heidi poised the cracker in the air as she reflected out loud. "He's nice, I suppose. But . . . well, this sounds awful—he's rough around the edges. Not really the kind of boy you'd hope your daughter would bring home, you know?"

Gabby didn't know if she should speak up or not, but Heidi seemed to be looking at her as if waiting for a reply.

"Maybe that's why she picked him. I mean that in a good way, of course. Katie seems so good-spirited. Like she'd go all out for the underdog. Even mangy dogs." Gabby grinned and shook her head in amazement, recalling how Katie had bravely sought out Hazard, making it a personal challenge to win him over by the end of their trip. "I mean, calling Hazard precious? Ack! I'm with you. I think that animal is plain scary. But evidently Katie sees something else in him—the boyfriend, I mean. And the dog too, I suppose." She paused. "Or maybe she thinks she can turn him around, turn him into a prince. Again, the boyfriend, not the dog."

Heidi smiled. "Or maybe there's another reason. Maybe she's doing it to irritate me simply because I'm the mom."

"True." Gabby had been around enough kids to know that was a possibility. "Every kid does that to some degree. I know I did."

Heidi sighed. "I admit we do our share of arguing; that's for sure. But she gets decent grades. She's not into drugs. I know I should be thankful. I am. I guess I wish things were the way they used to be. Before Jeff died, Katie was so into sports—basketball, lacrosse, soccer. Always trying out for different things at school. After he passed, she seemed to lose interest in everything for a while. Maybe we both did." She looked away, staring at the crackers in her hand as if seeing them for the first time. "Then overnight it was no sports, black hair, new friends whose parents I didn't know."

"Maybe she's trying out things for herself," Gabby suggested.

"I'm sure you're right."

"Again, Katie's really sweet. How many teenage girls wouldn't be complete pills in a place like this? All sulky and whining. She's been none of those things. In fact, she's actually been a joy to be around."

"Yeah, except for our tiff today, it has been nice. Maybe that's why I hated having him—the boyfriend—contact her here. Things have been so pleasant on this trip. Well, obviously not the accommodations." Heidi glanced around the grungy room. "It's not the Hilton, but even in these awful conditions, I've been enjoying Katie. In some ways, I feel like I have my old Katie back."

Falling silent, they both listened to the sound of the kids' laughter wafting through the open window from the courtyard below.

"Are you sure you don't want a cracker?" Heidi offered again.

"Maybe one." Leaning forward, Gabby plucked a cracker from the pack.

"Take two," Heidi insisted. "And, please, feel free to sit down. I don't know if this bed can hold both of us, but if not, we'll go down together."

"Right through the ceiling." Gabby smiled as they gingerly attempted to distribute their weight evenly with Heidi at the head of the bed and Gabby sitting near the foot.

All settled, crunching on another cracker, Heidi confided, "She gets it from her dad, you know. All that bigheartedness."

"A good guy, huh?" Gabby crossed her legs, feeling at home in Heidi's company. "Your parents didn't mind when you brought him home to meet them, I imagine?"

"Unfortunately, my parents never got to meet him. They had me when they were much older and had already passed by the time Jeff and Katie came into my life. I was in my late twenties and teaching kindergarten. Katie was in my class, as a matter of fact."

"I think I see where this is heading." Gabby wagged her brows.

"You're right. When Jeff came to school on parents' conference night—*bam!* That was it. They both pretty much swept me off my feet." There was a trace of laughter in her voice. "I didn't have a chance."

The joyful glow that broke out on Heidi's face told Gabby she had a heart overflowing with precious memories. The story of how they met made her smile too.

"Do you have any other children?"

From what Gabby knew of her, Heidi seemed to be such a pro at the mom thing. She certainly mothered all of them—providing snacks, always having a tissue handy, looking for the best in things, encouraging them all. And of course, doing a bit too much worrying, but only because she loved like a mother too.

"Oh no," she answered, without a note of regret attached. "When I met Jeff, I'd never been married. Had never had a child. Katie hadn't had a mom for years, nor Jeff a wife. So there was an adjustment period for sure when we were simply settling into a life together. Happily settling into a life together, I should add. Just the three of us. It felt perfect, actually. I didn't even think about getting pregnant. Well, not until later, when Katie started getting older, the thought began creeping into my mind. But by then, Jeff started having health issues. Problems that seemed to go from one thing to the next until finally the years of fighting cancer."

Gabby couldn't believe they'd found each other just to lose each other again. "It must be difficult being a single mom."

"Yeah, but there are so many single moms out there, I really don't have the right to complain. And can you imagine what it's like for someone like Jaleela?"

"The woman's remarkable, isn't she?"

"Incredible. And here I am whining in the midst of AIDS and poverty in South Africa." Heidi shook her head. "You must think I'm awful."

"No, not at all." Gabby had felt like whining a time or two herself since they'd been here.

"So how about your husband? Tom, right? Did your parents like him right away?"

"Actually, yes. But I'd brought so many other characters home before that, by the time I brought Tom Phillips home my second year of college, he seemed nearly perfect." Gabby's pulse quickened just thinking about the year they'd first met. "Plus, he made it past my brothers' inspection. They were tougher on my dates than my parents. Tom fit in with both of them from the very beginning."

"They really liked him, huh?"

"Oh yes. He was smart." She mused, her memories of those early years pure and clean. "We had a pool table in our basement, and he always let my brothers win. Until we were married, anyway."

"And then the tables turned?" Heidi laughed.

"Oh, that's a good one. I'll have to remember that."

"It sounds like you have a fun family. Have you and Tom thought about a family of your own?"

Hadn't Gabby known the conversation would naturally lead to questions about her and Tom and a family? And yet she hadn't done anything to steer Heidi away from the subject.

Gabby wasn't sure why she hadn't, except for in a weird way, it felt comforting talking to Heidi. But then, Heidi had no connection to her, wasn't someone Gabby was disappointing in her inability to carry a child. Now that she'd fled as far away as she possibly could, to the other side of the world to grieve and escape her problems, she realized she didn't want to be alone with her loss anymore. If she didn't talk about the baby, it would be like the baby had never existed. And that wasn't true. For a while the baby had lived and thrived inside her.

She sucked in a deep breath before answering. "We've done more than think about it. We've been trying almost ever since we've been married."

"Oh, I'm sorry to hear that."

"Yes." Swallowing hard, she fought the sudden swell of emotion rising in the back of her throat. "I had a miscarriage. Right before I came here, I lost my baby."

Heidi scooted closer and squeezed Gabby's hand. "I'm so sorry," she repeated. "I can't even imagine. How terrible that must be!"

"This was our last time, our last attempt. We said it all along. Emotionally. Financially. This was it." Gabby closed her eyes, forcing back the tears that wanted to pour out and spill over.

The room went silent for many long moments until Heidi filled the void. "Would you possibly . . ."

Gabby looked at her.

Heidi tried again. "Have you ever thought about adopting?"

"We've talked about it over the years." Gabby raked the hair from her forehead. "Tom has always been comfortable with the idea. He would have adopted years ago if it hadn't been for me. But I wanted so badly to give birth. And even more than that . . ." She could feel the heat creeping into her cheeks, the quickening of her breath. She wasn't sure if she wanted to go on. "I've never told this to anyone before."

"You don't have to explain. It's okay."

"No. I do want to tell you." Or at least she finally wanted to tell someone. She'd been carrying the secret around, struggling with it by herself for so long—too long. Why hadn't she said something to Tom years ago? Even weeks ago? Why had she let her fear tear them apart? "The truth is, I've always been afraid to adopt a child."

"Afraid? You mean because of the complications?" Heidi's voice was void of judgment, just filled with curiosity. "Kids searching for their birth parents? That sort of thing?"

"No. This is really going to sound awful, especially coming from the director of children's ministries." Gabby could feel her face coloring even more fiercely, but she felt pressed to explain. Although in some ways, she didn't even know where to start. "My mom's youngest sister adopted a baby when I was about ten. He was so cute. Everyone said how perfect Timothy was because he hardly ever cried. My aunt absolutely adored that baby, but then . . ."

A chill ran through her and she shuddered, remembering. "That sweet baby was nothing like the boy Timothy grew up to be. He had severe mental and health issues, so maladjusted. My aunt was torn between loving him and not being able to take care of him. In the end, she had to turn him over to the state, but the guilt and sadness destroyed her life and her marriage. Ultimately she ended up nearly penniless and alone."

"That sounds horrid." Heidi gazed at her sympathetically. "No wonder you have reservations about adopting."

It wasn't just reservations. It was all-out fear. Panic. Acute anxiety. And she knew it might sound irrational to some, and that's why she'd never said anything. Not even to Tom. But the fear had always been very real to her.

Yet in the past couple of days something within her was softening. She could feel it when she looked at Nomvula and Tumi. At the parentless children Mama Penny had stopped to hug in the village. Even when she looked at Katie, something inside her felt different.

When she'd first arrived here, she'd dared God to let the sun burn off the chilled layers that had built up around her heart. Could He have heard her?

Gabby was just about to confide in Heidi and tell her that. But someone's shoes clacked on the concrete stairs, and their conversation ceased without another word.

"Private party?" Cassandra appeared in the bedroom doorway.

Gabby couldn't believe the woman was nearly ten years older than she was and always so fresh and vibrant-looking, even after the long afternoon they'd had. Even in the middle of a poor village in South Africa, Cassandra Albright looked like she could step onto a cruise ship if one happened to be sailing by, her white capris and navy safari-style linen blouse as neatly pressed as when she'd put them on this morning.

"No," Gabby answered quickly, then felt bad she didn't want to divulge what she had shared with Heidi. After all, Cassandra wasn't naive. She would surely sense they'd been talking about something serious. Something personal and secretive.

True, just days ago, she wouldn't have been concerned about Cassandra's feelings at all. She had seemed so rude, crude, and self-centered, everything about her rubbing Gabby the wrong way. But that had started to change. Gabby now found most of the woman's flippant remarks to be somewhat amusing and her stories entertaining. Plus she was an interesting combination, wasn't she? So polished and refined but then resourceful and hardworking too. All in all, there was more to her than the annoying know-it-all Gabby had first perceived her as.

Even so, while Gabby felt friendlier toward Cassandra, she didn't feel quite ready to open up to everyone all at once. Thankfully, though, it appeared Cassandra didn't feel slighted.

"Well, here's the deal, ladies," Cassandra said pointedly. "I think Jaleela is fabulous. She truly is. I can't help but like the woman, and believe me, there are not many people in this world I can say that about. But this thing she believes about God providing and the money just appearing . . . I mean, please. Money doesn't just appear, as we all well know. I don't want to put the whammy on a sick woman's dying wish or her visions or whatever. But I'm thinking, if this is going to work and the money's going to show up, it's going to be up to us to make that happen."

"Us?" Heidi got up and retrieved a bag of Twizzlers from her suitcase, offering licorice all around. Gabby accepted, while Cassandra, of course, declined. "I can maybe come up with a couple hundred dollars or so," Heidi offered. "But not the few thousand we'll need to purchase the jewelry from the women. I wish I could, but I already spent thousands for Katie and me to come on this trip."

Gabby wished she could finance Jaleela's dream too and hated to confess that their savings was almost nonexistent.

"I don't necessarily mean for us to take money out of our pockets. But we should brainstorm, start thinking about people who might contribute. When the ladies make the jewelry we've asked for, we need to pay for that inventory. And that's when? The day after we come back from the safari—the day before we head home? Because hellooo—" Cassandra snapped her fingers as she drew out the word—"that day will be here before we know it."

"Right." Heidi bit her lip, her voice growing soft. "But then again, look at Jaleela; she has faith the money will be here by then."

"Yes, well, I don't know about you all, but I'm the 'ye' in 'O ye of little faith.' And isn't there that saying, 'God helps those who help themselves'? Am I wrong about that?"

Gabby racked her brain for a moment. "Tom has an aunt. She's always giving to the arts and city programs. Maybe something like this would appeal to her. I could try it out on her. I could call Tom and get her phone number."

"Could you call him today? Maybe now, while we're waiting?"

Gabby looked at her watch. They'd already put in a full day, but the morning was just getting under way in Ohio, a little after nine o'clock. Tom might still be at the house, working from their home computer. Or chances were, he'd already left for the day. But at least it might be worth a try. "They said we can get into the pastor's house to use his phone, right? As long as we use it sparingly?"

Both Heidi and Cassandra nodded.

"Okay. I'll go give it a try, then."

"And I'll start thinking about it too," Heidi promised.

Meanwhile, resting her chin in her hand, Cassandra appeared to be seriously lost in thought. Until an idea sparked, igniting a smile that illuminated her entire face. "There's always Jack, my boss."

"He's that generous?" Heidi closed the licorice bag. "He can spare thousands of dollars?"

"Well, if I blackmail him, he would." Cassandra wiggled her brows.

Gabby looked at Heidi, whose mouth hung open at least as far as her own.

"Oh, come on, you two. Business is business. Look," Cassandra added after rendering them speechless, "he's the one who's stupid enough to be having an affair. I can't help it if that information might find a way back to his wife."

"You're not serious," Heidi said. "I mean, you wouldn't *really* do that."

Cassandra flashed her colorful nails in the air. "Who knows? When it comes to survival, who knows what one will do? Am I right?"

Gabby had promised Cassandra she'd call Tom to get his aunt's information right away. But now that the caretaker had let her into the pastor's house and she stood with the phone to her ear, she didn't know if she could do it. Her hand wouldn't stop shaking as she punched in the international code and their home phone number. Her stomach cramped so violently she thought she'd have to put down the receiver and run to the bathroom any second.

Not exactly the way a woman should feel when calling her husband. Not exactly the way she'd ever thought she'd feel about Tom.

No, no. She couldn't do this. What would she say? How would she start? It felt too awkward. There was too much to be said between hello and asking for his aunt's number. Too much that she'd been thinking about lately. And even more she'd left unsaid before.

But then . . . Gabby missed him. So simply, so much. She missed him and wanted to hear his voice. Wanted to feel the way she used to when the deep, sweet sound of his hello washed over her.

Let it ring. Let it ring. She gripped the phone, willing herself not to let go. She could hang up right after he said hello. *Just let it ring.*

"You've reached the Phillips residence, Gabby and Tom. We're not here right now, but if you'd like to, please leave a message." Her own robotic voice greeted her ears, instead of Tom's.

Because he'd already gone to work?

Or because he'd already gone forever?

25

Cassandra felt totally at ease with the video camera pressed up to her face. It was the uncomfortable feeling of the ankle-high grass scratching at her skin that bothered her. That is, until she got lost in her task, deliberately lagging behind the other women, filming their approach to Lydia's dilapidated house.

"Did you hear that?" Heidi suddenly turned around, questioning Gabby and Jaleela. She even looked directly at Cassandra, right into the lens of the video camera. Cassandra could easily see lines of concern creasing her forehead.

"Hear what?" Gabby's voice came low and hushed, but Cassandra was fairly certain the camera would pick up her audio.

"It sounded like someone crying."

"Perhaps it is a bird finding its way home from the day." Cassandra turned the camera in Jaleela's direction in time to record most of her response.

"Maybe," Heidi said uncertainly.

Without a square of concrete in sight, Sipho hadn't felt comfortable taking the passenger van off the dirt path that lay to the west of Lydia's house. That meant the four of them had to walk a few hundred yards through the unkempt brush to her front door. Trying to keep the camera from jiggling too much was no easy task as Cassandra traipsed over the uneven ground.

There had been plenty of daylight when they left the pastor's compound, but it had been a long ride out to Lydia's place. Now it was apparent that dusk would come soon, erratic stripes of mauve and gold already hinting at it in the sky. A random cricket belted out a screech over the open field, a prelude to the cacophonous racket that hordes of the noisy insects would crescendo to when night fell. But that wouldn't happen for at least two more hours, when total, consuming darkness set in. Even so, Cassandra flipped on the light attached to the video camera for good measure.

She needed to get to work and get as much footage as she could. Wasn't that why she'd come to South Africa in the first place? She'd almost forgotten; she'd been getting so involved with Jaleela lately.

With Jaleela and her dream, to be exact.

Zooming in on the brown-skinned woman, Cassandra watched as Jaleela held up her calf-length skirt in order not to dirty the limp, frayed thing in the patches of dust and grass. Her feet must've felt scratched or at least itchy at every step, with only cheap, rubbery flip-flops to cover them. But, of course, Jaleela didn't complain. Nor did she mention feeling fatigued even though, in the eye of the camera, she looked that way, her legs seeming to slow more and more with every step.

The full day of activity seemed to have left everyone spent, if the lack of conversation on the ride to Lydia's place had been any indication. And it had to be a strain on Jaleela, Cassandra imagined, given her poor physical condition.

But evidently the woman was never too tired to visit a sick friend. Or to start a women's movement, right? Cassandra had to smile at that. Where she got her strength, Cassandra couldn't fathom. She also couldn't fathom the attachment she felt toward Jaleela. Was that rare for her, or what?

She'd fallen asleep thinking about it the night before and could only figure maybe it was because they had something in common. After all, Cassandra knew about wanting to make something from nothing. She'd gotten really good at dreaming too. She'd had to. Those dreams had been all she'd had in her horrific childhood.

But to make those dreams come true? Oh yes, therein lay the irony. She'd learned as much over the years through her many trials. More often than not, attaining great dreams didn't just mean a lot of hard work. It meant getting down and dirty too.

Heidi and Gabby had looked shocked when she'd mentioned blackmailing Jack. Once she really thought about what she'd said, she didn't even know if she was serious about that either. But the point was, life hadn't been, wasn't, and would never be nice.

Cassandra hated to burst anyone's bubble, especially Jaleela's, but to get what you wanted, to get the job done, a person couldn't always afford to be nice.

But she admired Jaleela's indomitable faith, her belief and trust in God, in their group, and in the other South African ladies. She couldn't totally relate to it since she'd grown up having faith in nothing or no one but herself. But she did appreciate the other woman's perseverance and dogged pursuit of her dream. And she'd try to let Jaleela do it her way—or in Jaleela's terms, that meant God's way. She'd try to wait patiently for the money to come by way of some supernatural intervention as Jaleela completely expected it to.

Just in case that didn't happen—and there was a 99 percent chance it wouldn't—Cassandra thought they all needed to be thinking of alternative ways to get their hands on a few thousand dollars.

She couldn't think about all that at the moment. She needed to focus, really focus on her work. She twisted the lens just the slightest bit. No way she could go back home without a great story to pitch. What would be the point?

The fading sun caught on Gabby's red hair, glimmered for a moment, causing Cassandra to blink into the viewfinder. What were the three talking about?

"Does your friend have any neighbors?" Gabby asked.

"I have heard Lydia mention a man, a much older man who lives in the place over there." Jaleela pointed to a place at least three football fields away that looked to be about a third the size of a double-wide trailer and several times larger than Lydia's homestead. "But I do not think they talk, actually."

"Why does she live so far out here by herself?" Heidi stopped, waiting for the others to catch up with her.

"I have asked her to come live near me." Jaleela's skirt fell from her hands. "More than once I have asked. But I have a feeling Lydia thinks her husband may still be coming back to her. If she moved, she is afraid he would not know where to find her and their son." She paused. "He has been gone many years, though. He made her sick before he left."

Of course he did! Cassandra ground her teeth. The camera jolted and she worked to right it.

"Have you known Lydia for a while?" Heidi asked.

"Oh yes. She is my oldest friend," Jaleela answered with a grin.

"So, the ladies from the hospice were here a few weeks ago?" Gabby kicked at a clump of weeds blocking her path. "How was Lydia doing then?"

"All right, I am told. But sometimes, you see, Lydia is not always so truthful."

"What do you mean?" Heidi halted in her tracks again, appearing not to be going anywhere until she had an answer.

Jaleela sighed. "Sometimes she plays a dangerous game with her health. Though she doesn't mean to."

Cassandra filmed Gabby and Heidi exchanging questioning looks.

"Meaning?" Gabby prodded.

"If you are being treated for AIDS and they test your blood and your CD4 count is at a certain low level, you can receive money from the government. They believe you are sick, and they are trying to help you and your family."

"That's good, isn't it?" Heidi sounded optimistic.

"Yes, except then if you get better, the level gets higher. When the level is higher, over a certain number, the government does not pay. If Lydia needs money to feed her Daniel, she would make any sacrifice. Sometimes she lets herself get sicker and sicker, does not take her medicine. Does not follow her treatment plan. So her level will become low and she can get her money again." Jaleela paused, her mouth turning down. "Do you see? This is what we do. This is what the women do for their children. To feed their starving children." Her voice cracked with emotion. "Now do you see?"

Cassandra didn't want to. Not at all. She had never wanted to see. She'd seen enough in her life. Now, as often as possible, she preferred staying at a distance the same way she reported the news—at arm's length and without a second thought about all the bad and fatal things that didn't concern her.

After all, if you never let the words sink in, the news was only words on a printout, words on a monitor. News of shooting fatalities, car accidents, fires, floods, death only meant well-paid career moves if she did a good job of reading about it while pretending she cared.

So, no, she didn't want to see. She wanted to tug the camera away, but she couldn't take her eyes—or the camera—off Jaleela. Standing there in her modest skirt, a scarf wrapped around her head. So thin, so resilient. So tired yet so tenacious. Jaleela with her arms outstretched and her hands clenched into fists. Her voice, her ardent plea, echoing into the evening.

Suddenly as Cassandra peered into the lens, unable to tear her eyes away, the frame was filled with color. Life-jumping color.

Jaleela's pleading silhouette wasn't stark anymore. Strips of honey and lavender seemed to drop from the sunset sky, cloaking Jaleela's shoulders from behind like a beautiful shawl. Like a caress from something otherworldly. Yes, that was what it looked like—surreal and real at the same time. Making words tumble through Cassandra's head. *Almighty. Omnipotent. All-loving. Celestial.* Words that had never had a place in her vocabulary, her life. Making her almost trust in a thing called heaven. Making her almost believe in that moment heaven had bowed down to meet earth in this powerful, meek woman named Jaleela.

Unaware of the ethereal aura surrounding her, Jaleela turned and started walking again toward Lydia's house.

Cassandra blinked, but the image was still there, burned into her mind. Like nothing she'd ever witnessed before. Nothing she'd ever be able to explain.

Had Gabby and Heidi seen it too?

It took a moment before Cassandra gathered her wits and resumed filming the three of them, their arms wrapped around each other's waists, making their way to Lydia's front door.

"Shall I knock?" Heidi asked for Jaleela's consent.

"Yes, try it." Jaleela nodded.

Heidi knocked on the door, then stood back and glanced at the camera, shrugged, and tried again.

"Lydia!" Jaleela inched closer to the door. "Lydia, are you there?"

Obviously the place was so small, like Jaleela's home, it would have taken Lydia only a moment to cross the length of her home and open the door to them.

After a polite moment of waiting, Gabby pushed at the door. It opened at her touch. She looked at Jaleela questioningly.

Without a word, Jaleela walked past Gabby and Heidi into the dimming shack that was her friend's home. The other two women followed Jaleela, and Cassandra fell in behind them with the camera still recording.

She thought she'd gag from the smell. No, make that smells. There was more than one, each more horrible than the last. She tried to hold her mouth open, not sniffing any of it in.

Poor Heidi began coughing instantly, and Cassandra couldn't tell if she was attempting to be polite, putting her hand over her face to cover her mouth or trying to close off her nose from the odors.

Probably the latter. The smells seemed to seep right into them, making everything Cassandra saw through the viewfinder even worse, if that were possible.

Because everywhere she turned the camera, filth reigned. A pair of mice scuttled around an abandoned pot on the stove, insects parading along next to them like close companions. In the sink, amid scraps of decaying food, soiled clothes sat, reeking with rot and urine that had never been rinsed clean.

And in the bed, in the folds of tousled, dingy sheets lay Jaleela's dear friend Lydia. The woman's body lay twisted and rigid in her own feces, the stench of death all around her.

As a lone spider crawled up the dead woman's sunken cheek, making its way to the bridge of her forehead and into her hair, Cassandra dropped the camera to the floor. She couldn't do it anymore. Couldn't keep her distance.

She'd never had a best friend before. And had never been much of a friend. But no one—no one—should have to live or die this way. That she knew for sure.

Jaleela wailed. A sound so gut-wrenching Cassandra was glad it wasn't on film. Who wanted to ever hear that awful, heartbreaking sound again?

"Oh, dear Lord, take care of my Lydia. Please, good and gracious Almighty. Please take care of her." Jaleela swayed, her legs unsteady.

Cassandra stood stiff alongside Jaleela as she cried out, but Heidi stepped forward and put her arms around the sobbing woman.

"We have to find her Daniel." Jaleela looked up through her tears. "She would want me to find her Daniel. Where is her precious little boy?"

Breaking free from Heidi's hug, Jaleela turned around and began searching. But there weren't many places to look in the small place. Under the bed. Alongside the stove. In the corner by the front door.

"Maybe he's outside," Gabby suggested.

Heidi nodded. "We'll go look for him, Jaleela. Don't worry. We'll find him. He's probably outside."

But a sick feeling came over Cassandra even with their words so full of hope. She knew better. She knew exactly where he was. Yet for a moment, she couldn't move.

Standing still, she watched as Heidi and Gabby ran outside. She listened to them call the young boy's name, hoping so much that he would answer them. But knowing he never would.

Because he wasn't outside. He was here. Inside. She knew it as sure as anything. He was here.

Taking four hesitant steps from the bed, Cassandra stood in front of the garbage-filled sink. A stained yellow curtain hung down from the basin. She reached out her hand and stopped. Oh, how she didn't want to push the flap of material aside. Didn't want to open the past and unleash the hurt again. Too many times she'd hidden from him . . . from the man who called himself a surrogate parent. Her foster father. Hid from the unwanted feel of his rough, chapped hands. From the stiff, harsh prickles of his whiskers that burned her cheeks. And from the smell of him, the repulsive unclean smell of him.

But he'd always found her. As she cowered in the darkness of a closet, trying to coil herself into the smallest ball possible. He found her as she tried to press her body flat into the dusty wooden floor under her bed. Or as she hid among the cobwebs underneath the cellar stairs. The sick excuse for a father had always found her. He'd dragged her out, yanked her by her feet, pulled her by the hair, repeatedly laughing, scoffing at her cries. He wasn't good at much else in his life, but he'd always excelled at finding her, hadn't he?

The revulsion rose from her gut with the memories of him. She tried to fight it as she flung the material wide open and found a shell of a boy sitting there. Hidden beneath a sink full of trash, hidden in full range of death's grasp.

Wide eyes stared back at her. Eyes too blank to even look frightened anymore. She knew the look well. She'd seen those same eyes staring back at her in the mirror when she was a young girl. When she'd felt so alone. So empty. So forgotten.

She tried to hold out her hand. Gently, encouragingly, to the dead woman's son, to Lydia's little boy. But the nausea rose and swelled, wave after wave, till it overcame her. As Jaleela rushed to the near-lifeless child, Cassandra bolted out of the death-filled hut, spewing her vile, undeserved, insufferable past onto the sun-baked ground in the glow of the glorious sunset.

Shaken, Cassandra watched as the others led Daniel out of the hovel he knew as home. Standing in the scruffy grass of his front yard, he simply stared straight ahead.

Gabby took off her flip-flops and put them on his small bare feet. Heidi untied the gray sweatshirt from around her waist and placed it around his shoulders, the fleece arms dangling past his skinny waist.

But still, Daniel stared. No eye contact. His expression blank. Not a whimper. Mute.

Once they boarded the van, Jaleela attempted to comfort him. She tried to draw him to her bosom, cooing to him about the kind Mrs. Olomi and all the wonderful children he was going to meet. But still his body remained rigid and upright.

And rightfully so, Cassandra thought as Sipho drove them deep into the starlit night, away from the boy's home. Away from everything Daniel had ever known.

The shock of his mother's dying had been too much. Now the well-meaning attention from them was also too much. Suddenly Daniel had too many people—strangers—mothering him.

But he no longer had the mother he wanted. And knew. And loved.

Cassandra got it completely. She knew he didn't want her or any of them in his present state. But back in the shack, she had stared into his eyes for a moment. And she couldn't stop herself. As soon as the van slowed to a stop at Mrs. Olomi's house, she hoisted her bag onto her shoulder.

"What are you doing?" Gabby frowned at her. "I thought Sipho was dropping Jaleela and Daniel off."

"I'm getting off too." She slid out of her seat. "A woman who takes in orphans could be a good interview. I'll see you all later when Sipho comes back to pick me and Jaleela up."

"You're feeling better?" Heidi asked, ever the concerned mother.

She shrugged. "Why wouldn't I be?"

Even as she said the words, she felt as if Heidi and Gabby were seeing right through her. Even she wasn't buying her businesswoman act at the moment. Reality was, she'd been the one to find Daniel. Odd as it seemed—even to her—she wasn't sure if she was ready to lose him yet.

Especially without knowing the woman she was losing him to.

Mrs. Olomi must have seen the pastor's familiar van from the window of her modest brick home. Immediately her front door opened, and she padded down the uneven walk, unlocking the steel gate that barricaded her place.

Aunt Bee! Crazily, that's the first thing that Cassandra thought of when she spotted the benevolent woman. Obviously *The Andy Griffith Show* reruns during her workouts were making a deeper impact than she imagined.

Only, of course, Mrs. Olomi's skin was as brown as a pecan pie that Aunt Bee would've baked. Aside from that, though, the two women could have been sisters. Mrs. Olomi wore the same sort of apron over a plainly designed housedress. She was just as squat and round as Aunt Bee and as cheerful-looking too. She didn't look in the least perturbed to have her evening interrupted by visitors and another orphaned child.

As the van rolled away, the gate closed behind them with a heavy clank, and Mrs. Olomi ushered them into the house.

She'd always felt comfortable with her medium size and height. But now, inside the house, as with Jaleela's shack, Cassandra felt like an Amazon woman. The low ceilings hovered closely overhead, seeming to accentuate the fact that the living room was scarcely big enough to turn around in. She hugged her camera bag close, attempting to minimize the amount of space she was taking up.

A lone light from the kitchen overflowed into the dark living room, providing enough of a glow that she could detect clumps of color dotting the floor to the right of her feet. Adjusting her eyes to the dimness, it took a few seconds to distinguish the colors as swaths of material and the clumps as bodies—sleeping children with their arms and legs shooting out beyond the makeshift sheets.

Certainly Mrs. Olomi knew how to make use of her small space.

The woman led them into the kitchen, slightly smaller even than the living room, and before Cassandra realized what was happening, Mrs. Olomi hugged Daniel, sat him down in a plastic chair at the table, and set a bowl of some kind of porridge in front of him.

Cassandra sat quietly, looking away from Daniel, hoping he would feel free to eat but not really expecting him to. She listened while the two women spoke softly in a language she didn't know. Zulu, maybe? The only part she understood was when tears began to stream down Jaleela's face and Mrs. Olomi reached out and squeezed her hand.

Yes, Jaleela had lost a very dear friend. And Daniel had lost even more.

As she suspected, the boy didn't raise a hand to eat; he only stared some more.

But Mrs. Olomi didn't press him. "Every day will be better," she promised him instead. "You are safe now. You can rest." She patted his head, then taking him by the hand, led him to a room off the kitchen where he could sleep. Jaleela trailed them.

Alone in the empty room, Cassandra stared at her camera bag. When she'd stepped out of the van, the camera had been more of a cover-up. She really hadn't had much intention of doing any filming. Certainly she had no desire to film Daniel. No way did she want to be haunted by his catatonic expression and know what the unseen villain fate had done to the poor child.

But all things considered—most notably her past and Daniel's future—she couldn't help but be protective. And somewhat suspicious. Who was Mrs. Olomi? Who was the woman *really*?

"Mrs. Olomi, how about an interview?" she asked the moment the caregiver and Jaleela stepped back into the kitchen. "People where I live need to know about you and the story of the orphaned children."

Mrs. Olomi suddenly didn't look so self-assured. Fidgeting with the skirt of her apron, she hesitated.

"It is a good thing," Jaleela urged her, taking a seat next to Cassandra.

The woman of the house eyed Jaleela steadily. "A good thing?"

Jaleela nodded. "It may help the children if others see."

"For the children then," Mrs. Olomi acquiesced. She settled down into the same plastic chair Daniel had sat in. Pushing his full bowl of porridge aside, she laced her chubby fingers together.

Cassandra wondered at the woman's nervousness as she took her camera from the bag, turned it on, adjusted the lens. Were Mrs. Olomi's intentions not as pure as they seemed? Or was she simply anxious about being filmed?

"This will be simple. I just want to ask you a few questions," she said, focusing on Mrs. Olomi's round face through the camera. The woman's eyes looked kindly and her demeanor appeared sweet, but so had Cassandra's foster mom's. Cassandra shuddered at the thought. That still hadn't stopped her foster mother from looking the other way, ignoring the abuse her husband doled out. "First question, why have you opened your home to the orphans?"

"Why?" Mrs. Olomi looked away, presumably to gather her thoughts. When she turned back to the camera, she spoke softly but firmly. "It is because I have been greatly blessed in my life. I live in a government house. Now I rent the house. In thirty years, I can own this. It will be my home," she said proudly of the house that was smaller than most two-bedroom apartments. "My husband and I lived here with our son. My husband, he has passed. He is with God. My son, he has married. He is with his bride's family. That being so, it is simple. I have room in my house. I have room in my heart. And there are many children whose parents have died from HIV and AIDS."

"How many orphans do you care for at one time?"

"I do not keep count. God brings them to me as He wants."

"God does that?" Cassandra hadn't meant to grind the words out. But she couldn't keep the facetious tone from her voice. *God makes orphans and then dumps them off at Mrs. Olomi's?* Why couldn't He not make orphans at all? Wouldn't that be the most sensible solution?

Apparently Mrs. Olomi didn't question God's ways. Cassandra steadied the camera in her hand as the woman explained, "Yes. The first orphan came to me many years ago. Right after my husband died. A child sat at my gate. I cannot tell you why. There are many gates along the dirt road here. But I found the girl there. She was weak and dirty, hungry and tired. I took her in. I have been doing so ever since. Others know that and at times they bring little ones to me. Perhaps you could say I have been made 'for such a time as this.'" She smiled.

Jaleela chuckled and leaned toward Cassandra. "Her first name is Esther. Esther Olomi."

"Esther?"

"Yes, Esther. As in the Bible. You know of Esther? Mordecai? King Xerxes?"

Cassandra blinked, feeling slightly intrigued, but more than anything, excluded by the Bible talk. She swiftly changed the subject. "The children feel safe here, Mrs. Olomi?" Her voice sounded brusque, even to her own ears. Like she was interrogating instead of interviewing. She couldn't help it. She had to know.

"It is my hope. They have the company of each other in this house. They are not raped here."

"Raped?" The word shook her to her core. Instantly a trembling started within her, bringing with it emotions and memories nearly as old as she was.

"At times young children are sexually abused by infected men who believe they can be cured of HIV by having sex with a virgin," Jaleela explained.

The thought sickened her, the bile rising in the back of her throat, threatening to overcome her once again. Still, she had to know more. She had to be sure. Was the woman like her foster parents in any way? "Where do you get your money, Mrs. Olomi? How can you afford to feed the children?"

"We do not always eat the best. Yet we eat. I sell my beadwork in the market. I have taught some of the children the skill too. Others are kind and help us as well."

"Others?"

"She is speaking of Mr. Terrence." Jaleela grinned. "He is very kind. Especially to Esther."

"Oh, Jaleela." Mrs. Olomi covered a bashful smile with her hand. "Mr. Terrence is only a friend. You make that face as if he is something more."

"He would like to be; I am sure of it." Jaleela giggled, then explained to Cassandra, "He grows vegetables at his house. Some he gives to Esther to feed the orphans. Other vegetables he sells to make money for the orphans."

"He sounds like a decent man," Cassandra replied.

"He is that." Mrs. Olomi nodded, looking at her above the eye of the camera. "There is something we say here. You may have heard. We say, 'Even if you are not infected, you are affected.' In some way HIV, AIDS, touches us all. It is in everything around us. The sickness. The poverty. The sadness. We lose so many. We see so much. We can either let ourselves become ill in spirit. Or we do what we can to make things better. I do not know another choice."

Cassandra had interviewed many a powerful woman but none quite like the women she sat between. If either Jaleela or Esther Olomi wasn't the real deal or didn't have the purest motives, then Cassandra was really losing her touch. She could usually spot a con a mile away.

Mrs. Olomi appeared to be just who she was made out to be—a loving, concerned advocate for the lost children. Given Daniel's sad situation, it seemed doubtful he could do any better, though he could certainly do a lot worse.

"Thank you, Mrs. Olomi," Cassandra said, feeling strangely relieved as she turned off the camera and packed it away.

While the other women talked about Lydia's funeral arrangements, she excused herself. Unlike Jaleela's shack, Mrs. Olomi's house had indoor plumbing, though no toilet paper or hand soap in sight. Coming out of the bathroom, shaking her hands in the air to dry, she considered, *Turn left and go back to the kitchen, or . . .*

Something inside her tugged the opposite way. Turning right, she took three short steps and peeked into a tiny bedroom. Pale white moonlight seeped through the threads of the thin curtains over the only window, enough that she could make out more bodies of children resting on the bare floor. She studied the forms covered with homemade sheets, searching for Daniel.

Would she even be able to tell him apart from the other children? she wondered. Then, as her eyes adjusted more, she caught a glimpse of a gray sweatshirt. But not on the floor, rather on top of the twin bed pushed against the far wall. She was sure Daniel lay underneath Heidi's sweatshirt. Evidently, kind Mrs. Olomi had not only taken the child in, but she'd given up her place of rest for the newly orphaned boy on his first night here.

Gingerly she stepped around the sleeping children and stood next to the bed where he lay.

Staring down at his face, she realized how she'd never been around kids much. She'd never had much reason to get to know a child. Or the desire to know one either. Yet today she had come to know Daniel. In a moment she'd seen past his eyes and she knew him. She understood. She actually felt . . . something.

And she remembered much too. Like all the dark, lonely nights as a child she'd lain in bed, longing for a comforting touch. Just to know she wasn't as alone as she felt. Just to know she wasn't forgotten. That someone, somewhere, cared.

She lifted her hand. Her fingers shook slightly. But the trembling stopped the moment she touched Daniel's cheek. He was asleep and hopefully, finally, wrapped in some sort of consoling dream. She was certain he didn't feel a thing as she stroked his soft skin. But she did.

She felt more than she planned to as she wiped away his tears.

26

Hearing Cassandra slowly plod her way up the cement steps, Gabby poked her head out the bedroom door. "How's Daniel?" She spoke softly, not wanting to wake anyone up.

Usually the epitome of poise and put-togetherness, Cassandra had never looked so undone to Gabby. Black smudges underscored her eyes. Gray lines streaked her white capris.

"He didn't eat any of the food Mrs. Olomi gave him. But thankfully he was sleeping by the time Sipho came to pick me up. Jaleela decided to stay with him tonight at Mrs. Olomi's. I offered to trade places with her. She was so tired; I could tell. But you know her." Cassandra sighed, then rolled her eyes. "The woman has a mind of her own."

As if Casssandra didn't. Gabby almost smiled.

"She assumed Nomvula and Tumi would already be asleep and wouldn't miss her till Sipho picked her up tomorrow."

Gabby nodded. "Apparently Katie wore them out. They were all bedded down by the time Heidi and I got back."

"It's been one long day. I can't believe I'm actually looking forward to my lumpy bed." Cassandra shook her head and started for her room.

"Cassandra, I . . ."

Cassandra turned and looked at her, her brow furrowed as if she couldn't imagine what more needed to be said. "Yes?"

"You know, earlier today, when you came upstairs and Heidi and

I were talking . . ." Gabby found herself stammering under Cassandra's gaze. "I was telling Heidi something, and I sort of acted like . . . well, I didn't want you to think—"

"It's okay." Cassandra held up her hand. "You don't have to tell me. I'm fine."

"I had a miscarriage." The words came out despite Cassandra's protest. "No, it's more than that. I've been trying to have a baby for all the years of my marriage. And it's just not going to happen for me. For Tom and me."

"I don't know what to say," she replied in honest Cassandra fashion.

"You don't have to say anything. I just wanted you to know."

"Oh. Well, thanks. I mean, thanks for trusting me. And I'm, uh, sorry."

Gabby accepted the condolence with a nod, then offered a faint, tight-lipped smile. "Well, like you said, it's been a long day."

"Yes, it has." Cassandra headed for her room again, but this time she was the one who turned and stopped Gabby. "Will you pray?"

"For you?"

Cassandra chuckled. "Oh no. If there's a God, I don't think He cares to hear from me or about me. It's a little too late for that. But will you pray for that little boy? for Daniel?"

Gabby tilted her head, taking a moment to consider Cassandra's request. "Yes, I'll pray. For him, I'll pray."

As soon as she closed her bedroom door, her stomach tightened. Pacing the dust-covered floor, she suddenly felt trapped in the small space with her thoughts and regrets.

Could she? Could she really pray for Daniel? Why had she said she would? Would God even listen to her?

Obviously it hadn't been right to pray over the food on Jaleela's table, not when the words rolled off her tongue with so little meaning. No, that hadn't been virtuous at all.

But Daniel was a child who had lost so much—his mother, his

innocence, and the light that should be shining in his young eyes. If he was going to be lifted up to the Lord, shouldn't it be by someone who hadn't shunned God's presence like she had?

Distraught, Gabby collapsed to the floor. The rough wood dug into her knees, but she barely noticed. Hanging her head, she closed her eyes and all she could see was Daniel, his young face lifeless. His expression so hollow. His eyes so sad and heartbreaking. He needed to be kept safe, and he needed to be loved so he might smile again one day.

Even though Gabby's heart ached for him, how did she have the authority to pray for him? Why had she promised Cassandra she would?

"Oh, Father! I have no right to come before You!" She began to weep. "I have no right after turning my back on Your love. I don't even know why You'd listen to me. But there's a boy, dear Lord. You know him. Daniel. Oh, Father, hold him close to You! Please!"

As the prayer tumbled from her mouth, more and more words came. Begging comfort for Daniel, begging forgiveness for herself. When her words ended, a gentle pitter-patter of rain began to fall. Gabby opened the window to better hear the light sounds on the palm fronds and broad leaves of the trees.

Listening to the mesmerizing rhythm, she breathed in the cleansing moisture. So calm. So soothing. She was sure she could hear His whisper, comforting her in between the raindrops. For hours and hours she stayed that way, halfway through the night. It had been a long while since she'd opened herself up to listen. She didn't want to miss a sound of it.

◈ ◈ ◈

Gabby's eyes flickered open. She blinked into the blinding morning sunshine lighting the tiny bedroom like a thousand-watt bulb. Chatter sifted up the steps from downstairs. Buoyant, it poured into the room, and right along with it came the comforting aroma of something cooking in the kitchen.

Causing a familiar warmth that tugged on her heart.

Many a summer's morning, pleasing scents of cinnamon and bacon had wafted up to her pink and lavender little girl's bedroom along with the voices of her mom and older brothers. How she'd always hated to be the last one up, feeling like she'd missed so much by staying in bed too long. She couldn't wait to make her way down to the kitchen, nearly tripping over her own feet in her teddy bear slippers, wanting so badly to catch up with the day and the others who were already enjoying it.

Just like this morning.

Grappling her way out of the sinking mattress, she slid into the flip-flops waiting at the foot of the bed and threw her light cotton robe over her OSU T-shirt. Then she made a quick, loose braid on the side of her head, not even bothering to take the time to secure it with a rubber band.

Sandals smacking down the concrete steps, she felt oddly happy about the prospect of seeing everyone this morning. She'd started out the evening before with a heavy heart, but miraculously, it seemed a prayer had changed all that, brightening her outlook like the new morning sun.

Seeing everyone gathered together, Gabby felt as if her fondness for them had multiplied during the night. Cassandra sat at the nicked-up kitchen table with her pinkie in the air, sipping a cup of tea, talking to Heidi, who was already dressed and manning the small, one-cook kitchen area.

Meanwhile, Tumi bobbled a beach ball in the air while Katie and Nomvula sat side by side at the table, sharing crayons and a coloring book. Heidi must've packed both the ball and the coloring book along with the Frisbees, candles, paper towels, Band-Aids, snacks, and other goodies in her suitcase full of surprises.

As Gabby approached the table, Tumi accidentally bounced the ball onto the girls' artwork. They laughed and tossed it back.

"Good morning." Heidi greeted her with a wave of the spoon she was using to fluff the scrambled eggs in the skillet.

"Good morning to all of you too."

Sweet young Nomvula scooted back her chair and ran to Gabby, giving her a waist-high hug before resuming her coloring again. Tumi must've figured he needed to follow suit because not two seconds later, ball in one arm, he also hugged Gabby loosely with the other.

Both of their faces looked freshly washed, and Gabby wondered who'd taken the time to brush their hair neatly into place. Probably Katie. It definitely had to be Katie who had given Tumi the T-shirt he was wearing. It was dark brown and way too big for him, with the outline of a guitar and some obscure band name printed on it.

"One of the pastor's helpers delivered a dozen eggs this morning along with a loaf of bread and a quart of milk," Heidi said by way of explaining the feast she was preparing. "There was a little butter too." She pointed to the small refrigerator. "I don't know how long it's been there, but hopefully it's fresh enough."

It appeared Heidi had already browned and buttered slices of French toast and that the eggs she'd scrambled were almost ready. Clearly she had the gift of making much out of little, just like Gabby's mom. And like her mother, too, Heidi didn't seem to need an expla-nation for Gabby's sleeping in late. Although Gabby would've gladly shared the reason with her.

In fact, she wished someone would ask so she could tell them every-thing. Like how she hadn't prayed, or at least not said any words that meant something, for so long. How she'd been hurt and angry, desolate for so many weeks. And how last night, she finally cried out in pain for little Daniel—and for herself—and she'd heard God's soothing whisper of mercy and grace in between the beats of the cleansing rain.

But instead of saying all that, she asked Heidi, "What can I do to help?"

"I've been asking Wonder Woman the same thing all morning," Cassandra quipped. "She hasn't given me an assignment yet."

Heidi laughed. "All right then. Cassandra, how about you pour milk for the kids? And, Gabby, want to see if you can salvage anything from those?" She motioned to a couple of brownish bananas lying on the counter.

Cassandra poured three cups of milk, which had never looked frothier, and set the brimming glasses on the table. Gabby did the best she could with the overripe bananas, lining up slices like a smile with two eyes on a section of the kids' plates. Meanwhile, Heidi sprinkled the French toast with sugar from the tea set before serving the fluffy, nutritious eggs and sweet treat.

As soon as breakfast was set on the table, the ball stopped bouncing and the coloring halted. All grew quiet while Nomvula's and Tumi's eyes grew as round as their plates.

Nomvula gaped. "For us?"

"For you." Heidi nodded.

The breakfast was lavish, Gabby knew. For two kids who often shared one meal a day, it was over the top. Extravagant. But after what Gabby and the others had witnessed the night before at Lydia's, it seemed perfectly fitting.

It seemed to be just right.

"Can I get anyone more tea?" Gabby asked, filling her cup with hot water.

"No thanks," Heidi murmured.

"I'm about to float more than my boat," Cassandra cracked.

Hot cup in hand, Gabby sat at the table again, which seemed so empty now that Jaleela's kids, stomachs filled and faces smiling, had begged Katie to take them outside to play.

Blowing on the steamy brew, Gabby took a quick sip, then set the cup aside and pulled the trip itinerary out of her robe pocket. "Well, ladies, you know what this morning is."

With a few hours of free time, they'd talked to Mama Penny two days ago about how to fill the void. She suggested some sightseeing to get a feel for the surrounding cities. Among her suggestions was a trip to the zoo in Pretoria, which Cassandra wrinkled her nose at because of the upcoming safari. Or a visit to the beadworking women in KwaNdebele, although it was then decided there wasn't enough time to drive that far and back. There was also a mall in Johannesburg, with its African and European influences.

"You like to shop in Dallas," Mama Penny had said to Cassandra. "Maybe you would like to shop in Johannesburg too?"

A side trip to the mall seemed to be something they could all agree on. At least, it had been the other day.

"Gabby, about the mall . . . Cassandra and I were talking this morning, and . . ." Heidi glanced at Cassandra, presumably to see if she was still in agreement. Cassandra nodded for Heidi to go on. "We were thinking—"

"You don't want to go either?" Gabby blurted.

The two of them shook their heads.

"I know. After last night . . ." She searched for the right words to describe her feelings, but it really came down to a few simple ones. "It just doesn't feel right, does it?"

"We were thinking Sipho could take us to a store, though," Heidi said, "so we could buy food for Jaleela's family and for Mrs. Olomi."

"I wish I could buy them new homes to live in too." Cassandra looked distant, staring across the table out the window. She must've felt their eyes on her because she suddenly shifted her stare and almost sounded defensive about her plaintive wish. "Well, I mean, seriously, no one should have to live in those kinds of places." Her voice rose. "Why, where we live, people keep their lawn mowers in sheds that are nicer than those awful huts. It's pathetic."

They sat quietly, lost in their private thoughts. Minutes passed before Gabby spoke up. "We'll plan on buying food today. We can chip in whatever we feel comfortable with. I'm sure Sipho will know where to take us."

Almost all at once they got up to start clearing dishes, to clean up from breakfast before starting the day. Little by little, Gabby noted their dispositions began brightening as they went about the task, chatting like old friends.

Gabby had just started to wipe the table when Nomvula came running in the door. She appeared stricken. At first glance, Gabby thought perhaps she was simply in search of a restroom. But it was far more than that, Gabby realized, seeing Nomvula's entire body tremble, her hands shaking uncontrollably as they dangled at her sides.

Gabby ran over to the girl, trying to still Nomvula's hands with her own. "What's wrong?"

Nomvula didn't seem able to speak.

"What's wrong?" Gabby repeated.

"It is Katie Blue Eyes," she cried, her eyes filled with panic. "Come! You must come quickly!"

Gabby turned to Heidi, whose cheeks paled in an instant.

"It's the dog, isn't it?" Heidi dropped a plate, the clatter harsh and loud as it hit the counter. "How many times did I tell her not to get near that dog!" She bolted past Gabby. "How many times?"

27

"It is not the dog, Mama Heidi. Not Hazard," Nomvula cried. "It is Katie. She is not moving!"

Heidi tried not to hear the high-pitched alarm in Nomvula's voice. Tried not to see the look of panic in the girl's wide eyes as they both ran out the door. She couldn't handle all that too, not when she could feel her own eyes bulging and the strangling tightness of fear closing around her throat.

"I tried to hold the ladder like she asked of me. I did." Nomvula began to sob as soon as they reached the outdoors. "I tried." She balled up her fists, ground them into her eyes.

The entire sun-filled courtyard was quiet except for the echo of Nomvula's crying. A silence that felt eerie, ominous, causing the blood to leave Heidi's legs, bringing her to her knees alongside Katie's body.

Her hair looked almost too perfect, unnatural, with nothing out of place as Katie lay flat on her back on the rock-hard ground. But then it didn't feel any better to see the rest of Katie's appearance in such a state of disarray. Her pale yellow peasant top was pulled to the side, askew on her chest. Her knee-length, rolled-up dark jeans, covered with dirt and dust. A lone sandal dangled on her left foot, and the other one was wedged between the rungs of the ladder that lay near Katie. The ladder was at least ten feet in length.

Making for a very long fall.

"Oh, Katie. Katie!" She leaned down to Katie's nose, holding her own breath while waiting to feel the heat of Katie's breath on her cheek.

How many times had she done that since Katie was a young girl? when she'd been sick or seemed to be sleeping too long?

"I did not mean to kick the ball so high! I am sorry." Tumi began to wail too. "I am sorry."

Thankfully, Gabby and Cassandra moved in quickly to take care of Jaleela's young children, both shell-shocked and crying. Because all Heidi wanted was to focus on Katie. Her precious girl. Her only child. And how could she forget the baby growing inside her?

It wasn't hard to figure out what had happened. Especially when the multicolored beach ball—the one Tumi had apparently kicked—was still stuck on the pastor's rooftop. No doubt Katie had plucked the ladder from somewhere near the unfinished house, from amid the wheelbarrow and buckets scattered around. And in attempting to retrieve the ball, everything had come tumbling down except for the toy.

Everything in the world that mattered to Heidi.

"Sweetie? Kay-kay?" Heidi tried to get Katie to rouse, but she wasn't making a sound.

Beads of sweat instantly broke through her skin, dotting her hairline and forehead. Hadn't she just been kneeling by her side at Lazarus East Hospital? She fought to swallow a sob lodged in the back of her throat. Could this really be happening again? here? in a place so far from home?

"Katie!" Heidi yelled louder. Frustration and anger at the unfairness of it all fueled her fear. "You've got to wake up," she commanded.

Grabbing Katie's limp wrist, she checked her pulse. It seemed to be within the normal range. So why wasn't she responding? Why wasn't she making a sound?

"Katie, come on now." She rubbed her cheek vigorously. "Please, Katie. Please say something."

Finally, a moan. Deep and painful. Gut-wrenching and primal like the low groaning of an injured animal.

"Katie, can you hear me? Can you move your hand? your fingers?"

"Is she all right?" Suddenly a male's voice sounded at Heidi's right side. Sipho! He dropped down on the ground next to her, like a guardian angel descending from the sky. "I need to move her to the van, Mama Heidi. We need to get Katie to a hospital."

"Can you call an ambulance? Please." Heidi laid a hand on his shoulder, pleading with the young, resourceful man they'd all come to depend so much on. "I will pay anything. Please, an ambulance."

"It will be much quicker if I take you both, I promise." He started to put his hands under Katie's back to lift her.

One hoarse word from Katie stopped him. "F-foot," she stammered.

"Your foot, honey? Your foot is hurt?"

Katie closed her eyes as if to signal yes.

"Katie, we're going to lift you into the van."

Katie's eyes drifted open at the sound of Heidi's voice.

"You've got to stay awake," Heidi told her, recalling what the doctor had said years ago when Katie had gotten shoved and tripped and had slammed her head against the unforgiving floor of the basketball court, resulting in a concussion.

Getting to her feet, Heidi moved around to Katie's right side, bent down again, steadying herself. "Okay, Sipho." She placed her hands underneath Katie and nodded for Sipho to do the same. "Can we lift her on three? One, two—"

But Sipho had already swept Katie off the ground. In his long, strong arms he carried Heidi's angel to the van.

Sipho placed Katie on the long backseat of the van, and after that everything blurred, happening so fast. Gabby and Cassandra had emptied out Heidi's two plastic bags of snacks, filling them with ice—one for Katie's head to cool her and one to soothe her foot. Nomvula and Tumi popped into the van for a moment, quickly giving their older friend kisses. Not a moment later, Sipho took the wheel, promising to "drive like they were going to meet Jesus, only just a smidgen slower."

As the van rolled out of the compound, Heidi crouched on the floor next to Katie.

"S-sorry . . ." Katie's mouth twitched.

Heidi tried to soothe her, smoothing back the bangs from her forehead. "Nothing to be sorry about. It was an accident."

"It knocked the breath out of me, and then I couldn't . . . I couldn't get a word out."

Heidi shifted the ice pack on Katie's foot, so thankful that Katie seemed conscious enough to talk; still, she didn't need to be expending energy, didn't need to be getting herself upset. "Shh. It's okay now. Everything's going to be all right."

"But the mall. We were supposed to go. I ruined it for everyone."

"Another day." Heidi shushed her daughter again. "We'll go to the mall another day."

"But not in Johannesburg." A muffled whimper crept into Katie's voice. "And you wanted those linens. The ones from Europe, didn't you?"

"Katie, it's not a big deal. Truly, it isn't."

In fact, nothing was anymore. Since being here, Heidi realized, the world had become so much bigger than Heidi Martin's wants and whims, so much larger than pure damask linens and embroidered pillowcases from France and Belgium, no less. From her talk with Gabby and Cassandra this morning, she knew they felt the same way.

Oh, that didn't mean she wouldn't ever go shopping again. Of course she'd go to a mall again at home. But she didn't think she'd ever look at the trendy clothes and designer merchandise, the brimming shelves and racks aplenty, in quite the same way again.

At least she hoped not.

"We'd already decided not to go anyway."

Katie held her hand over the ice bag, lifting her head. "No mall?"

Under other circumstances, Heidi would've chuckled at the dramatic, shocked expression on Katie's face, her eyes wide as the South African sun. But instead, Heidi shook her head. "Long story."

Now was not the time to tell Katie of the horror, the sadness they'd witnessed the night before. But she would tell her someday. Definitely. About Lydia's sacrifice. About Daniel, Lydia's orphaned son.

Just not now.

"I'm so glad you weren't hurt any worse." Heidi sighed, feeling like she could finally breathe, even just a little.

She started to close her eyes, offer up a moment's praise, when Katie abruptly turned her head to the side. As if hearing something? feeling something?

"What? Is there a sharp pain? weird pains in your head?"

"No. I feel like . . ." Her lips tightened and her eyes narrowed. She paused as if detecting something. "I feel like I'm bleeding."

"Bleeding?" Heidi tenderly raised Katie's left arm and examined it. Sifted her fingers through Katie's thick hair. Let her eyes roam, up and down, over Katie's legs. "I don't see anything, honey. Just a few scratches on your legs. Some of those bushes got the best of you on your way down."

"No," Katie whispered, causing Heidi to lean in closer. "Down there." She raised her head just a bit, nodding toward her stomach.

The baby?

"I'm bleeding. I know I am." A mixture of fear and sadness filled Katie's eyes. A look of pain that tore at Heidi's insides.

"Oh, sweetie." Heidi grabbed Katie's hand and squeezed as if that could help. And she squeezed tighter still when Katie's eyes pinched shut and a lone tear slid down her soft cheek and across her pink lips.

28

Heidi reached for Katie's hand once again as the doctor approached the hospital bed. But this time, not as a gesture to comfort Katie, more as a matter of strength for herself.

If they held together strong like a chain, like a force that couldn't be penetrated, maybe they could block out anything bad where the baby was concerned. And where they were concerned too.

There couldn't be any more loss in their lives. No more. It was as simple as that. Heidi couldn't let it happen. It would devastate Katie to lose the baby now. Heidi knew it with all her heart.

Heidi had seen so many sides of Katie in the past days, qualities her daughter possessed that she'd never witnessed before. And other qualities had resurfaced on this trip too. Parts of Katie's personality—her humor, her heart—that had been lost to her, lost to both of them, for a very long time.

While it was unlikely Katie was ready to be a mother twenty-four hours a day, Heidi admired how her daughter appreciated life unequivocally, without restrictions or prejudices. From the South African children she played with to the dark-skinned women she embraced. The boy Dominic she tried to comfort and the dying older woman at the hospice she delivered a flower to. She loved every color of people and all the brilliant shades of the beads, of the sunsets, and of the birds in the courtyard. Katie even had a space in her heart for not-so-friendly Hazard. Though she might not be into typical high school stuff like cheerleading or sports, though her hair couldn't be any blacker, as Gabby had said just yesterday, there was nothing dark about Katie. Nothing that wanted to lash out and hurt. And Heidi didn't want her hurting in return.

If the baby died, Katie would blame herself indefinitely, Heidi knew. For not being more careful, for being so daring. Even if, in the end, they decided giving the baby up for adoption would be best, as hard as it would be, she felt Katie could live with that. But hurting the baby? No, Katie would never be the same.

Oh, dear God, please let this baby live! Let my baby, my Katie, be happy again, Heidi prayed, holding her breath as the doctor greeted them with Katie's prognosis.

"The results of the X-rays show the ankle is not broken," the physician told them. "It is merely an acute sprain. Recommended treatment would be rest," he continued dryly, as if he'd said all this far too many times, "along with ice, compression, and elevation when possible until there is a significant improvement."

Heidi got the impression he might've thought they'd overreacted by coming to the private hospital. *Private,* meaning not government operated, Heidi had quickly learned from an aide when they first arrived. It was a hospital for people who had insurance or the means to pay with cash.

However, she'd also discovered *private* had nothing to do with privacy. There were no individual rooms for patients, only large rooms called wards, divided down the middle with three beds on either side. And the beds didn't appear comfortable at all, with thin, flat mattresses, no electronic controls, and tall side rails. They looked odd to her, almost like large, adult-size metal cribs. Even the hectic emergency room at Lazarus East offered more seclusion and comfort for patients.

"Do I have to use crutches?" Katie asked the doctor, which Heidi found to be very brave of her, considering the doctor's curt bedside manner that conveyed as much warmth as their surroundings.

"For the next couple of days, that would be my suggestion."

Maybe he had blue eyes, and maybe he wore a white lab coat, but Heidi couldn't help but draw a quick comparison. And in her mind, he was definitely no Dr. Kevin Peterson.

Kevin's eyes were warm and made a person feel cared about. Whereas this doctor's eyes were the opposite, inset deep into their sockets on his flat, round face. He hardly opened his mouth to speak, but when he did, his teeth appeared narrow, uneven, and small, as if he'd whittled them away on a diet of small rocks. From his stone-faced expressions, that seemed entirely possible.

Of course, who wouldn't prefer Kevin's compassionate, reassuring manner to this doctor's businesslike air? It made her appreciate the doctor—the man—she'd remet just weeks ago.

"What about the other issue?" she asked. "What about the bleeding?"

Though it was a relief to hear Katie wouldn't need a cast or any kind of operation to mend her ankle, the injury had become secondary to both of them compared to the well-being of the baby Katie was carrying.

If she'd had her way, she wouldn't have chosen this unresponsive man to talk to about such a personal, delicate situation, but given she had no other choice. . . .

"I cannot control the course of nature," he answered.

"Excuse me?"

"It is simple. The fall from the ladder created trauma to the baby." Looking past Heidi, he directed his answer to Katie. "If the bleeding continues and is heavy, you will ultimately miscarry. If the bleeding decreases and ceases, however, most likely the baby will be all right. But again, that is entirely out of my control."

Heidi could feel her emotions rising. How could this doctor be so blunt? "And there's nothing, absolutely nothing, you can do?" she ground out.

"She may stay overnight to let everything calm down and we will observe her, if you wish." The doctor shrugged. "But as I said, I have no control over the matter of the bleeding."

Heidi took a deep breath, gathering her nerve. Even though the doctor appeared to be close to her age, she felt almost as if she were challenging someone's father. "And that means what? We just have to wait? Without knowing anything?"

"I realize waiting is more difficult for some than others."

Was that supposed to be some kind of gibe? Like she was an impatient American? "Can't you do an ultrasound? a sonogram? something that will show us, tell us something?"

"If that would put you more at ease." He gave her an indifferent look. "Yes, we could perform an ultrasound to determine if the heart is beating, but that is still no guarantee. If the bleeding persists, there may be other complications. Like I said, a possible miscarriage. You could be paying for something that means nothing in the end."

"I don't care," she nearly screamed. "I don't care. I'll pay whatever I have to pay. We want to know about our baby. We want to know how our baby is doing now. Right now."

The doctor flipped open Katie's metal chart cover, jotting something down as he spoke. "An ultrasound technician will come to get you shortly." He slapped the chart closed. "Good luck."

Heidi worked to calm herself. He was definitely no Dr. Kevin Peterson.

The ultrasound room was small but more private than the ward, and the female technician slightly friendlier than the doctor had been. Although it seemed she, too, had no place for small talk in her schedule. After a few attempts at trying to engage the young woman in conversation, Heidi gave up.

The ultrasound machine didn't appear as up-to-date as the machines Heidi had seen in her gynecologist's office, but she imagined it would still give them answers and mostly, she prayed, some hope.

As the technician placed a paper sheet across Katie's lap and pelvic area before raising the hospital gown to a spot just under her breasts, Heidi glimpsed Katie's exposed belly and couldn't help but wonder for a moment how they'd ever gotten to this place. Couldn't help but be a little bit melancholy about where the time had gone.

And where the innocence had gone missing too.

How she remembered so vividly Jeff bent over Katie's five-year-old belly, placing goofy, noisy, slobbery kisses there. She could still hear Katie's shrill, exuberant, uninhibited laughter, the joyful sound of a child who is loved. Could still recall the look of delight on Jeff's face, knowing he could make his little girl laugh and light up that way.

And then when Katie couldn't take any more and had to catch her breath, she'd jump up and come running, right into the safe haven of Heidi's arms. Shrieking, she pretended she needed to escape a big bad monster, while every second she checked over her shoulder, making sure that her daddy was coming for her.

And he always did. Stomping his feet as loud as a giant, he'd plod toward her slowly while her squeals rose higher and higher. Then he'd raise his arms in the air and let out a deafening growl before swooping down on them, enveloping both of his girls in an embrace.

Oh, Jeff, you made it so magical. I tried to do that too. Tried to keep Katie safe. I really did try.

"Ack!" Katie sputtered, bringing Heidi out of her reverie. "That's cold!" she exclaimed as the technician applied the jellylike stuff to her belly. A belly that appeared to be slightly swollen if you didn't know any better.

The technician clicked some buttons and flipped a switch before swirling the oval-shaped handpiece around on Katie's belly as if she were operating a metal detector and looking for buried treasure. After some moments, she lit on a spot, clicked a few more buttons, zooming in on the area.

"Do you see that?" The young woman nodded to the screen.

Katie rose up on her elbows, eyeing the monitor. Heidi leaned over her, trying to see too.

"That is your baby."

Baby. It really was there? Even though Heidi knew the tests said

Katie was pregnant and even though she believed those results, she hadn't fully comprehended it. Not until now. But it truly was there. She could see the evidence inside Katie. She could see proof of a new life growing there.

"It's so . . . tiny." Katie's voice came soft, incredulous.

"It is. Only about six centimeters in all."

"And what about . . . ?" Heidi couldn't finish the question.

"The heartbeat?"

Heidi nodded at the technician and clenched her teeth, bracing herself.

Circling and circling the hand piece over Katie's belly, glancing at the screen, the technician searched for movement there. "I am looking."

The moments may as well have been millennia while Heidi waited, holding her breath, covering her mouth with her hand, ready to muffle any cry that might break out.

"Ah!" The handpiece stopped. "See the movement there?" The young woman pointed to the screen. "The flutter? That's it. That is your baby's heart. It's beating over one hundred times a minute." She turned to Katie and her gray eyes seemed to finally warm. "Just like it's supposed to."

Katie sighed and turned to Heidi. "I want the baby to be okay. It's got to be okay."

Moved beyond words, Heidi wrapped her daughter in her arms.

For the slightest moment, it felt like Jeff had his arms wrapped around the two of them too.

Hours later, Heidi sat in the vinyl chair next to Katie's bed, watching her daughter nap. Though it was still daylight, with the late afternoon sun filtering through the window at the far end of the ward, Katie had drifted off to sleep.

They'd been so relieved to know the baby's heartbeat was strong and amazed to see it "flutter," as the technician had described the motion, with their own eyes. But following their exhilaration came the waiting and the worry. Also the hoping and the praying the bleeding would stop.

Seeing the movement on the ultrasound made the baby seem more real to them than ever before. It also made the possibility of losing the life inside Katie even more profound.

And now there wasn't only one person's well-being for Heidi to be concerned about and feel responsible for. There were two.

As Heidi rolled her shoulders, there was no mistaking every muscle from her neck to her calves felt tense and achy. She knew the tepid coffee the aide offered her earlier would only make her feel shakier and more agitated. Yet she accepted the instant brew and drank it even after it had grown altogether cold, taking in the last sip of caffeine.

More important than how she felt, she needed to stay alert and keep vigilant with all her motherly might. The bleeding had to stop—and it would—but only if she remained focused and concentrated and continued to will it away with every ounce of resolve she had inside her.

Setting down the empty coffee cup on the tiled linoleum floor, she stood and began to shake out her taut, stiff limbs. Starting with her arms, she took a turn jiggling each. That done to her satisfaction, she moved on to her legs. She was just about finished when a familiar voice came up from behind her.

"You look like you're getting ready to run a marathon."

She turned around to see Cassandra and, of course, saw Gabby standing there too.

"Hey, you two. Thank you for coming," Heidi said, her voice low so as not to disturb Katie. After squeezing Gabby's arm, she turned to Cassandra, patting her shoulder. "It's so sweet of you," she added, though the tension she'd just shaken out of her arms and legs was beginning to return. Swiftly.

"Of course we wanted to come. As soon as Jaleela picked up Nomvula and Tumi, we had Sipho rush us here." Gabby chuckled. "I'm sure we drove him crazy, leaning over the back of the driver's seat, staring at the speedometer, begging him to go faster. We were so worried. Jaleela is concerned too."

"I know." Heidi clutched the neck of her peach T-shirt. "Can you believe Katie fell like that? And then there she was lying on the ground, not moving. It scared me to death. But she only hurt her ankle and got the wind knocked out of her."

"Yeah. What a relief!" Gabby agreed.

Meanwhile Cassandra was taking in the not-so-pleasant surroundings. When it seemed she'd seen everything she needed to, she leaned in to them, scoffing, "Remind me never to fall off a ladder in South Africa." Her upper lip curled in distaste.

Fortunately the bed next to Katie's wasn't occupied, but the four others in the ward were. And the white-haired lady curled up in the corner bed had started moaning and whimpering again. Heidi had to agree it was disturbing, especially if you weren't a medical professional and somewhat accustomed to the sounds and sight of someone suffering.

But did she have a choice?

"So, is Katie's ankle . . . ?" Gabby stammered. "Is her ankle broken? Does she need to have surgery on it or anything?"

"No. It's just a bad sprain." Heidi felt her face redden. "Thankfully."

"Yes, that is something to be thankful for," Gabby said.

But Heidi could feel Gabby eyeing her warily. Cassandra was, too, for that matter.

Less than a moment passed; then Gabby abruptly shot out a hand, placing it on Heidi's forearm. "Oh! Does she have a concussion or an internal injury?"

"Um, no." Heidi rubbed her palms together. "Just her ankle. It should be better in a few days. With proper care, of course."

"Okay, I don't get it," Cassandra spoke up, true to form. Unfortunately. "If her ankle isn't broken, and there's no concussion, et cetera, et cetera, then why for the love of pete is she still here? Frankly, hospitals give me the willies." She gave the ward another dubious once-over. "But this place, especially so."

"Yeah," Gabby chimed in. "We need to get Sipho back here—"

"Forget Sipho." Cassandra interrupted. "If he's too busy, I'll pay for a cab to take us back."

Gabby nodded at Heidi. "I have a little bit of cash in my wallet. I'm happy to chip in on a taxi."

"Good. It's settled. Heidi, while you wake up Katie, we'll go make arrangements for a ride," Cassandra half suggested, half demanded in that way of hers.

Heidi could feel her nervousness stirring again, her agitation increasing quickly from a simmer to a boil. She tried to keep her voice controlled, but it wasn't working. "I'm not waking her up."

"Really?" Gabby frowned. "Don't you think she'd rest better back at our place?"

"The compound isn't the best, I agree." Cassandra never could shut up, could she? "But at least if anyone's moaning," she chortled, glancing at the lady in the corner, "you'll know who it is. Me."

"Yeah, we need to get you guys out of here."

"Hospitals are no place for well people; that's for sure."

Their voices kept coming at her, over and over. They wouldn't be quiet. Wouldn't leave her alone. Wouldn't let things be. Interrupting her vigilant watch. Causing her to lose focus. Until finally something snapped inside her.

"Look, you two! Katie is not going anywhere, all right? She's here because she's pregnant, and I'm afraid she's about to lose the baby."

29

"I'm sorry. I can't talk about this right now." Heidi started crying.

Gabby stood in shock, staring at her. The most Gabby could manage to do was place a hand on Heidi's arm.

But Heidi shook her head, dismissing that small attempt to comfort her.

Cassandra seemed to be the only one in control, the tone of her voice even and unusually sensitive. "It's okay, Heidi. We'll just be on the other side of that door. If you need anything, that's where we'll be." She pointed toward the main door of the ward and nodded for Gabby to follow her.

But when Gabby tried, she couldn't make her legs move of their own volition. Cassandra noticed and stepped back, gently taking hold of Gabby's elbow, leading her to the waiting room.

Scooting two chairs from across the linoleum floor, Cassandra placed the vinyl cushioned seats side by side and motioned for Gabby to sit.

Cassandra remained standing, however, hands on the hips of her chocolate-colored capris. "Obviously you didn't know about Katie."

"No. I knew she had a boyfriend Heidi wasn't too fond of," Gabby offered.

Cassandra clucked like a mother hen. "Well, now we know why."

Gabby nodded, thinking back over the course of the trip, realizing other things that now made sense too. Heidi's overprotectiveness. Katie's nausea.

"I'd say whoever's in charge of this universe sure has quite the imagination." Cassandra's voice snatched her from her thoughts.

"What? What do you mean?"

Cassandra leveled narrowed eyes at her. "Oh, come on. You look as devastated as Heidi does. Only not for the same reason, I'm guessing. Not that you're not a nice person and all. But you are human. This has to hurt."

"Well, it's . . . um, it's hard." She stared down at her hands. "It makes me remember the times I went through the same thing."

"Uh-huh. And it doesn't make you feel just a little jealous? frustrated? angry? all of the above?"

Gabby's insides churned with every word Cassandra threw at her. Still she pretended not to understand. "About what?"

"Oh, please!" Cassandra rolled her eyes. "Well, it's your choice. You don't have to air your feelings to me. It's not like I'm that keen on hearing it anyway. But I guarantee we'll go back to that dive we're staying in, and you're going to feel like a pressure cooker every time you look at Katie and—"

"Okay, you're right!" she yelled, unable to contain herself any longer. "You're right!" Tears came to her eyes. "I'm jealous. I'm angry. And I hate it. I thought all those feelings were behind me, but I guess they're not. It's just so . . ."

"Unfair?" Cassandra offered.

"It's totally unfair." Curse words dared to fly off the tip of her tongue. "You don't know how hard we tried to have a baby. How long we've tried. And then a teenager . . . I mean, Katie's a sweet girl. But she's not married. She's not emotionally ready. She hasn't yearned and cried and dedicated her life to having a baby all the years I have. For her, it was just some night. Probably a night that things got out of hand. With a boy her mom isn't even that crazy about and—"

Cassandra held up her hands, cutting her off. "Whoa! I know I asked for that, but . . ." She sucked in a deep breath, attempting to square her shoulders beneath her knit beige shell. But by the time she exhaled, her shoulders slumped ever so slightly. "You know what? I need a drink," she confessed.

Gabby blinked. *What in the world?* "A drink?"

"You know, a tea or a coffee. A strong tea or coffee." Cassandra dug through her purse. "I'm sorry, but it all just hit me. This is too much drama. Between last night and now today . . . You have to understand, I live alone. No husband. No kids. No friends. Not even a cat. Not that I'm complaining. But at the moment, I'm on overload."

Cassandra Albright on overload? It seemed unbelievable, given the woman's profession. "But you report the news."

"Exactly. Report. It's all about lights, cameras, action. Excuse me." Cassandra held up a finger. "Makeup, lights, cameras, action. I read words; I don't digest them. I'm sure some news people do, but I'm not one of them and never have been. But this is different." She spread her arms wide. "Heidi's fear. Your disappointment. This is real and happening in front of me."

For the first time, Gabby noticed Cassandra's well-manicured hands were not poised or flashing in the air but trembling ever so slightly.

She cared, didn't she? Just like last night with Daniel, she cared. Which was hard, Gabby knew, because caring still didn't guarantee things would turn out right. Caring only meant being vulnerable, and who liked that feeling?

"We probably all need a minute," Gabby answered, giving Cassandra a way out and a moment to collect herself too.

"Can I get you anything?"

"No, I'm fine."

But as Cassandra walked away, they both knew that was a lie. A girl who had grown special to her and a woman who almost overnight had become a dear friend were both on the other side of the waiting room door, struggling to do the impossible. They were grappling to keep a baby alive.

And who knew that feeling of helplessness better than Gabby? She'd described it to Heidi just the day before. Yet as badly as she felt for them, she couldn't seem to squash the awful bitterness that had clamped down on her heart again.

She cradled her face in her hands, trying to think back to the prior afternoon and all they'd said while sitting on Heidi's bed. She'd felt so relieved to finally be talking to someone, especially a sympathetic listener like Heidi. But never once had Heidi intimated anything about Katie.

Judging by Katie's slim figure, Gabby estimated she'd probably only be in her first trimester, meaning her baby would possibly be due . . .

In the fall?

Gabby swayed in the chair, gripping the metal armrest for support. Yes, it was too hard to believe. That's when her baby—her and Tom's baby—was supposed to be born. The prospect had made her so happy when she'd first heard the news. It had seemed fitting and right. She really believed with all her heart it would finally be their time of harvest, their time to receive the greatest, richest, most bountiful blessing of their lives.

So often, she'd touch her barely swollen stomach and daydream, picturing the day they'd take their baby out on a sunshiny autumn day, gold and russet leaves swirling all around them. And how if the baby was a girl, they'd take photos of their daughter surrounded by pots of pink and cranberry-colored mums. If they had a son, how cute and boyish would he look sitting in front of a carved pumpkin?

It's not possible.

Is it? That Katie's baby would be born around the same time theirs was supposed to be?

Burying her face in her hands again, she tried to squelch the emotions rising inside of her. But before she knew it, her chest racked with sobs.

How can You, Lord? How can You do this to me?

The familiar painful emptiness filled her once more, and she couldn't decide which hurt more—the thought that God had played a cruel trick on her or the thought of feeling separated from Him again.

She didn't want to say hollow, unfeeling prayers anymore. She didn't want to feel apart from Him. She thought that was all behind her since last night, when Daniel had been brought into their lives. A child so tragic, she couldn't help but offer up prayers for him. And in her crying out for him, she cried out for herself too, begging for God's forgiveness, sorry she'd given up trust in Him, sorry she'd turned from His light. And God had listened. In between the raindrops, He heard her voice. She knew it, could feel it as the burden of her anger and hurt lifted from her heart.

But suddenly her heart felt shattered. No, she didn't want anything bad to happen to Katie's baby, Heidi's grandchild. Of course she hoped the best for them. But Cassandra couldn't have been more right. Gabby was human. She felt jealous. And beyond that, frustrated and betrayed. All the things she'd felt before. All the things she didn't want to be feeling again.

"Gabby. It's time. Time to wake up."

How she'd ever managed to doze off in the uncomfortable waiting room chair was nothing short of a miracle. But evidently she had, because there was Heidi bent over her, laying a gentle hand on her shoulder, saying her name softly.

"Oh, I'm sorry." She sat upright immediately. "I didn't mean to fall asleep on you like that."

"It's okay. I fell asleep too."

"You did?" Now that she looked more closely, Heidi's eyes didn't appear to be as lined and tired-looking.

"Mmm-hmm. Katie woke up about 2 a.m. and told me she felt different. She checked, and thankfully the bleeding had stopped. There hasn't been any blood this morning, either."

"Oh, so the baby's all right? Katie too? That's great." Of course it was good news—great news. Even so, Heidi's joy seemed to only intensify Gabby's hurting.

"I know. I ran in here to tell you and Cassandra, but you were both zonked out. And rightfully so."

They glanced across the room, where Cassandra was sleeping. She'd taken two chairs and pulled them together, using her purse for a pillow and a towel she'd found from somewhere to make a blanket for herself.

"After Katie told me, I curled up in that awful old chair next to her hospital bed and slept like a baby." Heidi laughed, shaking her head. "Like a baby? Did I really just say that?"

Gabby managed a weak smile as Heidi buoyantly hugged her, then rushed over to wake up Cassandra to tell her the good news.

"I knew everything was going to be okay," Cassandra said adamantly, the stiff vinyl cushion crackling as she hoisted herself up on her forearms. She didn't appear surprised in the least, but she did look happy, the faded lipstick on her lips breaking into a smile. "I wasn't worried. Not one bit."

It was a bit of a fib, Gabby knew, but it was Cassandra's way, and there wasn't any reason to call her on it.

"Well, I wish I could've been so sure." Heidi's eyes misted as she bowed her head in apology. "You two were such good friends, waiting here all night, just in case I needed you. I'm sorry I yelled like that." She looked up, seeming to focus more on Gabby than Cassandra. "Can you forgive me?"

"You were out of your mind with worry." Gabby shrugged off Heidi's words as if they weren't necessary. "I've been there. Trust me, I know." Didn't Heidi remember their talk? She didn't seem to.

"Well, it's not only that." Rubbing her palms together, Heidi drew in a deep breath. "Ever since we started out on this trip, I kept Katie's pregnancy a secret from both of you, and that disturbs me. Well, it didn't bother me when we first met. But now that we've become friends, I feel bad that I lived such a lie."

Her comment caused Gabby to wonder how the three of them had become close so quickly. They were all such different personalities and at different stages in their lives, yet an unexpected bond of friendship had formed in this time and place. Even though Heidi seemed insensitive to Gabby's hurting right this moment, it didn't mean their group wasn't near and dear to Gabby's heart. "We were still virtually strangers. You didn't owe us an explanation."

"Yes, don't be so hard on yourself. Nothing is shocking to me, if you haven't already guessed. The living-a-lie scenario? Familiar with it. Been there, done that. Am still doing it, actually." Cassandra smiled as they both eyed her curiously. "Oh no. Now is not the time or place, ladies. But someday. Someday I'll tell all. Maybe."

Funny. Only days ago Cassandra had been the one to put them on edge. Now, oddly, she seemed more apt to put them at ease, making them smile at her antics and the almost-too-honest observations she made. Gabby felt thankful for that and didn't have to wonder if it was just her feeling that way. She could see it in the way Cassandra's words settled like a canopy of calm and absolution over Heidi.

"Well, thank you." Heidi turned to Gabby, hugging her before bending down to hug Cassandra too. Then, crossing her arms over her chest, she hugged herself. "I hope you know I really appreciate you both. I haven't known about Katie's pregnancy for very long. I'm still a bit stunned, trying to adjust to it myself. Here, all along, I was so nervous about you two finding out and about how you'd react, yet you've both been very sweet and—"

"Can we finish talking about this back in our luxurious accommodations at the compound?" Cassandra asked.

Gabby was thankful Cassandra interrupted. She had had about enough baby talk too.

Pushing apart the chairs that made up her makeshift bed, Cassandra sprang to her feet. "Who has Sipho's number?"

"I already contacted him," Heidi told her.

"Great!" Cassandra slipped on her sandals sitting at the foot of the chair. "Have I mentioned hospitals give me the willies? I can't wait to get back and take a shower. Even a freezing cold one."

In less than a half hour, with all the paperwork completed for Katie's release, their group stood outside the hospital in the sunshine, waiting for Sipho to arrive. In between their mindless chatter, Gabby couldn't help but keep glancing at the heavens dubiously.

"Be joyful always; pray continually; give thanks in all circum-stances . . . ," the verse of Scripture came to mind.

Oh, how she longed to. How she wished it were that easy.

The hugging was going to last all day long, it seemed to Gabby.

Sipho would have never initiated a hug with them, but when they saw him and embraced him first, letting him know Katie Blue Eyes was okay, he didn't hold back. A big grin replaced the worried look on his face, and he whistled intermittently all throughout the ride back to the compound.

"You looked relieved," Gabby told him from the front seat.

"Yes. The others will be relieved too."

"The others?"

Sipho laughed in that hearty way of his. "You will see."

As the van turned in to the driveway of the pastor's property, Gabby realized she hardly saw the barbed wire and electronic fence anymore. Or if she did, it didn't make her heart clutch in panic like it had initially.

What she did see were the tall, graceful palm trees scattered over the property and the pastor's unfinished home that only gladdened her heart. Clearly to her, it meant the pastor was more interested in saving lives and souls than in finishing his house. Even in its incom-plete state, it appeared homier to Gabby now than it had before.

And then she spied something else—a bevy of dark-skinned women standing in the dogged heat of the day, hovering in front of the building where her group was staying.

As the women turned at the sound of the van's wheels crackling over the pebbled dirt, she recognized their faces. Mighty and Jaleela with Nomvula and Tumi, plus two beadworkers she'd met, Lindiwee and Chloe with her son, Khomotso.

"Mama Penny was here last night too. I hear they had to be quieted down in the middle of the night so that some of the other guests at the compound could sleep." Sipho chuckled. "And so that Hazard would stop his howling. They were praying far too loudly, praying for their Katie Blue Eyes. Asking God for her to be all right."

They'd been there all night? praying?

While she'd been feeling sorry for herself?

What warriors these women were! Loving prayer warriors who'd seen so much of illness and death yet would never let it get the best of them or their faith. They were always ready to pray. To give thanks. And to fight for and celebrate life.

Humbled, Gabby turned to the others in the back of the van. "Hey, you really need to see this. I can't believe it. Sipho says they've been here all night praying for Katie."

Katie immediately got on her crutches and moved to the front of the van. Heidi and Cassandra followed right behind her.

"They're here for me? They've been praying for me?" Katie asked, her face brightening, visibly touched and awed by the sight of the women.

As they got out of the van, the group of women dressed in blues and yellows and pinks descended on them, surrounding them like a laurel of pretty flowers. Laughing and smiling, they hugged Katie profusely and openly as if she were one of their own.

"We knew God had you in His hands." Jaleela beamed at Katie. "We prayed all night for you."

Their South African friend embraced Katie again as Heidi leaned over and whispered in Gabby's ear, "Wait until they hear Katie's having a baby."

"You're going to tell them?"

"Katie wants me to, and you know what? For the first time, I'm okay with it. I feel comfortable. I want to say the words out loud."

Gabby understood completely, especially in this place where

women loved, not judged. "They're going to be so overjoyed," she said, knowing it to be true without a doubt.

"I know." Heidi grinned. "Be prepared for more hugging and words of praise."

Gabby stood by as Heidi delivered the news, then watched as the women whooped to the heavens and hugged some more and even shed a tear or two. Even with her unsettled heart, she couldn't help but be astounded by them as always. In a world that had robbed them of so much, these women seemed rich, enriched beyond belief.

36

Even if she wasn't particularly feeling up to it, Gabby knew inviting the women and their children inside their living quarters, out of the sun, and up off the hard ground they'd been sitting on all through the night was the right thing to do.

Not that the conditions inside were that much better. But at least she and Heidi could offer them some juice to drink and a small bite to eat in the way of peanut butter and jelly sandwiches, compliments of Heidi's seemingly bottomless suitcase. While the two of them worked side by side in the kitchenette, Cassandra forgot about the shower she'd been looking forward to and took care of getting everyone situated, scooting kitchen chairs over to the couch and tossing a worn blanket on the floor for the children.

Everyone settled in, seeming happy just to be together despite the stark surroundings. Katie in her usual way helped make the gathering more intimate too. Touched by the women's prayers for her, she wanted to reciprocate right away.

After cleaning up the small mess in the kitchenette, Gabby helped Heidi locate a pad of paper and pencil, per Katie's request; then they both followed the teenager as she hobbled into the living area. Gabby grabbed a spot on the tattered blanket with the kids and Chloe, while Heidi opted for a kitchen chair by Cassandra. Katie, on the other hand, stood in the center of the small room, hovering over Chloe and

Khomotso. Poised with pencil and pad in hand, she resembled a wait-ress taking orders, except for the crutches she leaned on. And except for the kind of order she was taking.

"Katie Blue Eyes, you are asking, do I have a prayer request?" Chloe smiled hesitantly.

The few times Gabby had seen Chloe, the young mother had been wearing colorful wraps around her head, and at those times, Gabby didn't think Chloe could look more beautiful. But she'd been wrong. Even despite her lack of sleep the night before, Chloe looked even lovelier without the head covering. Her black-as-night hair was pulled from her forehead, showing off her naturally arched brows, and crowned her head in dozens of perfectly neat cornrows tied together at the base of her neck.

"Yes," Katie answered. "I mean, if there's something you'd like to share."

Chloe bit her lip, her smile widening. "May I have more than one request?" She laughed, the wake of her humor rippling through them, making everyone grin.

"Go for it. I have lots of paper here." Katie riffled the blank pages. "And a lot of time to pray."

As a sleepy Khomotso laid his head in his mother's lap, Chloe paused, seeming to consider her answer. "Mostly I pray for a home." She patted her son's back in a gentle, soothing rhythm. "A home where the roof does not let rainwater seep on my son. And where the cold weather does not keep me up at night, rubbing his hands to keep him warm."

"I know what you are saying," Jaleela spoke up from the couch, and Lindiwee, sitting next to her, nodded too. Jaleela had looked especially tired when the women came inside, and Cassandra insisted she lie down on the couch. But of course, their South African friend resisted. The only way she'd sit on the couch was if she shared it with someone else. Cassandra had gotten Lindiwee to comply. "The heat, it is a problem. But the cold can be worse," Jaleela agreed with Chloe. "There are not enough clothes to keep the children warm."

Katie scratched more words on the pad. "Anything else?"

"I pray for an education for my son," Chloe added. "Also, I would like to be good at my beadwork so I may provide for him and help others. I ask my Father every day that the HIV that has entered my body will not make me sick so I may do these things." She bent over, caressing Khomotso, who had drifted off to sleep in the folds of her skirt. Gabby could hear his even breathing and see how the peace of it made his mother smile.

"Okay." Katie scribbled more notes on her pad before addressing Jaleela. "Would you—?"

"Oh, may I say another thing? I told you I had many requests." Chloe grinned, making everyone laugh again. "I also would like to give thanks to God for women like Gabby, Cassandra, Heidi, and you too, Katie Blue Eyes, for the hope you bring. And for women like Jaleela who make us strong to face our illnesses. There. Now you may have your say, Jaleela."

"Finally!" Jaleela gave her friend a teasing glance, and even though her eyes appeared tired to Gabby, the enthusiasm in her voice didn't hint at her weariness. "For now, I only want to praise God for your baby, Katie, and to give thanks for adorable Khomotso and also for my own babies, my treasures, Nomvula and Tumi. It is my prayer that God and His angels watch over the children and protect them always."

Gabby looked at Jaleela's children, sitting next to her on the blanket. They'd quickly devoured their sandwiches, and Nomvula brushed the remnants of bread crumbs from Tumi's lips as both of them grinned at their mother at the mention of their names. Gabby guessed there were probably other things weighing on Jaleela's heart, but a protective mom always, Jaleela didn't want to share all her concerns in front of the two of them.

"Lindiwee, you're next, if you have a request." Katie flipped the pad to a fresh page.

Lindiwee pushed against the couch cushion, trying to sit up a bit taller as everyone's attention turned to her. Her smile glowed from ear to ear, epitomizing everything Gabby loved about the woman. Plentiful. Abundant. Those were words that came to mind when she thought of Lindiwee. From the plumpness of the woman's body to the ripeness of her round cheeks to the joyful spirit that exuded from her like bursts of sunshine.

"I also pray for a home," she said. "A home where I can live together with my children."

"Did you say earlier you have one girl and two boys?" Heidi leaned forward in her chair to ask.

"Yes, but we have never lived altogether. I live with my daughter at my aunt's house. It is very crowded there. My aunt has two older daughters who live there as well with their little ones. You have seen the places in the Squatter Camp. You know they are not so big."

"Where do your sons live?" Cassandra asked quietly, surprising Gabby that she was sitting still and hadn't taken out her video camera. But maybe she thought filming the women might inhibit their requests.

"They live with my mother, who makes room for my sister and her children too. In either place, there is not so much room for us." Her smile faded somewhat. "I miss my sons. I long to see them each day. I want us to be a family. Though I like beading, I hope someday to become a teacher. Then I could have a home for all of my children. It seems impossible, but every day I pray that God will show me a way. He is a big God; He is. As Pastor reminds us many times, we cannot think small and praise a big God."

"No, we cannot," Mighty said. "But there was a time my faith struggled, and I did forget how big our God is."

All eyes turned to where the young woman sat on the floor next to Cassandra's chair. The plain green T-shirt she wore was roomy on her, as were most of her clothes, leading Gabby to wonder if they were hand-me-downs and who the donor might be.

"Many know the story of how my parents died. How I took care of my younger sister and my brothers." Mighty took a deep breath.

"Many know that I cared for my sister and brothers, feeding them, nursing them until they also passed from the earth." She paused, cupping her hands together.

"What most do not know is what happened after, when I was all alone. I went to the hospice, and I asked Mama Penny to test me for HIV, for AIDS. I so hoped that my prayers would be answered. I prayed that the test would say I too would die soon. I did not want to live any longer without my parents, without my little sister and my brothers. I was very lonely, very sad. But the test Mama Penny took on me, it did not say that at all. How I cried, how I screamed to learn that I would live."

The room was drenched in silence except for the sound of Mighty's calm, firm voice as she went on. "When Mama Penny realized how much I wanted to die, she gave me help to live. She let me stay at the hospice. She said I could have a bed and food in exchange for my help there. Some people say, 'Oh, it is so sad, a young girl living at a place where people come to die.' But I feel comforted that God has brought me there. Caring for others, it is what I know best. And I know it is not the only plan God has for me. As I told Mama Heidi and Katie Blue Eyes, someday I hope to come to America. It is in my heart to go there to learn nursing skills."

"God will make sure you get there." Always positive, Jaleela's promise sounded more like a final word.

"He has already started, I believe. You have seen the stacks of bricks by the side of the road sometimes, have you not?" Mighty glanced around the room.

Cassandra was the first to respond. "Yes, I've wondered what those are for. Are they from buildings that have been torn down?"

"Oh no. No buildings." Mighty laughed. "For many years people save bricks. They set them together in a spot, hoping someday to have enough bricks to build a home on that spot. I do not have bricks, but Mama Penny knows of my dream. Each week she gives me a few rands for my work, from her own pocket, I think. It is not much in American dollars, but it is something. Like the people who save bricks, I save the rands for my dream. For the day when I come to America."

"You can be sure when you get there, you have a place to stay," Heidi told her, the invitation bringing a bright gleam to Mighty's eyes.

"You'll get there, Mighty. I know you will. I can't wait," Katie gushed and probably would've jumped up and down if it hadn't been for that sprained ankle of hers. "Is that, like, your all-time, biggest prayer request?"

"Yes." Mighty grinned, for once looking as young as Katie, as youthful as her years. "Yes, it is."

Jotting down more words on the pad, Katie looked up, taking in all the South African women. "Thanks again for praying for me, everyone. You are so sweet. I think your prayers probably went for the baby too, and you didn't even know it. I'll be sure I pray for you." She balanced with the crutches under her arms, hugging the pad to her chest. "Unless, well, do you think . . . ? Would you all want to pray together right now?"

A murmur of yes started around the room, growing stronger with each person.

"Okay, we should pray. It's just, well, believe it or not, some things make me a little shy, so . . ."

Gabby could've predicted the way Katie turned to her to lead them in prayer. She didn't even make her ask. How could she? After hearing the women's heartening requests firsthand, after having spent days growing closer to them, she held out her hand for the pad of paper listing the items they were so certain God would take care of—in His way, in His time.

Throughout her life, Gabby didn't think she'd ever encountered women so endearing as these. Oh, she loved her mother immensely; it went without saying. And her sisters-in-law. Her old, chummy sorority sisters. Her good friends at work. And many of the mothers of children at Graceview Church too.

But the South African women lived half a world away in harsh conditions, a life seemingly condemned from the start. They felt every emotion she did, yet somehow they thrived. Remarkably, they didn't let the bad steal their joy away.

"Be joyful always; pray continually; give thanks in all circumstances...."
The Scripture from earlier in the day repeated in her head once again.

How could she dare to sulk? to go through the days of self-pity again?

Oh, but I need Your help, Lord. I don't want to slip away from You again. Please help me to live Your words.

Gabby closed her eyes for a moment, offering up her own prayer request. Then opened her eyes and started reading at the top of Katie's list.

As Nomvula knelt next to her on the blanket, she stroked Gabby's arm. The children still seemed mesmerized by the light covering of hair there. So different from their own bare arms. "We played a game with Katie the other day," Nomvula told her.

"You did?"

"The game was hide-and-seek. Do you know of it?" Tumi asked offhandedly, sitting back on his heels.

Gabby knew he wasn't feeling as nonchalant as he was pretending to be. She knew where this talk about the game was leading. Understandably, the two of them were growing restless. After the praying, they began wriggling around on the blanket. Luckily, Khomotso seemed to be sleeping soundly and wasn't bothered by their commotion. "Yes, I just happen to know that game."

Their big brown eyes stared at her just like Katie's big blue ones had about twenty minutes earlier. And again, just as she'd let Katie off the hook, she didn't make them ask.

"Would you two like to go outside and play hide-and—"

The kids popped up off the floor. Nomvula kissed her mother and told her where she and her brother were going; then the two of them flew out the door, well ahead of Gabby.

As she stepped out into the courtyard, the early afternoon sun had retreated momentarily behind a passing cloud. Hiding in high branches, gray louries cried out to each other. Hazard gave a lazy yip at them and then seemed to give up on quieting the birds down. But suddenly even those noises were blocked by the singing pouring from the open windows of their dormitory. Boisterous, glorious singing that swelled and seemed mixed with praise and laughter.

Gabby couldn't make out the words the South African women sang. She didn't know any of the tunes. Still, the foreign sound felt familiar and comforting. It seemed impossible for her heart not to be affected by it.

"Are you listening to the singing too?" she asked Nomvula and Tumi, who had run over and planted themselves in front of her.

They shook their heads.

"Are you ready to go hide, then?"

They shook their heads again.

"I thought you wanted to play."

"We do. First, Tumi has a question for you." Nomvula gently pushed her brother to the forefront.

"No." Tumi took a step back. "You ask." He grew unusually tight-lipped.

Nomvula shrugged and sighed. It seemed she'd been left no choice. "A boy in the village said to Tumi that there is the orange color starting in Tumi's hair. He said it is like what happened to his sick brother."

Gabby's stomach dropped. She remembered seeing the clump of orange in Tumi's hair the first day she'd met him. But she'd dismissed the idea of it being anything at all because Mama Penny had never said a word about it. And Mama Penny always filled them in about every-one's lives and health conditions. Surely if the orange meant anything, she felt confident Mama Penny would've said so.

Wouldn't she?

"But I said, 'Tumi, Gabby's hair is orange. And she is not sick.'" Nomvula grabbed her brother's hand and held it tightly. "Are you?" she asked in a hushed voice.

"No. Not to worry. I'm not sick. I'm perfectly fine. Where I live, people have all different colors of hair. Orangish hair, reddish hair like mine. They also have yellow hair, white hair, brown hair, and—"

"Black hair?" Nomvula asked.

"Yes, black hair."

"And purple hair?" Tumi snickered.

"No, silly. Not usually." She laughed, putting her hands to her hips. "Okay. Now are you two going to go hide or what?"

"You need to close your eyes," Nomvula reminded her.

"Oh, right."

"And put your hands over your eyes." Tumi's voice grew fainter as he and his sister skipped off to separate hiding places.

Doing as she was instructed, Gabby began to count slowly. "One . . . two . . . three . . ."

But the sound of her own voice couldn't drown out her thoughts where the children were concerned. She felt terrible that they had to worry about such things as a potentially deadly virus and a loving but sickly mother. And luckily, the echo of her voice reverberating across the empty courtyard also couldn't drown out the life-lifting singing and the brave laughter of the women who carried on for them.

31

"I'll take ten packages of those juice boxes," Cassandra directed Niyi, the South African stock boy who was pushing the wooden pallet behind her. "How many in each of those flats? Twenty-five?"

"Yes, ma'am." Niyi nodded.

"All different flavors?"

"Yes, ma'am."

Waiting patiently while Niyi and another young helper loaded the flats of juice onto the platform, Cassandra looked around, still not quite believing she was in a wholesale warehouse. She'd never stepped into one in her life. Not that she didn't watch her pennies and make sure the dollars she paid for classic, designer clothes and other expensive luxury items were money well spent. But shopping in any place that had a concrete floor wasn't exactly her style. Plus, why would she? Living by herself, it would take aeons to go through forty-eight rolls of toilet paper. And in her condo, spacious as it was, where would she store it all?

"Don't let me forget. After we gather the food, we'll need toilet paper and paper towels. And antibacterial wipes. Bars of soap, too. Oh, and toothbrushes. And toothpaste. Lots of it."

Niyi paused long enough in hoisting the juice onto the cart to comply with another "Yes, ma'am."

No, this generous spirit simply wasn't like her, she knew. She had never even put change into those little plastic boxes at a restaurant cash register before. She had a hard time trusting the money went to some noble, worthy cause. How could she know for sure the cashier or cook didn't have sticky fingers? So many people did these days.

But there was something about this country, about these people . . .

She let her gaze fall on the brown, smiling faces around her, so eager to help and eager to please. Good thing she would be leaving soon; otherwise she had a feeling she'd go broke staying here.

Of course, her friends—a new term in her vocabulary—Gabby and Heidi had chipped in their fair share of money in an effort to host a gathering at the hospice. Where else?

Initially they had planned to buy a supply of food for Jaleela, but that was days ago, before Katie got rushed to the hospital. Since then, after getting to know the beadworkers and those who had prayed for Katie so earnestly and realizing any food they got for Jaleela she'd give away anyway, they decided they wanted to do something more. An afternoon get-together where the women could come with their children, share a meal, and take home a bag of groceries seemed like a better idea.

And better yet, maybe she'd even get to see Daniel again.

Everything in her hoped that Mrs. Olomi would bring Daniel to the hospice for the event. The kid had really gotten to her. If only she could lay eyes on him, know for sure that he was healing in some small way, she'd be okay. Then maybe she'd start sleeping through the night a little better and not start the day with him on her mind.

"Macaroni and cheese? And fruit cups? Where would those be?" Cassandra asked Niyi when he and his helper finished loading the juice. "Can you lead the way?"

Her job was to purchase all the food for the gathering. Gabby would go to the hospice to make preparations. Heidi had to stay back at their place to care for Katie, whose ankle was still slightly swollen and needed to stay elevated for part of the day.

The store wasn't far from the village in terms of miles. But from what Sipho had told her, it might as well have been a world away in relation to the villagers' reality. None of them had a way to get there nor the means to purchase anything from the warehouse. The place may as well have existed on another planet entirely.

Sipho had dropped her off and was going to be so surprised, she knew, when he picked her up and she had enough food to fill the van. At least she hoped it would all fit.

She hoped, too, she was doing a good job and making wise purchases. But who knew? Food buying wasn't exactly at the top of her list. She rarely shopped for groceries for herself, so shopping for a group of strangers made her atypically nervous.

Especially wondering what a young boy like Daniel would like most.

Nomvula and Tumi may not have had a house full of food, but they had Jaleela, who nourished them with love.

But what did Daniel have?

"Do you like these?" she asked Niyi, pointing to a bag of toasted oats once they landed in the cereal aisle.

"I do not know, ma'am."

She broke open a bag and offered him a handful. "Here, try some."

Scooping up the oats, Niyi flung the cereal into his mouth like a handful of popcorn. "Good."

Cassandra nodded, satisfied. "Let's add on twenty bags of those too, then. And something else. Maybe cornflakes?"

As Cassandra watched the young men load the cereal, her mind drifted, thinking about prayer and God, wondering, not for the first time, how it all worked.

Daniel lived. But Lydia died. Katie and her baby survived a fall. But many a mother's child would perish from AIDS that day. Jaleela seemed to accept it, take it in stride. "Too much sun produces a desert. It is rain that makes us grow," Jaleela had said, referring to life's hardships. "God hears our prayers. But He is the one in control."

It still didn't make sense to Cassandra. Maybe there was something else involved that decided which prayers got answered. Something mathematical, like the laws of probability. Or some giant equation no one had figured out yet.

Jaleela laughed when she mentioned things like that. That wasn't the sort of way her new friend viewed her faith. Whatever their differences, however, Cassandra felt a strong kinship with the AIDS-stricken woman. In a way, she wished she could pack Jaleela up and take her home with her. Put her in front of a TV camera, and *voilà!* Everyone would fall in love with Jaleela, just as Cassandra had, and there would be her news story. No problem.

So far she didn't know what her feature story would be. The thought overwhelmed her, made her panic at times. There seemed to be too many stories to tell.

She needed to relax. And wait. Stand back. Oftentimes, as she'd learned from experience, a person needed to get to the end of the story before knowing the beginning.

"Excuse, ma'am," Niyi interrupted her thoughts. "Will you be getting more?" He glanced at the mountain of goods topping the wooden platform.

"Yes, of course. We haven't gotten the flour and sugar or the paper goods yet. You'll need to grab another pallet, boys."

Niyi smiled obligingly and started to walk away to retrieve an empty pallet.

Cassandra stopped him. "Before you do that, why don't I buy you and your friend lunch?"

"Ma'am?" He appeared baffled.

"Over there." She motioned to a small sandwich and coffee bar within the huge store.

"Really, ma'am?"

"Yes, really. You boys are far too skinny. I need strong, muscle-bound men to move these heavy things, don't I?" She flipped a hand at him. "You two need to put some fat on those bones of yours."

"Yes, ma'am. Thank you, ma'am." Niyi bowed with a gracious smile that went beyond his words.

Cassandra followed Niyi and the other young man as they pushed the laden pallet to a holding area at the front of the warehouse and then as they shyly walked over to the sandwich shop.

Hmm, all this niceness and generosity. She shook her head. She certainly didn't know where it was coming from.

Yes, it was good she'd be leaving soon. From the giant warehouse. From the massive continent of Africa.

A girl could absolutely lose herself in this place.

32

Gabby stopped on her way into the hospice, plucking several tall magenta flowers growing by the door, their petals as soft and delicate as silk. How such a beautiful, perfect flower could grow out of the hard, red ground, she couldn't begin to fathom.

"Would you like a glass for those?" Mighty asked, sitting at the front desk as Gabby entered the building.

"That'd be great. Is it all right that I picked them, I hope? I thought they might be a pretty addition to the conference room for our get-together."

"It is fine." Mighty's tone sounded more clipped and efficient in her work environment and so adult for her age. In contrast though, her relaxing smile exuded much warmth. "They grow wild here. More will come in their place," she said, before coming out from behind the desk. "Would you like to see the conference room?"

Even though Gabby was aching inside, eager to get to the computer and send Tom an e-mail telling him about Jaleela and the wonderful ladies she'd met; about Nomvula and Tumi, the children she'd come to adore; how coming to know these children and the people here had changed her and her views of adoption, she tried to steel herself.

First things first. She'd been delegated to get the conference room in shape for their gathering, to arrange chairs and talk to the cooks. That had to be her top priority.

But, oh, how she didn't want to think about anything but Tom and what the changes in her could mean for them and their hopes of having a family. Excitement and anxiety blended, daring to steal her breath away. Difficult as it was, she tried hard to concentrate on the task at hand as Mighty led her down the hallway to the conference room.

Standing inside the doorway while Mighty went to fetch a container for the flowers, Gabby realized there wasn't much more she could do to make the conference area more festive. She'd brought two decorative vanilla candles that Heidi dug out of her suitcase, and the wildflowers she'd picked would help too. So would the two landscape prints that hung side by side on the west wall of the room, although they were faded by age or sun or both.

But the things that stood out most in the room were the posters, providing colorful and thorough information about AIDS and HIV, describing everything, including testing, treatment, prognosis, and also education, support, and supplies the hospice so willingly provided.

Party or not, those signs weren't coming down. Nor should they. Gabby moved to straighten the corner of one of them.

"There are a few more chairs scattered throughout the building," Mighty said, handing Gabby a glass container half-full of water for the flowers. "I will be glad to get them for you."

"You don't have to do that." Gabby set the flowers on the table, flanking the glass container with the candles, which helped brighten the room to some degree. "That's why I dropped by—to set things up. I don't expect you to do that. Believe me."

It wasn't the only reason she was more than happy to come spruce up the hospice's conference room. There was the matter of the e-mail she needed to write to Tom. If she could send it out soon, he might respond to her when he first woke up.

"It is not a problem. But first—" Mighty checked the clock on the wall—"I must serve breakfast to our patients. After that, I would be most happy to help you."

It seemed like a perfect time to make a beeline for the computer, but Gabby couldn't be that rude, especially to a sweetheart like Mighty. "Would you like me to help? If you're helping me with the chairs, it's the least I can do."

Mighty warned, "It may take a while."

"I have time," Gabby said calmly, despite the way she felt—rushed and anxious as if there wasn't a moment to waste. She wanted so much to talk to Tom and to pull all the pieces together. Maybe then she could have the happy little family she'd always yearned for before the chance slipped away again.

It took only a few minutes before Gabby realized why feeding breakfast to a couple dozen hospice patients might take more time than one would imagine.

The two young women in the kitchen had prepared two types of breakfasts: one a lighter fare for those who were most ill and another for patients with heartier appetites.

Mighty didn't have to be told which trays were for which patients. As she explained, she served meals a couple of times a day during most shifts. She knew the grim or hopeful condition of each patient by heart.

With no hospital-style carts to transport the food, Gabby and Mighty got plenty of exercise, ducking in and out of the kitchen to gather trays in their arms, first serving patients on the second floor, who were capable of feeding themselves. It wasn't an easy task without an elevator. But then it wasn't pleasant delivering trays to the patients on the first floor, who were critically ill and couldn't raise their heads or speak a word, either.

Gabby was sure her legs would give out when they'd carried trays upstairs, but it was her heart that concerned her when they served breakfast to patients on the ground floor. She was certain it would break in two.

Unlike in the private hospital Katie had been in, some thoughtful person had had the foresight to paint the walls of the downstairs ward a soothing pale blue. Billowy cotton curtains in the same tranquil shade hung at the windows, shielding against the intensity of the sun, but they were still lightweight enough to let its therapeutic cheeriness shine through.

"Good morning, dear." Mighty's sweet voice encouraged a small-boned woman in the bed nearest the door to hold up a limp hand in reply. "It is time for breakfast. Let us sit you up a bit, yes?"

Laying the tray next to the bed, Mighty deftly slid her hand under the small of the woman's back, lifting her up ever so tenderly in the bed. Following her lead, Gabby propped the thin pillow behind the frail woman.

The woman's head rolled to the side, she had so little strength. The only sound she made was a gasp. A gasp, a pause. A gasp, a pause. One right after another.

"You'll like what the cook made for you today," Mighty spoke over the gasping, taking one of the woman's hands in her own. "She knows what you like. God does too. Shall we thank Him for the food?"

Mighty prayed over each patient in the ward before feeding them their breakfasts one spoonful, one sip at a time. Her maturity combined with her ability to care and then care some more mesmerized Gabby. It would be a shame if the girl didn't have a chance at nursing someday. No doubt, as she told them before, she had a gift for caring.

As she watched the young woman lovingly perform her duties, a slight morning breeze drifted in the window, parting the light cotton curtain. The flash of another magenta wildflower caught Gabby's eye, making her think how Mighty was so much like the dainty flower with its roots embedded in rock. Truly an example of grace growing out of hardship.

As Mighty took another patient's hand in her own, Gabby watched and cursed at herself vehemently—and not for the first time in the past couple of days—for how wrong she'd been. She spent so many years dwelling on what wasn't perfect in her life instead of being thankful for the one thing that was.

Her loving husband, Tom.

After the patients were prayed over and fed and chairs moved into the conference room, Gabby felt like a swimmer who'd finally paddled her way to a far-off shore when at long last she sat down at the computer adjacent to Mighty's desk.

"Allow me to get you started." Mighty tapped on the keyboard with both hands. "There, now you are free to use the e-mail as you please. If you have any problems, do not hesitate."

The moment Mighty stepped away, Gabby typed in Tom's e-mail address, her fingers flying. She also typed in the subject "Hello from South Africa."

Clicking down to the body of the e-mail, fingers poised over the keys, she stopped. She stared at the blank screen.

How should she start? What should she say? She wanted so badly to tell him about her experiences halfway around the world that made her feel so much closer to him. About how her fear had disappeared because of everyone she'd met and everything she'd seen. She wanted to tell him all of it.

But all Gabby could see was his face, the hurt in his eyes the night her lack of words and caring pushed him away.

She wasn't pushing anymore. Except for them to be together.

Finally her fingers struck the keys.

Tom,
   I'm sorry, so terribly sorry. So many things have changed.
Can you ever forgive me?

                                           All my love,
                                           Gabby

It looked like such a little message. But she meant each word, syllable, letter so earnestly with every inch of her heart. Her hand trembled slightly, hovering over the mouse, studying the script one last time.

Were they the right words? the ones that could bridge what had happened in the past to what could be in their future? She couldn't be sure at all.

Pushing Send, she could only hope and pray they would be.

33

"I'm so bored," Katie whimpered from the beat-up couch, her right foot elevated on top of a mound of pillows.

"Of course you're bored. You're not bounding up ladders, scaling tall buildings, or racing across rooftops." Smiling, Heidi handed her a glass half-full of mango juice.

Taking the glass with one hand, Katie murmured, "Thanks. You make me sound like Spider-Man."

"Well, if the shoe fits . . ." Heidi chuckled.

"Cute, considering I can't even get my gym shoe on."

"And that's why we're here resting. So the swelling will go down and you can enjoy the rest of our stay. There's the party today and the safari tomorrow. You'll want your ankle as good as it can be for that. You know you'll love seeing all those animals."

"But Jaleela and the ladies were so nice. I really wanted to do something to help with the party, like go to the store with Cassandra. Or help Gabby at the hospice. I still can't believe the women were here praying, waiting for us to come back from the hospital."

Every time Katie spoke about the South African women and their kindness, an amazed expression settled on her face.

"You can thank the ladies again later today at the reception. For now, you need to rest as much as you can. Dr. Mom says so." Heidi raised an authoritative brow. "Do you need any ice for it?"

Katie looked down, moving her foot slightly. "No, it's fine." She paused. "But I'm not. I'm so—"

"Bored. I know," Heidi cut her off. "You've only said it a dozen times in the past fifteen minutes."

"Well, there's no computer. No TV. I wish Dominic would stop by." Katie sighed. "He must be working nonstop. I usually see him every morning. I didn't see him the day I fell, and he didn't come to visit yesterday."

"You two seemed to have really hit it off."

"I thought so too." Katie sipped at her juice thoughtfully.

"Well, like he said, he feels lucky to have a job." Heidi motioned for her to lift her leg while she propped up the pillows underneath it. "He'll drop by whenever he has the chance."

"I hope so because I'm really—"

Heidi raised her hand. "Don't even say it!" she threatened, a chuckle following her warning.

"My bad." Katie's eyes glimmered with playful mischief.

"Didn't you bring any books to read?"

Katie shook her head. "Just magazines. And I read them all on the plane."

"Maybe you should sit still and meditate." Straightening her back, Heidi held out her hands in the air, palms up. "Like this." She pinched her thumbs and forefingers together and closed her eyes, trying to remember the meditation class she'd taken during her college years. "Now you chant. Ohmm . . . ohmm . . ."

Katie broke into giggles. "Oh yeah, that looks really exciting—and kind of lunatic-ish too."

Heidi opened her eyes. "Well, I'm running out of suggestions, dear girl. What about your iPod? Would that help?"

Katie nodded. "More than 'ohmm . . . ohmm . . .'"

"Where is it?"

"Right where I left it."

"Katherine Elizabeth!" Heidi tried to give her a stern look, but her tight lips curled into an involuntarily smile. "That ankle of yours better heal quickly, because you're driving me crazy already."

"What?" Katie's eyes went wide with mock innocence. "Isn't that what you always tell me? My stuff is right where I left it."

"Cute," she mimicked Katie's earlier comeback. "Your iPod's upstairs, then?"

"I think so."

"Okay, I'll be back in a minute." Heidi headed for the concrete flights of steps. "Don't die of boredom while I'm gone."

She paused at the bedroom doorway, a vision of Katie's room at home flitting across her mind. What a comparison!

Painted a pale yellow when Katie made the transition from young girl pink to tender teen, there'd be no telling where she might have found an iPod in that sizable space, amid the furniture and extraneous mounds of stuff sitting and hanging everywhere. Tapestries push-pinned to the walls. Posters taped to the ceiling. Piles of pillows flung on the bed and floor. While hooks and containers sat all around to hold purses, backpacks, scarves, barrettes, earrings, pencils, digital camera disks, and other mementos of good times and bad. And then there was the only preteen item that had escaped the storage box—a lone stuffed dolphin Jeff had given Katie. It camped out near her pillow at the head of her bed.

But in this particularly sparse room, laying hands on Katie's iPod shouldn't be a problem. Where was there to look? On top of the two beds? Under them? Inside their suitcases sitting on the floor, all zipped up tightly in order to keep the ants from making a home there?

And also Katie's purse. Picking up the paisley-printed sack from the bed, Heidi glanced inside for her daughter's only salvation for combating boredom. Not seeing anything, she felt along the bottom with her hand. Nothing again.

She was just about to unzip the suitcases and search inside when she recalled waking up a couple of nights before to see a sleeping Katie with her earphones on. She remembered because she'd actually felt a twinge of envy that Katie had something to soothe her, melodies to muffle some of the foreign sounds of the night.

It was probably still there, right under her pillow. Heidi lifted the pillowcase by its end. The pearly white iPod lay in a wad of earphone cords. But there was something else next to it. Heidi leaned closer. A gray-blue spiral notebook. A notebook with *History* written on the cover in Katie's handwriting.

A history notebook? Under her pillow?

Heidi froze with the pillow in her hand, a sense of déjà vu overwhelming her. This had happened before, hadn't it? years ago in Katie's room?

Now she remembered how she'd smiled, seeing the notebook back then, figuring Katie had hidden it under her pillow, thinking the history terms and dates might enter her brain by osmosis while she slept.

But why now? Why bring the notebook here?

Beyond curious, Heidi lifted the notebook from its hiding spot and held it in her hands, wanting so badly to open it. But then again, suddenly nervous about what she might find inside.

Finally she flipped open the cardboard cover.

Dear Dad . . .

The sight of the words cramped her chest. Feeling for the bed, she eased down onto it slowly. It took a moment before she could turn the pages, revealing more and more of Katie's handwriting. Sometimes words were written in sweeping, flowery penmanship. In other entries the ink-printed letters were etched so deeply on the page, the stabbing hurt, the sharp pain seemed almost palpable. Some passages were neatly written and lengthy, others rushed and sparse, and many punctuated with splotches. Water spots? Katie's tears?

Each entry started with the same words: *Dear Dad.*

Wisely, Katie had camouflaged her diary from Heidi with a title like History. Leaving Heidi to assume exactly what she had. That the pages chronicled events that had gone on in the world instead of everything going on within Katie's heart.

"Hey, Mom," Katie yelled from downstairs. "Did you find it? my iPod?"

Startling at the sound of her daughter's voice, Heidi shut the notebook quickly, feeling like she'd been caught red-handed. "Yes. I did." Her heart double-thumped. "I'll be right down."

But she stood for a moment, staring at the cover, trying to decide what to do. Finally she hid it under the pillow again, then shakily made her way downstairs to deliver Katie's iPod.

When the earphones were in place, a look of contentment settled over Katie. She appeared so comfortable, Heidi leaned over her and spoke loudly. "I'm going to get a bath now."

"'Kay." Katie gave her a thumbs-up, happy to retreat into her favorite songs.

I'm going to bypass the bedroom and head straight for the bath. I will not look at that notebook again. Katie deserves her privacy. Her space. I need to give her space.

Heidi walked by the bedroom and started to pause but forced herself to keep moving. To open the bathroom door. Close it. Set her towel near the edge of the tub. And then she stopped.

Space? When she's twenty-one, she can have all the space she wants. Right now she's living under my roof, and there can't be any more secrets.

She turned on her heels, crossing the landing to the bedroom they shared. Reaching under the pillow, she pulled out the notebook once again and held it in her hands.

But it's a diary. Katie's diary. A personal journal. How would I feel if I were her? She's seventeen.

But she'd glimpsed the word *mom* so many times when she'd brushed back the pages, she couldn't imagine how she'd stand not knowing what Katie had written about her.

True, she knew she wasn't supposed to be Katie's best friend. But she did want to be her ally—support her and love her in her journey through this world. Is that how Katie saw her? Or as something else? How could she know for sure if she didn't peek inside?

"Mom?"

Heidi's entire body jerked at the sound of Katie's voice coming up from behind, causing her to clutch the notebook even more tightly against her chest.

There was no way out of it now. No way to disguise her actions. She turned and faced Katie. "You shouldn't be climbing the stairs with your swollen ankle."

"I didn't climb. I scooted up on my bottom."

"Oh, that's good." Heidi sounded inane even to herself.

"I just realized." She paused. "My iPod was under my pillow, wasn't it?"

"Yes."

"And so was . . . that." She pointed to the notebook.

Heidi stared at Katie, wishing so much she'd never laid eyes on the notebook in her hands. "I didn't read it. I saw it was notes to your dad, and I didn't read it."

"But you were going to."

She stiffened at the near truth. "I wasn't sure if I was going to or not. I admit I glimpsed the word *mom* a few times. It did pique my curiosity. But it's yours." She held out the book to Katie.

Slowly, Katie took it from her hand, her cheeks cherry red. Without a word, she turned and limped over to the top of the stairs.

Before she could settle down on the step, Heidi put a gentle hand on her back to stop her.

Katie turned around. Heidi could see her eyes cloud, something almost resembling embarrassment. It was exactly the reaction Heidi had been afraid of. She didn't want Katie to feel that way at all.

"I just want to say, it's good you have the notes to your dad. I'm glad you do. Your dad was the best. He was the greatest husband to me, my best friend, the most wonderful man I've ever met.

But he was also something else quite, quite special. He was your dad. And you were his one and only daughter, the most precious girl in his life. That's a relationship only the two of you can share, whether it was when he was here with us or whether it's here—" she pointed to Katie's heart—"where he'll always be. I know what it's like to miss him, honey. I do. It's good you want to keep him close."

"I wish . . ." Katie hesitated. "I wish we talked about him more."

Heidi drew in a deep breath. "You know, you're right. When it first happened, I wouldn't mention him sometimes because I wasn't sure if it would upset you. I didn't want to see the hurt look on your face. But we need to remember him as much as we can, don't we?"

Katie nodded.

"Are you all right?" Putting her arms around Katie's shoulders, Heidi could feel her nodding. Heidi hoped it was true, hoped she'd said the right things to help Katie. All she knew was that she'd said what was in her heart.

"Do you need some help getting back downstairs?" Heidi asked once they'd broken apart.

"No." Katie pointed to the bed. "I think I'll change scenery for a while."

"Well, I'm going to take that bath I've been talking about." Heidi smiled wanly. "Finally."

By the time Heidi finished the brisk bath of sorts and went into the bedroom to grab her clothes, Katie had already vacated the room. But there was a part of her she'd left behind lying on Heidi's bed.

Wrapping the towel tightly around her, Heidi picked up the papers on top of the stained comforter. In an instant, she recognized they were pages intentionally torn from the notebook. She also immediately recognized the date at the top of the page. How could she forget? It was the same date of Katie's first appointment with the obstetrician, the appointment they never made it to.

Dear Dad,

I always felt so awful that I didn't know my real mom. Some nights when I was little, I'd lie in bed crying, wondering how she could just walk out on me that way. It made me so sad. What did I do that was so awful? I was only a little baby. I always wanted to ask you. Did I cry too much? Wasn't I pretty enough? Did she not like my nose or the way I smiled? I've always wondered.

But today, for the first time, I realize I don't need to think about that person anymore, the mother I never really knew. Because I have a real mom. I've had a real mom for a long time. You may not have picked so good the first time around, Dad— no offense—but the second time, you nailed it. And here I am, screwing it all up.

I don't know why I've made such a mess of things, why I've been so mean to Mom over the years, arguing, doing everything she doesn't like, even when sometimes I didn't like those things either. I've been so dumb. All she ever tried to do is keep me safe and happy.

I don't know. I think when you weren't here anymore, a part of me got so scared. What if Mom left me? What if she walked out too? And instead of being a better kid, I was so awful. Like I just had to keep testing her and pushing her to make sure she really loved me.

And now here I am pregnant. Shocking, isn't it? Me? Katie Martin? Your daughter? Yes, I'm pregnant, and I'm not proud of it. It was only once. But I guess once was enough.

You know what Mom said to me today? You won't believe it— or no, you would believe it. She said, "It's okay, Katie. You made a mistake. We'll figure it out."

No kidding I made a mistake! All you asked me to do is stay true to myself and be good to Mom.

But I haven't done either of those things. I've ruined Mom's life around here. And I've made a mess of my own. I don't know how *to change it, but I want to. I just hope it's not too late. Dad, please forgive me.*

Anyway, thanks for picking her for my mom. I know the reasons why you loved her so much. They're the same reasons I love her too.

Tears blurring her eyes, Heidi gathered her clothes and threw them on as fast as she could.

"Katie," she called out, running down the steps. "Katie."

"Hey." Gabby took her by surprise, carrying a case of bottled water through the front door. "Cassandra got it for us from the store this morning."

Halting at the bottom of the steps, Heidi smoothed her wet hair. "Great. Have you, um, have you seen Katie?"

"Yeah, she hobbled outside when we pulled up in the van. She and Cassandra are talking to Sipho. We're heading back to the hospice in about an hour." Gabby set the case on the kitchen floor.

"She's outside?"

"Yeah, but she's using the crutches. Don't worry."

"I was just checking on her." She tucked her hair behind her ears. "I guess I'll go finish getting ready." Heading up the stairs, she paused on the second step. "Thanks for doing all the work at the hospice today. I'm sorry Katie and I weren't there to help set up."

"It wasn't a problem." Gabby shrugged. "Did Katie rest her foot? Did you two have a good morning together?"

"Yes, it was . . . good. Thanks." She ran up the steps before she blurted out anything more.

34

Gabby wished she could keep her mind on the present—namely, the gathering with the South African women—and not dwell on the past, like all the mistakes she'd made with Tom. And certainly not let her imagination jump to a future dream where Tom forgave her, they adopted a baby, and they all lived happily ever after.

But it was extremely difficult. Even in the company of the gracious, smiling South African women and their adorable children filling the conference room.

To say that her mind and heart were both preoccupied was an understatement. Yet she did all she could to focus on what Jaleela was saying.

"The women are beginning to trust you." A proud, content smile smoothed out the few premature lines on Jaleela's face. "You and your friends have made a good impression to be sure. That is a good beginning for the job we are facing together."

Gabby followed Jaleela's gaze as she surveyed the clusters of women and children around the room. Grinning and socializing, the South African women looked so pleased to be able to feed their children—actually even the children who didn't belong to them—from the food spread out on the table. Mama Penny and Mighty had asked if they might invite some of the child-headed families they knew of too. It tugged on Gabby's heart to see the faces of the older children of those broods. How relieved they looked, the worry of feeding their younger sisters and brothers put at bay if only for a couple of hours.

Meanwhile, Cassandra and Heidi floated through the room chatting and offering cold drinks while Katie had crutched over to a group of younger kids, visiting with them. There did seem to be a sense of ease and comfort with the gathering, exactly what they'd hoped. Some of the beadworkers who looked familiar to Gabby also seemed far less shy than they'd been a few days earlier.

"The women here are amazing, Jaleela. All we're doing is reciprocating the good feelings we received from them the moment we met. They opened their arms to us, prayed for us. Ministered to us. We wanted to give back something in return. That's why we decided to host this get-together today."

"Still, it is kind of you," Jaleela added in her typically gracious way. "And it is kind of you to provide food for their families. I know they will be happy and proud when the day comes they may do that for themselves."

"It *will* be a good day, won't it?" Gabby smiled, forgetting herself for a moment and thinking—hoping—there would be many good days to come for the South African women. And for the children.

Especially for Jaleela's children, whom she'd come to care for and know so well. Tumi just wouldn't be Tumi if he wasn't standing there across the room, grinning, with a cookie in each fist. And Nomvula wouldn't be Nomvula either if she wasn't breaking a cookie in two and giving the larger portion to Lydia's little Daniel, standing at her feet. It reminded Gabby of a situation the other day with her last piece of gum. She'd given it to Nomvula, putting her finger to her lips, urging Nomvula to keep it a secret from the other children since there'd been only one piece. But minutes later, Gabby noticed three other children chewing their hearts out. Nomvula had split the one piece four ways.

There was no doubt where Nomvula had learned such generosity. Gabby was still as awed by Jaleela as when they'd first met. If Gabby had the chance, would she be as good of a mother as her South

African friend? She wasn't sure. But if the possibility ever came to be, with all her heart she would try.

"Are Nomvula and Tumi excited about going on the safari tomorrow?" She turned to their mother. Large beads of sweat had suddenly popped out on Jaleela's face. Blinking hard, she appeared to be having a difficult time focusing.

Gabby's heart pounded. "Jaleela? Are you all right? I'll go get Mama Penny." She started off.

"No, no," Jaleela panted, laying a hand on her forearm to stop her. "I only need to sit."

"I'll get a chair for you."

"No. I will walk to the chairs."

Not wanting to waste time or Jaleela's energy by arguing, Gabby took her friend's frail hand in hers, leading her one slow, short step at a time toward the seats against the far wall. Walking alongside her, Gabby thought back to last week when they'd met. Jaleela's grasp had felt stronger then, hadn't it? So wonderfully warm and welcoming. But now her hand felt more fragile. Had she actually grown thinner in the days since they'd been here?

It would make sense that she had, considering all the extra running around she'd been doing since their arrival. Not to mention, Jaleela had lost a dear friend. Even if her health wasn't compromised, even if she lived in the best of conditions, surely all of that would wear on a person.

"Let me get you a cool drink," she offered after settling Jaleela into one of the folding chairs.

"You do not have to fuss over me."

"I know I don't have to." Gabby smiled. "I want to. And I'm not fussing. I'm caring for you the way you care for others."

No doubt, Jaleela had been overdoing it. Organizing the bead-workers. Preparing a special meal for her American visitors. Spending the night at Mrs. Olomi's with Daniel.

"I think we've been wearing you out since we got here," Gabby told her as soon as she returned to her side with cold water. "I really think it's best if we cancel the safari tomorrow. You need to rest. Your health is too important."

Jaleela took small sips of the cool drink. "But it is a tradition. It is a vital part of the mission trip."

"We have traditions in our culture too," Gabby assured her. "Like Thanksgiving, for instance. But things happen. People get sick. Sometimes our plans just don't go as expected." She fanned Jaleela's face with her hand. "Are you cooling down any?"

"But we must go!" Jaleela protested, diverting the question. "You have seen the sickness of our country; you must also see the beauty of it. That is why the safari is a tradition for the mission people. All Africans are proud of our land and the beautiful animals God has placed here. Many, like us, have never seen such things outside the village. We have only been told about them. It is important to me to go also. It will be a journey to cherish."

"It would be an adventure, I'm sure. But again, if you're not feeling well, it just isn't worth it." Even the ride could get uncomfortable, Gabby thought but didn't mention out loud. The ride to Pilanesberg was close to an hour long.

"But I have already told Nomvula and Tumi. Last night I shared the news, and I thought they would never sleep." Jaleela smiled for the first time since she'd sat down. "I will be fine tomorrow, and we will go on safari. I do not want to miss this chance with my children. Or with my new American friends. The chance may never come again."

Gabby bent over, hugging Jaleela's shoulders in reply. There was no sense debating the issue with her, she decided. They would just see what tomorrow would bring.

Since Heidi would be chauffeuring them to Pilanesberg instead of Sipho, it had already been planned that Jaleela and the kids would spend the night at the compound with them. That would make for less driving for Heidi the next day. It would also make it easy to check on Jaleela's health, make sure she was feeling well before they took off.

In the meantime, what harm was there in letting Jaleela talk about the safari? The more she did, the more it seemed to lighten her spirits anyway.

"And did you know?" Jaleela filled her in. "Mama Penny will not be coming with us. She has work to do. She will send Mighty in her place. She will be telling her so before Mighty leaves here tonight."

"Oh, that would be so wonderful for Mighty and for us. She's such a sweet girl. I'm glad she has the chance to go," she gushed.

But her gushing was short-lived when reality set in. Leaving for the safari in Pilanesberg tomorrow meant they were that much closer to the end of the trip. Once they got back from safari, they'd have a day with the beadworkers again, purchasing product, and then the following day, they would be going back to the United States. Flying home.

Home.

Her stomach tightened involuntarily. Not because she didn't want to go there. But because she'd never given much thought to what she'd be coming home to when she'd left the way she did. When she simply ran away.

Not until now, anyway.

By the time Lindiwee came up to chat with Jaleela about a necklace she was designing, Jaleela's breathing seemed back to normal, the clamminess gone from her hands. Relieved about that—but not the other issue plaguing her mind—Gabby told her she'd be back to check on her and excused herself, heading straight for the lobby of the hospice.

She hoped she hadn't been driving Mighty crazy all day, running back and forth from the conference room to the front desk every fifteen minutes or so, checking to see if she had an e-mail from Tom. But she couldn't help it. She had to make the trip down the hallway once again. She had to look. She had to know. The words from Tom could set things right between them, maybe even back to the way their relationship used to be. Or at least better—far better—than the way she left it.

Gabby wiped the conference table with a damp cloth, sighing in the hushed room. The hospice's computer had been down earlier in the afternoon when she'd checked for an e-mail from Tom. But the last time she'd made her way to Mighty's area, the system was up and running again. And still no response from her husband.

"The get-together was a smashing success—don't you think?" Crouched over a splash of spilled juice on the floor, Cassandra sounded unusually cheery, especially given the fact she was cleaning up someone else's mess.

"Uh-huh, really good." Gabby let go of her cloth, cupping her hand around one of the flickering vanilla-scented candles. With a slight puff, she blew it out.

"Everyone loved the food. The women couldn't have been more thankful."

"Yeah, I know."

Cassandra stood up, holding a white rag now turned strawberry pink in one hand. She swiped her brow with the other. "I'm so glad we thought of this reception. It was perfect."

Gabby blew at the second candle. "Mmm-hmm."

"And didn't Daniel look nice, all cleaned up? Mrs. Olomi says she had clothes that another boy grew out of. They fit him perfectly."

"He's a cutie, all right," Gabby agreed.

"The one woman—what's her name? Nellie?" Cassandra disposed of the rag and began folding up a few of the extra chairs, gabbing all the while. "I thought she would break my hand off, squeezing so tightly, thanking us for the food." She leaned another chair against the wall. "I'm glad Sipho could shuttle them to their homes. I didn't know how they'd ever manage to carry the groceries that far."

"Yeah. Sipho's great, for sure." Picking up the damp cloth again, Gabby rubbed at a sticky spot on the table.

"Okay." Cassandra pulled over a folding chair. It squeaked as she sat down and crossed her arms over her satiny sleeveless gold top. "What's going on?"

Gabby turned from the table, the rag in midair. "What?"

"You know what I'm saying. Are you upset with Heidi for leaving so early and not being here to help us clean up?"

It was true Heidi and Katie had left while the get-together was in full swing. Sipho had gladly run them out to the pastor's compound. Later, once the party was over, he'd made another trip out there with Jaleela and the kids. But why Cassandra thought that would bother her, she couldn't imagine.

"Are you serious?" Gabby shook her head. "No. Nothing like that."

"Then what? I may be dumb, but I'm not blind. You seemed totally preoccupied through this whole event. And I don't know what's going on with Heidi. Or with her and Katie. She was gracious to the women, mind you, but with a pinched expression the entire time. She wasn't her usual, smiley self."

"You know, you're right. Now that you mention it, Heidi did look stressed." At the thought, Gabby pulled over a chair and sank down into it. "They said they were leaving early because of Katie's ankle. But . . ."

"I'm not sure that's all it was." Cassandra leaned forward. "Maybe after the exhilaration the other day, there's a realization. Maybe she's trying to figure out what to do about the baby now. Like she said, it's not as if she's had a lot of time to think about it." She brushed a clump of lint from her navy slacks. "So, are you going to talk about it or not? whatever it is that's bugging you? Because our five-minute break is half-over already."

She let go of a deep sigh. "It's just . . . I've been trying to e-mail Tom."

"And?"

Gabby glanced down at her hands, mostly at her silver wedding band. "We, um, we weren't on the best of terms when I left for this trip."

"Ha! No kidding."

"What do you mean, 'no kidding'?"

"Oh, dear girl." Cassandra waved her hands in front of her like she was trying to clear the air of some bad odor. "When you first got here, did you ever look miserable! And so out of it. Like you were in dire need of a makeover."

Good old, frank Cassandra. Gabby might've laughed if she wasn't so caught up in her anguish over Tom. "Thanks, friend."

"Well, now I know what that was all about," she said discreetly for a change, and Gabby knew she was referring to the miscarriage. "But it was about your husband too, huh?"

"Oh, I was so awful to him." She shook her head, recalling the quarrels, regretting so many things she'd said. "I was in hell, and even though I knew he was too, I only thought about myself, I'm embarrassed to say."

"Hey, it's me you're talking to. The Wicked Witch of the Midwest. Trust me, I can relate. We women can be that way."

"I sent him an e-mail, trying to apologize. But I haven't heard anything from him. That's probably not a good sign."

"Have you thought about calling him?"

Gabby remembered trying to reach him the other day on the phone about his aunt. She'd wanted to hear his voice so badly but then felt almost relieved when he wasn't there. It seemed easier to be rejected by the man she loved over the Internet than over the phone. Besides, she thought she was being kind not catching him off guard that way. "I didn't want to put him on the spot. I thought an e-mail would be better."

"If that's truly what you think, then be patient. It sounds like he was patient with you."

Cassandra's sage advice caught her by surprise. She blinked. "I-I think you're right."

"Good." Popping up out of the chair, Cassandra folded it and placed it with the others. Then she began stacking the leftover juice boxes. "You know . . ." She paused a beat. "I really can't believe this."

Gabby stood up too, then pulled over the trash can and tossed a few used napkins inside. "All the juice that's left? I wouldn't worry. It'll get used eventually."

"No. I can't believe me. Hosting parties. Giving advice on friendship, emotional issues, relationships. It's like I don't even know myself anymore."

For the first time that day, Gabby laughed. "Is that a bad thing?"

Cassandra shrugged. "I'm not sure. When I figure it out, I'll let you know."

35

Ever since she'd read Katie's note to her dad this morning, Heidi had been picturing all day how she was going to talk to Katie. How after Sipho dropped them off early from the hospice party, she'd get Katie situated on the couch with her foot elevated once again. They'd have some private time before Cassandra and Gabby got back. And since the beautiful tea set Dominic had brought by was still here, she would make some tea for them. They would talk, teacups in hand, woman to woman, mom to daughter in a quiet, ceremonious way, a way that they'd remember twenty years from now.

But when the van door opened, depositing the two of them in front of the place they'd been calling home for the past week, and Heidi unlocked the front door and turned on the fluorescent overhead light, she couldn't get Katie settled on the old sofa fast enough before her emotions spilled out.

"First of all, you need to know something," she said, the words tumbling out. "You have not ruined my life, okay? You are my life. No matter what, you're the best part of my life. Do you understand that?"

Katie blinked, looking surprised by her outburst. Heidi couldn't blame her. She was a bit surprised at herself. Who knew spending an afternoon at the hospice surrounded by the South African women and their children would move her so much? But it had.

Being in their company, watching some of the mothers tend to

279

their children weak with AIDS, seeing other women happy to stoop down and feed the children had made Heidi feel even more emotional than usual. The women had reminded her that all children needed to be loved and honored and guided. That knowledge was so powerful that her well of emotions kept rising and rising.

They all wanted the same thing as Heidi did, didn't they? No matter how difficult the conditions, no matter where in the world. Mothers just wanted to nourish their children body and soul, keep them safe, give them hope.

"Do you understand?" she repeated.

Katie's eyes started to fill, and it was a moment before she squeaked, "Yes."

"And another thing, I meant what I said earlier. I'm glad you keep your dad in your heart. I'm glad you have your journal. But don't you ever forget I'm here for you. How many ways do I have to say it? No matter what, I'll always be here for you. Do you understand that too?"

Katie nodded, a tear sliding down her cheek.

Heidi reached over, wiping it away. "Okay, then." She let out a deep, calming breath. "Do you want some tea now? Because there's something else we need to talk about."

Katie sniffed. "Could I have water instead?" she asked timidly.

"Of course." After grabbing two bottled waters from the case in the kitchen, Heidi sat down on the floor next to the couch. There was much to talk about, but it all seemed so important that she wasn't quite sure how to start. "Have you been cramping at all?" She uncapped her bottled water, taking a long drink.

"No, I've been fine."

"That's good."

"I know," Katie answered between sips.

"It's been a crazy couple of days. I'd never seen an ultrasound before. It was incredible, wasn't it?"

Katie's face lit up some. "Really awesome."

In the moment Heidi had seen the fluttering of that little heart, an answer had been written on her own heart. Where the baby was concerned, she knew what she was meant to do. "Do you honestly think Mark's mom doesn't want anything to do with the baby?"

Katie's eyes grew wide. She set her water bottle on the floor. "What Mark said is true."

"Okay. Well, I've been thinking about it a lot, about what's going to happen to the baby. And I'm sure it's been on your mind nonstop too." She looked her daughter in the eye.

Katie nodded solemnly.

"I think a decision would help us both. Then mentally and mostly emotionally we can prepare ourselves for what's ahead. The months will fly; they'll be here and gone before we know it. And the way I see it, we have only two choices: do we raise the baby ourselves or put the baby up for adoption? Have you thought about it in those terms at all?"

"Some." Katie's head bobbed. "And I . . . well, I don't think adoption is bad. I mean, in a way you adopted me, and it was way better than anything I had from my birth mom. But . . ."

Heidi didn't have to guess what the *but* was for, not after reading the note earlier. She'd never imagined Katie was still stinging from the indifference of her mom after all those years, still feeling less than worthy because of it. But then why wouldn't she be? It wasn't that her mom was too young. Or not financially sound. Or didn't have a husband to help her raise a child. No, she simply didn't want her. The thought of how that must've hurt Katie pained Heidi deeply too.

Capping her water and setting it aside, she asked, "What would you think about keeping the baby?"

Katie sat straight up. "You would let me do that? You would do that for me?"

"No, I would do that for all of us." Heidi smiled at Katie's astonished expression. "I realize this isn't perfect timing, and I'm guessing someday when the time is right, you'll have more children. But I have to admit, after seeing the ultrasound, in my heart nothing else feels right. Not only that . . ." She paused, remembering the anguish from days before and how hard she prayed. "Now I know what it feels like to almost lose this baby. I don't know if I could stand the thought of losing the baby for good, even if it was to a deserving couple."

Katie reached down, hugging her. Heidi soaked it up. So uninhibited and honest, the hug felt like one from a much younger Katie. "I can't believe you're saying that. It's like I'm scared to have the baby. The physical part. But I don't want to give it up either. I didn't want to say that. I didn't want to burden you."

"You have to stop doing that. You have to start talking to me and being honest with me."

"If you want me to be honest . . ." Katie tilted her head, her expression suddenly turning from joyous to pensive. "I want to keep the baby, but the problem is, I don't know how good of a mom I would be. I mean, at this age. There's still so much I don't know."

Heidi laid a hand on her arm. "I'm not asking you to raise the baby alone, honey. I want to help."

Heidi didn't think she'd ever forget how Katie looked at her in that moment. Appreciation and realization shone in her glistening eyes. She looked as if she'd glimpsed the meaning of love with a woman's heart and not as a child any longer.

"I can't believe how lucky I am," she said softly. "The kids here . . . It's so hard for them. The orphans, Mighty . . ." She shook her head sadly. "And then me. I've been so spoiled."

"Trust me—you're not alone in those feelings."

"I can get a job after school until the baby's born. I can save some money, and after graduation next spring maybe I can take some classes at the community college. Besides taking care of the baby, I mean." Her hands rested protectively on her still-mostly-flat stomach. "I need to plan for the future."

"I think you have a good sense of yourself now, my darling daughter. Step by step, it will all get figured out. And again, I'll be there to help."

"What about your work?" Katie chewed her lip. "And having time to do what you want to do? It's not going to be easy helping to raise a baby."

"No, it's not. But giving the baby away wouldn't be easy either. The baby's already a part of our family. We'll just have to make it work together."

"People will gossip about us—you know they will."

"You mean like they already are?" Heidi rolled her eyes. "Whatev'."

"'Whatev'?" Katie giggled. "Mom, really . . ."

"Yeah." Heidi laughed. "They'll be saying, 'Those Martin women, have they lost their minds? They're a different breed.'"

"And we'll be saying, 'Good!'" Katie reached down to high-five her.

"Okay, then," Heidi said with some finality as if they'd just signed a contract. "It's decided. We're going to keep the baby."

Katie's exuberant smile told her they'd made the right decision. The light feeling inside her heart said the same thing too.

36

After she and Cassandra finished cleaning up, Gabby checked for an e-mail from Tom one final time, only to be disappointed once again. Then she and Cassandra said good-bye to the night nurse and rode along in companionable silence as Sipho shuttled them through the dark streets of Mamelodi back to the compound.

She wondered what thoughts filled Cassandra's head along the way. Almost all of Gabby's thoughts were about Tom. So much so that once they'd arrived at the pastor's place, she slid out of the van, suddenly feeling a need to be alone. "I'm going to stay out here for a little while." She pointed to a rise of grass at the edge of the courtyard.

"Whatever you want to do." Cassandra slung her camera bag over her shoulder, a look Gabby had grown accustomed to. Then she tilted her head, her gaze sympathetic, a look Gabby was just starting to get used to. An expression she wouldn't have thought could possibly come from Cassandra when they first met. "Isn't this the part where if you were me, you'd be saying, 'Have faith'?"

The truth of her words caused Gabby to smile weakly. "I know. I just need a minute."

Cassandra nodded as if she understood before heading inside.

Meanwhile, Gabby made her way across the common area and settled onto the grass. Hugging her knees to her chest, she gazed at the comforting sheen of white lighting up the darkness. Like thousands of giant fireflies flung into the skies, far more stars than she'd seen in a long time.

In a very long time.

Nearly ten years ago, when she and Tom had moved into their neighborhood, they had one of the first homes built in the subdivision. How quiet and calming it was, especially moving in the dead of winter, without even songbirds to break the morning silence or owls to herald the night. And how dark and isolated too. There were no porch lights from nearby homes. No streetlights to shine protectively on their property. There were only the two of them and a few displaced deer traipsing through the backyard from time to time.

Only the two of them and so many stars!

Standing on their deck in the crisp cold, Gabby had felt like they were queen and king of the universe at times, looking at the splashes of white dotting the broad, black sky.

It hadn't been just the stars that moved her to such over-the-top contentment. It was Tom, coming up behind her. Wrapping his arms around her. Swaying to music there were no notes for, unless you counted the beating of her heart.

Yes, they'd been to hell and back since then. And she'd been hurt, anesthetized by pain, numb for such a long while. But even with all of that, Gabby could still feel his arms around her as she leaned back against him on their deck those wintry nights. The fresh scent of his sandalwood cologne teasing her senses. His warm lips nuzzled into the crook of her neck.

If Tom looked up in a sky full of stars, would he remember? He'd feel it too, wouldn't he?

Didn't that count for something? Didn't that mean they were supposed to be together?

Staring at the sky, she searched the vastness there, somehow hoping to find the answer to her so-called life on earth. But everything was still and quiet. There seemed to be nothing for her to take away from the night.

Dismayed, she started to get up when Hazard's bark shattered the silence. She startled until she realized what had unsettled him— Nomvula and Tumi racing toward her.

They plopped down on the ground on either side of her with all the easy, graceful aplomb of youth, and she could feel the warmth of their skin on her arms as they leaned against her.

"Mama said we could come outside to be with you." Nomvula puffed out the words as she caught her breath.

"You are sitting in the dark?" Tumi asked. "Why?"

His question caught her off-balance, almost making her laugh out loud. It sounded so simplistic and yet somewhat profound at the same time. Why was she sitting here? She'd agreed with Cassandra she needed to be patient. She agreed she needed to believe. And yet here she was, questioning everything over and over again.

"I was wishing on stars," she said to them because in a way it was almost true.

Nomvula laid her head on Gabby's shoulder. "How do you wish on a star?"

"It's easy." *Easy like being with Jaleela's children,* she thought. With Nomvula and Tumi at her sides, she didn't feel like she was sitting in the dark anymore. No, her heart had felt lighter the moment she'd set eyes on them running toward her. "First, you pick out a star you want to wish on." She pointed up to the sky. "I see one I want. Do you guys see a star too?"

Mimicking her, they both used their index fingers to point to the heavens. Nomvula settled on a star right away.

But Tumi kept jabbing into the air. "I want that one. No that one. No—"

Gabby chuckled. "We don't have all night."

"We do not?" He looked at her, puzzled.

"Tumi, pick a star. Please!" Nomvula took her finger off her star, shaking it at him instead.

"All right!" He pointed to a star close to Gabby's. "That one! That is my star."

"Now that we've got our stars, think of a wish you want to make," Gabby told them in a hushed voice. "After you think of a wish, we're going to say, 'Star light, star bright, the first star I see tonight, I wish I may, I wish I might have the wish I wish tonight.'"

The kids studied her, mesmerized.

"But say your wish in your mind. To yourself. Don't say it out loud or it may not come true," Gabby warned. "Okay?"

They both nodded.

"Ready? Look at your stars and say the words with me. 'Star light, star bright . . .'"

She had to smile at how deliberate they were, saying the words clearly, seriously, their eyes riveted on their special star in the white sea above their heads.

"'I wish I may, I wish I might,'" they ended in a singsong rhythm, "'have the wish I wish tonight.'"

Just as she and Nomvula closed their eyes to make their wish, Tumi shouted, "I wish Gabby would read a story to us."

"You were not to say your wish out loud," Nomvula squawked. "Now it will not come true."

He grabbed Gabby's forearm, his voice sorrowful. "You will not read a story to us?"

Putting her arms around both of them, Gabby felt laughter bubbling up inside her. "You didn't have to use a wish for that. You could've just asked me. Of course, I would love to read a story to both of you."

Tumi broke free from her embrace. "Then come. We have had enough of the dark. Let's not sit in it anymore." He tugged on one hand and Nomvula on the other, and she let them think they were pulling her up all on their own.

Tumi's words kept coming back to her as she brushed the loose grass from her capris. What good advice, she thought. The boy was a regular little philosopher, and he didn't even know it.

37

"Tumi, you must stop." Jaleela sat on the other side of the picnic table, shaking her head as her son crawled into Gabby's lap. "You are behaving like a monkey."

Even in her frustration, Jaleela looked so pretty, Gabby thought. Sitting there between Cassandra and the younger Mighty, Jaleela even appeared rejuvenated, as if the attack she'd had at the party had never happened, as if the night of rest had been enough to fortify her for the trip to Pilanesberg. The chartreuse scarf curled around her head should've clashed with her mint green top and blue printed skirt, yet it didn't seem to. Around her wrist dangled the blue beaded bracelet Nomvula had given her from the Christmas box. Evidently she'd taken it down from the cross on her wall, wearing it for the special occasion.

And though she scolded her youngest child, Gabby knew how much Jaleela adored him. The twinkle in her brown eyes said so.

"He's fine," Gabby told her as Tumi wriggled. "All boys this age act like monkeys."

"It's true," Heidi said, sitting right by Gabby's side. "My first-grade boys are the same way."

"Even some older boys are too," Katie added.

Cassandra rolled her eyes. "Not to mention the man-size monkeys I've run into."

"You mean apes?" Heidi laughed.

"Oh, do not tell me that. Please. I will not want to come to America any longer," Mighty said, making everyone laugh.

Everyone chuckled again when Tumi smiled. While the women had been talking, he'd been sucking on a lemon from Gabby's plate. When he parted his teeth, nothing but the yellow peel showed. Nomvula leaned into Gabby, giggling behind both hands at her brother's silliness.

"Monkeys are not allowed in restaurants." Jaleela shook her finger at her son. "Soon they will throw you out."

Gabby doubted if any of the other diners around them cared or even noticed. Halfway to their destination, bellies growling and ready for food, they'd stopped at a casual outdoor restaurant right off the main road.

Picnic tables dotted the grassy ground in between the trees. Brightly colored flags hung overhead, strung high from tree branch to tree branch. Thatched grass umbrellas shaded some of the smaller tables made just for two. The restaurant's menu hadn't been fancy either. Their group had filled up on something that resembled a hamburger plus side dishes of fresh fruit.

Beside the restaurant area was a rather large souvenir shop, another attraction for anyone who cared to pull off the road and take a break from their travels.

"The food was very good. Thank you," Mighty remarked.

"Yes," Jaleela said. "Heidi, thank you for driving the large van all this way."

"It was really nice of you to take Sipho's place," Gabby added, "since he had other work obligations."

"I'm used to driving vans from the whole soccer mom thing when Katie was younger. Although none of those vans were quite the size of this one, were they, Katie?" Heidi leaned forward to smile at her daughter. "I don't mind, though, as long as you all keep navigating for me and deciphering some of the road signs."

"Oh, I love the signs here," Katie chirped. "They're made like our road signs, and some are even boring like ours with the speed limit and stuff. But others are so funny." Amusement flickered in her eyes. "My favorite was the one that said dung beetles have the right of way—whatever a dung beetle is."

"What about the one with cows?" Cassandra interjected. "What did it say? Something like 'Cow and Pedestrian Crossing—No Fences.'"

"Not everything on our roads is funny. They can be dangerous." Mighty was the only one not so amused by it all, Gabby noticed. "Mama Penny warned me so."

"You mean like those boys collecting donations for their so-called traveling cricket team? I don't know. I thought they looked fairly harmless," Heidi said. "At least they were being creative about asking for money."

"And didn't a sign say 'Ostrich Crossing'?" Katie asked. "I would love to see that. I'd jump right out of the van and pet them."

As the lively conversation swirled around the table, Gabby tried not to think about Mighty shaking her head when they picked her up at the hospice. No one knew what Mighty meant by the gesture except for Gabby. No, there hadn't been word from Tom. The realization of what that could mean pulled at her heart. Even so, hard as it was, she didn't want to appear sullen. She didn't want to ruin the trip for the others. Especially for Nomvula, giggling beside her, and Tumi, sliding off and on her lap. She didn't want to be sulking like she had been the first time she met Nomvula, preoccupied with herself and her problems.

None of them had ever been on safari before. It wouldn't be right to put a damper on their good time. Hadn't Jaleela mentioned they'd never been beyond the dreariness of their village before? Who knew if they'd ever be again?

Still, it wasn't easy. Her thoughts strayed, out of her control, wandering from the present to the past and all the way into wishes for the future.

"So who wants to do some souvenir shopping?" Heidi laid her napkin over her plate. "Any takers?"

"Believe it or not, I've already eyed some art in a shop at the airport," Cassandra said. "But I'm content to sit here. By all means take your time."

"Gabby, can you go with Mom? I don't feel like hobbling around. Besides, you can help her pick out something special for me . . . and for the baby." Katie grinned. "Can I tell them?" She glanced down the picnic bench at Heidi, who smiled and nodded her consent.

"I hope you'll be glad to know, we're not giving up the baby," Katie announced, beaming. "Mom and I decided last night. We're going to keep the baby." She hugged her tummy, her smile off-the-charts happy.

"That is wonderful news!" Jaleela squealed. "I am most excited for you."

Mighty clapped in approval. "It will be a beautiful baby; I am sure!"

"And if you're ever in need of a surrogate aunt, I might know of someone. Someone incredible," Cassandra quipped. "Of course, I don't do diapers. Or that burping business. Actually, come to think of it, I've never babysat a child before. But for your baby, little Katie, I might give it a whirl." She smiled, looking suddenly moved, as if she might shed a tear or two. "With proper advance notice, of course. I *am* a busy woman, you know."

Katie laughed and turned to Gabby. "I'll bet you're already a really great aunt. Think you can add one more niece or nephew to your list?"

Heat flushed Gabby's cheeks as the familiar pangs of jealousy started to rear once again. Oh, how she didn't want to give in to the temptation to feel sorry for herself. Or to feel anger toward Heidi or Katie. This fall they'd be reveling in the joy of a newborn child. Just the way she and Tom had been expecting to be. But it wasn't Heidi and Katie's fault that she'd lost her baby. Or that perhaps she'd lost Tom in all the hurt too.

Dear Lord, I need Your help to keep a kind heart, she prayed.

"I think—" she swallowed hard, making stabs at a slight smile—
"I can manage that."

Katie didn't seem to notice her stammering one bit. "Oh, Gabby,"
she gushed, reaching over Tumi's head to hug Gabby around the neck.
"Thank you."

"So, Gabby." Heidi slipped her purse strap over her shoulder.
"Are you ready? You really don't mind cruising the souvenir shop
with me?"

All eyes around the table were on her as she nodded. But she
didn't get up right away. Not until she hugged Tumi tighter, gathering
strength and comfort from the warm joy of him.

"It's so much to look at." Heidi scanned the rows of African
mementos that stretched half the length of a football field.

Gabby had to admit she was overwhelmed as well by the vast
amount of hand-carved bowls and masks, jade elephants, batik wall
hangings, ceramic mugs, beaded jewelry, straw purses, and rhinoc-
eros belts and shoes. The shelves of souvenirs went on and on, with
displays in every direction.

But she wasn't as concerned about the African items as much as
she was keeping her emotions in check, fearing the envy could still
show its ugly self at any moment if she didn't maintain total self-
control. Meandering up and down the aisles, away from Heidi, she
attempted to keep some distance between them. But Heidi kept lighting right next to her.

"Who are you buying souvenirs for?" Heidi asked.

"Mostly my brothers' kids and my parents." And for Tom, though
she didn't even want to think about him right now. "How about you?"

"I'd like to find something for my classroom. I'm not sure what that
will be yet." Heidi tapped her lip thoughtfully. "And then I need to get
something for Jeff's parents."

"Do they live in Columbus?"

"No. They're not too far away, though. Just south of Chicago."
She pointed to a pair of mugs with an abstract design. "These are

nice—don't you think? They're big coffee drinkers. Or, I don't know . . ." Picking up a baby rattle from the shelf below, she gave it a halfhearted shake. "Think this would be a good way to tell them the big news?"

"You haven't said anything yet?"

Heidi shook her head, a blonde strand of hair falling across her cheek. "At first I thought about calling them. But it's not like we talk that often, so it seemed awkward." She placed the rattle back on the shelf. "And then I figured Katie and I would drive there. But that hasn't happened yet either. I guess I hate putting Katie through it. Especially since I'm not sure how they're going to react."

As they strolled down the aisle side by side, Heidi seemed to be looking at the floor more than the items for sale. "She's already been through a lot. Obviously it hasn't been easy on her. Not that I'm sanctioning what happened. But trust me, even in this day and age, people still like to gossip about a pregnant teenager and a baby out of wedlock."

Gabby hugged her purse to her side. "Oh, I'm sure." Sometimes she felt like people were pointing at her, talking about her behind her back, calling her "the poor woman who can't stay pregnant." She didn't think for one minute that it was all in her head.

"Plus—" Heidi stopped to look at a row of carved tribal masks— "I wasn't quite sure what to tell his parents. But now I know." She looked at Gabby. "Do you think it's awful, though?"

Laying aside a wooden mask she'd been staring at without really seeing, Gabby narrowed her eyes. "How is it awful?"

"That I wasn't sure? That I was so ready to make Katie give the baby away? Frankly, in my mind that was my first inclination, you know. A baby seemed so messy and overwhelming." She took in a deep breath. "I hate to admit it, but mostly it was too embarrassing."

"You probably needed some time to adjust to the idea."

"Or maybe adjust my thinking. I'm ashamed to say, I wasn't thinking about the baby at all. I was too concerned with what people at my school would think. What my neighbors—who I don't even know—would think. It was all about them and all about me. Me, with my liberal education. Me, who tells my daughter to be her own person. And then when she is, and it isn't exactly the way I think she should be, I'm upset with her." Noticeably exasperated, Heidi threw her arms in the air. "When did I get so small-minded? so hypocritical? I've hated how people have judged Katie for the mistake she made. But then what did I do? I turned around and did pretty much the same thing with her boyfriend."

Moved by Heidi's admission, Gabby reached out to touch her arm. She wasn't about to condemn Heidi for being so honest with her. After all, Heidi had been kind enough not to pass judgment on her when she'd shared her feelings. "Everyone gets caught up in that to some degree, right?"

"Not Jaleela." Heidi shook her finger kindly at Gabby. "Oh no. She's past all that. She's ready to embark on her dream. She's ready to help others at her own expense. She's willing to tell the entire world that she has AIDS. And here I am, anxious about a few gossipy women I don't even know? I came here thinking the trip would straighten Katie out. I'm not sure she was the one who needed it."

"Actually, I think we all needed it." Gabby knew by the way Heidi was looking at her that she expected Gabby to elaborate. But instead, as hard as it was to do, Gabby couldn't deny the feelings pressing on her heart. "I really think this baby—this new extension of your family—is going to be a blessing for you and Katie. Maybe even for Jeff's parents too. It's good you decided to keep it for your own," she said sincerely, though just a twinge of self-pity still wanted to pluck at her heart as she spoke the words.

"Thanks. I'm sure Katie's being pregnant can't have been that easy for you. You'd be a perfect mother, and here we are bumbling through the situation. It's been on my mind to tell you I appreciate how kind you've been."

"You don't have to . . ." She held up her hand, feeling guilty that she, too, was a work in progress. Still striving. That her innermost feelings didn't always merit such praise.

"I'm so glad we have the bead project to work on together. Glad you'll still be in our lives when the baby comes." Heidi took a Kleenex from her purse and dotted her eyes. "Katie adores you. I think she's already learned a lot from you."

Gabby couldn't imagine what. "I've learned a lot from her too." She paused, surveying the aisle they found themselves standing in. "So, back to the coffee mugs?"

Heidi nodded. "I'm thinking that's a safe choice."

"I think I'll grab two for my parents. They're both major coffee drinkers too."

As Gabby sauntered with Heidi back to the front of the store, she couldn't keep her thoughts from returning to Tom. She'd agonized over her e-mail to him, wanting so much to make it just right. But in the end, it really hadn't been accurate after all.

No. She had written to him that things had changed. But that wasn't quite true. Things hadn't changed—she had.

Hopefully Tom still had loving feelings toward her and she'd have the chance to show him all the ways she could now love too.

38

"Now this is more like it!" Cassandra winked at Jaleela as they crossed the threshold of their one-bedroom town house at the national park's resort. They'd already parted ways with the rest of the gang for the night and wouldn't be meeting up with them until 6 a.m. tomorrow for the safari.

As Gabby had told them weeks earlier, the cost of the safari adventure was included in the price of the trip for the missiongoers, and expenses for Jaleela and her children had been donated from the church's mission fund.

Yet Cassandra would've gladly paid that money herself, if she'd had to, just to see the look of amazement on Jaleela's face.

"Do they think we are queens?" Jaleela squealed, her gaze darting around the contemporary, furnished town house.

Straightening her shoulders, the South African woman cocked her brows, put on an imperious face, and strode in processionlike strides across the foyer and the kitchen area, into the sitting room adjacent to the bedroom, just like she was entering her very own castle.

Cassandra stood by and laughed, feeling unusually warmed and moved by the sight. She remembered the first time she had gotten a reporting assignment—one where she'd actually gone on location and the hotel room had been beyond luxurious. Oh, how good it had felt to sink into the bed, pull the downy comforter over her. In her desolate home life in Indiana, she'd never known anything so wonderful existed.

"Do you think the others have such a place? a place as nice as this?" Jaleela spun around.

"Larger, I'm sure," Cassandra told her, tugging her small suitcase upright and laying Jaleela's plastic bag on top. "Since there are six of them, their town house probably has three bedrooms."

Jaleela chuckled. "They will need the space with that monkey of mine."

"If you think you'll miss your kids, I understand. Maybe Mighty will switch places with you."

"No." Jaleela waved her hand. "Mama Heidi brought a game for them to play. They have far more energy than I. I know my children will come of no harm with the women. Me? I am tired from the trip. I am happy to rest."

Jaleela did seem to be breathing unusually heavily, Cassandra noted, from the short strut she'd made across the floor. The woman's mind, however, in contrast to her body, was still going a mile a minute. Her smile turned to an instant frown. "I hope Gabby will not mind my Nomvula's hugging and my Tumi climbing all over her."

"I don't think she'll mind." Cassandra opened her mouth again to tell Jaleela that Gabby couldn't have babies. But she stopped before she got started. Even though she was new to this friend thing, she didn't think good friends betrayed confidences. That, at least, was something she'd try to adhere to, even if it was going to be a struggle.

Instead, she made her way to the bathroom and flung open the door. A toffee-colored, tiled shower greeted her eyes like an oasis in the desert. "Oh, Jaleela, if you have the strength, you really need to come look. There's a shower. A real shower." Cassandra stepped in and turned the knobs. "With hot water too. It feels like heaven."

It took a moment, but Jaleela made her way. When she peeked into the bathroom, her amusement came out in a raspy chuckle. "God is good, isn't He?"

"And so is hot water. Do you want to go first?"

"Oh no. I am going to rest for a minute. You go ahead."

Cassandra didn't need any more of a push than that. Gathering her nightclothes and toiletry case, she made her way to the bathroom again, eagerly stepping out of her clothes and into the welcome, soothing heat of the shower. There was nothing on earth like a hot shower. Nothing.

When she came out in her silk pajamas and robe, she went into the bedroom to find Jaleela resting on her knees in front of her twin bed. Her hands and head pointed heavenward.

The South African woman struck quite a picture, the greens and blues of her outfit and headscarf against the tans and purples of the bedspread and wall hangings. With her hands together in prayer, the blue beaded bracelet had slid halfway down her forearm, emphasizing her thinness. She was so intent in her communion with her God, she didn't hear Cassandra enter the room.

Throughout the trip, Cassandra had gone hot and cold filming and snapping photos. She hadn't meant to, but some days there'd been so many other things to attend to, like Katie's baby drama or shopping for the party, that she hadn't gotten her camera out once. She told herself she'd remember everything she'd seen, but she knew that wasn't true.

Seeing Jaleela posed this way—being able to glimpse the very essence of the woman—felt too special not to record. It wasn't something she dared to leave up to memory alone.

Cassandra slipped her compact digital camera from her purse and stood as far to the right as she could, trying to capture the image of the woman in supplication, so engrossed she was oblivious to everything around her. Hoping there was enough light in the room so she wouldn't disturb Jaleela, Cassandra snapped the picture.

But the flash went off, lighting the room for a moment. Jaleela opened her eyes and turned to her.

"Please forgive me for that," Cassandra said. "You looked so intense yet so peaceful. I couldn't resist taking a picture of you."

"It is all right." Jaleela smiled, seeming to understand, even if she didn't. "May I see?"

Cassandra turned on the nightstand lamp and sat down on Jaleela's bed with her, placing the camera in her hands. "All you do is push this button. It lets you go back to see the pictures that have been taken. See, there you are."

Jaleela grinned at the photo of herself praying. "Oh, my. I do look so very serious."

"Yes, in that picture you do. But I have many others of you. You can see them all if you push the button."

"I push like this?" Jaleela pressed gently.

"That's all there is to it."

"Oh, there is Nomvula and Tumi. I am smiling with them. Though I do not remember you taking this picture."

"That's the trick sometimes," Cassandra explained. "To get candid shots."

Jaleela's brow furrowed. "Candid?"

"Pictures that are not posed. That are true. That show something happening in the moment."

"Oh." Jaleela kept pushing the button, grinning every now and then. Until finally she came to a picture and looked at Cassandra quizzically. "She did not come with you on the trip. Is she a relative? a friend?"

Puzzled, Cassandra took the camera from Jaleela to look closer. Evidently Jaleela had pushed the button beyond the South Africa pictures to the part of the disc that held photos from past events. Like Jack Hanna's Fall Fest that she had covered for the news the previous September.

Somehow, Trudi Miles had gotten word about the festival and had come to Columbus with her husband and kids in tow. Cassandra's so-called best friend tracked her down, buddying up to her all day. At one point she'd asked Cassandra if she had a camera, and Cassandra couldn't have been happier, offering hers to Trudi readily, thinking it might keep the woman busy for a while, taking photos of her not-so-attractive family. But, no. In a flash, Trudi was standing next to her again, hugging her like they were long-lost sisters or something, while Bobby, Trudi's husband, clicked away.

"You do not look so happy. It is candid, is it not?" Jaleela added when Cassandra didn't say anything. "She is someone you do not like?"

"It's a long story."

"Most often that is so. That is how you looked when you first arrived here. Without a happy face."

"And I look happier now?" Cassandra couldn't help but find humor in Jaleela's observation.

"Do not think I am being unkind. Yes, you have been getting better since you arrived. But at first, when you come here, you have this way about you like you are *aaahhh* . . ." Jaleela simulated a roar. "Like a lioness looking for prey."

Normally Cassandra would've felt affronted, but instead she found herself laughing. If Jaleela said it, then it must be true. "That bad, huh?"

Jaleela smiled, handing the camera back to Cassandra. "But now you are starting to behave more like a princess lioness."

"A what?"

"I have heard the animals can be regal at times. You are what I think a lioness, a grand lioness would look like. A princess lioness who moves over the land with grace and with her head held high."

"You have some imagination."

The virus and general living conditions had made Jaleela look older than her years, but still she was beautiful, her skin mostly smooth, her eyes soulful, and there was a joy and peace about her that was noticeable, almost tangible.

On the other hand, Cassandra had battled her way through hardships just like Jaleela had, and the result wasn't the same. Where was the peace? she wondered. The joy?

"Trudi and I knew each other as young girls. We're different," she tried to explain to Jaleela. And to herself for the hundredth time.

The two of them had always been different, hadn't they? Trudi could afford to be all nicey-nice and place others first in her life. She could think in terms of cookie recipes and homes for the scruffy-looking squirrels scurrying around her backyard. Even as little as Trudi's family had in materialistic terms, they'd still been a tight-knit, loving group. She always had a backup. Always.

But that hadn't been Cassandra's reality whatsoever. She couldn't relate to Trudi then, and she certainly couldn't relate to the mother-wife-homebody that Trudi was now.

"I can't like everyone. Not like you seem to. I'm not like you." Cassandra looked directly at her friend. "I'm not a saint or a hero."

"Hero? I am not a hero. I have made mistakes. Foolish mistakes. My husband, Kabul, left two years after Nomvula was born. There were no jobs near us. That is the sadness of how poverty tears families apart." Jaleela sighed. "He said he had work in the mines, but he never came back to us with money to show for it. Until years later. And then he came to me empty-handed."

Jaleela looked at her with brown eyes that suddenly seemed to dull and darken. Her breathing seemed to falter as she took a deep breath. "I should have never let him into the house. Though he was only there for a year or so. He made me swell with his baby, and then after Tumi was born, he left once more. In time, I felt the tiredness, the sickness, but I did not want it to be true. For many years, I thought, no, this illness cannot be happening to me."

"Did he tell you he had AIDS?"

"We did not talk of such things." A shadow of sadness crossed her face. "Children become orphans because we do not talk. Or speak up."

Cassandra waved a hand. "Don't go blaming yourself like that, lady. I doubt it would have mattered. Just because you talk to a man doesn't guarantee you'll get an honest answer from him. Trust me. There's nothing new about that where I come from."

"America is not perfect? not heaven on this earth like we think?" Jaleela asked, her question a soft probing.

"Oh no. We have our share of problems too." Cassandra was about to share some of the country's most recent dilemmas but instead asked, "Is Kabul still alive?"

"No." Jaleela looked down at her clasped hands. "I heard he died of the virus, but I do not know how many he infected first. I worried very much about Tumi."

Tumi? Cassandra's heart sank at the thought

"But he is fine. My children are well. I thank God every day for that." Jaleela bowed her head for a moment as if saying a brief prayer. "As for myself, I must keep fighting. More than the sickness that pains me is the hurt I feel when I think of my children growing up without a mother. But God whispers to me, 'Do not fear.' And so in this disease I have found my strength. I have found the will to fight. And perhaps my reason for being on this earth."

"See, that's where we're different." Cassandra got up off the bed and walked over to her purse on the dresser, tossing the camera inside. "I've been diseased too. I mean, you look at Nomvula and Tumi and see good things in them. You don't dwell on the father who abandoned them and infected you. But I look at Trudi and all I'm reminded of is my past. A past diseased by parents who didn't want me, by a foster father who molested me, abused me, and a foster mother who pretended to be blind to it." She felt her face heat with embarrassment yet still continued, needing to be honest with Jaleela. And, yes, maybe even honest with herself.

"Everything was so hard, too many evil people. I coped the only way I knew how. By concentrating on myself. I've only thought about lifting myself up, and I've never stopped. I've never considered helping another person along the way. Not like you have."

Now that she'd started revealing her darkest secrets, Cassandra steeled herself and didn't stop. "If you want to know the truth, I didn't come to South Africa to help anyone. No one but myself. I wasn't looking for a news story, thinking I might help your people by exposing the travesties here. No, I came to exploit. I came looking for something that would boost my career. That's why I came."

There! It was embarrassing to expose herself like that, especially to someone as selfless and kindhearted as Jaleela, but it was a relief, too. Why carry the load of that pretense? Who needed to?

She'd expected Jaleela to look shocked or hurt or both. But instead the woman smiled softly and spoke gently. "But you are helping others. Now that you are here."

"Well, sure, of course I am *now*." Still unable to accept any redemption, Cassandra shook her head and told her new friend the awful reality. "But I think I'm only helping you because . . . you're different."

At that, Jaleela laughed. "It is not because I am different. It is because *you* are different. He is seeping into you."

"He?"

Jaleela pointed heavenward. "He. He is pursuing you. You do not even know it." She chuckled. "And you are wrong. You are here because He wants you to be. He is letting the good pour into you. It is pushing out the bad. There will not be room for it soon."

She couldn't act as if she didn't know what Jaleela was talking about. Because in a way, she did. She'd started feeling differently ever since she'd been here. Ever since they'd gone to Lydia's and the past came spewing out of her. But just exactly how and why, she wasn't sure.

All she knew was that it must be wonderful to believe like Jaleela did. To believe when you put your hands in the air that someone bigger than you was actually looking down. To live without all the doubts and fears like Jaleela, who was certain her dream for the women would come true, certain the money would come and buyers would too. She was so sure of heaven in the midst of the worst kind of hell. So sure that all would be well. That God had a handle on it.

Cassandra sighed. It would be nice to put her fists down for a moment and just rest. Trust. Feel the peace and pleasure of the moment.

"Jaleela, have you ever had a slumber party?"

Jaleela looked at her quizzically. "I do not know what you mean. A slumber party?"

"I haven't ever been to one either. But I know you're supposed to stay up half the night eating snacks, talking, and laughing with friends." Cassandra reached into her suitcase, pulling out a plastic bag from Heidi. "And we have snacks." She raised the bag in the air.

"We can have a slumber party?" Jaleela's eyes twinkled.

"I'd say so. That is, if you would like to."

"I think I would like. But first, I will go bathe." Jaleela got up slowly. Her right knee buckled as she did so, but she steadied herself, reaching for her plastic overnight bag. "Then at our slumber party we will talk. You must tell me more about your exciting work in the United States. I want to hear all about my friend, the Princess Lioness," she said, adding her playful signature roar before she hobbled from the room.

39

"Do you think we will see many of the animals today?" Nomvula asked.

The canvas-topped Land Rover inched over the dirt path that cut through the grasslands and hills of the national park. Gabby could still smell the white tea and ginger shampoo in Nomvula's hair from the night before as the girl leaned against her.

At least, Nomvula was sitting there for the time being. She and Tumi kept trading seats, switching between Gabby and their mom, who was on the right side of the vehicle that sat eight in the back with an extra spot alongside the safari guide in front. Eagerly, the kids kept their eyes glued to the scenery on both sides of the path, searching out any animals they could find hidden among the leafy trees or curled up in the tall grasses.

"We'd better see them, for Tumi's sake." Gabby smiled as she and Nomvula watched Tumi, who was unable to sit still, bouncing up and down next to Jaleela. "And your mom's, too."

When they'd arrived at the resort the evening before, one of the guides had jauntily promised more animal sightings in the early morning. That was why they'd chosen a safari at the break of day, when animals would be rousing, coming to the ponds for a wake-up drink, or searching for a breakfast of foliage or prey.

Gabby hadn't minded starting at dawn, especially today. Even in the drippy mist of the gray early morning, she felt more awake and rested than she had the entire trip. Maybe because she'd finally slept in a bed that almost resembled hers at home. Or maybe because she'd had Nomvula and Tumi to keep her company.

Even after hours of playing Memory with Katie and Mighty last night, Nomvula and Tumi still had a hard time settling down. Too excited about the safari ahead, they wanted to play some more. But Gabby insisted on showers first and after that teeth brushing with their fingers, since Gabby didn't have extra toothbrushes. Then Nomvula and Tumi, wearing some of her larger T-shirts for night-clothes, piled on top of her bed and begged for more activities.

With Heidi's supplies, Gabby had come up with a couple of simple craft projects, having them make hearts and stars for their mom out of construction paper. Then she suggested they draw their versions of the "big five," the five most desired animals to see on any safari— elephant, leopard, lion, buffalo, and rhino. That kept them busy until their eyelids started to droop. Not long after, they said their prayers before drifting off to sleep at the foot of her bed.

After covering them with an extra blanket, Gabby had lain awake for a while, thinking about Tom, wondering how he was spending his afternoon. Wishing so badly he were here, cozy with her, looking forward to the new day together . . .

"Tumi, Tumi, look!" Nomvula cried, pointing out the window of the Land Rover. "An elephant. No, two elephants! There is a baby also."

Tumi practically leaped into his sister's lap, trying to see. When he managed to decipher the creatures, camouflaged in their own habitat, a broad grin lit his face. Using a pencil to circle the elephants they'd drawn on their papers, they stared out the window again, eager to see more.

Meanwhile, Gabby traded places with Tumi, letting the sister and brother sit together while she settled next to Jaleela.

"Children keep a person busy, yes?" Jaleela chuckled. "You did many things with them last night. I can see from the papers. I must thank you for the stars and hearts."

"It was fun. I enjoy Nomvula and Tumi a lot. I truly do." The Land Rover jostled momentarily, and she grasped the top of the seat in front of her. "They are so much like you. Warm and appreciative. Inquisitive. You should be very proud of them."

"They are a special gift from God." Jaleela's lips crinkled into a knowing smile. "Do you teach the children at your church?"

"I mostly oversee the teaching and everything that comes with it. But after last night with your kids," she said honestly, "it makes me think I'd like to teach a class again."

"You love children?"

"Oh yes," she answered without a thought, then paused, reflecting. "I always have. I guess children are my calling."

"I can tell that is true. I do not believe I have heard you speak of your own children."

"No. I'm sorry to say that's a special gift my husband and I have not received." Once again, like the refrain of a familiar sad song, a feeling of loss flowed over her.

Understanding filling her eyes, Jaleela gently touched Gabby's arm. "I am sorry too." The warmth in her voice soothed. "You deserve such a treasure."

"Thank you for saying that." Gabby bowed her head, feeling humbled by Jaleela's words. "I'm not sure if I'm deserving, but it would definitely make me happy." She smiled just as Tumi came up to them.

"We have seen a leopard and a rhino," he told them, excited as ever.

While she and Jaleela had been talking, Tumi and Nomvula had been busy scouting out more of the big five. He was showing the animals he'd circled on his paper when Nomvula spoke up from across the aisle.

"Giraffes!" She pointed in Gabby and Jaleela's direction.

As the Land Rover took a left bend in the path, everyone looked to the right, spotting a handful of giraffes bending their sleek necks to feed on trees beneath them. The giraffes were a spectacular sight to see, for sure, but so were Nomvula's and Tumi's faces. Their eyes were so lit up, their expressions so awed, Gabby couldn't take her own eyes off them.

The giraffes didn't begin to compare with the lion that came up so close to them, walking alongside the Land Rover for a minute or so as if he were escorting them along their way. Or the pair of female lions that suddenly shot up out of the grass, stretching their necks as if scoping out the area, making their plans for the day. In both instances, the kids had to cover their mouths so they wouldn't shrill out loud and agitate the beasts.

But by no means were the king and queens of the jungle the last of the free-roaming animals they'd see. By the time the Land Rover pulled into the parking lot over an hour later, Gabby couldn't believe all the creatures they'd spotted—monkeys, wildebeests, hippos, impalas by the dozens.

The guide had also pointed out some of the most exquisite birds she'd ever laid eyes on—a bright orange bishop weaver and a cape glossy starling with feathers blue as a peacock. It made her think of the cardinals and blue jays back home that she only had to step out on her deck to see each day.

And to make the safari complete, the kids had gotten to circle every one of the animals on their papers. Waving them in the air, they couldn't have been any happier.

"Thank you for making the safari so special for my Vula and Tumi." Jaleela linked her arm in Gabby's and motioned to a nearby bench where they could sit and watch Cassandra take pictures of the kids for about the hundredth time.

Gabby could tell from Jaleela's slow gait that the morning activity had taken a toll on her energy. It concerned her, too, that the short walk from the Land Rover to the bench left Jaleela winded. The day before, Jaleela had seemed more upbeat and rejuvenated, leading Gabby to think that the episode at the hospice party where Jaleela had nearly passed out was a fluke. But now she wasn't so sure.

"Jaleela, you seem a little tired. I haven't turned in my key to the town house yet. Would you like to go back and rest for a bit?"

But Jaleela didn't seem to want to talk about her health. "Nomvula and Tumi adore you. That is a good thing." She puffed out the words. "Thank you for caring for them so much."

Gabby patted her hand, trying to push aside her worries about her friend. "They made it special for me too."

Though it was way before noon, everyone seemed to be starving, more than ready for the lunch buffet that was part of the safari package.

"It's not like there's a McDonald's once we get back on the road to Mamelodi," Katie wisely reminded everyone. "We'd better load up." She rubbed her belly.

That in mind, Gabby helped Jaleela to her feet as Katie led the way to the dining room, where tables were filled with foods and desserts, some of which looked odd and foreign to Gabby.

But everything felt good and familiar once they all sat down at a round table with full plates. The easy chatter, sharing of stories. The laughter. It reminded Gabby of being with her family at home. How these people had become so dear to her in such a short time, she'd never know. But as they grasped each other's hands and a straight-from-the-heart grace spilled from the young Mighty's lips, Gabby could feel the love and warmth that flowed between them, filling the spot in her that had ached, giving her much to be thankful for.

◈ ◈ ◈

She was going to miss it, Gabby knew. The serene beauty of the country.

The afternoon sunshine poured through the open windows as the van journeyed over the wide-open road, the soft, rolling countryside spread out like a welcome mat on either side. Lanky sunflowers stood straight in fields that reached as far as the eye could see, raising their yellow faces high, paying homage to the bright sun. While the flowers saluted, the roadside vendors recoiled, snoozing in the heat of the day beneath their colorful striped umbrellas, their luscious fruits ripening even more in the heat.

Nomvula and Tumi had taken over the backseat of the van, and they yawned every so often, looking peaceful and sweet, Gabby thought, all curled up, taking turns listening to the iPod Katie had graciously let them borrow. At the front of the vehicle, Mighty was situated behind Katie's captain's chair and Heidi manned the wheel, her eyes peeled straight ahead on the stretch of road.

Taking a seat in the middle of the van, Gabby offered Jaleela the spot closest to the window. They both sat silently, gazing out onto the countryside. In the seat in front of them was Cassandra. Her head bobbed sleepily a few times.

Overall a quiet feeling of contentment filled the van. No one really spoke much for the first half hour.

Katie finally broke the silence when they'd gotten closer to home, about fifteen miles from the township. "Jaleela, have you thought about what you want to call the bead project? It's going to be kind of like a company, isn't it? I think it needs a name."

Gabby hadn't wanted to think about much, enjoying the lazy feel of the drive, the light breeze gently tossing her hair in all directions. But when Katie mentioned it, she realized how right she was. A name for the nonprofit project was a must, and Jaleela should be part of that decision, something they should all think about while they were together. Besides, it was something fun to brainstorm.

"I was thinking about Jaleela's Jewels," Katie offered. "You know, like an alliteration."

Jaleela shook her head adamantly. "Oh, I do not think I want it to be my name. It is not my dream alone. It is a dream for everyone."

"How about Beads International?" Cassandra suggested.

"Or—" Heidi looked into the rearview mirror—"something like Dream Beads?"

Taking everyone's suggestions into consideration, Gabby offered a few ideas too. "Maybe Beads of Dreams? Beads of Promise? Beads of Faith?" She turned to Jaleela. "What do you think?"

A shy smile crinkled Jaleela's lips. "I must say that I have thought about it before. Beaded Hope. That is the name that has come to my

"It is on the opposite side of the township from where you are staying. Nearly twenty minutes from here," Mighty answered.

As Heidi picked up speed on the roadway, the casual feel of their outing turned tense and frightening. An awful-sounding wheeze caught at the back of Jaleela's throat.

"No, Kabul . . . no," she muttered.

Gabby looked to Cassandra to see if she understood.

Cassandra nodded. "Her husband. He passed away."

Gabby shook her head at the sorrow of it all, a family torn apart so senselessly. As she did, she caught sight of Nomvula.

Tumi was still tuned in to a world of music, but Nomvula had seen her mother struggling as she undoubtedly had so many times before. And instead of the sweet sounds her brother was enjoying, she'd heard the panic in their voices. Now gone was the carefree smile on her little-girl face. Gone was the light that shone in her trusting eyes. Gone was the joy of the past two days.

All of it gone. Once again.

Oh, how cruel it was. How unfair!

Placing Jaleela in Cassandra's care, Gabby swiftly moved to the back of the bouncing van where Nomvula sat, hugging her knees to her chest, her body drawn up into a protective ball. She didn't reach out to Gabby as she usually did. She didn't even look at her. So Gabby did the only thing she could. Putting her arms around the grief-stricken child, she held Nomvula close.

"She's a fighter. You'll see." Gabby kissed the top of Nomvula's head. "She will fight," she repeated.

Because when it came to her children, she knew that's exactly what Jaleela would try to do.

◈ ◈ ◈

It felt surreal, standing at the entrance of the village hospital, so dingy and antiquated. Standing there in the heat of the afternoon sun, with

mind. Many times I have . . ." She paused, her excitement seeming to take her breath away. "I have thought we are each like a unique—" She stopped again, sucking in a breath. "A unique bead. Our God strings us together in ways that make Him happy. In ways that we may find His promises in each other."

As Jaleela's words settled over everyone, Gabby had to smile. Once again the eloquence of the woman's simple words had rendered them all speechless. "Well, I think it's settled," she said, doubting any of them could match the sentiment of Jaleela's heartfelt name. "Our project will be called Beaded Hope. Is that okay?"

Everyone nodded, then settled back in their seats.

"I think you've picked a perfect name." Gabby leaned toward Jaleela, squeezing her thin hand. "Oh, my goodness. Your hand's freezing."

Jaleela's icy fingers alarmed Gabby, especially since the air blowing in the window was as tepid as a baby's bathwater. It was peculiar, too, because even though Jaleela's fingers were cold to the touch, Gabby didn't have to look too closely to see perspiration beginning to dot Jaleela's face, outlining her upper lip, spattering her forehead, reminiscent of the other day.

Was she imagining how short of breath Jaleela suddenly seemed, her chest rising and falling noticeably? Apparently it wasn't her enthusiasm about the bead project that had been making it difficult for her to breathe.

"Are you sure you're feeling all right?"

The beaded bracelet jingled on Jaleela's arm as Gabby tried to massage some warmth into her friend's fingers.

Before Jaleela could answer, a giggle erupted from Nomvula at the back of the van, causing them both to turn toward the sound. Covering her broad smile with one hand, Nomvula pointed to her brother with the other. With the iPod earphones in his ears and his eyes closed tightly, Tumi appeared to be in a world of his own, swaying and wriggling to the music filling his head. Of course, the sight of his and Nomvula's pleasure made Gabby and Jaleela break out into grins too.

"Your kids remind me of the adorable cubs we saw on safari. They get along very well together, don't they?"

The depth of caring that existed between Jaleela's children had amazed Gabby since the day she'd first laid eyes on them. She'd been close to her brothers growing up, and she still was to this day, but it didn't seem to compare with the special bond Nomvula and Tumi shared. Of course, her family life had been so different. So protected, so secure. As kids, she and her brothers never had to depend much on one another.

"I do not know what they would do without each other. Nomvula, she—" Jaleela stopped and put a hand to her chest.

"What's wrong?"

But again Jaleela wouldn't say. She only shook her head and tried to finish relaying her thoughts. Her words, like her breathing, coming out in sputters. "Sh-she smiles when her brother smiles. And Tumi, he . . . depends so on Nomvula. Her strength. Like a mother to him since, since I . . ." She gasped. "Since I have been . . ."

Suddenly any peace or joy that had lit Jaleela's eyes earlier faded as quickly as a shooting star falling from the sky. Her features crumpled into a sad expression Gabby had never seen on her sweet face before. "They . . . ," she panted, her voice cracking with emotion, "they love each other so. I dream . . . I pray . . . they grow up together."

Gabby patted Jaleela's hand, trying to soothe her friend emotionally, hoping it might help to stabilize her physically too. "You need to calm down. You do."

"I am sorry. My thoughts . . ."

"It's okay. Mothers worry." Gabby took Jaleela's other hand and rubbed it. "It comes with the territory."

But it didn't seem she could soothe Jaleela in any way. Her hands trembled uncontrollably in Gabby's grasp. Her head bobbed and her chest heaved as she tried to catch her breath. "The hurt in my heart . . . far more than my body. God, help me. I do not . . . want to leave them.

Not let go. Of this life. Where my babies are with me. Not orphans . . ." Her chest rose and fell more and more rapidly. As if she'd just run a hundred-yard dash, she gasped, trying to draw in more oxygen.

Gabby could feel the panic rising within her own chest, could feel her heart pounding as the wheeze at the back of Jaleela's throat grew louder. And louder still.

Again, Gabby attempted to comfort her, to ease her breathing into an even rhythm. "Shh. It's okay, Jaleela. It's okay."

She kept saying the words over and over, trying to get Jaleela's symptoms to subside the way she'd managed to at the hospice party when she'd sat Jaleela in a chair and given her a cool drink of water. But the problem was, Jaleela was already sitting. And there was no cool water. Even if there were, how could Jaleela possibly drink it? She already sounded like she was drowning. Suffocating. Puffing and panting, her eyes wide, pupils dilated, she looked at Gabby, her expression as wild and panicked as Gabby felt.

"The cubs." Her eyelashes fluttered, her head rolled on her neck. "In the sun."

What was she talking about? What was happening?

The skin on Gabby's forearms prickled with fear. "Hold on, Jaleela. Hold on." She tried to steady the woman with a hand under her shoulder. "Cassandra! I need you. Help," Gabby yelled, nudging Cassandra out of her restful slumber.

"Mighty! Mighty, please! Jaleela needs a hospital," she barked toward the front of the van, immediately getting the young girl's attention. "Quickly. Please tell Heidi where to go."

Cassandra startled. "What's going on?" She hovered over Gabby's seat, appraising the situation immediately. "Why is she having a hard time breathing?"

"I don't know. I don't know what's happening." Gabby held Jaleela in her arms, feeling every movement as the woman panted, struggled for air, her eyes growing more distant, unfocused with every second.

"How far is the hospital?" Cassandra called out.

Nomvula and Tumi in shock clutching her legs. The entire past half hour or so had been one of the most terrifying times in Gabby's life as they rushed, Heidi flying over the unfamiliar roads to get Jaleela here, to this awful-looking place, the only place they could bring their friend for help.

Hugging the children to her sides, Gabby wished they didn't have to see their mother this way. A lady so full of spirit, hunched over, limp, and nearly lifeless in an old-fashioned wheelchair with a torn canvas back and spindly wheels that looked as dilapidated and broken and hopeless as Jaleela did.

"I am sorry. You cannot stay here with us. You cannot," Mighty told Gabby firmly as the young woman stood behind the wheelchair. Since they'd arrived, Jaleela's breathing had become shallower. A moist, rattling cough punctuated the quiet air around them. "Go now. Please go," Mighty begged.

Horrified, Gabby couldn't grasp what Mighty was saying. They couldn't just leave. She didn't want to. How could she when the very life seemed to be running out of Jaleela, their precious, precious friend?

Where was someone who cared? who would fix her? The hospital looked so broken-down. Could they really heal a person here? She couldn't fathom this was the only place Jaleela would be accepted.

"Leave? Leave her *here*? We can't," Gabby stammered, unable to fight back her tears, even for the sake of the children. "We can't go."

"But you must." Mighty shook her head at Gabby. At Cassandra, who ground her teeth. And at Heidi and Katie, their eyes wide with concern. Her eyes clouded with the hurtful reality—the truth. "For Jaleela's sake, you must leave. They will not trust you here. Her care will be worse, not better. Go now. Find Mama Penny. They will listen to Mama Penny."

"But—" Gabby's heart squeezed in anguish.

"Do not waste any more time. Please," Mighty pleaded, her eyes imploring them as her hands clenched the worn grips of the wheelchair tightly. "Nomvula. Tumi. Come," she said solemnly, nodding for Jaleela's children to follow her.

"No!" Gabby placed her arms more tightly around Nomvula's and Tumi's shoulders. "No, they can come with us. We'll take good care of them."

"Of course." Mighty's voice softened. "You would take good care of them. But they must come with us now. In case . . ."

So quiet were the words that came from Mighty's lips. So hushed. Barely audible. But Gabby heard them. Heard them very well. Nomvula and Tumi needed to be with their mother. In case there was a last moment. In case there was a last breath. In case Jaleela wanted to lay eyes one last time on God's most precious gifts to her.

40

Gabby's hand trembled as she opened the front door, not knowing who would be there. Not knowing if news of life or death waited on the other side.

"Mama Penny!" Gabby almost broke down at the sight of her friend, so thankful that she'd been the one to come to them. She embraced Mama Penny tightly, too tightly she knew, selfishly trying to soak up the strength that only the matriarch of the village could provide.

Over Mama Penny's shoulders, the night looked black enough to swallow them up, dark and starless, meaning the rains would come tomorrow. But it didn't matter. Nothing mattered at this moment. Only word of Jaleela.

That's all they'd been waiting for for hours. Sitting together numb and shocked as the daylight vanished and the nighttime came. They had been prayerful. They had been tearful. They had been frightened into silence, thinking about Jaleela's critical condition. And then overflowing with words, remembering all the things about Jaleela that made them smile.

Wordlessly, Gabby ushered Mama Penny into the somberness of their home away from home. Katie and Heidi got up from the couch, offering their seat to Mama Penny. But she shook her head, standing firm in the middle of the room, the dim lighting casting a yellow shadow around her.

"She is gone," Mama Penny told them before they could even ask. "She is gone," she repeated as if she were still trying to believe it herself. Gabby could see the shock in Mama Penny's weary, wet eyes. Yet the woman raised her head, holding it high. "Our Jaleela is with her Father now. She is with Him."

"No!" Cassandra hit the kitchen table with her fist, her teacup jostling in the saucer. "No! I knew they wouldn't save her at that awful place." She buried her face in her hands.

"You do not understand," Mama Penny pleaded gently. "Jaleela's condition was worse than anyone knew. It was not only the AIDS she warred against. It was lymphoma, too."

"Lymphoma?" Cassandra looked up. "Cancer? Why didn't you say something before? Why didn't she tell us?"

"I did not want to keep it a secret. Yet I promised that to Jaleela my friend. She wanted to battle alone quietly. She did not want to worry the children." Mama Penny bowed her head. "The truth is, our friends do not always die from AIDS. There are many fatal complications with the virus. TB. Infections. Cancer. Our poor Jaleela! She tried to be a valiant warrior. But we were not able to get the many treatments she needed. The cancer metastasized in her lungs. She died of respiratory failure."

Gabby noticed that Cassandra's expression seemed to crimp grievously with every word Mama Penny said. Heidi's and Katie's eyes looked bleak with sorrow as well. Surely the mother and daughter weren't only mourning Jaleela but reliving the loss of their husband and father too.

Gabby understood how the others were struggling because she certainly was. Her heart buckled as she tried to deal with the hurt, the frustration, the anger. How horrifying it was—how helpless it felt— to have their special friend torn out of their lives.

And then to be caught off guard by the intensity of her feelings for Jaleela too.

How had that happened so quickly? It had been less than two weeks since she'd come to know the South African woman. But it felt like a lifetime of emotions pouring out of Gabby. Jaleela and her family, Jaleela and her faith had touched her deeply in unimaginable ways.

From what Mama Penny said, their foursome had touched Jaleela too. "Ever since Jaleela got sick, I have not seen my friend so bright as she was with all of you." Mama Penny took a moment to study each of their faces. "In such a little time, you all became very dear to her."

"We came to love her too," Heidi managed through her tears. "She was so warm. So inspiring to us."

"Yes, I thought certainly there would be a miracle today with our Jaleela," Mama Penny told them. "She could not keep her eyes open, drifting in and out of consciousness, her breathing shallow, barely keeping her alive. But then came a moment, she rolled her head and spoke to me. So clearly. It seemed that angels had revived her, that she would be fine again the way she talked. But Jaleela must have known something I did not. She must have known her time was short."

Mama Penny's body swayed as she stood there, as if she were rocking an imaginary baby, soothing it to sleep. "Many of her words were about all of you. She talked much about how you would make her dream come true."

Absorbing Mama Penny's words, Gabby couldn't help but think of the first time she'd met Jaleela and how instantly she'd been moved by the woman's smile, by just the touch of her hand. With the memory of Jaleela's spirit warming her, she didn't know whether to laugh or cry, so she did both. "The woman never ceases to amaze, does she?" She smiled, wiping the tears from her cheeks.

"She felt thankful to each of you. She said you had become her sisters. She asked me to bring gifts to her sisters to give you thanks." Mama Penny held up a plastic bag, and Gabby realized she hadn't even noticed it when Mama Penny first came in. But seeing it now, Gabby recognized it as the bag Jaleela had used for their safari overnight in lieu of a suitcase she didn't own. "I do not only bring you news of Jaleela, but I bring a part of her too." She paused. "Cassandra, you are first."

"Me?" Cassandra had turned away after her outburst, looking out the window into the blackness. She'd been the quietest throughout the afternoon and evening, keeping most of her feelings to herself. But now she faced them, her face rigid with grief. She studied Mama Penny dubiously. "A gift?"

It seemed unfathomable that Jaleela, who had so little in terms of material things, would have gifts to bequeath to them. Plus, it seemed unnecessary. Hadn't she already given them enough by way of the example of her faith, the light of her spirit, the warmth of her love?

And yet it appeared there was more Jaleela had to give.

"Yes." Mama Penny reached into the bag, drawing out something so small Gabby couldn't even see what it might be. Walking over to Cassandra, Mama Penny placed the object in her hand. Something that glittered even in the dim lighting. The blue beaded bracelet!

"Jaleela wanted you to have the bracelet, Cassandra, the symbol of her dream," Mama Penny said. "You called her a businesswoman and a dreamer. She said you are both of those too. It was her hope you would lead the others to carry out her legacy."

Staring at the bracelet in the palm of her hand, Cassandra began to shake, and she finally started to cry. Gabby couldn't stand seeing her all by herself, so she went to her and put an arm around Cassandra's shoulder.

"I've never had a piece of jewelry that meant so much to me," Cassandra told Gabby in between her sobbing. "Or a friend who meant that much either."

"I know. I know. Jaleela was very special." Patting Cassandra's shoulder, Gabby tried to offer her some comfort.

"Mama Heidi and Katie Blue Eyes," Mama Penny addressed them. "There is something Jaleela has for you, too." Her hand disappeared into the plastic bag once more, and when she pulled it out, in her grasp she held Jaleela's chartreuse scarf, the one she had worn yesterday. "From one mother to two mothers, it is her gift to you. She hoped someday you may wrap your baby in it and make new dreams."

Gabby watched Heidi's eyes brim over as she took the scarf from Mama Penny's hand.

"Oh, Mom, I can't believe it." Katie's voice broke with emotion as she laid her head on Heidi's shoulder.

"And, Gabby." Mama Penny turned to her. "I have nothing that is hard or solid in the bag for you. But I have something solid from Jaleela. It is her word. As one person of faith to another, Jaleela wanted you to know that as soon as she gets to heaven, she will make sure to tell the angels about you. She admired you very much."

A week ago that wouldn't have meant anything to Gabby. But today it did. And she knew tomorrow it would too. To think Jaleela considered her a sister, in heart and in spirit, completely humbled her. What could be more precious than the thought of that to carry with her always? She only wished she could have been there in Jaleela's last moments to hold her soft hand and tell her so.

While Jaleela's promise was comforting, something kept troubling Gabby. Something she just couldn't let go of. It had her fidgety and disturbed, pacing the floor this afternoon and rocking back and forth in the chair like a crazy woman.

It was Nomvula and Tumi.

"Mama Penny, I have to know," she said. "What about Nomvula and Tumi? How are they doing? I can't stop thinking about them."

Mama Penny bowed her head momentarily as if the thought of Jaleela's orphaned children dearly touched her too. "Thanks to the Lord, Jaleela was able to speak to her children a few times before she passed. She comforted them. She hugged them. She told them she would always love them."

Gabby couldn't even begin to imagine being a child and going through what they had. She'd tried to protect them, hold them close to her heart on the way to the hospital. But who was comforting them now? now that Jaleela was gone?

"Where are they?" she asked.

"They are still with Mighty, but I will be going to get them soon,"

Mama Penny explained. "My granddaughter will help me take care of them for the time being."

And then what? Then who would care for them? Gabby wanted to know, but the time didn't seem right. Mama Penny had just lost a close friend, as all of them had. Surely she was doing the best she could do. Gabby didn't want to put Mama Penny on the spot or have her think Gabby was criticizing her decision.

"We need to change our flights," Gabby said. "For the funeral service. It doesn't seem right not to be here."

When she really examined her feelings, Gabby knew she wasn't making the suggestion solely out of respect for Jaleela. More than anything, she simply couldn't imagine not being there for Nomvula and Tumi on that day.

Yet even gone from them physically, Jaleela seemed to have something to say about that too, her message delivered through her friend Mama Penny. "Moments before she passed, Jaleela said she hoped nothing would change. She squeezed my hand, and with a light in her eyes she told me what to say at her funeral."

Gabby held her breath, waiting to hear and stealing glances at the others; they appeared equally anxious.

"She said, 'Tell them at my funeral, do not weep.'" Mama Penny's strong voice filled the room. "'As my body is being laid to rest in our homeland, celebrate. Because our new friends will be back in America, and a dream for all will be taking root across the sea.'"

"I cannot tell you right from wrong." Mama Penny shrugged. "I can only speak of Jaleela's wish. Her dying words about her dream. That is all I can tell you."

A hush fell over the room as Gabby tried to sort out the thoughts in her head and the feelings in her heart, neither of which seemed to go along with what Mama Penny was saying.

Cassandra stood, seeming to have a grip on the situation and on herself for the first time since the horrible events of the afternoon. "Then that's what we should do. I'm all for carrying out Jaleela's wishes. We need to get home and get the beads project started. Well...?"

Heidi and Katie looked at each other before nodding to Cassandra, and then, reluctantly, Gabby nodded too.

"But frankly, Mama Penny," Cassandra said in businesswoman mode, one step ahead of them, "we can't set up this nonprofit if we don't have product from the women. And they're supposed to bring their beadwork to the hospice tomorrow. But will they now, with Jaleela gone?" Her voice faltered as she spoke the last words.

Gabby hadn't even stopped to consider that, but obviously Jaleela had been their main link to the majority of the beadworkers. "Hopefully they won't think we had anything to do with their friend dying. We were the last ones to be with her."

"What if they don't trust us now that Jaleela isn't here?" Heidi bit her lip.

"Can you do anything to help, Mama Penny?" Gabby asked.

"I will remind the women you will be at the hospice tomorrow," Mama Penny assured them. "I can say to them they should act as if Jaleela were still alive. Some of the women know you well. But the others? No, I cannot force those women to trust you and to work with you. With so much death all around us, I wish I could. As it is, we don't have enough men left to shovel dirt on the graves. Now women must shovel the dirt too.

"In Jaleela's dream there is hope for the women if they would come." The thought of Jaleela seemed to make a smile creep onto Mama's Penny's lips. "Now that I think of her, she is probably talking to the Lord this minute about this situation."

"You're right." Gabby chuckled and walked over to Mama Penny's side. "I'm sure she's giving Him an earful."

As everyone laughed and smiled and even shed more tears in remembrance of their warm, faithful friend, Gabby squeezed Mama Penny's hand. "She was the best."

"Yes, she was," Mama Penny agreed softly. "And now I must go.

Though I do not want to leave your company, Sipho is waiting to take me home."

After a series of hugs, Gabby linked her arm with Mama Penny's as they ambled slower than usual toward the front door.

"Mama Penny?" Katie cried out, and they both turned to her. "What does the name Jaleela mean? I always meant to ask her."

"'Great exalted,'" Mama Penny said readily, smiling as if the name aptly fit.

And it did, Gabby thought as she closed the door behind Mama Penny. It surely fit the woman who had made such an impression on their hearts and souls and had made them part of something bigger than themselves.

Still, there were others who had made an impression on Gabby's heart too—Jaleela's children, Nomvula and Tumi. Gabby could only hope somehow they would be taken care of like the treasures Jaleela knew them to be.

41

Glancing at the clock across the hospice lobby, Cassandra clenched her teeth.

It was 12:45. She and Gabby and the others had been here over two hours and still no beadworkers. No jewelry. And no wonder. Who could blame the South African women?

Torrents of nickel-sized raindrops had been spattering against the red earth ever since they'd arrived at the hospice. Surely the women would have trouble walking here, their sandals sinking into the thick, gloppy stuff. Cassandra had even suggested driving out to Squatter Camp to pick up the jewelry, until Sipho reminded her that tires sank too. He'd never get the van out of the thick mud, which of course she hated to admit was true.

All Cassandra knew was that she couldn't sit and listen to the cursed rain any longer. The sound of the downpour drowned out the click of her sandals as she walked toward the glass doors at the entrance, away from the others.

She'd tried to be patient. She'd tried to stay calm. But she could only sit and wait so long.

Someone had to do something. They'd gone through so much to get to this moment. Cassandra couldn't let it slip away without a fight, without some kind of action. They'd already lost Jaleela. She'd never forgive herself if they let Jaleela's dream fall apart too.

But what? What could she do?

Staring out at the flooded parking lot, she could feel hints of helplessness seeping in. Just like yesterday when Jaleela had grown faint and weaker before their very eyes. More than frightened, Cassandra had felt powerless. So utterly incompetent and unprepared. It was not a feeling she was accustomed to. All she could do was hold her friend in her arms and rock her till they got her to the hospital. But that hadn't helped a bit. And now here she was, feeling inept all over again. But instead of trying to save her friend, she was attempting to save Jaleela's legacy. Her dream.

Cassandra needed to think. And think fast. What could she do?

Gathering her thoughts, she took a deep breath, smoothing the bodice of her dark green drop-waist dress. She'd gotten the chic and understated cotton designer dress half price last summer, not that it even mattered. She'd worn it because she wanted to look nice for the South African women. She'd put it on out of respect for them. But mostly she'd worn the dress because it looked good, complementing Jaleela's blue beaded bracelet.

Ever since she could afford it, Cassandra had been far more interested in gold and silver than in something colorful and whimsical like Jaleela's bracelet. But this bracelet was far different. With careful, almost reverent motions, she turned and righted the piece of jewelry on her wrist. And once again it felt like Jaleela was here with her.

But then she had been feeling that way all morning. Thankfully. Because crazy as it seemed, she missed Jaleela deeply, missed her so much already. Yes, she'd made friends with Gabby and Heidi and had come to adore young Katie. But Jaleela . . . In such a short time the woman had recognized the wall around Cassandra's heart. And she, of all people, had bothered to climb over it and touch her like no one ever had.

It made her ache profoundly every time she thought about never seeing Jaleela again. But at least there was a saving grace. At least she felt like Jaleela's spirit was near.

While putting on her makeup this morning, Cassandra had used a little less foundation and blush, all because of a remark Jaleela had made. They hadn't stayed up very late the night of their slumber party. Jaleela was clearly exhausted and not feeling so well. In just a couple of hours, she was sound asleep. But before she nodded off, she said more than a few things that had made a lasting impression. Things that would make Cassandra smile, she knew, for a long time to come. The woman had a way of doing that, for sure.

"Why do you wear so many colors on your face?" she'd asked, seeing Cassandra's face freshly washed for the first time. "You have a good face without it. Very pretty and smooth."

Touching her bare face self-consciously, Cassandra waved away the compliment. "Oh, please. You really need to have your eyes examined."

"My eyes?" Jaleela frowned, looking instantly worried. "You think my eyes are now sick?"

Cassandra had burst out laughing, and Jaleela did too after Cassandra had told her not to fret, explaining the phrase was just a saying American people used.

"Oh, Jaleela. I do miss you!" Cassandra whispered to the ominous-looking sky. But only the thunder crackled in reply.

Before Cassandra had even gotten out of bed this morning, she'd already decided she was going to finance Jaleela's dream and get it under way. She didn't even care if she ever got paid back. It was the least she could do.

After all, it wasn't lost on her that she'd been the one Jaleela had spent her last night on earth with. She'd been the one Jaleela had greeted the last morning of her life too.

Without the others knowing the details, Cassandra had Sipho drive her to the bank in Pretoria before coming to the hospice. Standing in the teller line, ready to make a cash withdrawal, she could've sworn she felt Jaleela's presence there with her too. Actually it was more like Jaleela's spirit weighing heavily on her, in a way almost scolding Cassandra for not believing the money would arrive on its own like Jaleela had promised.

But please get real, Cassandra wanted to tell her friend. They were already in need of one miracle for the day—just hoping the women would show up as planned. Cassandra wasn't about to expect a second miracle that the money would show up too.

"It's a backup, Jaleela." Cassandra hadn't meant to say the words out loud to her dead friend, a person no one could see, while waiting in line with the other bank customers. Everyone looked at her curiously, and one man must've heard the word *backup* because he moved away from her. All of which made Cassandra smile and shake her head at the memory of Jaleela once again.

But that had been hours ago. And now here she was at the hospice, dressed in a way she hoped would please others. With a purse full of money to pay the beadworkers for their work. Wearing a bracelet on her wrist that signified friendship, hope, and all the goodness that can come from bad.

But a key element was missing—the women with their jewelry. And now after all morning feeling like Jaleela was close by, it felt like she was missing too.

Jaleela, where are you? What would you do?

Again, the teeming rain overwhelmed every other sound— or answer—that Cassandra could hope to hear.

But it didn't matter because she knew it was a silly question to ponder anyway. Not because Jaleela wasn't there to answer but because she already knew exactly what Jaleela would do.

She couldn't say she felt entirely comfortable doing the same thing as her friend would. In fact, she felt awkward and unsure. Sort of ridiculous, too. But Cassandra decided she would try. For the sake of her Jaleela. For the sake of her friend's dream.

Oh, Jaleela. Look what you've gotten me into!

Folding her hands, pointing them upward like she'd seen Jaleela do, Cassandra gazed out the glass doors and high into the gray skies.

She didn't have any idea what to say. Certainly there were no fancy words she knew.

But it was now or never. Take it or leave it.

Closing her eyes, she began to put into words all that was on her mind . . . and in her heart. She wasn't sure if that was necessarily praying. But for now it would simply have to do.

42

"Chloe, these are just beautiful!" Heidi held up one of the dozens of bracelets Chloe had made, admiring the way it glittered in the sunshine pouring in the hospice window.

Chloe's hands were in tight fists of worry. "Do you think Jaleela would like them? I tried my best."

"I think she would love them," Heidi said, meaning every word. "She would be so proud of your work."

"I hope all is as she dreamed."

"I have no doubt that it is."

Nearly all morning and into the early afternoon, rain had pummeled the ground. The skies couldn't have been any darker or more melancholy-looking, so fitting for the intermittent weeping Heidi and Katie and the others couldn't seem to control over the loss of their dear friend.

Just as they were about to give up hope that the rain would ever stop and the beadworkers would come, the storm ceased. The clouds parted. And the sun shone as bold as ever overhead.

Within the hour, the hospice lobby was filled with women and children, once again wearing their best and brightest outfits as they had last week. Stretching from one end of the lobby to the other, they looked like a glorious rainbow.

And the women brought even more of their sparkling jewelry and beadwork ready for sale. Looking at the jewelry crafted with their sure, nimble fingers and worked on with hopeful hearts, Heidi could only imagine all the hours it took to create the pieces that could change the women's lives. And the lives of others.

"I have a feeling these are going to sell very well, Chloe. You should plan on making more."

Overall, Heidi wasn't always sure which women were victims of the virus and which ones might have more bad days than good. She didn't think she should get that personal. But knowing Chloe's story as she did now, she asked gently, "Would you be able to do that much work?"

"Yes, I can." Chloe beamed. "It makes me feel better to use my hands."

"Good. I was hoping you'd say that." Heidi hugged Chloe, gave her an inventory slip, and sent her to see Cassandra for payment.

While gathering Chloe's pieces and preparing a space for the next beadworker's jewelry, Heidi was interrupted when Mighty called, "Mama Heidi! Mama Heidi! Please, can you come?"

Was Mighty upset? excited? Heidi couldn't quite tell which as she hopped up from her chair and went to see.

Mighty waved her arms from behind the hospice's welcome desk, looking frantic but pretty, the bright Caribbean blue of her simple shift contrasting against her rich, chocolate-colored skin. "There is a new e-mail for Katie."

"An e-mail?" Mark had sent another e-mail already? *Kids and computers. There's no getting around it!*

"Yes. And I am sorry." A shadow crossed Mighty's expression. "I am sorry I read the e-mail."

"Don't worry. Don't even give it another thought. I'm sure it's nothing."

"Oh, it is something. It is good news. Good news from Katie's friend in America."

Good news from Mark? Heidi couldn't even begin to imagine. Maybe he'd gotten a car? or his job back?

Mighty held out the printed e-mail to her. "You should look at it too. You should," she insisted.

The day was supposed to be about the beadworkers. Their jewelry. And Jaleela's dream. There was no way Heidi cared to get distracted from those things, reading lovey-dovey exchanges between Katie and Mark. "No, I—"

"I hope you do not think my manners are gone, but truly, you need to see the words here." Mighty waved the paper in her hand.

Heidi had known Mighty was efficient, but she'd never seen her so assertive. What had come over her? Heidi wondered as the young woman came from around her desk and thrust the e-mail into her hands. Hovering over her, she refused to move until Heidi had read every last word.

"Oh, my! I don't believe this." Heidi clutched the paper to her heart, chills tingling up and down her arms.

"I know." Mighty held up her hands in disbelief. "I did not trust my eyes either."

"Where is Katie? She has to see this." Heidi searched the circles of females for any sign of her daughter. "Have you seen her?"

Mighty scanned the groups of women. "There. There she is." She pointed.

Coming out of the bathroom across the lobby, Katie was helping an elderly woman dressed in traditional African garb back to her seat on the couch.

Once Katie had settled her there, Heidi called, "Katie, can you come here, please?"

Although Katie's ankle was healing nicely, Heidi noticed she was still being careful, taking her time to walk to the front desk. As she did, she tightened Jaleela's chartreuse scarf turned sash around the waist of her denim skirt. Heidi didn't know if Katie would ever take the scarf off. She'd worn it last night as a shawl after Mama Penny had stopped by to see them. And then took it to bed with her too, almost as a sort of security blanket.

"What's up?" She smiled guilelessly, looking between Heidi and Mighty.

"You got an e-mail again," Heidi informed her. "From you-know-who."

"Oh." Katie's expression suddenly turned sheepish at the news that she'd received another e-mail. "I got a second one, huh?"

Heidi nodded.

"You saw who the e-mail is from?"

"I sure did. And it's not from Mark." Heidi narrowed her gaze on Katie. "Why didn't you tell me?"

"Um . . . tell you what exactly?"

"For starters about the first e-mail. It wasn't from Mark either, was it? And here I was, ranting and raving, going off on you."

"Exactly. You went off on such a rant." Katie rolled her eyes, but with the slightest smile on her face she added, "You were like Mom gone wild. I couldn't talk to you."

Heidi felt her face flush as she remembered just how over-the-top she had been. "I wouldn't have been so crazy if you'd told me the truth. You should've told me then."

"I know. But it's not a big deal, is it? And I wanted to see what would happen. I wanted to surprise you."

"Well, you definitely did that." Heidi laughed wryly. "This is quite a surprise, all right. Take a look." She handed the printed sheet to Katie.

As Katie read the e-mail, her eyes got wider and wider and her mouth dropped lower and lower. "I can't believe it!"

"I can't either and I . . . well, I just don't understand." Heidi squinted at Katie. "How did they know about this back home?"

"Because when I answered that first e-mail, that's all I wrote about. I talked about the women and the jewelry and Jaleela and what she hoped to do. About how brave she was and so sure there would be money and her dream would be real one day."

Heidi shook her head, amazed at her daughter and not for the first time in the past week. "I still have some questions, but I guess they can wait. But this news—" she smiled and lifted Katie's hand, the one still holding the e-mail—"is too good to wait. You need to read it to everyone."

"Me?"

"Yes, you, silly." Heidi hugged Katie's shoulder. "You're the one who instigated this whole thing. You're the one who got it started."

"I have to read it now?"

"Oh yes!" Mighty squealed. "You must! You must!"

Katie cringed, eyeing Heidi skeptically. "Will you sort of get everyone's attention for me?"

"No problem. That's one thing we teachers are good at."

But as she started to speak, Heidi could feel her throat grow thick with emotion. Why had she ever doubted the innate goodness of Katie's heart? Why had she thought for a second the sun wouldn't shine today?

Oh, to have the faith of Jaleela! Oh, to be so sure. Unwavering and true.

Thank you, Jaleela, for the person you were! Thank You, God, for bringing her into our lives!

Sucking in a deep breath, she tucked her hair behind her ears and faced the room full of women. "Excuse me, ladies. Could I have your attention, please, for just a moment?"

The buzz in the room hushed almost immediately as all the women and even their children looked at Heidi curiously, Gabby and Cassandra included.

"I just have a few things to say. First—" she swallowed hard— "I cannot express how saddened we are to lose the friend we found in Jaleela. But even more than that, I don't think I'll ever be able to put into words how thankful I am to have met her. To be inspired by her. And to have the privilege of being a part of her legacy, her dream. And I know, without even asking, that I can say the same for Cassandra and Gabby and my Katie too."

Cassandra and Gabby nodded at Heidi.

"All of you here today make Jaleela's dream real with the beautiful pieces of jewelry that are the work of your hands and the joy and dedication of your hearts. I just want you to know you are not working alone. It seems the dream gets bigger and becomes more real even as we join together today. Besides us, there are even more people who care and are thinking of you. In fact, Katie e-mailed someone in our hometown telling them about Jaleela and you ladies, and this is what they had to say." She nodded to Katie.

Katie looked at the women and smiled before lowering her eyes to the sheet of paper. "'Dear Jaleela, you are a courageous woman, and you remind us all of the power of faith and the hope that comes from humbly serving and loving others. We wish you and the other South African women much success in all of your endeavors. In an effort to assist your dream of helping others in becoming a reality, we hope you will accept our pledge of three thousand dollars, the sum of which will be wired directly to South Africa upon your instruction. Our best to you and those close to your heart.'" She paused. "'Sincerely, Dr. Kevin Peterson on behalf of the emergency room staff, Lazarus East Hospital.'"

They were the most beautiful sounds, Heidi thought—the shouts of praise that came from the South African women. The joyous shrieks and bursts of laughter. And the songs that erupted from the lips of the women that swelled and blended across the room.

"Jaleela knew it all along. She knew the money would come to us somehow. She never stopped believing," Katie said wistfully, watching the women celebrate.

"No, she didn't." Heidi hugged Katie close, treasuring the pure joy of the moment.

"And I have faith too. I believe I will come to America one day," Mighty said, a sure grin on her face. "I will work with the emergency nurses there."

After all she'd seen in the past week, Heidi didn't doubt it could happen. "Don't forget. You're always welcome to stay with us when you do."

"Perhaps you will introduce me to the kind Dr. Peterson?" Mighty's eyes teased and twinkled as she let go of a girlish giggle.

"He's a little old for you, Mighty. But he's just the right age for someone else we know. Right, Mom?" Katie snickered.

Silly as it was, just seeing his name on the e-mail and remembering his invitation had made her heart start to flutter erratically. And now hearing his name made her face flush.

Heidi swung away from Katie and Mighty quickly before they noticed. "Oh, you girls!" She grinned, dismissing the question lightly with a wave of her hand. "Are guys all you ever think about?"

Gabby picked up a carved miniature elephant from Mama Penny's bookshelf, rubbing the smooth wood with her thumb.

Tumi had liked the elephant the best of any of the animals on the entire safari, hadn't he? He'd circled the picture over and over again on his sheet and couldn't stop talking about how huge the creature's head and ears were.

A wistful smile crossed her lips, and she let out a sigh at the memory. Placing the carving back on the shelf, she glanced around Mama Penny's modest living room, full of things as interesting as the woman herself. A pair of angels in a painting on the wall seemed to be watching her every move, reminding her of Jaleela's two angels, Nomvula and Tumi.

Was she always going to keep doing this? Was everything she touched and everything she saw always going to remind her of Jaleela's children?

"I am sorry to keep you waiting." Mama Penny swept into the room, embracing Gabby warmly. "It is always busy times; is it not?"

Mama Penny didn't have to tell her that in addition to her daily jobs she'd taken on the task of arranging Jaleela's funeral, which in the village, meant a week's worth of visitations and commitments before the burial. Not to mention, the older woman had promised to care for Nomvula and Tumi until other arrangements could be made.

"You're always very busy."

"I am fortunate to have my granddaughter Mpumi to help me." Mama pulled a white kerchief from her skirt pocket and wiped her brow. "She let you in?"

"Yes, she's very sweet and attractive. Her face is strong-looking, full of character like her grandmother's."

"I will miss such nice words when you are gone." Mama Penny chuckled, slipping the kerchief back into its place. "I have a feeling you have come to say good-bye; am I right?"

Gabby nodded, sadness instantly making her body feel leaden. "Sipho is taking us to the airport in a couple of hours. I don't even know how we'll say good-bye to him. He's been so wonderful to us. And I know we said our good-byes last night, Mama Penny, but I didn't feel like I could leave without stopping by."

"I understand." Mama Penny gave her a knowing look. "It is the children. You want to say good-bye to the children."

Of course the other woman knew. She always seemed to know everything. Even so, Gabby couldn't help but explain. "I'm always thinking about them, I'm afraid. I can't stop. Not when I'm asleep or when I'm awake. I see their faces all the time, their smiles. Their tears. They're all I think about."

Mama Penny squeezed her arm. "Then you will lay eyes on them and you will see their faces. You can touch them and hug them. You will know they are whole. Then you can go." Nodding encouragingly, she motioned to Gabby. "Come. They are outside sitting with Mpumi. She just rejoined them."

Gabby followed the formidable woman down the narrow, dim hallway that led to the back of the house. Maybe Mama Penny was right. Maybe if she just saw the children and knew they were all right, she could feel freed from these possessive feelings.

But as the hallway emptied out into the natural light of the kitchen and Gabby could see the door leading outside to the back stoop, where the children were supposed to be, a queasy, hollow feeling came over her.

What was she doing? How could she really say good-bye to Nomvula and Tumi? Perhaps forever? How could she turn her back on the beautiful brown-skinned children who were hurting so? on the children with bright white smiles who had brought her so much joy?

How could she really say good-bye to them and possibly never see their sweet faces again except for in her dreams?

The thought nearly knocked her over, and she braced herself against the kitchen stove. "No, I can't."

Mama Penny looked puzzled.

"I can't say good-bye to them."

"You would like for me to tell them for you?"

Gabby shook her head violently. "No. I mean, I don't want to say good-bye at all. I don't want to leave them."

An unending well of compassion, Mama Penny reached out, caressing Gabby's cheek. "I know it is difficult, child. I know. But you have a plane and it is leaving. It will take you home to your Tom. To your family. And to your important work. To all you are a part of there."

"But you don't understand. Now this is a part of me too."

It hadn't been a conscious choice. It hadn't been anything she'd come looking for. It had just happened. Just like Heidi hadn't searched out a husband with a five-year-old all those years ago. And Jaleela hadn't planned on a debilitating disease that would ultimately give way to her dream and the hope of helping others.

Life just happened. And with help from above, a capacity to love and accept broadened the heart and deepened the soul.

Oh, Tom! Gabby's heart lurched with realization. He understood that, didn't he?

How she wished she'd heard back from him. How she wished he'd answered her e-mail. But more than anything she wished she'd listened to him long ago when he'd always been so certain things would work out for them. He'd always believed more than she had. Why had it taken her so long to open up and believe too? Why had she let fear cripple her and wreak havoc with their lives, their marriage?

"Mama Penny, I want to adopt Nomvula and Tumi." The words came out in a rush but completely from the heart.

Mama Penny's hands flew up to her chest. "Do you know what you are saying, dear one?"

"Yes, I do. I want to adopt them."

It would be perfect if Tom was still there for her. If he still wanted to have a family with her, it would be the best thing ever and she hoped for it with all her heart. He'd always been ready to adopt a child, to embrace a little girl or boy, to give them his name and call them his own. It had never been the slightest question for him.

But Gabby had hurt him greatly. She'd taken all of his love and spurned it. Pushed it away, shoved it back in his face. There was a good chance he wouldn't be able to forgive that. A very good chance he wouldn't want to look past the pain she'd caused him and start over again.

And yet, if he didn't, if he couldn't forgive her, what could she do? How could she turn her back on Jaleela's motherless children? They'd already grown to have such a special place in her heart. She wanted so badly to heal them and hold them, to love them and care for them always. If Tom had been too hurt by how she'd acted in the past, she would have to manage the future by herself. Wouldn't she? Like Heidi and Jaleela and so many other brave single mothers. She would have to find a way. She would simply have to.

"Did you hear me?" Gabby said when the other woman didn't answer.

But again Mama Penny didn't answer except to reach out and embrace Gabby tightly.

"You can't just hug me and send me off. You need to listen to me. I refuse to go until you do. I won't just leave." Tears choked her words as her body stiffened in the matriarch's arms. "I can't. Not when I want so much for them. Not when I want them to learn and grow strong in their studies and their faith. I'd never let them forget their culture, their traditions. I would bring them back here to see. And I would never, never let them forget their mother. Truly, I wouldn't."

"Oh, Gabrielle." Mama Penny laughed softly. "I am not trying to send you away. No, dear woman. I am holding you close so I can tell you a secret."

"A secret?"

"It was Jaleela's wish," Mama Penny said softly. "Her most pressing dying wish. Yes, she wanted her dream to live. But Nomvula and Tumi were her dreams too. Her most precious dreams. And she wanted them to be in your keeping."

Instead of fighting Mama Penny's embrace, Gabby suddenly yielded to it and was thankful for it. Because hearing that Jaleela could have possibly hoped that Gabby would care for and love her children was so humbling, her knees nearly gave out on her. Getting hold of herself, she straightened and pulled back. "She wanted me to be their guardian? You're sure?"

Mama Penny gave her a warmhearted smile. "The children have no blood relatives here, but in you Jaleela saw something like that. She saw the caring and kindness you showered on her children. She also saw a woman of faith in you." She squeezed her shoulder. "Jaleela knew you would teach Nomvula and Tumi many things and keep them safe. She had no doubt you would love them much."

Gabby squinted at Mama Penny, unable to contain her smile or catch her breath at what she was hearing. "When were you going to tell me?"

"I was not to tell you. That was part of Jaleela's wish. She said you must come to tell me it was your desire. She was nearly certain that you would."

"And what if I hadn't?"

Mama Penny shrugged and grinned. "I had not thought of it. You know our Jaleela—when she had something in her mind, she was certain it was meant to be."

It was true. The thought of the woman and her unwavering hope made Gabby smile. And she knew it always would. Unable—and not wanting—to suppress the joy that overflowed inside her, Gabby swiped at the tears of happiness sliding down her cheeks. "So it's possible? I can adopt them?"

"I know many people." Mama Penny winked assuredly. "It will take time, some months for certain, but I will make sure it comes to be. For now, you need to go home and prepare the way. We will be in touch. We will talk much too."

"Oh, Mama Penny, thank you. With everything in my heart, thank you so much."

After embracing the stout, huge-hearted woman once again, Gabby smoothed her hair and wiped the tear-induced smudges from under her eyes in preparation to face Jaleela's children. As she did, she felt something come over her. A tranquility. An assuredness. A sense of peace like she hadn't known for a very long time.

So this is it, Lord? This is where You've been leading me all along?

Stepping out onto Mama Penny's back stoop and into the sunshine, Gabby recalled how bold and striking the sun had been when they'd first landed in Johannesburg. She also remembered how empty she'd felt, so different from the fullness in her heart at this moment.

Even so, that didn't stop her from aching at the sight of Nomvula and Tumi, looking listless and lifeless as Mpumi sat nearby reading. With a twig in his hand, Tumi poked aimlessly at the dirt beneath a flowering bush at the back of Mama Penny's grassy, postage-stamp-size enclosure. Nomvula sat on the ground, twirling one of the red blossoms from the bush between her fingers, staring at the scarlet blur it made.

Oh, the pain they must be feeling, losing their mother, the special woman everyone adored. Gabby couldn't even begin to imagine. Seeing them that way made her want to crush them to her chest, longing so much to make everything right.

Gabby knew if Tom could meet Jaleela's children, he would want that too. He'd accept Nomvula and Tumi in a minute. That was the kind of sweet, loving man she'd married. If only he could forgive her first.

And then they wouldn't just have someone to mother them again. They'd also have a father. She could only hope and pray that it could be that way for the sake of the children and for her and Tom too.

Ever hopeful, she started to take a step toward them, toward her future and theirs.

"Gabrielle."

Her feet froze. Her heart did too. There was something uneasy and cautionary in Mama Penny's voice. A deep inflection that hadn't been there earlier. So unlike the typically encouraging, strong-willed woman.

Gabby turned, searching the woman's face. "Yes?"

But Mama Penny wasn't looking at her. Following her line of vision, Gabby saw the older woman's unwavering gaze focused on the children.

It seemed the impetuous, playful sun wasn't the least bit aware of Nomvula and Tumi's somberness. Dancing off the tops of their heads, its rays left the tips of Nomvula's dark chocolate hair glistening like tiny magic crystals. Then the capricious sunshine bounced and sparkled off Tumi's head, too, highlighting the colors there like an expert hairstylist. Deep browns. Medium browns. Colors pleasant to the eye.

But there was more to be seen, wasn't there? Threatening, fiery tints of gold. And orange. Colors alarming to Gabby's heart.

"I lied," Mama Penny blurted, her voice cracking with emotion. "To Jaleela. I lied."

Gabby's heart lurched in her chest. "What are you saying? She really didn't want me to have her children?" *After all this? After I've come so far? This can't be happening again.*

Clasping Mama Penny's fleshy forearm, Gabby tried to shake her out of her trance. "Please talk to me."

"I lied to Jaleela," she muttered, her gaze still fixed on the children. "But I cannot lie to you. When I tested Tumi for HIV, I said the results were negative. I had to. I had to say that to Jaleela." A tear escaped, a rare sight, running over the roundness of her cheek. "She was my friend. She was going to die. The cancer could only grow worse, and there was no way to save her. I could not let her go to her grave like so many others, worrying about her son. No, I wanted her to think about her dream. How it would help her children."

Mama Penny finally shifted her gaze from Nomvula and Tumi, and her moist eyes sought Gabby's. "I lied to my friend. Yes, I did. I told her the children only needed special vitamins. Nomvula makes sure they take them—the real vitamins I gave her and the antiretroviral drugs I bottled for Tumi." She hung her head. "I told Jaleela there were no worries, that Tumi was most fine."

Tumi was HIV positive.

Gabby had pretended not to see it. She hadn't wanted to think or ask about it. But there it was. The truth. Finally. No more guessing.

Standing under the daunting sunlight, she watched the children from a distance, letting the awful realization sink into her mind and into her heart. And then she waited. For the fear to overcome her. For the anxiety to paralyze her or to send her running. Far, far away. Back to where she came from.

But the longer she waited, all she felt as she looked at them were surges. A rush of something she couldn't even name, filling her, making her not want to cower. Causing her to want to stand strong and be bold and fight in any way she needed to for Nomvula and Tumi. For their well-being and happiness. For the unfairness of their pasts. For the dreams of their futures.

She wanted to battle for them with the same gut-driven fervor she'd felt for the nameless babies she'd carried in her womb. She wanted to hold them tightly and protect them with the same fierceness only a mother—any kind of mother—could know.

It didn't matter they weren't children she'd given birth to. It didn't matter they weren't perfect physically. All that mattered was that feeling—the undeniably strong feeling that she would go to the ends of the earth for them, without question, without a doubt.

She turned to Mama Penny. "No, you didn't lie to Jaleela. Tumi *will* be fine. He'll have the best care available. I'll make sure of it. Nomvula will too, in whatever she needs. They will be well taken care of always. That is the truth. I'll be there for these children, no matter. I will love them unconditionally . . . like my own. I-I . . ." She swallowed against the emotion rising in the back of her throat. "I already do love them like that. Honestly, I do."

Mama Penny took her hands, tears still glimmering in her eyes. "Oh, Gabrielle, Gabrielle, you really are like the angel Nomvula hoped you would be. The children will be so very blessed to have you as their guardian. Their mother."

Gabby smiled, tears misting her eyes too. "Believe me, they will not be half as blessed as I will be."

Moments later Gabby started walking over to Nomvula and Tumi. They appeared too lost in their thoughts to notice her at first, but then they looked up and seemed surprised and delighted to see her. Slowly, quietly, they made their way into her open arms. Nomvula instantly nuzzled her head into the crook of Gabby's neck.

"I do not know something," Tumi said seriously without saying hello. "If our mama went to her home in heaven, where is our home going to be?"

Gabby looked back at Mama Penny for her permission to be honest with the children. Mama Penny nodded, and Gabby was never so happy to be able to tell them openly, "I would like it to be with me."

"With you?" Tumi's eyes grew wide.

Nomvula's head perked up from Gabby's shoulder. "With you?"

"It was your mother's wish," Gabby told them. "And it is my wish too."

"You are staying here?" The slightest smile dared to creep onto Nomvula's lips.

"No, I'm going home." She hated more than anything to tell the precious girl that. "But soon you will be coming to be with me, and it will be your home too." She kissed the top of Nomvula's head. "And yours." She kissed Tumi's cheek.

Still the two of them looked at her skeptically. And why wouldn't they? They'd seen so much that the wisdom in Nomvula's eyes was beginning to shadow with cynicism. The light and hope in Tumi's gaze was dimming, more doubtful.

At a loss, Gabby reached into her purse, taking out the two-page itinerary stuffed in there. "Remember how we made hearts?" she asked as she folded each paper in half and proceeded to carefully tear a heart from each sheet. Holding the hearts in the air, she then gently tore both of them in half.

"Nomvula." She handed half of one of the hearts to the young girl. "Tumi." She gave him a half of one too. "Hold them up and see how your halves go together with mine."

As they held up the half hearts together, the children looked at her curiously.

"I want you to promise me that every day we're apart, you will look at your half of a heart and remember this day. Remember how the sun was shining. Remember how it felt to be here hugging each other. Remember that I promised we are going to be together again. Don't you ever, ever doubt that; do you understand?" she said sternly, earnestly. "Nomvula? Tumi?" She looked back and forth at them.

Both children nodded solemnly as smiles twitched at their lips and shimmers of hope began to shine in their eyes.

"When we're together again, we'll put our hearts together," Gabby promised them. "And we'll be whole. We'll be a family."

"When will that be?" Nomvula asked in that sweet, hushed voice of hers.

Gabby looked at Mama Penny for the answer.

"Soon." Mama Penny smiled on them benevolently. "I promise, soon."

44

Heidi shifted her gaze from the highway to Katie long enough to pay her a compliment. "Jaleela's scarf looks good with your hair. It's a great contrast with your coloring."

"Really?" Katie tilted her head. Satisfaction shone in her eyes. "Thanks."

All the way from the airport, Heidi had thought Katie looked so pretty with the start of a pink and topaz sunset coming in the window and the green band of color around her neck. She looked fresh, too, even after nearly an entire day of flying. Whereas Heidi had just caught a glimpse of her own tired-looking face in the rearview mirror and had promised herself not to look again.

"I'll miss having Gabby and Cassandra around," Heidi said, steering the SUV onto the exit ramp. "But it'll be good to sleep in our own beds, won't it?"

"Definitely," Katie agreed. "Plus we'll see them next week. We're going to meet at church and then go to Cassandra's for a dinner meeting, right?"

"That's the plan."

Earlier Heidi had mentioned to Katie that maybe coming back to Ohio from South Africa would feel similar to what the astronauts felt reentering earth's atmosphere after the quiet of space. But Katie had been quick to school her, saying the astronauts were probably more concerned about their spacecraft burning up upon reentry or hitting the atmosphere incorrectly and bouncing back to who knows where in the universe.

Katie's mind wasn't in science mode though when she turned to Heidi and said somewhat wistfully, "That was really nice of him, wasn't it?"

Heidi didn't have to guess whom Katie was talking about. Kevin Peterson had crossed her mind the minute she turned off the expressway onto Hawthorne Boulevard and spied Lazarus East Hospital up the street.

She nodded, glancing at Katie over the top of her sunglasses. "I never did get to ask you, how did Kevin get the e-mail address in South Africa, anyway?"

"Oh yeah. That." Katie chuckled. "I was wondering when you were going to get around to asking me." Dipping her head, she looked mildly sheepish. "Actually I saw him at the gas station a couple of weeks before we left."

Kevin had mentioned as much on the phone, but it still didn't make sense. "But you didn't have the e-mail address for the hospice at that point. We hadn't even met with Gabby yet."

"You're pretty good at this detective stuff, aren't you?" Katie smiled.

"Moms get plenty of practice, believe me. So?"

"When I saw him that day," Katie launched into an explanation, "he asked the usual sort of adult questions. You know, how I was doing and all that. And then he asked me about spring break plans."

"And you mentioned South Africa?" Flicking on the right blinker, she pretended to be hearing the story for the first time. Another little thing moms were good at.

"I don't know why I just started babbling to him. I told him I was a little nervous about the long flight and being pregnant and all. And then he gave me his e-mail at the hospital in case I had any questions. And so . . ."

"You e-mailed him before we left?"

"I wanted to ask him if I could take Dramamine or anything, and that's when—"

"You gave him the e-mail information for South Africa."

"Exactly." Katie nodded. "He e-mailed me there and asked how the flight went. Oh, and he asked about you, too."

"Just being polite, I'm sure," Heidi replied swiftly, but she had to admit her face seemed to warm involuntarily at the thought that he'd inquired about her.

"I don't know. Now that I think about it, he asked about you every time. When I saw him. And when he e-mailed." Katie turned to Heidi, wiggling her brows. "Do I detect possible romance in the air?"

"Romance?" Heidi took her eyes off the road long enough to give Katie a double take. "Now there's a leap."

Even though Katie was teasing, it seemed like the perfect time to mention that she'd been in contact with Kevin too. "But, uh, I do have to tell you, Dr. Peterson called me before we left for the trip."

Katie's brows went from wagging to furrowing. "He did?"

"He asked me out."

"Out?"

"As on a date. Believe it or not." Glancing out the corner of her eye, she tried to gauge Katie's expression. Did Katie look happy about the possibility of her mom and Kevin going out together? Or concerned? But in that instant, Katie's face didn't give anything away.

"I do believe it. I mean, like I told you, he asked about you every time." Katie grew thoughtful for a moment. "But you didn't go out with him, did you?"

Heidi shook her head.

"Why not?"

"A lot of reasons." She shrugged.

"You mean like me? and the baby?" To her surprise, Katie suddenly looked almost crushed. "Because seriously—" she held up her hand as if ready to take an oath on a Bible—"this is the new Katie you're looking at, remember? I want you to be happy. Really. I do."

"It was a lot of things." Heidi paused, weighing her feelings more than her words for a change. "Mainly, the timing just wasn't right."

"Yeah? So, like, is the timing better now?"

At some point on their return flight, high above the Atlantic Ocean, Heidi realized she'd made up her mind. She knew what she was going to tell Kevin.

Just weeks ago, before they'd left for South Africa, Heidi didn't think she could handle it all—being a single mom, becoming a grandmother in the not-too-distant future, and involving a man in her life again. But she'd been so busy trying to keep Katie's pregnancy secret from some people, while fretting about condemnation from the people who knew, it wasn't any wonder she had no energy left for anything else.

Now, however, she felt ready to deal with where she was and whatever came her way. And she was certain things would come her way. Futures and plans never stayed neat and tidy; that was for sure. Yet now she knew what Jaleela meant when she'd stood in her kitchen and bared her soul to them. Letting go of some of the worries, turning them over to God left room for love and hope. And life.

"Yes. Now it is."

Katie beamed like she'd just been given a great gift. "That's awesome. But don't make the date like the minute we get back. We need time to go shopping. Please tell me you're not going to wear your work clothes. Are you?"

"I haven't even begun to think about what I'm going to wear. And remember it's just one date."

"Exactly. So we need to find you something really special. Something cute."

Heidi laughed. She tried to resist the urge to think too far ahead, but even on the plane she'd daydreamed about a date with Kevin Peterson. Anticipating where they'd go. What they'd talk about. Wondering if he'd want to kiss her good night . . .

Feeling her lips seem to twitch in anticipation, she tried to veer her mind and their conversation onto other topics. "Have you missed Mark a lot?"

"Yeah." Katie nodded slowly, thoughtfully. "But it was good to be away. Good to meet new friends my age, like Mighty and Dominic."

"They're pretty special people, aren't they?"

"For sure. Plus, being away gave me time to think about stuff, and I don't know . . . I've been thinking Mark and I are almost better friends than we are boyfriend and girlfriend." She sighed, sounding tired for her years. "I guess at some point we'll need to talk about that, which is hard. Because he is nice, and he does have potential."

If anyone could possibly see potential in any person or thing, naturally it would be Katie. Heidi smiled to herself. "What kind of potential?"

"Oh, not like the I'm-going-to-marry-him kind of thing. I'm a little young to be figuring that out. But it's too bad he doesn't have help from his mom or dad, because he's really good with wood and making things with his hands. Actually I think he likes the smell of wood more than the smell of me." She looked as if the thought had just occurred to her.

Heidi laughed at Katie's surprised face. "Even with all those cherry blossom lotions and enchanted orchid–scented spritzers we buy?"

"I know." Katie burst into giggles. "Crazy, right?"

"It is funny."

"Trust me, it's true," she exclaimed, still chuckling some. "I just hope he gets to keep working at the lumberyard. It really does make him happy to be there. They give him scraps of wood, and one of the owners lets him come in and use some of the saws. He's already made a table for his mom. It's awesome how he knows how to put pieces of wood together."

"Really?" Heidi was surprised Katie had never said anything prior to this. But then neither one of them had initiated conversations about Mark before, had they?

"Maybe there are some things he can do around our house," Heidi suggested. "I don't know where we'll be storing the jewelry from the South African ladies, but maybe he can make some shelving for us. And you know I've always said I'd like to have a vanity with a mirror. The old-fashioned kind that you sit down in front of. Do you think he could build one of those?"

Katie looked at her with something like amused wonder. "I know you're the nicest woman ever, but he can only do one thing at a time."

"Hey, I'm not as nice as you," Heidi countered. "I wasn't the one petting Hazard on the head when we left. That dog scared me to death till the bitter end."

The full-hearted sound of their laughter filled the SUV, and Heidi felt blessed knowing the memories from this trip would be with them always.

But as she turned off the main road into their subdivision, her thoughts turned inward too. "You do know we'll have to tell Mark's mom, don't you? About the baby?"

Looking over at Katie, she expected to see a disgruntled face or to hear words of protest. But instead Katie nodded.

"I'm going to let her know she's not financially obligated in any way," Heidi continued, "so she doesn't have to worry about that. It's just that it's only right that she knows and—"

"Maybe a baby will give her something happy to think about too?" Katie interjected, adjusting the scarf around her neck. "Everyone needs something to hope for. Someone to hope in."

And to that bit of wisdom, Heidi had no reply. She could only look at Katie and think how far they'd traveled. And, my, how much they'd grown!

45

The hefty cabdriver carried her suitcases easily, as if they weighed no more than a couple of bags of groceries, right up to the front door of her condo. Meaning he was probably hoping for a hefty tip too.

Cassandra felt like she'd been getting nickeled-and-dimed to death ever since she'd left the village of Mamelodi. But what else was new?

She was just sorry she'd noticed the wedding band on his finger and the photos of his four kids on his windshield visor, one of the boys slumped over in a wheelchair. But she had noticed. Unusual for her, she had to admit.

Adding an extra ten to the already-generous 20 percent tip she'd figured on top of the fare, she handed the bills to him.

He fingered the money in one swift motion and, obviously quick at adding, broke into a smile that stretched across his entire round face. "Whoa. Thanks a lot, ma'am. Are you sure I can't help you get those bags inside?"

"No. I have it under control, thanks," she said, wondering if he'd be expecting another five bucks for that too.

He backed away, bowing, dipping his head, still looking grateful. "Well, thanks again. And welcome back," he said somewhat shyly, stuffing the cash into the pocket of his extra-extra-large sweatshirt.

When she tugged her baggage through her front door, it felt good to finally be inside her home after all the hours of traveling. She only made it as far as the kitchen before she pulled the suitcases to a stop, shrugged the camera bag off her shoulders, and deposited her purse on top of the island.

Long and rectangular, the kitchen was nearly three times the size of the cramped kitchenette in South Africa. With cherry cabinets and crisp white ceramic floor tile, it was obviously more contemporary and luxurious too.

Or at least it used to feel that way.

Crossing her arms over her khaki blazer, Cassandra surveyed the room and frowned, somewhat puzzled. Was it just because she'd been gone for a while that the room seemed to be so colorless and empty?

What would Gabby, Heidi, and Katie think when they came for dinner next week? Would they think it felt bare too?

Although why in the world did she care what they thought? Wasn't it enough she was hosting their get-together in memory of Jaleela? Wasn't it enough they'd named her as their leader in this venture ever since Jaleela had bequeathed the bracelet to her?

And now she had to decorate for them too?

Yet when she took a good look around the place, maybe it did need a little freshening up. Like a panoramic photo topping the three long windows by the kitchen table. Her shot of the field of sunflowers would fit perfectly there, wouldn't it? And there were other pictures she'd taken that would work well in the room too. Like the South African woman in a bright orange kerchief selling huge green-striped watermelons at the side of the road. Or the photo of the ice cream man, pedaling his sky blue bike with the ice-cold box on back that held frozen bars and cones.

And of course, the decor wouldn't be complete without a photo of the new guy in her life hanging on the refrigerator.

When she'd visited Mrs. Olomi's house again before their flight left, she'd gone with the intent of getting Daniel's picture. But when she got there, the other children had gathered around, clamoring to have their pictures taken the moment she pulled out her camera. All except for him. One kind little girl, however, took Daniel by the arm and led him over to the group. Once there, Cassandra had been able to coax him to smile—ever so slightly—for the camera. Only it hadn't been for the camera she needed him to smile. It had been for her, too.

Now that she thought about it, besides Jaleela's bracelet, the photos and video footage for her sure-to-be-thought-provoking news story were about the only other tangible keepsakes she had from the trip. She never did purchase the painting from the art shop in Johannesburg like she'd planned. The money she'd budgeted to spend on the artwork had gotten set aside for Jaleela's start-up inventory instead. But when that money showed up from Lazarus East's ER staff, Cassandra had found another use for her funds. She'd given the money to Mrs. Olomi, promising the sweet South African woman she'd help support the children by sending a quarterly check. She had to do it if she ever wanted to get any sleep again.

All she knew was that a conscience had a way of keeping a person awake at night. She'd had a lot easier time sleeping before she had one.

She took off her blazer, folded it in half, and laid it on the counter. Then she nudged off her shoes, freeing her swollen feet from their stylish prison. Dehydrated from the flight, she reached into her stainless steel refrigerator and pulled out a bottle of Evian. The blue beads on Jaleela's bracelet clinked noticeably against the metal frame as she closed the door.

Oh, Jaleela, you're not going to let me forget, are you?

Before Jaleela had drifted off to sleep the night of their so-called slumber party, she had made Cassandra give her word that she'd make a certain phone call. It seemed like the worst idea in the world then, and it didn't seem like such a great idea now. Still, Cassandra should do as Jaleela asked and be done with it. She should just get it over with if she expected to ever get a moment's peace. If not, she'd keep feeling Jaleela's promptings. Feeling like Jaleela was looking over her shoulder until she took care of unfinished business like she promised she would.

After taking a long, cool drink, Cassandra set the water bottle on the counter and turned to the phone behind her. Punching in numbers, she tried not to give even half a cognizant thought as to what she was doing.

"What city and state, please?"

"P-Plaines," she stammered. "Indiana." Just saying the name of the place rocked her off-balance, making her feel as if she were floating outside herself. It wasn't a sensation she liked.

"The name of the party you're trying to reach?"

"Miles. Trudi. Well, no. It's probably under Bobby. Robert."

"One moment, please. That listing is . . ."

Was it her imagination? Did Jaleela's bracelet seem to jingle happily as she tapped more numbers into the phone? Or was it just a case of the jitters getting the best of her?

"Hello?" For no logical reason, Trudi's voice took her by surprise.

"Hello? Trudi?" Suddenly she felt short of breath. "It's—"

"Cassie?"

Cassandra tried not to cringe at the use of the nickname. "You recognized my voice?"

"No, silly. Caller ID!"

"Oh. Right." That made her smile a little. And feel somewhat relieved. So Trudi wasn't as obsessed with her as she'd originally assumed?

"My word. I can't believe it!" She could almost feel her childhood acquaintance smiling into the phone. But even back then, Trudi had been a friendly, gregarious child. "It's really you, huh?"

"Yes, it's me."

Or was it? Cassandra wasn't even sure anymore. Jaleela had claimed God was working inside her, and Cassandra had started to sense something and had to believe it was true. She longed for the serenity Jaleela seemed to have. Jaleela had told her all she had to do was stop fighting. Stop fighting Him. Start receiving Him. Cassandra had promised she would try.

Since Jaleela wasn't only a spiritual woman but a knowing, realistic one too, she'd given Cassandra her thoughts on making peace with the past. As a result, Cassandra had given her South African friend her word about that too.

I called her like you thought I should, Jaleela. Cassandra looked up at the ceiling, phone still at her ear. *This better be good!*

After all, she'd never been a person who'd kept a promise to a friend before. That was something new about her too.

46

Gabby stood in the shadowy threshold of her front door as the golden sun was taking its time descending from the sky over Cantebury Court.

Here she was, home at last!

The very thought made her breath catch.

Oh, if only she didn't feel so nervous about being here. If only she knew what to expect.

Leaning her ear against the painted white door, she listened for sounds of life inside. A TV blaring, maybe? Footsteps shuffling? Someone talking on the phone? It would've been heartening to hear something. To know for sure that Tom was here.

Unfortunately, she couldn't perceive a thing. Nothing except for the dull pain throbbing in her temples. Nothing but the irregular beat of her heart pounding in her chest.

Her hand trembled as she dug the house key from the pocket of her jeans. In fact, neither of her hands would quit shaking as she tried to steady herself, fumbling the key in the lock.

How foolish she'd been, wishing that Tom would meet her at the airport. She hadn't even left behind a flight schedule for him, had she? Yet like a high school girl yearning for her special guy to stop by her locker at the end of class, Gabby kept hoping he'd be there waiting for her.

She'd searched for him in every group of people she passed in the concourse. She'd looked for him every time she turned a corner or rode up an escalator, watching for him on the opposite side, hoping he was rushing to find her. She'd checked her cell phone a dozen times, making sure she hadn't missed his call telling her he was on his way to the airport or already there and looking for her.

She just wanted, more than anything, to finally see his face—the same way she'd seen him in all her dreams during the long flight home. Tom, Nomvula, Tumi, herself. In her dreams, her mind kept slipping to a happy place, a place that felt so perfect and right, where the four of them were together.

But Tom hadn't been at the airport, and it didn't seem as if he was at home either. If it hadn't been for the Westie puppy yipping at her from the neighbor's yard, she wouldn't have received any home-coming greeting at all.

But really, what did she expect? She jiggled the key and finally turned the lock. When she'd closed the door behind her before she left for South Africa, she had a strong feeling that her life would never be the same again. And now she knew that to be true.

Opening the front door, she adjusted her eyes to the dim light inside, then hoisted her suitcases over the threshold and into the foyer. As she did, she caught the lingering aroma of . . . what? spaghetti sauce?

She paused, then realized it made perfect sense. She wouldn't put it past her mom to have let herself in earlier and have a home-cooked Rosalie O'Malley meal waiting for Gabby when she got home. And where there were spaghetti and meatballs, there would be a fresh salad and garlic bread too.

Gabby wished she felt hungry, but the combination of aching sadness and nervous uncertainty inside her hadn't left room for an appetite. Even so, she could put the food away and save it for later. Leaving her suitcases in the living room, Gabby almost felt like a stranger in her own home as she made her way into the kitchen.

She thought it might be the spring sunset pouring in the back window that created the amber glow coming from the kitchen. But as she rounded the corner, she realized it wasn't the setting sun.

There were candles. Lit candles everywhere.

Shocked, she stood back, gazing at them. Candles in pewter candlesticks shimmered on the kitchen table between two place settings of china and shining silverware. In the middle of the island, candles stood alongside a vase filled with spring flowers. Candles shone even on top of her grandmother's teacup hutch hanging on the wall. Gleaming, glimmering, casting a special glow on everything in sight.

Certainly her mom would never leave candles burning in the kitchen. It must be Tom. It had to be. Had he checked with the church about her arrival? Had he known when she'd be coming? Or had he prepared all of this—her heart sank even lower at the thought—for someone else?

Suddenly she heard commotion in the bathroom down the hallway—a faucet running and being shut off. She stood frozen, listening to the sound of footsteps scuffing across the carpeting, down the hall, and finally into the kitchen. "Tom!"

He stopped, obviously startled. "I didn't hear you come in."

"You must've been . . . You were in the bathroom," she foolishly stated the obvious.

It seemed forever that they stood there, staring at each other in the glow of the flickering candlelight. Oh, how she longed to touch him. He didn't resemble Beckham or any of the pro athletes daydreaming Katie had wanted to liken him to. No, he looked so much better. He looked just like her Tom. With the broad, strong chest she'd cuddled against for so many years. With clear blue, accepting eyes that had always seen to the depths of her being . . . and had loved her anyway. And tender, knowing lips she'd missed the feel of. So much.

"Tom, I . . ." She faltered, at a loss. There was so much she wanted to say, to ask, to know. She had imagined when she finally saw him again, she'd instantly know exactly where to begin. But now she found that wasn't true. She felt awkward and anxious.

"Are you hungry?" he asked. "I figured you would be, so I—"

"You did all this for me?"

"Well, who else?" Tom slipped a hand into the front pocket of his jeans, regarding her cautiously.

"I don't know. I just thought when you didn't return my e-mail . . ." She shrugged, not even wanting to say the rest.

"What e-mail?"

"I e-mailed you from South Africa."

"Oh." Tom rubbed the back of his neck, his gaze falling to the floor. "I, uh . . . I sort of took the week off." He looked up at her. "Went up to Dad's cabin. I had a lot of thinking to do."

"You did? You weren't here all week?" How many hours had she spent so stressed, sure he'd read her e-mail and didn't have any love left in him to answer her?

"No, I wasn't." His hand came out of his pocket as he nodded toward the table. "I thought we could talk about everything—about us—over dinner."

"Oh!" She grinned weakly, her stomach churning at the thought of what upsetting things he might have to say. "I hate to say this, but I feel a little too queasy to eat right this minute."

"Yeah, I know what you mean." His mouth formed a tight-lipped grin. "So—" he gripped the back of the kitchen chair in front of him— "what did your e-mail say?"

"It said, well, I . . ." Twisting the wedding band on her finger, she tried to gather her nerve. "I wanted to know if you could ever forgive me. It said things had changed. But that's not really true. No, it's not, because I'm what's changed. From this trip and the people I met." It seemed once she'd started talking, she couldn't stop. "Going away opened my eyes and my heart too. So much. And it said I love you, Tom, because I do. I love you."

Her words seemed to reverberate in the silence as he stood staring at her. The flames from the candles on the kitchen table danced merrily in spite of the unease she was feeling, waiting for his reply.

"You've changed?" He eyed her curiously.

She straightened and raised her chin, looking at him without blinking. "Yes. Yes, I have."

"Well, I hope not too much," Tom said, his words stunning her so that she couldn't move. Could hardly breathe.

Was he saying what she thought—what she hoped—he was saying?

"Because all that time at the cabin—" the side of his lips crooked into a slight smile—"all I could think is that it's always been you. I told you that weeks ago at Mancusi's, remember? I've never wanted anyone else. That hasn't changed."

Relief flooded her from her heart to her toes. Tears brimming in her eyes, she wasn't sure who took the first step forward, but suddenly they were together. Finally the distance between them no longer existed. Wrapped in her husband's arms once more, Gabby clung to him mightily. She knew she never wanted to let go.

"I love you, Gabby. I always will."

A familiar shiver of happiness rippled through her at the sound of his promise. "Oh, Tom, I was so awful, wasn't I?" she started to apologize.

His lips found hers, and he kissed her softly at first and then intensely at last, reclaiming all that they'd ever shared between them.

She'd never felt so loved as she did in those moments, absolved of all that had passed between them. Tom gazed into her eyes, pushing the hair back from her cheek, making her realize even more how much she'd missed the tenderness of his touch. "You were hurting, Gabby. It's okay."

"But so were you, and I made you hurt even more."

"Yeah, well . . ." He smiled into her eyes. "Just so happens I'm strong. I can take it." Teasingly he flexed the muscles in his arms, tightening his embrace on her even more, causing a giggle to erupt from her throat.

She grinned at him. "I never want to lose us. The good, the bad. I never want to forget any of it, because it's us. And there will never be another us, you know?"

Tom laughed, bending down to peck her lips. "And for the record, you don't have to worry. We don't ever have to talk about adoption again. I promise."

"Oh." Gabby pulled away from his embrace slightly, suddenly feeling a bit sheepish. "Well, we sort of do. We do need to talk about that."

He stared at her, baffled.

"It's, um, kind of a long story. A very long story, actually. But I think you're going to like the ending," she said, sweet thoughts of Nomvula and Tumi filling her head. "I really do."

"As long as the story begins with you." He pulled her into his arms again.

"You mean us, don't you?"

"Right. Us."

How long they stood kissing in the glow of their candlelit kitchen she didn't know. She only knew they had a hard time tearing apart from one another even knowing they had plenty of time, the rest of their lives, to be close. It felt too good—too right—to be in each other's arms. It felt like it had been far too long since they'd held each other and given thanks for all the blessings they'd been given, most especially the gift of each other.

As Tom offered her a kitchen chair and she sat down, he leaned over, brushing his sweet lips against her neck. His voice never sounded so good as he whispered in her ear, "I'm glad you're back, Gabby. Welcome home."

Epilogue

A few days before Christmas
Port Columbus International Airport

Tom squeezed Gabby's hand.

They'd gotten as close as they could to the passengers arriving on flight 1044, but Gabby knew it didn't feel close enough for either of them. No, not until they held Nomvula and Tumi in their arms—then, and only then, would it be near enough.

"They're almost here, honey." Tom brought her hand to his lips and kissed her there as passengers began trickling toward them.

"Do you see them?" Her cheeks tingled, and she couldn't contain her smile as she stood on tiptoe, trying to see around the people in front of her.

Though the airport had a special Christmas feel to it with evergreen sprays and wreaths topped with crimson bows hanging everywhere and the sound of bells jingling in the air, it was also much more crowded than usual. Gabby had lost count of how many times she'd teared up already, watching loved ones unite and lovers embrace, eager to be with each other to share the warmth of the holidays.

"No, not yet. But any minute, they'll be here." He turned to her, smiling into her eyes. "Any minute," he repeated, and she knew exactly what he meant.

After so many months of having only Nomvula and Tumi's photos to look at. After weeks going by without even speaking to them by phone. After all the praying and hoping the adoption papers would be completed swiftly. After what seemed like forever, Mama Penny was bringing Nomvula and Tumi home to them. At last.

Gabby didn't know how many times in the past few days she'd

gone into the rooms they'd decorated for the kids, fluffing pillows that were already fluffed, smoothing out comforters that had no ripples. She'd caught Tom doing the same thing, especially in the last twenty-four hours. Suddenly he'd disappear, and she'd find him out in the garage double-checking the tires on the bikes he'd hidden there, the bikes Santa would be bringing to the kids on Christmas morning.

Even before they walked out the door this morning, they'd both stood in front of the homemade stockings hanging from the mantel, straightening them so the embroidered words *Nomvula* and *Tumi* hung just so.

"Oh, man, I can't believe it," Tom murmured, peering over the crowd.

"What?" Up on tiptoes again, Gabby made another attempt to look over a head or two without much luck. "You don't see them?" Her chest started to tighten, but a moment later Tom began to chuckle. It was a deep, heartfelt sound that seemed like it was coming from the very core of him.

"Oh no, I do see them. I definitely see them. Tumi's much taller than I thought." Tom sounded like a proud dad already. "And Nomvula's so . . ."

Gabby could hear the emotion in his voice, his instant captivation with the kids making him grow hoarse. "She's so beautiful, isn't she? Nomvula's beautiful, just like Jaleela."

In the next moment, the crowd seemed to shift and Gabby could finally see them too. Nomvula and Tumi were walking slowly, holding hands, their eyes wide with anticipation. And Mama Penny was right behind them, looking somewhat relieved to have the long flight behind her.

"Nomvula! Tumi!" Gabby cried out, waving. "Mama Penny! Over here."

The kids' faces lit up as soon as they picked her out of the crowd. Though she'd been anxious wondering how they might react to seeing her and Tom, she didn't have to worry about that any longer. Smiling and laughing, Nomvula and Tumi came running to them.

Tears poured down her cheeks as she and Tom stood side by side, opening their arms to their beautiful children. Tom's eyes gleamed too, as the four of them finally embraced in a tight family hug.

But never one to stay still for more than a minute, Tumi wriggled out of their arms, giving Tom and her both a curious look. "You are my papa now? and my mama also?"

"Yes, Son." Tom's jaw twitched at the word. "We are your proud parents."

Tumi smiled broadly. "And Nomvula's papa and mama too?"

"And Nomvula's proud papa and mama too."

"Then we are a family?" Tumi looked at both of them, and Gabby didn't think she'd ever stop loving the boyish glint shining in his chestnut-colored eyes.

"Yes, we're a family now," Gabby and Tom answered.

Hugging once more, all Gabby could think was how thankful she was that she hadn't denied all of them this happiness. *And it's all because of You, Lord. Thank You for helping me overcome my fear, for healing my marriage, for leading us here. It's all because of You and only You, Lord, our hearts are so full on this day.*

"And we have more family for you to meet," Gabby told them as she kissed and hugged Mama Penny, thanking her profusely for everything she'd done to bring them together.

As all of them rode up the escalator together, Nomvula and Tumi appeared excited by the idea of more family. But the amount of people they saw waiting for them seemed to exceed their expectations.

Their eyes and their smiles grew wider and wider still at the size of the group that greeted them. Gabby's and Tom's dads were there, giving the kids big grandpa waves. And so were the grandmothers, who blew kisses to the kids with one hand, while swiping away tears with the other. Aunts and uncles clapped, grinning profusely. Cousins of all ages, holding balloons and signs, chanted their names over and over again, cheering their arrival. And then there were others faces too, ones Nomvula and Tumi recognized—Katie, Heidi, and Cassandra.

Along with them were faces that were still new even to Gabby, including Katie's precious baby and Kevin Peterson.

Nomvula squeezed Gabby's hand, looking totally awed by the sight. "It is like magic. It already feels like home."

"Yes, I love this family," Tumi exclaimed, his eyes zeroing in on his boy cousins, especially Mikey, who was close to Tumi's age.

As they reached the top of the escalator and everyone introduced themselves to Nomvula and Tumi, Mama Penny laughed in that hearty way of hers. "Oh, Jaleela is certainly singing with the angels today. I am sure of it," she said. "I know she is happy."

"We're happy too, and we couldn't have done it without you." Tom thanked the South African matriarch. "Christmas came early for us this year, didn't it, my beautiful wife?" He grabbed Gabby by the waist and kissed her cheek.

"Definitely." Gabby nodded, watching the children she loved blend into the family and friends she loved so dearly too.

Christmas had come early with some very precious gifts that would make them happy for a lifetime.

Reading Group
Guide

A Conversation with the Author

Authors are often asked where they get the inspiration for their stories. What prompted you to write this book?

Some ideas come from out of the blue. Some from snippets of an overheard conversation. Others from a headline or magazine article. But the inspiration for Beaded Hope *came to me from someone I met—Jennifer Davis.*

I work part-time at a hospital, registering people for outpatient and inpatient testing. One day, some years ago, a thirtysomething woman sat down across from me at the registration desk, and her jacket had a red beaded pin on the lapel. I couldn't help but ask where she'd gotten the pretty piece of jewelry. After introducing herself, Jennifer told me the pin was crafted by a woman in South Africa. Jennifer had just started a nonprofit called Beaded Hope that helps African women provide for their families by selling their beaded jewelry in the United States.

The day I met Jennifer I bought a piece of jewelry from her, but I never really expected to see her again. Looking back, however, I see that God had a different plan. It didn't matter which booth I was in—which week, day, or hour—when Jennifer visited over the span of the next few months, somehow she would always end up being sent to my booth. Since the continual crossing of our paths seemed too coincidental for us to ignore, we made plans to meet for tea the next week.

The tea grew cold as Jennifer shared her photos and journal entries from her earlier trips to South Africa. Though the faces in her photo album were completely foreign to me, I felt pressed to write about them. I'd published some romances prior to that and figured this would be a sweeping romance, covering two continents.

Try as I did, I couldn't get the first chapter of my romantic saga past my critique partners. They were right—it just didn't work. So I sat down and tried again. The story had to be about more than romance, I realized. It had to be all about women. Women helping women. Women bonding with one another through their struggles, dreams, hopes, and faith. Just like real life, that's what Beaded Hope is about.

You went on a mission trip that was similar to the one Gabby, Cassandra, Heidi, and Katie took. What was that experience like for you?

The flight was long—something like eighteen hours. I'm not a great flyer, and I kept repeating the first four lines of Psalm 121. It still seemed surreal to actually be in South Africa. We followed the proposed agenda and were busy each day. Even so, I feel like only after I had been home for a while could I really look back and process what I'd seen and experienced.

One thing I did realize while we were in South Africa was how truly attached you can become to a person in such a short amount of time. Near the end of the trip, I can remember feeling so anxious, wanting to be home, safe and sound, back on the same continent as my kids. On the other hand, I had a hard time leaving some of the people I'd met. In less than two weeks, it was amazing how close I'd grown to them. I'd felt such joy getting to know them and couldn't help the tears when saying good-bye, wondering if I'd ever see them again.

What was the most memorable part of your interaction with the people of South Africa?

We saw many terribly sad situations on our trip. Wheezing, nearly lifeless AIDS patients. Living conditions that were unfathomable. Children born HIV-positive. Things that made our hearts ache and brought tears to our eyes.

But even with all of that, the most memorable thing for me was that just when I would think I was there to minister to these needs in some way, I often felt that I was being ministered to instead. The smiles and hugs of the people there are so warm and genuine, they lift you up. And going to Sunday service with them is like nothing I've ever encountered. Their ardent prayers and songs of worship could take the roof off a building. They are just amazing people—you can't help but fall in love with them and want to help in some way. I definitely felt blessed to have had the opportunity to be there!

Were any of the characters in the story inspired by people you met on the trip?

Before I went to South Africa, someone told me, "Oh, you'll love the people. They're just wonderful—the best thing about the country." As I've mentioned earlier, I found that to be absolutely true. So through every character in Beaded Hope, I tried to portray the strong faith, warmth, and congeniality of the South African people we met.

But one character—Mama Penny—was inspired by a woman named Mama Peggy, who, as you'll see on the Beaded Hope Web site, is called "the Matriarch of Mamelodi." I don't know how the woman can possibly do all she does. She has her helping hands in everything— hands that never seem to stop moving.

It should also be noted that Mama Peggy and some of the other women we met working at Bophelong Hospice are well-educated women. They could live elsewhere. They could have very well-paying positions doing other things. But their hearts are with the people in the village. They sacrifice prestige and income to be able to help where they feel they are most needed. Going out to the villagers weekly, they counsel about AIDS, comfort the grieving, and bring hope, medicine, and food to the sick. They are incredible, admirable women.

Sometimes the needs of people in Africa feel so overwhelming it's hard to know how to get involved. What can readers do today to make a difference?

Without a doubt, the first thing the South African people I met would say to do is to pray. Really pray and believe that God is great and good, and He can and will do great things.

If it's on your heart (like it was for Cassandra) to sponsor a child, Compassion International (www.compassion.com) is a well-respected organization doing wonderful things for children in various parts of Africa.

Of course, if you get the chance to visit South Africa, you will be delighted by the genuine sweetness and pure joy of the people. But if you don't have that opportunity, you can also feel good knowing that nonprofits such as Beaded Hope (www.beadedhope.com) really do bring hope and means for a better life to the beadworking women and their families. The organization provides a hand up, not just a handout—and that's something the South African people are extremely grateful for.

Thank you, too, for purchasing Beaded Hope. *Obviously, I'm hoping you enjoyed the story. But please don't forget—since a portion of the proceeds from the sale of this novel will go to support Beaded Hope, that means you're creating a story too. A real story of hope and survival for another woman.*

Discussion Questions

1. Gabby is afraid to share her fears about adoption even with her husband, Tom. Do you think deep down she may have realized her fear was irrational?

2. Gabby, Cassandra, and Heidi didn't have their hearts in the right place when they left for the mission trip. Their reasons for going were egocentric. Yet they grew in spite of that, emotionally and spiritually. What does this say about God's constant love in pursuing a relationship with us?

3. What do you think made the women bond so quickly once they hit the foreign soil of South Africa? Have you ever been in a similar situation where you became close to a stranger in virtually no time at all?

4. Timing is everything, God's timing especially so. If an employee at Graceview Church hadn't had a family emergency, Gabby wouldn't have been invited on the mission trip. If she hadn't had the miscarriage exactly when she did, she probably wouldn't have gone either. How did God's timing play a role in Cassandra's and Heidi's decisions to go on the trip? Looking back, can you see where God's timing led you to a certain path or decision?

5. Katie's temperament improved once she arrived in South Africa. Why do you think that was?

6. When the women first saw Jaleela's tin-roof shanty, they were apprehensive about going inside. But after meeting her, they were slow to leave her home. What do you think they found compelling about Jaleela?

7. Tom was hurt that Gabby pushed him away. Eventually, he began to grow away from her too. Is there anything he could have possibly done to mend the situation earlier?

8. Mama Penny was larger than life. The people in the village depended on her for everything, much the same as many families depend on mom for most everything too. In Mama Penny's situation, her only source of comfort was God. If you are a parent, who or where do you turn to for renewal and help?

9. Cassandra's independent attitude came from a past history of hurts and disappointments. Do you think she would have been equally as successful if she'd had a loving environment to grow up in?

10. Jaleela's faith led her to surrender to God's will and the dream He placed in her heart. In surrendering, she believed He would be there to take care of the rest. To Cassandra that seemed as wistful as wishing on a star. Who was right?

11. At one point, Gabby looks at the pastor's compound and doesn't see the electric fence or the mess anymore. The place has become somewhat homey to her. Why do you think that was? Are we more adaptable than we think?

12. In two instances, a line of Scripture flits across Gabby's mind when she encounters the South Africans. Once was when Nomvula came running out of her dilapidated home (p. 136), and another time after listening to the prayer requests of the South African women (p. 243). Why do you think these verses pressed on her heart at those times?

13. Missiongoers often set out with the intent of ministering to the people they're visiting. But the South African women's faith was so strong, they ended up ministering to the Americans. Have you ever had this sort of instance occur in your everyday life?

14. Though the cultures and socioeconomics of the South African and American women were far different, in what ways were all of the women's dreams and wants very similar?

15. Hope is defined as "desire accompanied by expectation of fulfillment," but some would simply say hope can be a lifesaver. How has hope influenced a difficult time in your life?

16. Have you ever gone on a mission trip? If so, did it change you at all?

About the Author

CATHY LIGGETT knew writing fiction was for her after reading aloud a junior high English assignment and watching the class— at least the girls—well up with emotion. Yet it wasn't until much later in life that she seriously tried her hand at storytelling again. First came years of advertising copy, gift product development, and the publication of a nonfiction book.

Through it all, the urge to write fiction kept tugging on her, and a few years ago she published sweet romances for the secular market. After the release of these books, however, came an even stronger tug on her heart—a yearning to write inspirational fiction. *Beaded Hope* came from that desire.

Cathy and her husband, Mark, live in Loveland, Ohio, and are always happy when their greatest blessings—their two grown children— are home for a stay.

Visit her Web site at www.cathyliggett.com.

Look Good. Do Good. Give Hope.